'I am interested in pol
course I am.'

'The government isn't. You're the strong arm of
government. That's what you've allowed yourself
to become. You said yourself that fewer and
fewer policemen are looking at crime, but are
going armed to political demonstrations instead,
and offering more and more a strong-arm
response . . . That's what Paul is a victim of.'

'What's your first reaction when your house is
burgled or your mother attacked? I know what
you do, you call the police, along with all the
other liberals, radicals, blacks, racists,
conservatives. You call the police because there is
no one else to cope with all the problems.'

Also by G. F. Newman in Sphere Books:

THE MEN WITH THE GUNS

Set a Thief

G. F. NEWMAN

SPHERE BOOKS LIMITED

SPHERE BOOKS LTD

Penguin Books Ltd, 27 Wrights Lane, London W8 5TZ (Publishing and Editorial)
and Harmondsworth, Middlesex, England (Distribution and Warehouse)
Viking Penguin Inc., 40 West 23rd Street, New York, New York 10010, USA
Penguin Books Australia Ltd, Ringwood, Victoria, Australia
Penguin Books Canada Ltd, 2801 John Street, Markham, Ontario, Canada L3R 1B4
Penguin Books (NZ) Ltd, 182 190 Wairau Road, Auckland 10, New Zealand

First published in Great Britain by Michael Joseph Limited 1986
Published by Sphere Books Limited 1988

Copyright © 1986 by G. F. Newman
All rights reserved

Made and printed in Great Britain by
Richard Clay Ltd, Bungay, Suffolk
Set in Baskerville

Except in the United States of America, this book is sold subject
to the condition that it shall not, by way of trade or otherwise, be lent,
re-sold, hired out, or otherwise circulated without the
publisher's prior consent in any form of binding or cover other than
that in which it is published and without a similar condition
including this condition being imposed on the subsequent purchaser

'Fear acts visibly on those who break the law and invisibly on those who enforce it; making them all potential criminals.'

Prologue

Helen Daniels at thirty-five was in a crisis in her life. She was an actress who was becoming more and more involved in the animal rights movement and was finding increasingly that one activity was interfering with the other. Today she had turned down an offer which would have meant a week's filming to go on an animal rights demonstration. Not just one more demo, but one she had helped organize. The film director had seemed less than pleased when told she wouldn't have been able to film on that day; he obviously thought it a trivial pursuit and wasn't prepared to change his schedule to accommodate her. Had she said she was working elsewhere that day he almost certainly would have done so. It was his problem, not hers, she thought afterwards, and decided that he had probably never been committed to anything, or anyone, in his life. Her agent had been cross that she had missed the job for the reason she had. It was difficult to make people in general understand, but she had hoped that certain people – like her agent, solicitor, family and friends – would try a little harder. Did she want to remain an actress remembered for her public utterance against animal torture at an annual award-giving ceremony, rather than for the award-winning role itself? Her agent had known the answer, but still put the question. She sometimes asked herself if she shouldn't give up her career, which mostly involved her in trivia, and work for the animal rights movement full-time. But people in the movement thought it better that she maintain her public persona, which enabled her to make the sort of statements she did. Now it almost seemed as if she *was* working full-time for animal rights, only, like so many people, without pay. That had become a problem. Her agent had told her that he was finding difficulty in getting her work; potential employers were giving her a wide berth. Helen challenged their comfortable complacency over vegetarianism, furs, even the wearing of leather shoes. Most people, she believed, were basically kind and sensitive, and knew in their bones that what she said was right, that animals didn't exist simply to be exploited, but it was often easier to avoid her than to even think about changing the habits of a lifetime. Fortunately, she had landed a job in the theatre.

which restored her agent's faith in her even though it was the Royal Court, where neither radical nor loony stuck out. The job restored some of her faith in herself, as every job does for every actor, but it did not resolve her crisis.

The Citroën Dyane she drove was practically held together by the familiar clutch of ecology and animal rights stickers. They proclaimed what she was, and frequently got the car ticketed or towed away when it was parked where it shouldn't be. In a village in Essex where she had been hunt sabbing the previous winter, it had been almost totally vandalized by hunt supporters. The local police had smiled at her complaint, but she hadn't expected any other response from them. She knew they would enthusiastically defend laboratories against protesters, seeing them only as rabble threatening public order, while laboratory owners with their vile experiments were the 'protectors of health'. The police, like most other people, tended to believe the propaganda, but she knew that not one would fail to respond if brought face to face with a tortured animal.

Helen tooted the squeaky car horn when she drew up in the street outside a seedy Victorian terrace that had been converted into flatlets. Paul Bailey put his head out of the first floor window when Helen tooted a second time, and signalled that he'd be one minute. He was a medical student whom she had persuaded to come on the demo, and whose career was unlikely to flourish in view of his beliefs. Helen gestured impatiently. They were late.

'We'll miss the start of the march,' she said to her passenger. 'He should have been ready.'

'I'm surprised you persuaded him to come at all.'

Helen was also surprised, despite Paul's commitment. She suspected he'd agreed because he was a bit in love with her. She was no more than fond of him. He was twelve years younger than her and she had wilfully used his feelings to press-gang him into coming along. She wondered if her other passenger, Rose Willing, was going along for similar reasons. There were rumours about Rose being lesbian. Perhaps she was; it wasn't important in itself, but Helen was bothered that it mattered to her that Rose might be coming along because of her. It was nonsense, she argued with herself, Rose went on lots of demos; but lots with her recently. Trying to identify her feeling of sexual

8

vulnerability, she decided it was because there wasn't a man in her life, not one with whom she was having a relationship. That made her feel very unprotected.

The tall, gangly figure of Paul Bailey ducked out of the street door and leaped down the eight steps in two strides, carrying a placard declaring 'ANIMAL EXPERIMENTS DON'T MAKE HUMANS SAFE', a flask of coffee, a pack of sandwiches and two books.

'God, Paul, how do you imagine you're going to be able to read?' Helen raced the engine and let in the clutch. The car lurched forward.

'Oh, I thought if we were arrested, the police might not take my books off me if I told them I was a medical student reading for my finals.'

Rose laughed. 'They'll tell you you ought to know better.'

Parking too near to Hackney Town Hall, Helen hurried towards the assembly point, loaded with leaflets and smaller versions of Paul's placard to distribute.

Most people were expecting violence of some sort – that was the direction in which the protesters' frustration was taking them, especially when confronted by the brute resistance of the police; and judging by the large number present today, no doubt for the protesters' own protection, expectations would be fulfilled. Not one of the five hundred or so who were in the street at the side of the Town Hall, waiting to take their message to the Miracle Laboratories, had any doubt that it was entirely the actions of the police that provoked violence. It almost seemed to be police policy to be as provocative as possible in order to justify their huge presence.

Uniformed policemen from constables to chief superintendents were milling around, most in as much confusion as the protesters about what was happening. Senior officers were chattering to one another through their personal radios. The march was twenty minutes behind schedule and it hadn't even started. The police wouldn't let it move off for tactical reasons: there were four busloads of policemen coming in from other Districts to be placed inside the laboratories as reinforcements, but they were yet to get into position.

'Just what is happening?' Sheila Weymouth, one of the other organizers, said approaching a superintendent. 'Are we ever going to get started?'

'Your guess is as good as mine, Sheila.'

She had been liaising with this man over their route and where they would stand outside the laboratory; he tried to put on a friendly, human face. She hadn't invited him to use her Christian name; she certainly didn't call him Michael, not even Mr Regan.

Suddenly word came through that the reserve was in place, and the march got under way. The laboratory was two miles from the Town Hall, on the circular route the police gave them to avoid delays to traffic. The marchers chanted and gave out leaflets as they went. The hundred or so uniformed men and women walked alongside, while others maintained protection duty outside Boots the Chemist, butchers' shops and even a Macdonalds. When one of the marchers broke rank to leaflet the customers, he was stopped from entering. All that was left for him to do was chant 'Meat Is Murder' over and over, and he was arrested as others took up the cry. That precipitated shouts of 'Fascists', a label policemen liked considerably less than 'pigs' – a name the animal rights movement didn't use for obvious reasons.

Police officers dived into the crowd and pulled out a punkish-looking lad with a partial cockatoo haircut and wearing plimsolls. He was dragged unceremoniously along the pavement towards the police coach following behind.

No one could quite understand why this particular lad had been singled out. Demonstrators looked to Sheila Weymouth to find out as she hurried after the policemen, looking in vain for Superintendent Mike Regan to try and negotiate the release of the boy. At other, larger demos where the police had been unable to match numbers and feared being overwhelmed they hadn't actually arrested anyone, but had simply gone in with their truncheons marked with an oily substance and hit the offender, who was indelibly marked for easy identification and arrest afterwards.

Helen followed Sheila Weymouth, telling the protesters to stay calm and save their anger for the torturers in Miracle Laboratories.

'The police want to provoke you into being stupid so they can arrest you,' she said through the megaphone she was carrying. 'Don't let them stop us doing what we came here to do.'

'I should be careful what you're saying, miss, if I were you,' a chief inspector in uniform warned her cryptically as he came along the pavement with a hypertensive-looking sergeant. He moved on past. There was no need for Helen to say any more to the marchers.

These early arrests for such trivial incidents were an indication of what was to come. The more experienced protesters realised things might get heavy when they drew near to their destination and saw police Transit vans parked in the streets. These weren't ordinary policemen from the local station, but riot police from the District Support Units. They, more than any others, seemed to find it necessary to justify their existence by quelling riots; and if there didn't happen to be a riot to quell, it was an easy enough matter to create one. The commissioner was quick to proclaim the real need for DSUs in his annual report, pointing to the number of mini riots they had dealt with since being set up – riots that otherwise might easily have escalated into something similar to those of Brixton or Tottenham. About that, only he and those dealing with such affrays would know. These DSUs weren't simply parked at random along the route and in other side-streets, they formed a blockade around the lab, one the police could close once the marchers were inside. Helen Daniels glanced round at Paul Bailey, who was at her side, chanting with most of the other people, 'Human freedom animal rights, one struggle one fight!' He smiled grimly. She could see there was apprehension behind the bravado he got from the crowd.

'There are a lot of policemen around.'

'They've a lot to protect.'

Miracle Laboratories were housed in a new, anonymous, glass-fronted building with vertical venetian blinds and potted palms in the reception area. The building was situated on a fairly new industrial estate; dozens upon dozens of police were lined up on the lawned area and car-parking space in front of it. The numbers dismayed the marchers as they came along the main thoroughfare and were brought to a halt, confronting them. More than a few of them expected at least to get a stone or two through the windows, if not an all-out assault on the building, but the number of police present made any such action out of the question.

'Do you know what you're protecting?' Helen said, stepping forward out of the stunned silence and raising the megaphone.

'Do you know what vile, unspeakable cruelty you are protecting with your presence?'

As she stepped forward, so too did the people behind her. There was an uneasy stirring among the police ranks. They had the numbers, but not the commitment of any of those who came to see this place closed down.

A police chief superintendent raised his megaphone as if in challenge to Helen. 'That is as far as I want you to come. You may stand on the pavement and deliver your protests, but if any of you attempts to penetrate the perimeter fence of this establishment you will be arrested.'

The protesters stopped, not because they were afraid, rather because they were leaderless. It was considered undemocratic within the movement to have leaders, a position Helen wasn't in accord with, even though she knew that, in practice, leaders were usually the first to be picked up by the police. The crowd wasn't sufficiently frustrated to attempt an outright assault; only when they had been repeatedly thwarted would they respond in that way. Then it would be sparked off by an arrest, or a needless piece of aggression on the part of the police. The protesters were waiting, alert and watchful.

Helen raised her megaphone. 'Do you policemen know what you are protecting? Do you know what these sadists do to animals in these laboratories?'

Blank, uncomprehending stares came back at her through the chainlink fencing, which looked as though it had been recently erected. Two policemen together were smiling as though they were about to hear something funny. Helen's anger brought a sense of nausea. She wanted to scale the fence and slap those two policemen around their stupid, insensitive faces and tell them they were bad-mannered children – they each looked about eighteen. She wanted to take them inside this torture factory and show them what was being done in their name, and in the interests of producing more detergents and suntan lotions, anti-perspirants and insect killers – products that were ironically rendered no safer for humans for being tested on animals. What made it even worse was the possibility that these young men wouldn't care anyway.

She spoke slowly and carefully through the megaphone, not attempting to hide her emotion, but trying not to let it overwhelm the clarity of what she was saying. There was an uneasy silence when Helen finished listing both the long- and short-term toxicity tests on creatures from rats to beagles that went on here, with brief descriptions of the Draize eye-irritancy tests, where consumer goods such as shampoo were poured into the fixed open eyes of rabbits, and the LD50 tests, where substances were fed directly into animals' stomachs until fifty per cent of a batch suffered a lethal dose. Finally, the chief superintendent with the megaphone simply repeated the restrictions that were placed on the protesters, as though defying them to break them.

Almost certainly that response, that indifference to the suffering that had just been catalogued, prompted the reaction from the crowd. Had the senior policeman moderated what he had said, intimated that he understood and was sympathetic but had to uphold the rule of law, events might have unfolded differently. Either he had badly misread the feelings of the crowd, or he was contemptuous of them.

A missile arced up out of the crowd: a small vacuum flask, without cup or cap, spraying coffee and emitting steam as it flew towards the police ranks. There was an audible intake of breath from those police who saw it, they instinctively drew back, believing it to be a smoking petrol bomb, not understanding that animal rightists cared about the wellbeing of all animals including human animals; they stepped on each other's toes in their panic and confusion. The embarrassment of the police over breaking rank was compounded when the flask glanced off a well-padded shoulder and shattered harmlessly on the ground, splashing boots with coffee. The protesters pressed their momentary advantage. No one gave any order or signal, but it was as if an electric impulse had instantly sped through all those bodies. They surged forward to the fence, those in the front seizing hold of it, those behind pushing against them. They rocked and swayed, faster and faster. The fence, which hadn't been very sturdy to begin with, suddenly collapsed. This was something the police hadn't anticipated. Already rattled, they turned and fled through the metal gates at the side of the building as the protesters, flush with success, swept over the low parapet wall into the laboratory grounds. They stormed the gates, which were made of sterner stuff than the fence.

Quickly regrouping themselves, the first wave of police came at the gates with truncheons drawn, slashing at the fingers which clasped the wire. Protesters stood back and jeered and chanted, feeling a tactical advantage even though they had no tactics in this situation. In their general euphoria they seemed not to understand that the police couldn't simply take the humiliation of their rout lying down. Nor did they. The police called upon their well-rehearsed riot training. In the wide driveway at the side of the laboratory, their ranks parted like the Dead Sea, and through the space came not the Israelites out of Egypt but policemen with riot shields and batons. Other policemen fell into their noise-filled wake as they drummed on their shields. The gates were thrown open, but now there was no surge forward on the part of the protesters, who briefly fell silent. Shields parted and support policemen in snatch squads rushed at individual protesters and dragged them off, back through the police ranks.

This action animated the protesters. Some called out abuse at the police, others chanted. A group of younger activists started grabbing up stones from the garden and hurling them over policemen's heads at the windows of the lab. A dozen or so were shattered before the police moved. Then they drove a wedge into the crowd, slashing at them indiscriminately with their batons, and lifted the stone-throwers. These young people disappeared with more violence than anyone could have imagined necessary; there was humiliation to redress.

The situation was hopeless as far as getting into the laboratory was concerned, but then no one had expected to be able directly to help any of the hundreds of animals imprisoned there. By their actions, they hoped to bring some attention to their suffering. Helen would have liked to have called for a silent prayer, but this situation was beyond that. Instead she sat down and told those around her to do the same. Within minutes all the protesters were sitting in the forecourt to the building, chanting their familiar cries. The police stood back and watched them, uncertain what to do for a moment.

Senior officers consulted among themselves. They knew they couldn't allow this mob to control the situation a moment longer. They were trespassing and would be forcibly removed if necessary. The chief superintendent, stepping forward with his megaphone, brought a mocking cheer from those seated. He pointed out that they were trespassing and asked them to remove themselves and disperse or they would be arrested. That brought the response from Sheila Weymouth with a megaphone: 'What do we want?' The reply from the crowd was: 'Animal liberation!' Her question: 'When do we want it?' 'Now, now, now!'

The policemen waited as the chanting went on, each selecting their target with fear or hate in their eyes. They were impatient for the chief superintendent to give the signal. He was too slow and indecisive for this sort of operation. Superintendent Mike Regan was much better; he didn't put up with any nonsense from rubbish like this.

Pointedly examining his watch, the chief superintendent said, 'I'm giving you two minutes to clear these premises and disperse. After that you will be arrested. Two minutes.'

No one got up to leave and Helen felt proud of their commitment, regardless of the outcome here. She craned her neck and looked around at those people with her. The majority hadn't experienced personal violence on demos, certainly not from the police; perhaps they wouldn't today, but Helen felt there was a distinct possibility that they would. She had been going on demos from the very early days, and had seen the attitude of the police change – not just to animal rightists, but to all protesters who took to the streets. It almost seemed as if every police operation to deal with protesters was a rehearsal for some main event that had yet to be announced. This thought frightened Helen more than a little, because despite their always being on the opposite side or protecting institutions to which she was opposed, she had curiously trusted the police. She no longer did. Her thoughts were interrupted by the chanting going on around her. 'Vivisectors? Out. Vivisectors? Out. Vivisectors? Out, out, out!'

The time limit expired and the police went into action. They began to grab hold of the people at the front any way they could, and when arms were linked up in human chains they swung their truncheons or their feet to break them apart. Protesters went rigid or into tight balls to make their removal more difficult. It wasn't long before they reached Helen, who was linked up with three other people besides Rose and Paul Bailey. The police pulled and didn't succeed at first, so tried again. Some of the lines broke before swinging batons struck knuckles and forearms. A policeman thrust his arms under Helen's and clamped his hands on her breasts, with a sly grin to a colleague; Rose flew at him in that second's distraction. She was struck

15

from behind with a stick. Helen saw two policemen tackle Paul, but he hung on fast to the metal grating of a rainwater gulley until a third policeman started kicking his fingers. Anger rose in Helen at that unnecessary violence.

'You bastards,' she screamed. 'You sick sadists.' She lashed out at the policeman holding her, breaking free in her fury. All that was going on around her was immediately lost in the roar of protest that preceded the clatter of hooves as mounted police, who had been held in reserve behind the laboratory building, appeared on the service road and made a charge at the protesters. There was no arguing with mounted police. They bore down on protesters, swinging their long sticks. People no longer remained on the ground to be trampled on or struck over the head. They broke ranks and fled in the only direction they could, off the forecourt and along the street. The police on foot responded in the same way, drawing quickly back, releasing people they had held of.

The streets the protesters fled along were drab and littered with rubbish. Here was Victorian and Edwardian architecture at its worst, squat and ugly, grimed with decades of soot, uncared for. The streets invited no one; those who sought refuge there were intruders. The protesters were in flight, not knowing where they were going. Groups had scattered in various directions. About forty or so turned off Mare Street onto Well Street, with police coming up behind them. Helen Daniels and Paul Bailey were among them. Another group continued straight along Mare Street. Helen's party knew for certain that the police had the area completely closed off when two Transit vans full of them appeared up ahead on Well Street, blocking their escape. The vans stopped just below the junction of Tudor Grove, giving them the option of turning either back or into this narrow street. They chose the latter. Policemen from the vans wearing riot helmets and carrying shields and an assortment of weapons – from long American police night sticks to short saps that slipped easily into pockets – pursued them.

A thin youth of about eighteen with long fine hair that looked as if it hadn't been brushed in a while, wearing airforce dungarees, a blue airforce surplus shirt and plimsolls, was shaking as he ran. Paul Bailey who ran alongside him was scared also and felt empathy with the youth, feeling better himself that he wasn't the only one who was afraid. As he glanced sideways at him, he saw a long stave wielded by a policeman strike the boy on the shoulder, causing him to stagger forward.

Paul Bailey broke his step and called out as he tried to grab the boy and prevent him falling, thinking he would be trampled. As he did so, he felt something strike him a glancing blow on the shoulder. Someone in front shouted, 'They're up ahead!' and people began to turn back. The same object struck Paul Bailey again on the back of the head. The pain was colossal. He started to turn and saw a faceless, helmeted blue uniform. Another blow hit him on the head.

'I'm a medical student,' he said illogically, remembering he'd dropped his books somewhere. A great rushing filled his ears like the roar of water. Paul Bailey didn't hear Helen Daniels' screams of protest at this, or the abuse she lashed at the policemen as they fell back from where he lay in the road.

Helen knelt by him with a tremendous sense of foreboding. Protesters stopped about her, with nowhere to go. There was an oppressive stillness about Paul. She took his hand and watched a trickle of blood appear from his right ear. She noticed nothing else that happened around her just then, heard nothing. She thought only of how she had persuaded Paul to come on this demonstration because she was one of the organizers and felt she had to make it a success.

An Asian man from a nearby house approached and touched her on the shoulder.

'Would he want a glass of water?' he asked. 'Water?'

Slowly Helen shook her head.

I

His hand shook visibly in the mirror as he drew the razor down his face, and he stopped and steadied it on the side of the basin. He was thinking about what his wife had told him in the bedroom a short while ago and getting angry again.

After a few moments his anger subsided and he finished shaving. An indifferent effort, with bloodspots on his neck and a scraped chin and lip. He dressed slowly, not because he had time to spare, but because he was reluctant to go down and confront his wife, fearing that what she had told him was true, that she was really leaving him. Of course it was true; Sharon didn't make those kind of jokes. He was the one who was always joking around. He had a reputation for it; without exception, colleagues enjoyed his humour, but he amused Sharon less and less these days. When was the last time she had laughed at something he'd said? The children laughed, even the youngest of his five girls, who was only three. What would he do without them? Sharon had said the man she had met wanted them all to go and live with him. The thought made him quake. He knew other men whose wives had left taking the children. Most were desolate, staggering around empty spaces, waiting to make contact on the next allotted visit to their children. He shut the thought out, unable to bear it any longer.

The atmosphere in the kitchen as Sharon got the children ready for school was tense, and each in turn was affected by it. They were irritable or subdued. He wanted to go right off to work and pretend this morning hadn't happened. It was one where nothing would go right; he broke a handle off a favourite mug and spilt hot tea in his lap. Once upon a time Sharon would have taken the trousers and sponged them for him or offered to get his spare ones. This morning she just silently mopped the tea off the floor. Next his shoelace broke. He caught his wife's look, and wanted to say something, to ask why, after twelve years and five children, she had decided she not only didn't love him any more, but didn't even like him enough to try and work through their difficulty. He supposed he had asked something similar when she had told him earlier that morning, but couldn't remember her reply. He could scarcely hold a thought in his head.

'Will you be here tonight still?' he managed to say.

It seemed an eternity before she replied and he felt enormous relief when she said she would. From now on he would live his life in inches until one evening when he returned from work she wouldn't be there and nor would the children. Would this other man care about the children? He suddenly felt a great surge of resentment for this man he didn't even know, hating the influence he would have on his daughters without their realising it. He wondered how they would respond to him in the future.

The middle child, who was six, gave him an extra long kiss when he said goodbye, as if saying goodbye forever. He resisted squeezing her tightly and hugging her face to his, for if he did he knew he wouldn't be able to let go without crying, and that might upset them. He didn't want them going off to school upset.

Fragmented thoughts raced in his mind as he set out for the bus to work. He remembered the coupling that resulted in his middle daughter, but couldn't remember his last coupling with his wife. The harder he tried the more fragmented his thoughts became. Last weekend was it? He remembered a girl from before he was married. Maybe he could find her number and ring her up. Hello Sharon. Long time. My wife's left me. Only her name wasn't Sharon. He couldn't remember what it was. Last Sunday! That's when they had made love. They had woken before any of the girls, he had brought her tea and toast in bed, and she had rewarded him. Anger rose again when he realised that she must have been rewarding her boyfriend in the same way and at the same time. What made him especially angry was the fact that he had been completely unaware of their relationship. He was grateful that it wasn't someone he knew, without being sure why; he suspected it was in case he liked the man.

'Are you with us this morning, Roger, or still at home in bed?'

'Just five more minutes,' Roger Grainger said, snapping out of his reverie, 'then I'll get up.'

Most of the thirty-one traffic wardens in the muster room of the old police station in Walton Street laughed. Roger Grainger never missed an opportunity, and not one of the three senior wardens took exception to his quips. Unlike most humour, his was rarely at the expense of someone else's misfortune, apart

20

from when it was directed at the 'enemy' and their pathetic excuses for parking illegally.

'You're covering King's Road, from Sloane Square to the Town Hall. See if you can't recoup the cost of putting you on the street this morning.'

The reference was to Roger Grainger's tour of duty the previous day when he had issued only three tickets. He preferred to give motorists warnings; after all, life was difficult enough for most people without parking tickets.

Having been given their duties and told what the police were asking them to be on the lookout for today, most of the wardens were taken to their beats by Transits. But King's Road was an easy walk along Sloane Avenue from Walton Street. Roger Grainger enjoyed the streets, especially on sunny mornings in late summer before the air became laden with exhaust fumes. Now he was at work the domestic troubles that he had woken up to were pushed to the back of his mind, although they wouldn't go away entirely.

His work partner, who was ten years younger, quickened his pace without warning as they approached King's Road. It was a familiar move, sometimes it would happen on the way back to the station for a meal break, when they would find themselves having a walking race. Roger Grainger lengthened his stride. He wasn't particularly tall but had long legs and a fast stride and not many could beat him if they kept to the rules of the game. But not many kept to the rules as closely as Roger Grainger. His wife popped into his thoughts again.

Grinning at each other, both wardens jockeyed for position, each trying to prevent himself bursting either into laughter or into a run. Roger Grainger began to pull ahead when his partner suddenly grabbed his arm to drag him back, then sprinted ahead. Both stopped as suddenly as they had started.

Roger Grainger grinned and nodded across the street at a car parked on double yellow lines. He could have claimed it as technically he had won the race, but believed it was a bad way to start the day. Tickets were a last resort. He watched his colleague cross the street pulling his book from his black shoulder bag, thinking how he was being rewarded for cheating. He wondered briefly, as he turned left towards Sloane Square, if Sharon would be rewarded for cheating him. Roger Grainger

21

didn't consider that he may have in some way cheated her.

The driver of the silver stretch Mercedes 380 SE smiled to himself as he drew up on the double yellow lines outside the bank in King's Road. He parked the car deftly at the kerb some eight feet behind the dark blue Brinks-Mat security truck, giving himself space to pull out easily without manoeuvring. He smiled to himself again as he glanced through the mirror at the four lumps in the back, each in black robes and yashmaks. He didn't fancy any of them! Climbing out and straightening the grey cap of his livery, he walked briskly round and opened the rear passenger door. One by one the four black-clad lumps shuffled inelegantly across the seats, clasping their gowns about them as if in terror of showing something they shouldn't. As the last clambered from the car and accidentally exposed a fat hairy hand by pulling on the doorpost to gain leverage, the driver couldn't resist giving a wink. A blank cold stare came back from the vivid blue eyes, which were all that was visible of the face.

As the four crow-black figures filed into the bank, the Brinks-Mat security guard on watch by the door glanced over at the driver, who accommodated his prejudice by raising his eyebrows: we are us, mate, and them are them.

He walked back around the car, climbed behind the wheel and started the engine, as if indicating that he wasn't going to be there for long. He wasn't anticipating parking trouble this morning; drivers of diplomatic registered cars weren't usually harassed. He glanced across to the doorway of the bank as two other customers went inside; a woman came out leading a dog.

The driver realised that his mouth had gone inexplicably dry. He tried to moisten it but couldn't, and searched around the car for something. There was nothing. The man who had hired him had been very strict about that. He wished he were in a Roller and could dive into the cocktail cabinet for a quick drink. Coke or lemonade would have been all right, and he thought about going to find one, but knew the sort of trouble he'd be in if they came out while he was gone. He needed a drink then more than at any time in his life, and couldn't work out why; never once had he taken a drink while he was working. A tremble ran through his hand and he steadied it by gripping the wheel, then noticed that his palms were wet. Cautiously he glanced across to the security guard, then surreptitiously wiped his hands along his grey trousers.

Three minutes had passed since his passengers had gone into the bank and he wondered what was taking them so long. To add to his anxiety he saw a traffic warden along the street writing a ticket for a taxi. He assumed they had the same immunity as diplomatic cars and security trucks delivering and collecting money at banks. He glanced at the door again, then at the clock on the dashboard and back to the bank, wishing they would hurry. Calm down, he told himself, it's only a traffic warden. But his unease wouldn't leave him.

All fourteen of the customers in the bank would, if asked, probably have denied any feelings of prejudice towards foreigners, and especially towards those from the Middle East. Chelsea was, after all, one of the most cosmopolitan districts of London, and if people couldn't tolerate their neighbours, however strangely attired and oddly behaved, life would be very difficult indeed; nevertheless not one of the bank's customers had any compunction about pushing in front of the four crows, who hung back somewhat demurely, as if unfamiliar with the customs of the country.

The sharp-elbowed manner of the customers suited the four figures in black, and there was nothing they wanted from the service tills. When finally a bank employee, embarrassed at their being pushed aside, came forward to a vacant till and signalled to them, speaking in an Arabic language that none of them understood, the watchful blue eyes that were peering from behind that black veil were merely averted. The bank employee made an embarrassed comment to a colleague, trusting he had not given offence, and went for a more senior assistant to help them. These people were used to being dealt with by those at a senior level.

Bolts drawn on the door at the end of the bank counter caused each of the four crows to turn. They weren't expecting the manager, nor did they get him. What appeared was a small bogie on which sat three metal money boxes, each measuring about half a metre in length and half as deep and wide. As the two security guards trucked them across the hall the four Muslim women suddenly became animated. From under their black gowns two of them produced sawn-off shotguns, the other two pick-axe helves. The security guards were as surprised as anyone, and their visored helmets provided little protection as those shafts of hickory impacted. Rather like the motorcyclist's helmet, theirs provide cover against lacerations, but not against the hammer-effect, the head jarring into the body as the neck is compressed. The blows rendered one unconscious; the other guard reeled and received a body blow which knocked him to the floor.

'Don't anyone move!' the crow with blue eyes ordered in a deep Cockney voice. He fanned the bank with the shotgun.

Although they had been told that shotgun lead would not penetrate the protecting glass grille along the counter – it was also generally assumed that the guards' helmets gave them adequate protection, but one of them would suffer recurring pain from a compressed vertebra for the rest of his life – the bank staff became as immobile as the customers. There were no thoughts of heroic deeds as they watched one of the robbers grab a customer and push the shotgun into her neck. The bank rewarded its staff for saving it and the insurance company money; there was fifty pounds to be had for the capture of a fraudulent cheque card, only there was no risk in that. Fool-hardy heroism wasn't condoned.

The crow who fanned the bank with the second shotgun anxiously signalled to those with the pick helves to get going, but one of the guards was lying across the floor and they were having difficulty manoeuvring the heavy truck around him. Anxiety increased in everyone present as the bank robber ran forward and tried to kick the dead weight of the unconscious guard out of the way. It was a flash-point that might extend to further violence and any one of them could be at the receiving end.

Anxiety was making the driver of the Mercedes more un-comfortable. He had a sickening feeling that something had gone wrong and considered driving away, but he knew that that would be more than his life was worth. If he stayed he knew he might shit his pants; he could feel his bowel moving as he watched the traffic warden approach. The driver reached into the door pocket and touched the handgun there. Rather than give him comfort it distressed him further and he felt a faint trickling warmth in his back passage.

Roger Grainger was angry as he moved along the pavement past the Brinks-Mat truck towards the Mercedes. He was more angry with himself than his wife, angry for having given that taxi driver a ticket, and knowing the only reason he had done so was because the man Sharon was going off with was a taxi driver. He remembered the occasion he had arrived home to see a cab pulling away from the house. The incident had stuck in his mind. His wife had said the driver had come to the wrong house. She had lied, he realised now. That was last year. Perhaps it was the same cab driver he had given a ticket to. It didn't make him feel any better.

When Roger Grainger glanced over at him the security guard raised one finger to indicate they'd only be a minute, then smiled and nodded approvingly as if to say, 'One of them not getting away with it', as the warden stepped around the parked car to speak to the chauffeur.

'Are you going to be long?'

The chauffeur shook his head and opened the electrically-operated window. 'The cultural attaché's wife is in the bank.' He glanced anxiously towards the doors, which had just opened.

'Could you drive around the block?' Roger Grainger asked. Their business could be no more important than a taxi driver earning his living and he didn't want to have to issue a second ticket.

The chauffeur started to shake his head as the alarm bell started up in the bank and galvanized everyone's attention.

The robber with the vivid blue eyes flew at the pavement security guard, bashing him in the face with the shotgun, breaking his visor. Meanwhile the other three robbers spilt across the pavement and started hefting the security boxes into the car.

'C'mon, c'mon, for fucksake,' the blue-eyed robber screamed as he swung back to the car in time to see the traffic warden diving around the rear end at him.

There was no thought at all in Roger Grainger's head as he did this. He was neither courageous nor particularly foolhardy, but when something needed doing he tended to do it. He didn't like the way that man in uniform was battered to the ground, and he responded on pure impulse.

The flash of the shotgun exploding only three feet from him stung his eyes, and he wondered in an instant how he would cope without Sharon if he were blinded. He didn't feel anything as his chest tore apart. He was blown sideways over the boot of

25

the car, and slid down into the road, leaving a wide smear of blood across the brightly polished paintwork.

No one else did anything as the four robbers piled into the car, which then pulled straight out into the traffic and sped away along the King's Road towards Sloane Square, merging instantly with the traffic.

2

'A nation beset by economic decline, where the gap between the haves and have-nots continues to widen, must inevitably face the daunting prospect of rising crime. That nation must be judged by the way it tackles such problems. We know from a number of speeches at this conference how some senior policemen would have us deal with them.' The speaker paused and slowly shook his head in disagreement with those earlier speakers, feeling his audience weren't in accord, but quite enjoying that – being thought of as different, radical even, but succeeding despite the fact. 'A nation must deal with these problems in a fair and impartial manner. Bigger police forces, or a national police force – as has been proposed from this platform – more manpower, bigger prisons, these are not the answers to the problems; nor is more power for the police under the laws held in the Home Secretary's new White Paper, proposals which he will doubtless expand on when he speaks tomorrow. If you think these are the answer, then you're clearly not thinking, you are deluding yourselves about that. What we must not do is panic the politicians into that same deluded belief. Just because the feeling in your gut tells you it's right, doesn't make it right. Certainly the police need help from the politicians, and unless we get the right sort of help and soon, the situation is going to get worse. But don't go away with the idea that the current concern being expressed in political circles is going to bring the right solutions, or even any solution at all. The concern expressed in political circles has, I fear, little to do with better policing within the community through the improvement of relations between the police and the public, or even with the improvement of democracy. What it is instead is the first conscious step towards direct political control of the police. If we're not very careful, the police will more and more be used as a stick with which politicians beat their opponents. You have seen how the plank of consensus policing is daily being whittled away. You heard an earlier speaker express concern at the directive to the police from the Home Office about reducing CID overtime – that's one way it's being eroded; to concentrate not on capturing criminals, other than for serious crime, but on policing public

27

order is another. These moves are something all policemen should be warned about, and hopefully will resist. We ignore these danger signals at our peril.'

Jack Bentham didn't expect rapturous applause when he finished speaking, that was hardly likely with only about a hundred delegates present in the main auditorium at the Brighton Conference Centre, but the long silence was un-nerving. What eventually followed was spasmodic clapping, which only came when the chairman of the Association of Chief Police Officers rose to the lectern and politely clapped. The content and tone of his speech had obviously gone too far for most of these policemen, including his boss Assistant Commis-sioner (Crime) Peter Vyvyan, who had left the hall half-way through – no doubt on urgent business. However, it hadn't gone far enough for Jack Bentham. It had gone only as far as he dared in railing against politicians who wanted to use the police as an aid to the executive. He had nineteen years of conditioning as a policeman to struggle with, and this wasn't something that could be dismissed lightly. He had managed to avoid some of the more obvious prejudices of policemen, possibly because he had gone to university before even considering the police as a career. He had got a reasonable second in psychology at Exeter University. Even so, he felt an affinity with these men, that feeling springing up in people brought together in adversity, and he was disappointed that they hadn't gone at least some way towards sharing his views. The truth was that most of them probably didn't care that they were being used politically, just so long as it was the political party of their persuasion. But perhaps it meant he was changing more than he realised, and if that was the case it didn't bode well for his future in the Metropolitan Police.

'Thank you, Chief Superintendent Bentham, for a stimulat-ing, thought-provoking speech,' the chairman said as Jack Bentham left the stage.

He was the last speaker of the morning on the second day. Bentham wasn't planning to stay the full length of the con-ference because of the pressure of work. He had delegated a lot of it, and a number of the meetings with other senior officers couldn't take place as they were here also, but even so there were mountains of reports to get through and nothing would happen in Brighton that he felt he couldn't miss, not even Peter

Vyvyan's speech; Bentham could have written that for him without thinking. Vyvyan was a hardline reactionary who would make a passionate appeal both for the restoration of the death sentence for capital murder and for a further increase in police powers. He had made a similar speech the previous year, and had won some extra powers for the police since then, but he failed to see the rocks of reason upon which his deterrent argument in favour of the death penalty foundered. Bentham knew he was in a minority with his own views on capital punishment. His reason for being against restoration wasn't that it might encourage more villains to carry firearms, but sprung from occasional self-doubt over such cases. To lay the evidence before a court that said the accused did the deed and let the judge and jury take the decision was one thing, but to rely on a gut feeling in bringing a case when the defendant could be executed was quite another. Jack Bentham knew how evidence was collected and presented to the courts, that there was always a bias against the suspect; the police weren't in the business of proving innocence, only guilt. Jack Bentham would stop being a policeman if the death penalty were reintroduced – and he didn't trust politicians not to vote it back when the pressure for restoration increased.

After an indifferent lunch, which he ate alone in the conference centre, wondering if he was being purposely avoided, he had his driver drop him off at an address on the west side of the town – two large Regency terraced houses made into one on the ground and first floors to make a ballet school, which let space in the evenings for other activities. Climbing the uncarpeted stairs to the first floor. Bentham stood and watched a ballet class in progress through a glazed section of wall. The dancers were all girls aged from twelve to sixteen. Like most policemen he was fairly accurate at guessing age, especially the age of youngsters; age determined criminal responsibility as far as the courts were concerned.

From the more than passing interest he took, Bentham could tell the girls were all quite proficient and a few possibly hoped to become professional ballerinas. Probably less than five percent of that few would go any further in the ballet world. Watching their young, muscular limbs, which glistened slightly from a fine film of perspiration, Jack Bentham found them sexually very exciting and noticed that his cock was getting hard. So captivated was he that he didn't notice the middle-aged woman who approached along the corridor until she was alongside him.

'We aren't open to the public,' she said in an accusing tone.

Jack Bentham glanced at her and almost smiled. 'I'm looking to get some lessons for my daughter,' he lied. The woman, whom he recognized, seemed prepared to play his game. He assumed she knew who he was.

'You'd better come along to the office.'

She turned and went back along the corridor, expecting Bentham to follow. Instead his attention returned to the dance studio, where the girls were now at the bar. He could find himself arrested for such pursuits if he weren't careful; he quite understood how men who weren't got themselves in that sort of trouble. Young girls were resistable, Bentham found, but only just.

The dancing school office was very small and crowded with posters of both past and future ballet productions. Jack Bentham hadn't seen any of them and realised his story about his non-existent daughter wanting to take up ballet probably wouldn't stand close examination. Also on the wall was a scoreboard showing how many of their pupils went on to better things, and he wondered if such a device in squad offices and police stations might spur detectives on to make more arrests and so get to the top of the league. Possibly it would make them less careful, and arrests that with care would ordinarily end in a conviction would get a throw instead.

'How are you, Mrs Lane?'

Mrs Lane rose from behind the cluttered desk and closed the door, then cleared some clothes from a spare chair. 'Do you remember me?' She had asked the same question when she had telephoned Detective Chief Superintendent Bentham in his office over three weeks ago. He didn't remember her, only her husband, and told her so.

'We're not married any more.'

'Didn't fancy living in Spain? From what I've heard the life isn't all it's cracked up to be.'

Mrs Lane nervously twisted the wedding ring she still wore. 'He wants to come back.' She looked at the detective, then away again and qualified her statement. 'To England.' There was no question of her and David getting together again, even though he had telephoned her and asked her to approach Jack Bentham about giving himself up.

'Could cost him a lot of time inside. There's no way he wouldn't go – with a bit of work.'

'He feels he's in prison where he is, Mr Bentham.' She expected him to laugh and was pleased that he didn't. Her ex-husband had sounded more unhappy than she had ever known when she had spoken to him on the telephone, but she knew it would be difficult to convey that misery to anyone, especially as David not only had his freedom, but had it in a holiday resort. 'He wants to do a deal.'

Now Bentham did laugh. 'London's crawling with policemen from Wiltshire looking for police corruption. They'd love to talk to him, I'm sure. You should have telephoned them.'

'David doesn't trust them to give the sort of deal he wants.'

'Well I can't give him any guarantees. Not the sort he'd want.'

'You helped his brother.'

'He wasn't a regular villain.'

He remembered David Lane's younger brother Charlie, how he had been made the body by a firm who had robbed a warehouse. Charlie Lane was the only one they had arrested. He was like a child and Jack Bentham could have got him to put his hand up to anything he needed to clear up. He hadn't needed a high clear-up rate that badly in a long while.

'He's out of the mental hospital now,' Mrs Lane said, sensing the policeman's interest, and understanding a little now why David had asked her to ring him in particular. 'He's even got a job.'

'If David gets in touch, I'll do what I can.' He scribbled his numbers on a sheet of paper from her desk. 'We've a lot to talk about.'

He could have promised Lane his liberty, or anything else, to get him back, but didn't.

The ballet class was over by the time Bentham got back along the corridor. He was disappointed; but thought perhaps it was just as well.

'That was a fucking awful speech you gave this morning, Jack. Thank God there was no one there to listen to you.' He meant from the media. 'What are you, a fucking Marxist?'

31

'They wouldn't take my subscription, Peter.' Bentham turned to the tall, slightly paunchy, slightly stooped, slightly balding Assistant Commissioner Peter Vyvyan in the circular corridor of the conference centre. 'I thought you were going to America with the commissioner.'

'Not for a fortnight.'

'You going in Concorde?'

'If he is,' the ACC said defiantly. 'Did Harry Streeter reach you? He wants you to take on the investigation into the death of that medical student out at Hackney.'

'Needs a Marxist viewpoint, Peter, does it?' Bentham was smiling.

'Needs someone a bit fucking sensible to take it on. Should be CIB2 – the biggest department in the CID and he wants to tie up detectives on complaints. Why he wants you to take it on? D'you know why?'

Bentham shook his head. It was easier than lying directly. But then he could only guess why he had been elected. 'It might look better if someone from outside took it on.'

'Haven't we got enough of those with this lot from Wiltshire. Widespread police corruption! Fucking nonsense. We don't need an outside force looking up our arse or anywhere else.' Peter Vyvyan was never shy about making known his views over what support the police should get. He believed the police had an increasingly difficult and dangerous job, which they did very well, and that they shouldn't be criticized or penalised whenever they responded in kind to any especially dangerous situation. 'We've always taken care of our own wrongdoers.'

'Isn't that part of the problem, Peter?'

Ordinarily Jack Bentham was inclined to agree with him, that the police should get a lot more support than they got; but this killing, allegedly by a policeman out at Hackney, looked nastier than just another case of the press with their knives out. Whether or not it was, he still didn't want to take on.

That wasn't Harry Streeter's view and, as deputy commissioner, he outranked him somewhat. He could have ordered Jack to take on the job when he called him into his seventeenth-floor office the following day, but Jack knew that wouldn't happen.

He couldn't think why the deputy commissioner would want him to take on this complaints inquiry when there was CIB2. Jack was sure he'd only thought of him on account of another-problem that he had recently raised with him, directly rather than through the deputy assistant commissioner or even the assistant commissioner at the appropriate meeting. If Bentham had gone through the usual channels the problem wouldn't have ceased, it would have been circumvented.

'It looks very messy, Harry. I'd hate to find myself having to take the official line.'

'That's why I thought of you, Jack. The last thing I want is for you to trot out the regular police line and hope press and public alike will swallow it. I don't think they will. But nor do I want you to find those lads guilty just because someone is screaming for police heads.'

'Fuck it,' Bentham said, finding it difficult to resist. 'Why doesn't CIB2 take it on?'

'Having those lads from Wiltshire here hasn't exactly enhanced their credibility,' the deputy commissioner said. 'They got their hands full with that lot.'

'I'm not exactly scratching for work.'

'If there were anyone better, I wouldn't ask you. You don't seem to give a fuck about other policemen's opinion of you. You're prepared to stick your neck out, and do too often for your own good. I want a conclusion to this, Jack. I think those lads out at Hackney deserve a little better than the nasty odour that's floating around at present. It needs to be seen to be as impartial as we can make it.'

'That's why you should call in someone from outside.'

'No one wants that, least of all the commissioner.'

Policemen all over London were realising to their cost what a mistake it had been to bring in the Wiltshire Constabulary to investigate the Met. But it was too late to do anything about that now, with their inquiries spreading from one District to another.

'What if I find it's as messy as it seems, that Old Bill was entirely responsible?'

'Well, we'll see what we see if and when we come to it.'

Jack Bentham wasn't reassured and knew it was naive of him to ask such a question when so many outside factors would determine the answer, most of them political. But, reluctantly, he accepted the job.

33

3

The sky was blue and cloudless, and with a light south-easterly breeze it was a day to be setting out for the Channel Islands, not returning. But both Terry Sneed and the other half of his crew, Judge Anthony Wertham, had work commitments. Work wasn't all that was on Terry Sneed's mind as he manoeuvred the forty-foot sloop into Brighton marina on its fifty-five horsepower Perkins diesel engine. The sails were stowed. Terry Sneed had had this boat for going on six years, having bought it when the bottom was falling out of the market; he had decided that that was the time to buy anything large or luxurious. He had had several offers for the sloop since then that would have returned him a nice profit. Only occasionally did he think about selling, usually when he had to put in time on maintenance. He wasn't one of those enthusiasts who were prepared to spend fifty weekends a year doing up their boats for two weekends' sailing. He saw no point in hanging on to anything once there was pain involved, be they objects or people. Terry Sneed hung on to nothing other than information, which he equated with power, especially when it concerned people. Just then, Terry Sneed was thinking about a meeting he had set for that evening, even though it was business that he now wanted to be as far removed from as possible.

Sneed throttled back on the engine and swung the wheel hard to port, then watched the aft of the boat come gently around towards the berth. Pushing the engine into reverse he edged the stern against the quay. Judge Wertham, who was fifty-two, sprang ashore to tie up like an enthusiastic teenager. He seemed to enjoy these trips more than anything he did, and Sneed still wasn't sure if the pleasure came from the duty-free scotch and cigarettes he brought back, or from the fact that it was illegal and he was living so dangerously for a man in his position. Sneed suspected it was the latter, for he had been living danger-ously when they had first met, when he was still only a recorder and not a full circuit judge; then his interest had been young girls, and Terry Sneed had helped him out of a potential black-mail situation. He had said at the time that he thought perhaps he should resign, until Sneed pointed out that it wasn't necessary as all the evidence was contained. Wertham hadn't felt compelled to do the honourable thing; he liked being a judge, the law was his life, and Sneed saw more value in his alliance with a judge than with an ex-judge.

'Not the tiniest bump, Terry,' Anthony Wertham said, coming back on board as Sneed shut down the engine. 'You could have had a box of eggs over the side.'

'I wish some of the other boat owners were as careful.' He would sometimes find scuffs on the varnish where other boats had manoeuvred alongside. Their owners were like car owners who scraped other parked cars – they felt that they had got away with something if the owner of the damaged vehicle wasn't there to protest and demand insurance details.

The judge went below and started bringing up the three seabags which he had brought on board nearly empty. Now they were full of bottles of scotch and cartons of cigarettes. Sneed had one small grip bag. He kept clothes on board, along with the scotch he bought in Jersey, though nothing like the amount that the judge got on each trip.

'Do you fancy going down to Spain the weekend after next, Anthony?' Sneed invited as they moved along the jetty. He was taking his boat down to its winter berth in Marbella, although that wasn't the sole reason for the trip, just the excuse. He had to see a man to collect some money. The judge would make an even better cover.

'I'd love to, but I fear that might be too long a weekend for me. I've got the West Midlands circuit.'

'The Wellington boot crime,' Sneed said cryptically.

The judge smiled knowingly. 'They have their entertaining moments, Terry.'

'We wouldn't take that long. We'd get the plane back.'

'There's always the risk that we might not get back to meet my schedule. You know I'm not one to take risks.' He stopped by a Rover 2300 parked on the quayside, unlocked the boot and put two of his seabags in. Sneed lowered the third in and Wertham relocked the boot. Sneed smiled to himself. That was fifteen litres of Johnny Walker and five thousand Benson and Hedges cigarettes that weren't going to be declared at the customs house.

'I'm tempted though, Terry. Do you require an immediate answer?'

'No. But if you can't do it I'll need someone handy to go down with me. Ring me next week some time. Take care with that lot.'

The judge smiled and climbed into his car. Sneed walked further along the quay to where a dark blue Ford Sierra was parked. The driver didn't get out from behind the wheel to open the door. He was there to drive, and had to be ready to do that the whole time, which would be impossible if he was in and out opening and closing doors.

'Been waiting all weekend, Roger?' Sneed threw his bag onto the back seat and picked up the folder which was lying on the front seat; it contained urgent reports which he needed to read for meetings that day.

'Good sense of timing, guv. To the office?'

'Go past my flat.' It was more or less on the way.

Sneed had a three-room flat in Crystal Palace with an old cast iron conservatory on the back room. It stood on the hill overlooking the basin of London. It was a stunning view, if not a particularly pretty one. He had sometimes considered a flat on top of a highrise, but decided the view alone wouldn't have been sufficient compensation for the rest of the hassle tenants in these modern slums had to put up with; the debris, the crummy neighbours, a high percentage of whom were black or out of work, broken lifts. Sneed wasn't someone who was affected one way or the other by his environment, but there were limits.

His current flat had been converted out of a large Victorian semi-detached house, and converted cheaply, which meant badly. Panelled doors had been taken away and replaced with flush, asbestos-filled fire doors to meet local authority regulations, but why thirteen-inch skirting boards had been replaced with modern four-inch ones wasn't clear. The rooms were large, painted white and furnished mostly out of Peter Jones in Sloane Square, not because he thought them the acme of style in furniture, but because he had known a woman who worked there as a floor supervisor and she had got him a good discount. The rooms were anonymous and told a visitor very little about the occupier, other than that he didn't mind very much about his surroundings and probably didn't spend a lot of time there. There was a television, but no video, a radio, but no stereo system to play music; few books, and only a couple of prints on the walls which blended blandly with the decor.

Walking into the bedroom Sneed changed his shirt, and put on a suit and a tie. He didn't wear the emblem tie of the Old Flying Squad, which had since been reorganized and renamed the Robbery Squad. He didn't need that sort of identification. Reaching into the closet, he took out a tracksuit, which like all the other clothes in there was hanging in a Sketchley cleaning bag. He removed the hanger, rolled it into his grip, then took his jogging shoes, a towel and socks from a laundry parcel in the bottom of the cupboard. Jogging wasn't his religion; sometimes he left it off for months, at other times he would get his driver to drop him on the way to work and he would jog the rest. He found running in the morning good for hangovers. Tonight he would jog on Barnes Common; it was business.

Nothing that had happened on any of the jobs the Squad had in hand in any way startled Terry Sneed when he got to the second floor office which he shared with a chief inspector on the Regional Crime Squad out at Barnes police station. The RCS had all but disappeared in the reorganization of the Flying Squad. It had become integrated into the new Robbery Squad, which had been moved out of the Yard and into the eight Districts. Met officers from the Flying Squad, with their old loyalties, dominated the new set-up and expected the remnants of the RCS to be dispersed at any time out into the regular CID within the Districts. Sneed thought it would be a move in the right direction, as no real integration had taken place; both squads kept their own identity where possible, often pursuing the same villains, and showed a reluctance even to swop information when it came in. Sneed suspected that this was happening with the one across the pavement in King's Road. The RCS had got something on it and were keeping it to themselves. He also suspected that their information was coming via C11, which was run by the ex-governor of the RCS. But he wasn't particularly bothered.

As the most senior detective chief inspector on the Flying Squad at the time of the reorganization, he had been offered the reserve squad, which was posted at the Yard, but had turned it down – it was nearly all administration there. There was always enough of that on an active squad. Most of his time seemed to be taken up with policy meetings about how best to interpret the latest cost-saving proposal, and checking that his men didn't exceed their overtime quota. For his part, Sneed would have let them put in all the overtime they wanted; 'pubbing and clubbing' with lads who were at it was sometimes the only way to get results. But now if they did over fifty hours of overtime a month the computer would throw their names up and they'd have to take time off. At any one time half his men might be off duty for having exceeded the overtime quota, and he would have to go and make a case to the DCS to allow them to put more hours in. Without that authorization, they would be working without pay. Fortunately, the chief superintendent who ran the Squad was easily manipulated, but there were rumours that he was on his way out, to be replaced by a more efficient administrator. Before that happened, Sneed would have moved on himself as his time on the Squad was nearing its end. Every three years all officers to the rank of superintendent were rotated to stop them getting too comfortable in their office, or too well known and accessible to those involved in wrong-doing on the manor. He wouldn't quite spew out from the computer to a random posting, as the lower ranks did. He had made it known to his commander, Ernie Wiseman, that he had fancied going across to C Division; Wiseman had spoken to the commander for that District, and that's where Terry Sneed would be heading. He might not get Chelsea police station, which was his first choice, but if he didn't he'd get Notting Hill or Kensington.

He checked through the huge pile of papers in the tray on his desk. He might have been away a week instead of a weekend and a day. About the only thing that wasn't on his desk was the individual Squad officers' duty logs, which were checked on a weekly basis for overtime and expenses against investigations worked on. They were seen first by the Squad inspectors and then by the DCIs before going off to the computer. Despite overtime restrictions, there was still a lot of fiddling, and the unserialized duty log sheets made bogus claims easier to spot. But unlike the old system of detectives' diaries which had been examined by senior officers in a similar way, the duty log sheet could be easily changed if mistakes were made or found out, but no record of them was wanted. The detective simply took a fresh set of sheets and started over again. Sneed had often given detectives he had caught fiddling a second chance, and he had found that it always paid off. Nicking detectives for such misdemeanours and getting them landed with a disciplinary offence and possibly sent back to uniform was rarely useful. Sneed had decided a long while ago that the system got what it deserved for having become increasingly restrictive and bureaucratic. Being run as it was more and more by policemen who had never felt a collar, he was surprised that the men in the job, and especially detectives, weren't more pissed off with their lot.

Another three of his fourteen detectives had been thrown up on the computer as having exceeded their overtime limit; DCs Troy, Kennedy and Martin would have to take a day off. He had five others who had exceeded theirs and they were only half-way into the month. At times he believed there was a conspiracy to prevent them capturing criminals. There was a meeting of Squad DCIs and inspectors at the Yard this afternoon. He would pull the DCS and ask him to prise loose some more overtime, even though he knew one of the main items on the agenda would be the amount of overtime that was still being worked despite directives to the contrary. Even capturing criminals had to be cost-effective, regardless of how the alternative impaired the quality of life. The problem was, of course, that those on high who formulated policy were totally out of touch with what was happening on the ground, and certainly didn't have villainy forcing its way into their lives.

The remainder of the paper work consisted of reports of investigations in progress, which kept him informed so that he could keep those ranks senior to him informed, enabling them to make cost-effective decisions. Investigations on the Squad were never abandoned, quite simply because they only dealt with major robberies which *had* to be investigated, unlike crime reports on District where offences were awarded points of priority based on the value of the theft and the amount of violence involved; if an offence didn't achieve ten points, it wasn't investigated. The more successful an investigation, the less needed to be written up in a report – only the salient points for the legal aid report upon which the prosecution would be based were necessary; the less successful the investigation, the more was required in the report, which would sometimes run to two hundred pages or more; every last detail had to go down, almost to the colour of witnesses' socks. Those sort of reports were 'the hate', and always left to the DCIs to write. It looked to Sneed as if that one across the pavement in King's Road where the traffic warden had been shot dead was going to be like that, unless the RCS came up with something; but Sneed had little expectation that they would achieve anything worthwhile.

Sneed looked at the shape of his day. There was a Squad meeting at 2.30; a meeting of DCIs at the Yard at 4.30; a meeting with an active villain at 7.30. The last wasn't entered in his diary; it was the one that held most interest for Sneed.

Sneed was numbed by the meeting at the Yard and felt pleased when he could finally get away. No one had talked about capturing villains, not even in general terms; they only seemed interested in who was keeping track of overtime. When he complained that lack of overtime was stopping them capturing villains, the Squad DCS, Geoff Lyle, told him to go up and complain to the DAC. He was amused that the DCS hadn't got the front to argue for overtime himself when the deputy assistant commissioner rarely denied special requests for overtime for Lyle's CID officers. The DAC was a chain-smoker with a persistent cough and was called Doc Holliday. Sneed was happy to go up to the fifth floor to talk to the DAC, if only to see his secretary. She was worth a visit any time.

'When are you going to come out on my boat, Vanessa?' he asked as he waited to see her boss.

'When are you inviting me?'

'How about this weekend?'

'I'm not a very good sailor.'

'We needn't leave the marina,' he told her.

She smiled invitingly and reached for the phone as it rang. She had a brief, guarded conversation with another secretary, then replaced the phone.

'Mr Vyvyan's secretary,' she explained. 'The commissioner's going to Washington on Concorde and the ACC's getting very jumpy in case he and his wife are supposed to go Club.'

'Can't say I blame him.'

'He doesn't like to ask directly.' The intercom buzzed. 'You can go in now, Terry.'

'I'll pick you up on Friday,' Sneed said, 'from your flat in Streatham.'

He got what he took to be acquiescence from Vanessa as he went into the DAC's office, holding his breath as if to resist taking cigarette smoke into his lungs.

'Terry, I can't get your squad another hour of overtime,' Doc

Holliday said, between coughing and drawing on his cigarette. 'There's not a squad in the department that isn't short. The Home Office is saying we should cut back further.'

'We'll stop functioning, that's what it amounts to.'

'I know that, and they know it because I keep telling them.'

'But they don't do the job, guv.'

'I keep on fucking well telling them that, too. All goes on public fucking order.' He coughed, then said, 'Can't you borrow some men from the other squads?'

'The trouble is we can never pay them back. It's like the national fucking debt.'

'You'd better nick a few more hours. Tell Geoff Lyle.'

The ease with which the DAC capitulated indicated that he wanted something.

'There's a DI who's been nicked out your way, Terry, Martin Skelhorn. He's at Putney. He was putting a bit of dope back in circulation – only pills. Probably do less harm than these.' He lit another cigarette. 'Couldn't you have a word with someone on CIB2? Skelhorn's in my lodge. In fact, I introduced him. If nothing can be done then nothing can be done.'

Sneed agreed to talk to someone, quite willing to oblige a brother officer in this way.

As the lift doors opened in the basement car park, Sneed saw Jack Bentham just getting out of his car. He'd expected the DCS to be at the meeting earlier, as so much of the information the Squad acted upon came via C11, but Bentham probably liked such meetings even less than he did.

'Terry,' Bentham greeted. 'How's that one across the pavement going?'

They had known each other since they were young officers rising fast in the system. Terry had risen through the ranks to become the youngest ever DCI, but at forty he had lost a lot of the impetus of his earlier career, and no one knew why better than he – his deep involvement in corruption. No charges had ever pursued him, or were likely to, but he suspected that he represented an Achilles heel to all those senior officers he did business with, business they would sooner not have been involved in, but in which they were too deeply involved to extricate themselves with any ease. Jack Bentham wasn't one of those, and Sneed recognized in him someone as contained as himself. Bentham would never prove to be a weak link, any more

41

than he would himself. Sneed would have loved to know what the DCS was having; he had no doubt that Bentham was having something from somewhere.

'No one's putting their hands up. Then after killing that traffic warden, I can't say I'm surprised. He was a very popular lad. Had five kids. Things seem well closed up on it. Especially your lads over the Water.'

Bentham knew he was referring to the ex-RCS officers. 'S'all the same firm now, Terry.' He stepped into the lift while Sneed held the gate.

'Try telling them. S'like a fucking egg and spoon race.'

'I heard you were all keeping your heads down with Wiltshire making themselves busy.'

'Them cunts.' There was a note of contempt as he dismissed the outside investigation. Then he laughed. 'Just means being a bit more careful, Jack.' He smiled, his pale blue liar's eyes revealing nothing.

He let the lift door close on Bentham, and noticed before he did that the other man smiled too. Sneed didn't enjoy that smile. It was an 'I'm waiting' sort of smile. For an offer, or to feel his collar? Sneed was never sure, and that's what made him uneasy about Jack Bentham. He was a working copper, one who preferred to be out working rather than coping with the bureaucratic arithmetic, and one who would go out on a limb to back his men; but that didn't endear him to Sneed, since Bentham had never been his governor. Bentham, having been until recently operational head of the Regional Crime Squad, which strictly wasn't part of the Met, didn't have those same loyalties to brother officers simply because they were Met officers. The RCS was a creature of the Home Office and that was why the Met was taking so long to bury it. Had it been a squad designed and got up by them, they would have disbanded it the moment it was no longer of use to them. Now that Bentham ran Criminal Intelligence, C11, and operated secretly, as detectives there did, he was possibly more dangerous. Sneed felt unnerved at not knowing what senior policemen were up to.

Dusk had fallen when Sneed had his driver set him down on Castelnau by the edge of Barnes Common.

'D'you want me to wait here, guv?' his driver asked from behind the wheel. He guessed at the kind of activities Sneed was into, but his unswerving loyalty was bought with all the overtime he got from driving him.

'Go round the river side. I'll see you on Horne Way. That'll be far enough to run for tonight.'

There were a number of people about, even though darkness was closing in by the time Sneed had been jogging for about twenty minutes. He had built up a fine sweat, which he assumed was the scotch he had drunk during his trip to Jersey. Other joggers were going past him, some obviously fitter, keener than he'd ever be; a woman jogged past in the opposite direction with three dogs on leads. Sneed turned and went backwards a few paces to watch her, physical exercise always made him horny and he might have pursued her in other circumstances. He lost his stride when he turned back and slowed towards a bench near the pond, where a man of about his age, but fatter and more out of condition, sat sweating in his tracksuit and gasping for breath. Despite his breathing difficulties, he drew on a lighted cigarette as if it were a source of oxygen. Sneed recognized Brian Cayman at once and felt slightly angry that, having arranged this safe, inconspicuous meet, Cayman should bring attention to himself by sitting around in a tracksuit smoking a cigarette. He was a reformed smoker himself and fairly intolerant of the habit anyway.

Sneed didn't speak as he reached the bench, but put one leg onto it, straightened it and leaned forward to stretch the ligaments. He did the same with the other leg, while Cayman looked at him as if he were mad. Bending to the ground between his spread out legs to touch his toes, Sneed reached for a small package from under his seat. He opened it and briefly fanned the edges of the banknotes inside before straightening up and zipping it away into the top of his tracksuit.

'That looks a bit sick, Brian, after what happened to that traffic warden.'

The edginess under which Brian Cayman had been labouring at the prospect of meeting this detective was due to that very fact. He knew the shooting was likely to bring all sorts of problems, not least financial ones; it wasn't something that had been accounted for, and was quite likely to negate the deal.

'The thing is, Terry, that was an accident. Know what I mean?'

Sneed looked at him with utter contempt. 'You'd be nicked 'I thought otherwise. But it's still got to come to a lot more than what we agreed. A lot more. Especially in these dangerous times.'

A thin, distressed sound issued from between the villain's thick lips. Having a detective like Terry Sneed pissed off at you was one thing; having to pay more for his help was something else again.

'It was an accident.'

Sneed nodded, but saw no reason not to benefit out of that.

'Aren't you going down to Spain to see Ronnie for the other bit? I thought that was what was happening.'

'I still want double off you, Brian. And as much again off him when I get down there. He's got to know that, after what happened. You cunt.'

Cayman sighed again. He wanted to argue and try and beat him down on the price, but was afraid to. He thought about the alternatives. There were two, neither of them very attractive.

Capable of out-thinking most people in these situations, simply because his emotional responses were always in control, Terry Sneed said, 'You could always leg it, Brian.'

'S'right fucking mug's game.' There was no way he believed he could survive on the run from the police. He rose off the bench as Sneed started away without so much as a thanks or goodbye.

A few paces along the path, Terry Sneed turned and jogged backwards. 'Oi! Don't forget we want a body.'

Cayman didn't answer, but he knew that someone had to be put up, and soon. That was standard, only the election was rarely democratic. The body was usually a surplus member of the firm who was taken on without suspecting his true role, often chosen for what he wouldn't tell the police when interrogated rather than what he would. It was time for some sort of result on that robbery.

Sneed smiled encouragingly at the unhappy Brian Cayman but suspected he didn't notice. Finally, he turned and jogged away towards his waiting car.

4

The theatre had only been half-full, the audience fairly dead, and the play on stage generally dull. Helen Daniels regretted the insecurity that had forced her to take the part, regretted her dilemma and the lack of any valued advice on which direction her future should take. It would have helped had there been a clear path through the animal rights movement, had they been winning some battles; but the sad fact was that there were too many clashing egos, too much in-fighting, too many people putting themselves before the animals. They needed one single person or winnable goal to rally behind, to unite the entire movement on a single front – the total abolitionists, the absolutists and all those prepared to compromise over anything from eating dead animals to allowing them to be subjected to some degree of pain in laboratories. Helen had hoped Paul Bailey's death at the hands of the police would have provided the focus, if only as a tribute to him, so that he wouldn't have died completely in vain. There were further meetings planned concerning his death and people did feel very angry and upset by it, but she wasn't convinced it would provide the impetus that was needed. If she got a decent contract, went off for a solid stint of work, away from all the animal rightists, and took a fresh or different look at things her mood might change, the dilemma resolve itself. Or perhaps she was, as a psychiatrist friend had suggested to her recently, making such a huge investment of emotional energy in animals because she couldn't cope with people very well – that diagnosis had come after she had resisted his advances. His suggestion had made her furious at the time and she had almost retorted that he was a psychiatrist simply to avoid confronting his own very confused feelings.

'Oh, Helen,' the young man in the stage door telephone cubicle said, catching her attention as she picked up her message slips pinned to the notice board, 'there was someone looking for you earlier.'

Rose flashed into her mind and she felt irrationally angry. Rose had telephoned twice and she hadn't returned her calls, because Rose seemed to be pushing her into a corner. They had spent the night together following Paul Bailey's death, at least

45

what had remained of the night after a group of them had tried to talk out their anger. It had been 4.00 a.m. by the time she had curled up on the bed with Rose, grateful for her support, her comfort, the physical contact she provided. Nothing had happened between them other than that they had given each other mutual support in their desolation, but now Rose had been ringing her on a daily basis as if she had some expectation of a relationship starting. Helen didn't think she wanted a physical relationship with another woman, not Rose or anyone else, even though she felt in need of a relationship with someone, if only for the physical contact she often craved, a need to be touched intimately, held by someone; it had been a long time. Both the actors in the play with her were homosexual, as was the director. Her last affair had been with an actor. It had lasted three weeks, the duration of rehearsing and recording a television play in Manchester for Granada.

'I think he was a policeman. He had that look about him. They do, don't they.'

'Oh, how nice for me. Thanks, Colin.' She pushed out of the stage door and started along the alleyway at the side of the theatre, intending to catch the tube back to her flat, fearing Rose would be in the pub next door.

Jack Bentham was walking towards the stage door; his car was parked beyond the pavement at the mouth of the alley. He recognized Helen, having been in earlier to see the play. He thought it a pointless exercise, but didn't think it deserved quite the degree of anger some of the reviewers had reserved for it. He didn't often read theatre reviews, and he went to the theatre even less frequently, but on this occasion tended to agree with what he took to be the author's message – that we each create our own reality. What made the play pointless in his opinion was the author's railing against the pricks without offering the solution. Bentham thought the best thing to do in the dark was light a candle, rather than complain about it.

'Helen Daniels.'

'Right,' she said. Colin on the stage door was exactly right also. You could tell about policemen, even those not in uniform. She was intentionally curt, guessing why he might be pursuing her, and intended being as obstructive as she could. The police had after all murdered Paul, and whatever the outcome of any internal inquiry they might conduct, or the verdict of the coroner's court, nothing would change that fact as far as Helen was concerned. 'If you want a signed photograph, you must write to my agent.'

It was clear she knew who he was. 'I think I can probably get by without a photograph. I'm conducting the investigation into Paul Bailey's death out at Hackney. My name's Bentham.'

'How very reassuring, Mr Bentham. Now we have the police on the job looking at other policemen, our minds will be put completely at ease.'

'I didn't expect you to fall over yourself to talk to me. It is important that we do talk. In fact I'd say it's essential. I understand you were the one who brought him along to the demonstration.'

Helen closed her eyes momentarily. She had been over that time and again, and no fragmented rationale she grasped at could assuage her sense of guilt. She remembered clearly her arguments to persuade him, as she had others. But none of the others had been killed; nor had she blatantly manipulated them through any feelings they may have had for her.

'I also saw the police strike him down.'

'Look, do you want to have a cup of coffee or a drink somewhere while we talk?'

Helen wouldn't have minded a drink. She pulled her coat protectively about herself, even though it wasn't cold.

'Not really.' The words came out like brittle glass. 'You'd better ring me sometime and make an appointment.'

She hurried past him, making for Sloane Square. As Bentham watched her she turned at the end of the alley and glanced back at him, as if to measure his reaction. He wasn't going to pursue her, not now, and started back to his car. He needed to talk to her, and soon. All in all he wasn't progressing very fast with this inquiry. Some of the witnesses weren't being very forthcoming, not least the police who were directly involved.

When he got to Hackney police station the following day to interview four of the eight policemen on duty in the first DSU Transit van – designated Uniform Carrier G/59 – to stop in Well Street just before Paul Bailey's death, the uniformed Superintendent Mike Regan came down to meet Bentham and DI Joe Russell. He had spoken to Superintendent Regan several times on the telephone, but had got only a hint of the resentment he felt coming off him now they met face to face.

47

'Pick your fucking feet up, sooty, or we'll put you in a wheelchair.' The statement came from one of two uniformed constables who looked about nineteen, as they manhandled a black youth through the back door, interrupting Bentham and Regan's preliminary niceties.

Their gaze followed this trio through the rear reception area to the charge room, then Superintendent Regan finally turned back to Jack Bentham with a trace of a smile in his look which challenged him to say something.

'There's a lot of the lads here resent this inquiry, sir,' he said, thinking it best to get that statement in so the DCS knew exactly where he stood. 'They think it bloody unfair. I'm inclined to agree. You do the job the best you can in the circumstances.'

'I'm sure Paul Bailey's friends think his death here was unfair. In fact we know they do. That's partly why you've got this sort of inquiry. Now I didn't put my hand up for it. I'd sooner be out nicking villains than policemen. But it affects everyone in the job when something like this happens. It causes aggravation, makes the work harder, causes the public to have less confidence in us. The investigation has got to be done, and the more obstructive your men are the longer it takes.'

'I can't do anything about the feelings of the men, sir.'

Bentham stopped at the foot of the back stairs and looked at the man in uniform, who had very coarse facial features, pores like craters and a waxy bulbous nose. He wondered if he had listened to anything he had just said.

'It's up to them. I could talk to the deputy commissioner about suspending them during the inquiry.'

'I think we'd lose them, and half their colleagues. Even lads who aren't part of the DSUs.'

Bentham simply nodded. He understood that sort of loyalty.

'Let's get started. You have an office we can use?'

'You're welcome to use my office,' Superintendent Regan offered in a conciliatory way.

'It might be better if we see the policemen directly involved down here. An interview room will be fine.' He reached for the folder of statements DI Joe Russell had taken and opened it. 'We'll start with constables Strong, Sanderson and Westbrook, and Sergeant Morrison.'

There was a pause. It was almost as if the uniformed superintendent didn't want to give him the next piece of information. 'They're all on leave.'

Bentham didn't say anything, but felt his anger rising. He became quiet when he got angry, fearing his own temper, and those who worked around him knew the danger signs.

'I did provide a list of officers for you to interview today, guv,' DI Joe Russell said breaking the silence.

'It cut across their leave, sir.' Superintendent Regan didn't enjoy the silence from the DCS.

'What about any of the other men from Uniform Carrier G/59, or those from G/60?'

'These men are out providing back-up for the policing of pickets out at the docks. I'm not sure they can be pulled off that at short notice.'

Bentham nodded slowly. He understood the importance of DSU back-up in such situations. Policemen could get dangerously stretched, psychologically, emotionally and physically, when on duty at industrial disputes or demonstrations, especially when feelings were running high. Possibly that fact had contributed to Paul Bailey's death.

'I am going to get this investigation done,' Bentham said calmly, not allowing this man the satisfaction of seeing he was being got at. 'Either the easy way or the other way. In future when I ask for officers to be available to be interviewed, they'd better be here.'

Fortunately things were progressing better for Bentham's squad on another front. They had had a break on the robbery in King's Road. Detective Inspector Bill Senior had been on duty in the C11 squad's office at the Yard when an anonymous piece of information came in about the silver Mercedes 380 that the police had been looking for. The caller obviously knew his way about the Yard; it was strange that the call should come to Criminal Intelligence. For that reason, DI Senior didn't pass it on to the Robbery Squad. He called on some of his own detectives for a visit out.

The car, with its diplomatic index plates lying behind the front passenger seat, had been parked in the basement car park to the flats of St George's Field, just off Bayswater Road. At first glance it seemed as if any number of stolen cars had been dumped here – there were Jaguars and Jensens with an inch of dust on them. There were a number of newly-arrived cars, all of them police vehicles: two area cars with uniform officers in, an unmarked Ford and an old Triumph, with two C11 detectives, one of them DC Denis Marsh, who had been on the RCS with Jack Bentham. An oldish but well-maintained Saab came down the ramp and along the line of parked cars to where the Mercedes was. Detective Sergeant Kingham, another ex-RCS man, got out with a detective who was new to C11. A third area car came down the ramp, shortly followed by a fourth.

'That took its fucking time turning up,' DS Kingham said, joining the other detectives by the Mercedes.

'S'right result, skip.' DC Marsh opened the rear door, reached into the car and pulled back a coat lying on the seat. Beneath it were the two sawn-off shotguns used in the robbery and the pick-axe helves.

'S' almost like someone dumped it here for us to find.'

He glanced around at the dusty cars. The Mercedes didn't look like it had been sitting in this underground car park since the robbery. Reaching into the car he picked up one of the shotguns to examine it, using the corner of the coat to do so, hoping there might be prints, but very much doubting it. Even so, he didn't want his on the gun.

'S'odds on they went missing from somewhere.' The guns looked fairly expensive, may even have been custom made. 'Better get this driven in, have C5 check it for prints. The guns had better go to forensic – we'll get a trace on this.' He indicated the filed serial number. His statements covered the routine checks. Someone had to go through the things to be done or there was a chance they wouldn't get done, and he was the most senior detective present. He dropped the gun back onto the seat and closed the door with his elbow as yet another area car arrived.

'Fuck me, who called the woodentops?' He thought from DI Senior's information that this was something special, which was why C11 were getting involved post-robbery. Usually they would gather all the information that was to be gathered on crimes about to be commissioned, then they would hand it over to the Robbery Squad for a result.

'Looking for a bit of overtime, skip.'

'We'll give them something to do. Have them catch hold of

people who park here, see if anyone noticed when the Merc was dumped. Who left it here. They can start knocking on the flat doors above.'

'We following this up, skip?' Marsh asked.

'Bill Senior seemed to think it might be worthwhile.' He shrugged. 'Maybe he's forgotten what it's like to feel a collar.' C11 detectives rarely made arrests themselves.

No one had seen the car being parked or could remember how long it had been there. The flat owner to whom the bay had been assigned rarely used the space as he usually left his own car in the country, so couldn't throw any light on whether it had been occupying his space for long. Flat owners didn't strictly adhere to assigned parking spaces, and when he did drive into town he usually had to park elsewhere. There were no fingerprints on the car at all, and only two flecks of blood caught in the corner of the rear window matched to the traffic warden's. The index plates had been professionally made, and inquiries would be pursued at all possible sources – the expectation was that nothing could come of this other than details to fatten the report that a DCI on the Robbery Squad would eventually have to write.

There was one development that cheered those immediately involved; it concerned the shotguns.

'They were stolen just over a year ago in a burglary from a house outside Marlow,' DCI David Evans told Bentham in his fourth-floor office at the Yard. Evans, who was big, with a ruddy complexion and more London than a Bow Church mouse, despite distant Celtic ancestors, was another ex-RCS man. He ran one of the sections of C11, along with about twelve detectives who had investigations ranging from drug smuggling to armed robbery.

'Anyone nicked?' Bentham asked, leaning back from his desk as a blue overalled lady brought in tea from an urn on a trolley in the corridor. She asked if Evans wanted his tea in there, calling him Mr Evans, as she addressed all the detectives whose names she knew. Those she didn't were simply 'mister', and all women police officers were 'love', regardless of rank.

'There's a lad doing a three in Bradford. He claims he sold the guns to a lad who does a bit of dabbling. Could be true. Bill Senior's looking to pick up the gun-dealer.'

'What about the bank manager? Did you find anything on him, David?'

The manager of the bank that had hosted the robbery in King's Road hadn't shown up too well when the entire staff of the bank, as well as everyone working at the Brinks-Mat depot, had been interviewed by the Robbery Squad. Bentham had got this, along with Xeroxes of their statements, from an ex-RCS DI who was stationed out at Barnes on the Robbery Squad. The DI didn't question why Bentham had wanted them. Possibly Bentham was only focussing on the bank manager out of dislike for his breed – prejudice born of past experience, most of it when he was at university and lived beyond his means and the bank's tolerance. He had a vague feeling that something wasn't right with the man, but didn't often trust such feelings.

'He has a second mortgage on his house, and not through the bank.'

'So do a lot of people. Sign of the times. I suppose it might give him a reason for putting someone in there. But there are a lot of big jumps we'd need to make. There were no rumours about the books not quite balancing?'

'None that anyone heard. You want someone to pull him down to the local nick? He might look like something then.'

Bentham smiled at Evans's dry sense of humour. 'See if you can find out why a man in that position, that age, is over-stretched rather than having got his mortgage paid off.'

Bank managers were probably more feared by people than policemen, Bentham decided. The idea of nicking one might settle the score for all his anxious visits in the past. The notion was a real possibility, for someone in either the bank or the security trucking company had parted with information. C11 had picked up some of that information, and as soon as they had got enough to know a robbery was going off they had given it to Chelsea CID. DI Fred Pyle had been involved, but nothing had happened, apart from a robbery and murder taking place without a single detective in sight. That was why Jack Bentham was taking a personal interest in an area where his department should no longer be taking an interest at all.

5

'God, this place is the fucking pits. How about having this as your manor?' Detective Constable Michael Farr asked from the passenger seat of an Astra car as it turned off Old Compton Street into Frith Street. 'Look at that. It's a brass.' He nodded towards a young girl with spikey blond hair in black fishnet tights and a chrome-studded leather bomber jacket.

'It used to be my patch a few years ago,' the older detective said, 'when I was working out of Vine Street.' Soho was a bit different in those days, he remembered. Not that long ago, either. He was thirty-two. Every week seemed to bring changes to this place, bring more sleaze as the owners of the sex emporia leaped upon whatever bandwagon earned the most money, attracted the most punters to satisfy a need they could probably have satisfied as easily elsewhere. Prostitutes were still fairly popular, but getting pricey; rising rents and rates on property forced many of them away from the centre and out into the suburbs. But what currently entertained the punters was porn video, both takeaway and the kind the punter paid to see in a booth of his own.

'It's not so bad during the day. You get ordinary people here.'

The car stopped outside narrow-fronted premises which couldn't seem to decide whether they were a cinema club or video shop, and were in fact both.

'Imagine having to resort to this to get yourself off,' DC Michael Farr said, casting a disdainful eye over the store front where a man sat in a blazer and open-necked shirt, displaying a huge medallion around his neck. He seemed more like an obstacle than an invitation to potential customers.

'What would you do, have all these places close down, Michael?'

'Wouldn't do any harm at all. Probably get AIDS from just walking into the place.'

The older detective smiled and nodded towards the door. 'Come on, we haven't got all day.'

DC Farr slid out of the car and with a glance around at the passing dross – a habit long established on such visits in case there was anyone waiting around whom he wouldn't have welcomed seeing – he stepped across into the porn emporium. He nodded in a familiar way to the man in the blazer, even though he had only seen him occasionally before.

'S'Warren about?'

Without awaiting a reply the detectives walked through into a room at the back of the store, where Warren Moles, who claimed he was only the manager but who Farr suspected owned the place, had been alerted by the buzzer signalling arrangement on the front counter. The room was small, windowless and untidy, stacked with magazines and videos, catholic enough to cater for everyone's taste, or lack of it.

'It's like a fucking rat's nest back here, Warren. How do you ever pass fire regulations?'

'I bung them greedy cunts, too,' Warren retorted bitterly. He was from the eastern end of the Mediterranean and was very familiar with the system of paying officials to stay in business in a relatively hassle-free fashion. But he never paid without whining first and trying to shave the percentage. 'My earnings are well down t'is week, man.'

'I understand how it is, and don't think I'm not sympathetic. Everyone's feeling it in these constrained times. We've had our overtime cut,' the detective said.

'The punters, dey ain't spending their money no more.'

'I suppose they stay at home and have a wank instead,' Farr commiserated. 'I can't say as I blame them.' He broke open a shrink-wrapped magazine and flicked through it. There were photographs of young girls, and seeing them made him realise how effective their help was on the ground. This establishment would certainly have been busted by the local uniform branch but for the money that was being spread around.

'We take almost nothing this week.'

'You're still open, Warren. You know what it comes to.'

Warren reached for the money he was due to pay over, but each payment to the police was made as reluctantly as the last. He hesitated. 'I had dose other detectives in asking me questions about dis money. From Wiltshire. You know.'

No ground at all was given by Farr. He suspected Warren was lying, but accepted that there was a possibility that he was telling the truth; only it made no difference. All the Wiltshire detectives were doing with their inquiry, apart from pissing off a lot of Met policemen, was causing everyone to be more careful. Well, almost everyone.

Reluctantly Warren passed over the £260 that was due. Farr didn't know how the price was arrived at. All he did was collect it each week. Not all of his stops were prepared to pay what was due regardless of their take.

He smiled. 'S'gotta be better than being turned over and having all your videos confiscated.'

The look on Warren's face posed the question: Is it? but set off no alarm bells in the detective.

This was one of several calls that DC Michael Farr fitted in with his regular work on the Robbery Squad, none of which ever appeared in his duty log, and which culminated in his visit to Heston Service Station on the M4 near the airport, with his black, standard issue briefcase. The final location was arranged by phone at the last moment for security reasons.

Michael Farr was a good and observant detective and spotted his party immediately on entering the barn-like cafeteria. He was sitting at a table reading the *Daily Telegraph*, immaculately dressed as usual, his black briefcase, exactly similar to his own, on the floor by the end of the table. By the time he had got himself a cup of tea and a packet of biscuits, Michael Farr had checked out the other twenty customers and staff in the place and had decided that that was what they really were – customers and staff, not plants. He knew Terry Sneed would have checked out this location even more thoroughly, but gave one final look around as he approached him.

'How's it going, Michael?' Sneed asked as the young detective sat down. He knew by the way the fleshy face crumpled into a grimace that it was going to be bad news and hard-luck stories.

'S'about thirty per cent down. Everybody's blaming it on those Wiltshire detectives being on the ground. They reckon they're stopping them doing all sorts of business. Everyone's getting very jumpy, guv.'

'Of course they are. What they don't realise is the greedy cunts above have still got their hands open. They want their whack just the same.'

That wasn't quite true, but only Terry Sneed knew it. If need be he would simply say that the percentage of the take was down and, as disappointed as they might be, it would be accepted by those senior policemen who were on the firm above him. He

could have cheated them every month or any month he chose to
and they wouldn't know; but he didn't. However, if he suspected Michael Farr was short-changing him it would be a fairly
simple matter to check at source, and the DC knew that.

He knew Farr wasn't pulling any kind of stroke when, after a
moment's embarrassment, he said, 'The thing is, guv, we feel
we've got to go and draw a bit more ourselves. I mean, putting ourselves on offer like we do, it's got to come to a bit more,
guv.'

Sneed nodded and folded his paper. It was an easy enough
problem to resolve.

'How much are you looking for your end?'

Surprise sped briefly across Farr's face. In serious negotiations
with an astute negotiator who didn't want to give anything
away, that look would have signalled that a rise wasn't really
expected.

'You reckon it's down thirty per cent? Up the prices your end
by thirty per cent, Michael. We'll all have an increase. It's
about time. I should think we've been doing more to hold down
inflation than anyone.'

With a tight smile Sneed rose, taking with him the briefcase
that Michael Farr had brought in and leaving his own.

The safe-deposit-box vault that Sneed headed for was situated in Lloyds Bank on the corner of Baker Street and Marylebone Road. It was the securest of all possible locations, Sneed
felt, because it had been robbed a number of years ago; Lloyds's
credibility was at stake and he couldn't see such a disaster
striking box keyholders again. It was a very real disaster for
people with valuables in such places, as insurance companies
were as reluctant to pay out claims as victims were to declare
what they had in their boxes. There was nothing in Sneed's two
that he could ever be able to make any sort of claim for, but the
loss would be a very real tragedy. He had two other security
boxes, both with private security firms who had opened up
deposit-box vaults in high-street locations as people became
more and more panicky about keeping valuables at home and
didn't like the inconvenient hours of banks. These new security
enterprises operated a twenty-four-hour service and Sneed
tended to move his valuables between them.

'Good afternoon, sir. Beautiful day.'

Sneed passed over his key at the basement desk in the bank. 'I don't suppose you see much of it in here.' The room was brightly lit with fluorescent tubes.

The elderly clerk laughed as he matched Sneed's key with the bank's. 'They let us out for lunch. They could replace London buses with dinosaurs for all we'd know.' He released the catch and let Sneed in.

'I think that's the plan.'

Their conversation was similar each time he went there. Sneed had heard the man have similar conversations with other customers and had emulated them so as not to stand out.

Besides quite a lot of money inside the ten-by-fifteen locked metal drawer that Sneed carried into the private cubicle, there were statements, tapes, written evidence, most of it in Sneed's hand, on every worthwhile bit of business he had done, especially with policemen senior to him and anyone who held high public office. This was his insurance and made him feel more secure than any money he accumulated. The future, for Terry Sneed, lay in his continuing to be a policeman. There was nothing he would rather do, and nothing else he intended to do, and what he held in this drawer would guarantee his continuing in the job for as long as he wanted to. From his early days in the job as a detective constable he had recognized the value of getting other policemen involved in ramps and keeping a record of all they had earned, and when. The practice had got to be a habit with him, and had almost become an obsession.

Handling large sums of money was something Terry Sneed was quite familiar with and his long, elegantly-manicured fingers quickly sorted the notes into shares. There were nineteen that he was to deliver personally today; other shares were delivered by detectives lower in rank. DI Fred Pyle, who was now out at Chelsea, did quite a bit of ferrying. Every pound was accounted for and listed against whose bin it went into.

Sneed's visits weren't in order of seniority, but in as direct a line as possible from central London to his office in Barnes.

Nor did the shares vary according to rank. A superintendent drew the same as a commander. One was often as useful as the other where help was needed.

The fourteenth call Sneed made was to a post-war semi house in a tree-lined road in Esher. He knew the woman who opened the door and she told him her husband was in the garden, and said for Sneed to go through. The house was comfortable but fussy, and the furnishings didn't blend too well together. The grandfather clock looked cramped on the quarter landing of the stairs and out of keeping with the modern barometer on the wall. The washed Chinese rug through the hall had a clear plastic tread cover over it that looked like a permanent feature.

'Doing a bit is he?' Sneed said in his familiar way, and smiled.

The lady of the house, an ex-policewoman, raised her eyebrows.

The rear garden of lawn, patio, flower bed and small vegetable patch at the end, screened by a trellis, exactly complemented the house. The same person obviously kept both, and it wasn't Peter Vyvyan. The assistant commissioner was stretched out on tubular garden furniture, catching the late afternoon sun of the Indian summer. On an orange-topped garden table was a small portable television set, with a cable leading back into the house.

'What won the three-thirty at Chepstow?' Sneed asked, disturbing the ACC.

'Oh, it was just an option, I wasn't watching it,' Vyvyan said almost as an apology.

'When Mrs Vyvyan said you were in the garden, guv, I thought she meant doing a bit.'

That brought a smile to the spaniel-like features which belied a ruthless streak in his character. Peter Vyvyan had been known on occasions to be both vindictive and unremitting in hounding villains and policemen alike into court; the latter, however, not until every alternative avenue had been explored. Generally he was more supportive of policemen than most senior officers.

'That's her department, Terry, gardening. Even the slugs do as Vera tells them.' He straightened stiffly in the chair. 'I had two days well earned leave due me. Just down from town?'

'I made one or two stops on the way.'

'You're a bit later than you said. It made me wonder.'

'I was going to give you a bell. But I thought it best to give the phone a miss.' He sounded a cautionary note, but didn't feel apprehensive about the telephone, despite knowing how large a number of phones were tapped.

'The Wiltshire have taken enough liberties one way and another, but they're hardly likely to tap my phone.'

'They've had a go at just about everyone else, myself included.'

'They are making absolute pests of themselves. They mostly seem to be investigating irrelevant tittle-tattle from anyone who rings them up. I told them so at our last meeting.'

Obligingly Sneed said, 'If they got a tap on your phone, guv, I wouldn't fancy anyone else's chances. I was just being cautious.'

'That's no bad thing. Some policemen have been getting very greedy, and very careless. Greed I can understand, but not carelessness.' He paused and seemed to experience the momentary embarrassment of someone about to try and borrow money. 'What have you brought for me?'

'Comes to one nine eight four.' Sneed said. He could have rounded the figure up with the extra six pounds, but saw no need to. He acknowledged the ACC's sulky, disappointed look. 'Reflects what those cunts from Wiltshire are doing to business.'

Peter Vyvyan drew in his breath at Sneed's language, not at the word itself, but because this was his garden and he had neighbours. He didn't challenge Sneed's assessment of the situation. He was more concerned by the fact that he was being given an odd amount of money. It was difficult enough keeping such loose cash in his head in round figures. Half the time he didn't know what to do with the money, so simply deposited it in his wife's name. He had never thought it through properly or imagined there would be so much, otherwise he'd have made serious alternative arrangements. They spent some, on such luxuries as the spring holiday they had taken in Venice at the Danieli, a converted Venetian palace on the Rivi Degli Schiavoni, only to run into the DPP and his wife, who were also staying there. So he purposely didn't spend very much.

'I don't know what the solution is for all this spare cash. You've obviously found one.' He waited as if hoping Terry Sneed might give him a hint. When he didn't, he asked, 'What do villains do with their money, Terry?'

'Mostly they splash it about – and get themselves nicked.' The reliable ones did as Sneed did with any money he shouldn't be seen to have, they placed it where it was safe, reachable and couldn't easily be connected to them. He wondered why the ACC was asking, if he was trying to draw him out. He could as easily have blanked him, for the topic was as delicate as sex. No one was obliged to tell an inquirer how often he had had it in. Sneed didn't fear giving offence, but he changed tack all the same.

'I hear more detectives are being brought in from Wiltshire – to tie the fucking laces of those already here, I suppose, stop them tripping over. That's not exactly spreading cheer.'

'There was nothing I could do,' Peter Vyvyan said quickly, feeling this reflected badly on him. 'I suggested introducing Met officers to push their inquiries along to some conclusion. It wasn't very well received.'

'It's all ballocks, guv. And for what? A big fat fuck all at the end of the day. A lot of good detectives are getting thoroughly demoralized, a lot are putting in their papers, men the service can't afford to lose. You know as well as I do what's happening. Villains we've had too many results with are settling old scores. What's worse is those cunts from Wiltshire are taking notice of them.'

Peter Vyvyan shifted uncomfortably in his chair and started to rise. His Esher neighbours expected senior policemen to restore olden-day values, not lower the standard in the neighbourhood.

'It's a terrible fucking situation we're getting into. No one wants to believe a policeman any more.'

'That's a very dangerous situation. When the general public can no longer trust its policemen that's a very sorry day for the general public,' the ACC said, as if believing that situation could only arise out of public stupidity, rather than any action of the police. 'I think we'd better go inside, Terry. We'll have some tea if you've got time.'

Sneed hadn't. He had five more calls to make, and work to clear up back at his office before the weekend.

6

There was something to be said in favour of simply inviting suspects or witnesses down to the station and conducting an interview in that slightly intimidating atmosphere; convenience mostly. Giving up an evening made little difference to Jack Bentham as most of his evenings seemed to be spent in the pursuit of work of some sort, if only reading or writing policy reports, but he wondered if he wasn't putting a little too much into the inquiry surrounding the death of the animal rights demonstrator out at Hackney, especially as he was likely to get no thanks for it at the end of the day. If his report favoured the police, the animal rights organisations would be in a fury. If at the conclusion of his inquiry the DPP was forced to prosecute any policemen, and it was becoming fairly clear from interviewing witnesses that the police struck the fatal blows, the police on the ground would get angry. Possibly Bentham was responding to Deputy Commissioner Harry Streeter's encouraging words – about there being no one better or less partial for this job – but it was more likely that he was responding more and more to the political pressures of the job. No longer was it sufficient for a policeman to go out and capture villains; in fact that original objective had slipped very badly in the order of priorities. Instead he was increasingly becoming the enforcement arm of the Executive, a more acceptable agent than the army.

Bentham disliked that trend, but he knew the only alternative was to stop being a policeman; if he did, there would be other policemen to replace him, policemen who possibly wouldn't have the interest he had in moderating the effect of political interests. The last miners' strike had signalled the real change of direction for the British police, and there was no way to undo the lasting damage which the government had done by forcing the police into that overtly political role. They could no longer pretend to be apolitical, or even impartial. At every street corner the police were geared to support the status quo, and would do so wherever and whenever government indicated a potential threat. Bentham was determined to show that, despite being forced into this position, he could be fair, but it was a bit like an intellectual exercise in outwitting one's own conditioning and the prevailing political wind. And so he found himself giving up another evening to go out to see Helen Daniels, who had broken two previous appointments, one without letting him know. This was one witness he could easily have given an ultimatum to: come to the station to make your statement, or don't make it. After all it was her friend who had died, so presumably it was important to her, as well as to Jack, that the truth should be allowed to surface. She and her fellow protesters were convinced the police murdered Paul Bailey, for a reason that Bentham was unable to get his head around. Perhaps he should have let her make the running. But instead of issuing that ultimatum, he was being the arch diplomat as he rolled along the West London street wondering if the lady would keep this appointment, and if what she had to say would make it worthwhile. There seemed little prospect of her ever being won back to a position of faith or trust in the police.

The street was generally depressed and uncared for. Spools of litter and plastic bags of refuse in the gutter fought for space with parked cars; household rubbish spilled off builders' skips. In this sort of street people filled the skips almost before the dump trucks had deposited them. The number of skips parked in the kerb all the way along the road, together with the clutch of estate agents' boards, indicated that the street was upwardly mobile. Original leases which had held the houses in affordable squalor were fast running out. The converters were buying the properties and turning them into luxury flats to sell at three times their original price; suddenly the poor couldn't live there any longer. It was happening all over London, but especially in West London. Bentham made a mental note of one or two properties and agents. He saw the street as a good investment; not if he had to borrow money to invest, but he had enough money tucked away to pick up one of these and leave his current mortgage intact for the tax break it gave him.

'Here. Eighty-six,' he said seeing the number before the driver did. There were three different boards outside the house, each representing prosperous, upmarket agencies.

The step was littered with a bike, a pram, empty bottles and flower pots. As he waited Bentham turned to consider the street again, wondering if the local beat copper had got his informer sorted out on this street. 'Street Watch' was a policy of Bentham's that had been adopted. Constables from the local nicks found someone on each street to feed them information about what was happening on their street. Usually it was a kid who was out of work, and so was around the whole time. The scheme was successful, even though it was creating a nation of grasses. He counted eleven skips, one of them being filled by four large black women who had brought an old mattress and a fridge from a house and were heaving them over the end. The fridge didn't arc high enough and rolled back across the rim of the skip and crashed on the road, which brought paroxysms of giggling from the women. Eventually they left it where it lay. It might take a couple of years for an investment here to fully appreciate, Bentham thought, but his money was doing little else.

Helen Daniels opened the door behind him, and as Bentham turned he saw what he decided was disappointment in her face.

'I'd say he's not coming, if he's not here by now.'

'What?' She was puzzled. She had forgotten the detective was coming and felt slightly irritated.

'You didn't phone and cancel our meeting and you're not out, so I assume you're going to give me a statement.'

He stepped across the threshold uninvited, surprising her more.

'I do have to be at the theatre by seven forty-five,' she informed him.

He looked at his watch. It was a little after six. 'We can *not* do it if you want. It's up to you. We can *not* have an inquiry. It was only your lot screaming foul that brought it about.'

'For the good it will do Paul or anyone else it may as well not take place.'

Bentham followed her into the ground-floor flat. It was one large Victorian room with most of its original features retained, including a marble fireplace with two gas lamps on either side, now connected to electricity. Along the back wall of the room there was a platform bed which had a cast-iron staircase and a low matching balustrade along the front of the platform, making this very modern space-saving feature appear almost original.

'Why are you so hostile towards the police?' he asked, his glance sweeping the room, taking in the profusion of protest posters showing monkeys with agonized expressions wearing head-clamps fitted with electrodes, scalded guinea pigs and blinded rabbits. He wondered how anyone could live with all this around the place without having constant nightmares.

'I don't like the way you force your presence into my life. How you poke into things that don't concern you.' She retrieved the postcards he had picked up off the mantelpiece before he had a chance to read them. 'Perhaps you'd like to have a look at my diary.'

Jack Bentham smiled at her hostility, determined to be diplomatic. If he managed to make someone like this change her view of the police it would be an achievement indeed. 'It might help. What about the police on the street?' He had started his interview, but didn't need to take notes at this point. He would probably get more out of her before she realised what he was up to than he would after she had. 'How do you feel about them?'

'All the police are the same, if you ask me. They're offensive and belligerent and intimidating. They only vary in degrees. They're certainly nothing like the policemen I remember as a child.'

'Different age,' he told her, making a mental note for the next policy meeting he attended. They should make an all-out effort to cultivate policemen on the street like in the days of yore, the helpful, kind bobby who would win back the respect of the general public. Nothing got that respect like the fair and decent policeman who stopped someone for speeding, then let the grateful offender off with a warning. In practical terms that probably did as much to cut down speeding offences as fines and endorsements.

'There weren't all these activists around in those days.' He guessed her age right. She had probably been involved in those anti-Vietnam demos around at the American Embassy. He had been on some of those as a student. That was really a different age again, the start of the loss of innocence for both the public and the police.

'God knows what sort of society we'd have if some people didn't show they cared by protesting. The things that are going on are already a complete horror show. They'd be worse if no one cared.'

'You think policemen don't care? They care passionately about order and decency, freedom for the majority. Do you think they'd really risk their lives every day otherwise?'

'Of course they care, and they're prepared to squash anyone down to prove it. To ride into strikers on horseback and smash them back to work, to crush any spark of decency and turn it to fear when people cry out at the inhumanity to our own kind, much less poor animals who don't have a voice.'

Silently, without feeling the need to defend his position, Bentham held her look, until finally she avoided his eyes. 'I don't think so, Helen,' he said quietly. 'Policemen have the same problems you have, or anyone else. The same feelings, ambitions, fears, failings. They're not really different.'

'You make them sound almost reasonable,' she said, finding it difficult to maintain her anger in the face of such reasonableness. 'They're not reasonable at all. They're not kind or helpful or caring. Certainly not on our demos. They see us as a threat that they have to smash at all costs.'

'I don't suppose you've ever faced an angry mob of protesters, hurling sticks and stones and petrol bombs. I don't suppose you've experienced anything like it. There isn't a policeman on those lines who isn't scared for his own safety and that of his colleagues. And very often they don't know what the hell they're doing there, apart from protecting something or someone for no other reason than that it's enshrined in law.'

'They can question, can't they, like everyone else?'

Bentham slowly shook his head. 'If they did that they would then start to make judgements. They would lose their impartiality. They'd prefer the politicians to make the judgements, make and amend the laws according to the dictates of the electorate.'

Through her anger Helen suddenly realised this man was very dangerous. He was presenting the acceptable face of policing, when it was much much easier to cope with that oafish intolerance that was so frequently encountered in policemen.

'Have you ever faced a mob of policemen who are determined you shouldn't do what you're legally entitled to do?' she countered, clinging to the remnants of her anger. 'It's terribly intimidating, especially for a woman, especially when they sexually assault you. If you don't believe that you can ask any of the women who go on demos, whether it's against nuclear missiles or animal torturers. They grab your breasts, or take hold of you at the crotch. One said to me the other day, "Oh, I always wanted to feel an animal rightist's bits."'

'Did you make an official complaint?'

Helen laughed derisively. 'You must be joking. What on earth for? So that we can be completely humiliated all over again, and at the end of the day have the police report back that they are unable to identify the officer involved?'

'I'm not going to pretend that the complaints procedure is anything but flawed. The trouble is, no one has come up with a better alternative. Not one that will work.'

'Well, at least you didn't say you have the choice – not to go on such demos, that then you wouldn't get rough treatment from policemen.'

Bentham almost smiled; he *had* nearly said that to her.

'Look, what happened to Paul, it's terribly unfair. He didn't even go regularly to animal rights demos. He was only exercising the freedom that policemen care so passionately about.' Anger was beginning to surface again as an alternative to tears; there was still a well of those to be shed over his death and her feeling of culpability.

'I suppose it's regrettable that police all too often respond to the situation that they find themselves in. They meet violence and because they're only human they respond with violence. What we have to do is a lot of work on the young man just coming into the job. More training, shrewder psychological assessment of his character. It will make a lot of difference to how he shapes up under stress. There's not much we can do about those we've got at present – try and weed out the really disturbed ones.' Bentham usually found that in situations such as this if he gave something he got something back. It was the same in most situations where barriers of reserve, suspicion and uncertainty were erected. He saw the fight pass out of the woman opposite him; her face relaxed slightly, almost from relief, he felt.

'Why don't you make some coffee and let's talk about Paul Bailey. I'd like to know about his background, his character, to try and help me form a picture of him before you tell me in detail what happened that day.'

Perhaps he hadn't given enough, Bentham thought, when Helen Daniels said coldly, 'I don't have any coffee. I don't drink it. Or tea.' When he simply shrugged as if her uncharitable response were a matter of no importance, she felt still more uncertain of the position she was maintaining with this particular policeman.

'I have some herb tea – I don't suppose you'd like that.'

Bentham smiled at her assumption. 'Herb tea will be all right. I'll have mint.'

It suddenly occurred to her that he might be humouring her, but she wasn't certain, and didn't know whether or not to be annoyed.

'I suppose you're vegetarian, too?' she challenged.

It was obvious that she was, for plastered on the window, among her tortured animal faces were notices pleading, LET VEGETATION FEED THE NATION, and stating that MEAT IS MURDER. He hadn't thought about that before. He smiled. 'As a matter of fact I am.' It was a winsome smile that helped him to carry off his lie smoothly. He knew then he was half-way along the right path with this woman.

During the time he had spent as a DS on the Arts and Antiques Squad, Detective Inspector Les Norman had become quite knowledgeable about the subject through his continuous dealings with the trade, but that knowledge didn't affect his taste in any significant way, and just because he knew certain abstract or modernist paintings were valuable he didn't like them any better. Those along the wall of the Serpentine Gallery, lit by the evening sunlight that bisected the room, were neither valuable nor appealing, but he was no longer on the Arts and Antiques Squad and was a bit out of touch. He was still quite happy with the reproductions of famous paintings that hung on the walls of his own house.

He had welcomed this meeting with a grass who gave him worthwhile bits from time to time, but was slightly regretting it now that the man was late and he faced the prospect of having to go around these walls again. He was doing just that when a short, edgy man entered and joined him. Lee wasn't the sort of person who would pass unnoticed in an art gallery – his whole manner marked him for what he was – but Les Norman accepted that he might be biased. He looked as if he dressed straight from a menswear shop window.

'You do pick some fucking places for a meet, guv.' He looked around to check who was about, showing no interest in the paintings. There were few people in the gallery, which would soon be closing anyway.

'You said you were on this side of town. Who are you likely to run into in here, Lee? I'm glad you were on time.'

'I'm reliable where it counts, guv. You know that. The sort of information I put up.'

'What have you got?' The informant had rung him up and intimated that he had something on the robbery across the pavement in King's Road. The policeman had been like a hungry gannet, but tried not to show it. The last thing he wanted was to put himself in the power of grasses; they lived by his grace and favour, not the other way round.

Hesitating a moment, his head bobbing in and out of his collar as he checked about, he said, 'You won't like it. I heard it was Old Bill what put those villains into that one. It's what I heard.' He repeated himself, as if apologising for the information.

'I wouldn't be surprised, Lee,' Norman said, with no flicker of emotion. 'They seem to be into every other kind of villainy nowadays.'

That information was only secondary, a whisper Lee had picked up from sources other than the one who had provided the name of one of the villains actually involved in the blag. Norman's hunger was momentarily satisfied and he gave his grass a fifty-pound note, with a promise of something more out of the reward, if and when.

This information he took to DCI David Evans, as there was nothing he could do with the name himself – apart from passing it directly to the Central Robbery Squad who were handling the case. It might simply end up there whatever he did with it, as too many complications arose out of too many separate squads chasing the same crime – as if there wasn't enough to share between them. The DCI thought it important enough for Jack Bentham to be informed.

'How reliable is your informant, Les?' Bentham wanted to know. He knew this detective was reliable, and that the evidence he assembled was usually sound, even if it was best not to question the quiet, willowy Les Norman's methods too closely.

'He's always been pretty good.'

'Any axe to grind against the police?'

'Probably,' Les Norman said in an offhand manner. Most grasses and villains had the needle with someone when they grassed them. That was why a lot of good information came to light. 'I'd like a few more like this lad on the firm.'

'He didn't name the corrupt policeman involved?'

The DI shook his head. 'He said there was more than one involved. But like I said, he's probably no particular liking for the police. What with the Wiltshire lot looking under stones, it probably seemed like a good time to stick some more poison in.'

'He did say he had some rank.' Evans confirmed.

Bentham thought about that. If they weren't careful about how they handled this they'd probably find the Wiltshire detectives in on it, trampling on delicate police–criminal relationships that sometimes led to arrests and convictions.

'Treat that for what it is, Les. An unsubstantiated rumour. If we took notice of a quarter of the allegations villains made against the police there wouldn't be CID enough to nick a flasher, much less a blagger. You'd better have a look at any connection between anyone involved in the money in transit and policemen – anyone locally who knew the stop, no matter how high or low the rank. I mean, has that bank manager ever been burgled and had the CID visit his place? He might have let something slip.'

Evans gave a thin, humourless smile at his governor's obsession with nicking a bank manager.

'Pursue the villain whose name your grass stuck up, Les. Make sure the lads are all armed.'

'Is the Robbery Squad going to be involved?' Norman asked, expecting that they might be.

'It might not come to anything,' Bentham said non-committally.

Bentham went along the fourth-floor corridor to where a briefing on the same robbery, resulting out of the lead on the shotguns that had been sold to a greengrocer who dabbled in weapons for villains, was taking place. The grocer was nothing big, but he did enough to have a reputation for reliability, which was what his customers were looking for. It was no good villains buying a gun which in the event of arrest landed them with not just a robbery, but a murder charge, because the gun's previous owner had shot someone with it. The grocer had taken them no closer to the blaggers out of King's Road, as he'd only dealt with a disembodied voice down the telephone. The first half of the money for the shotguns had arrived at his shop by registered post, the second half had been waiting in an underground car park belonging to Tesco's when the guns had been dropped off. That was the way he did business. He'd said that if he had known who was involved in the shooting, he'd have put up the names to the detectives interrogating him, as he was keen to help in any way he could, and in fact put up the name of another gundealer he had done business with – Tony 'Mars Bar' Rice. This the Robbery Squad had reluctantly passed over to C11, as at this stage it amounted only to criminal intelligence.

'Right, what have we got?' Bentham said in a businesslike way when he entered the long room and took a chair at the side of the oblong table. Although chairing this briefing, he didn't feel the need to sit at the head of the table. That was something that always happened upstairs, as it did at the Home Office policy meetings he had attended, as if no one at the meetings could tell who had seniority until they sat down.

'That lad who handled the shotguns on the King's Road blag has put us onto a firm in Reading that's looking for shooters,' DCI Frank Burroughs said, ponderously looking at his notes. He wasn't the quickest brain in C11, not by a long way, and by normal criteria he was not an ideal candidate for the job he was doing. But Bentham knew him to be a good practical copper who could find a way round most problems that the more academically inclined would be making drawings of.

'There's a meet going off tomorrow,' he continued.

'We going to be there?'

'If we have to tie ourselves under Mars Bar's car.'

'It might fucking well come to that, guv.' It was a familiar whine from Bill Senior. Never one to steam in and take a chance, he always examined the shortcomings of any proposal. 'Our only fucking contact is this lad Mars Bar who's s'posed to be collecting the shooters. We've got to make a fucking tail all the way to Reading. We don't know where the meet is or who it's with or nothing.'

'We can follow his trail of Mars Bar wrappers,' a young DC put in, and flushed scarlet when Senior turned and looked at him.

'Fuck me, Bill,' Frank Burroughs said. 'You want them to put their hands up. We'll get in on the ground floor, go right to the blag with them.'

'I'd be satisfied with seeing them nicked if and when they collect the shooters.'

'Why don't we know where the meeting is?' Bentham asked.

'Because Tony Rice doesn't know. He has to make a phone call when he gets to Reading.'

'Sounds well iffy to me,' Senior said, but ironically there was no way he would stay behind. Staying cooped up in an office gave him claustrophobia, but spending hours parked in a car waiting for a suspect's next move was something different.

'What's the connection with King's Road?' Bentham asked. 'Apart from the lad who dabbled with shooters.'

'None as far as we know, guv. The word is that the lad we're tailing, the Mars Bar kid, was involved in that Securicor van that was cut open with chainsaws in Kent last year. We've yet to get it firmed up.'

The Animal Liberation Front's supposed poisoning of Mars Bars – because the Mars company allegedly used monkeys in experiments – popped into Bentham's thoughts, and he wondered if it had affected Tony Rice's confectionary habit. His thoughts moved on briefly to Helen Daniels, who interested him outside his contact as a policeman. He suspected that it was because she was intellectually challenging, as well as the fact that she was living on the edge of lawlessness, which made her attractive to him. He wondered how he might see her again, apart from just telephoning her and inviting her out for a nut cutlet and some dandelion tea, feeling instinctively that she would blank him. Perhaps he'd decide he needed to check some information in her statement about the demo.

'That wouldn't be a bad result at all, putting someone else away for that robbery,' Bentham said, coming back to the matter in hand.

That would indeed prove more than ordinarily satisfactory, as the one person arrested for that robbery had all the hallmarks of a body. He had quietly gone down for twenty-five years without any mention of others involved. The Robbery Squad had handled that investigation along with the Kent CID; together they had almost turned the whole thing into a game. It really was about time someone shouted 'Foul!', Jack Bentham decided, and suspected the Wiltshire police weren't the ones to do it. But he wasn't sure that he was either.

7

There was a palpable trail of Mars Bar wrappers floating out of the Volvo 720 that cruised along the middle lane of the M4, keeping just a fraction below the speed limit, even when overtaking slower vehicles. Popular classical music bounced around the four speakers of the stereo system; Gilbert and Sullivan didn't have to try very hard to be heard over the effectively sound-proofed engine. The squeaking sound of celophane being torn off the next five-pack of Mars Bars was clearly audible inside the car as the thin, dark-haired Tony Rice opened his sixth bar since leaving London. He hadn't had any lunch, and stress caused him to burn sugar at a fast rate.

'How the fuck isn't he as sick as a pig?' said the driver of the Sherpa van, which bore the name of a roofing contractor on the side, as yet another wrapper came out of the car two vehicles in front. 'That's eight.'

'How come he isn't as fat as a pig?' said Detective Sergeant Kingham, who sat next to him. He was overweight and would have loved to have eaten just one chocolate bar of any kind, but seemed to put on weight just thinking about chocolate.

They watched the Volvo signal left at the last moment and zip across to the exit ramp for Reading. The van could have made the same manoeuvre, but it would have been a last-minute decision and might have alerted Tony Rice.

'Go past, go past,' Kingham ordered from the passenger seat. 'Back up on the ramp.'

Braking past the on-ramp to the motorway, the driver reversed the van along the hard shoulder and up the on-ramp, ignoring the blasts from drivers of cars coming down. The manoeuvre was slow and the Volvo would be way ahead of them by now, but there were three other vehicles involved in the tailing operation: a BMW, which not surprisingly DI Senior had chosen to travel in, a Ford Cortina and a Renault 5. The Renault had preceded the Volvo up the off-ramp and would have rejoined the tail via the on-ramp had Rice not taken this exit. The BMW and the Cortina both passed the Volvo, which had stopped on the A4 outside a phone box; the Mars Bar kid, one in hand, was arranging the drop. The detectives in each vehicle were delighted that their tail had so far been successful, and that it looked like Rice was proceeding to collect some guns. They each found a place to park and wait. If the Volvo doubled back, the Sherpa and Renault would pick it up.

Minutes later the Volvo appeared, with Tony Rice tapping out a melody on the steering wheel, completely oblivious of his tail. The vehicle went into Reading and entered a multi-storey car park, the driver stopping for his ticket. The BMW did the same, shortly followed by the Renault.

There were about twenty cars on the top level where Tony Rice reversed his Volvo into a space with its nose facing towards the exit. He got out and carefully locked the door and, despite the car's central locking system, checked all the other doors. Satisfied finally that he had safeguarded his car against casual theft, he walked along the line of parked cars to a Morris Ital, unwrapping another Mars Bar.

The man sitting in the Ital was smoking and throwing his cigarette ends out of the window. Tony Rice knew he would be. He found it a filthy habit, and deplored the way smokers spread all their rubbish around. He didn't allow people to smoke in his car.

'Have you got the time, please?'

The man in the Ital, who hadn't taken his eyes off Tony Rice as he approached, didn't bother to look at his watch. 'Five past two.'

Tony Rice lowered the Mars Bar from his mouth and looked at his own watch. 'I'd say you were a bit fast, pal.'

They each knew they had made the right contact before this exchange; now there was apprehension in each of their looks, and a moment's hesitation before the gundealer reached for a set of keys off the seat next to him and passed them over. Rice passed in a packet of money from inside his bomber jacket, and waited while the older man examined it.

'S'all there,' he said. 'The notes yoú wanted.'

'The blue Escort down there,' he said, nodding along the line of cars. 'It's hired. The papers are under the seat. Make sure you return it on time.' He started his car.

'You'd better wait while I check the goods, hadn't you.'

'It's all there in the boot. Everything you asked for.'

The gundealer backed his car out of the space as the Cortina, with two detectives in it, nosed off the ramp and swung towards a parking space. The detective in the passenger seat reached for the radio phone below the dashboard, bent out of sight and gave a description of the Ital and its driver. As that disappeared down the ramp the BMW came up from the lower floor.

Tony Rice opened the boot, showing no interest in the car that had just parked at the opposite end of the line. Inside, in a canvas bag, were three sawn-off shotguns and a handgun, with cartridges. Satisfied, he drew the zip closed and shut the boot. He unlocked the Escort and climbed in. At that point he realised he hadn't brought any Mars Bars with him. He started from the Escort, then saw two cars, one reversing, the other driving along the aisle, and knew instinctively what that meant. He didn't move as detectives sprang out of the cars, levelling their own guns at him. The two without guns slammed him against the car and began to search him.

'Don't move, don't move!' DI Senior screamed, the gun trembling as his hand shook. He looked in alarm at his trembling hand and jammed the barrel of the gun into the back of Tony Rice's neck to steady it. 'You're nicked!'

'Leave off!' Rice protested. 'Leave off.' He had a real fear of being shot.

Leaving the protesting villain Senior heaved himself across to the parapet in time to see the Sherpa van and the Renault swing out after the Morris Ital as the driver paid his exit fee and went off, oblivious to what had happened.

There was real jubilation in the squad office at Reading Divisional HQ. The detectives who had brought Tony Rice in swaggered around with their tea and scotch like football supporters celebrating their team's win. Bill Senior was known on this manor as he was provincial police liaison officer with C11. It made life easier for all concerned. The Reading CID felt no particular resentment, knowing that everything would be passed to them and they would get a result for anything that was going off on their patch.

'He's gone back to work, guv,' DS Kingham said across the office, cupping his hand over the mouthpiece of the telephone. He was on the line to one of the detectives keeping obo with the gundealer. 'Is he gonna be nicked or what?'

'No. Just tell them to stay put. I'll get some of the lads here to relieve them later,' Senior said, and glanced up at a uniformed sergeant who had approached the desk.

'That lad you've got in the cells is wanting to talk, sir.'

'Got a few names has he?' Bill Senior speculated, rising from the chair. He had not forgotten the ignominy of his gun-shake, and needed in some way to be assuaged. Another result would do it.

'Fucking sick'ning, right fucking sick'ning,' Tony Rice said, pacing about the modern cell in the basement of the police station. Light through the glass-brick windows was sufficient to obviate the electric light. 'One minute you got your liberty, plenty of dough, nice car, one swinging on your dick, the next you're facing plenty of fucking bird. Sick'ning.' His whole body moved agitatedly, not coping with all the sugar that was being pumped into his blood.

Standing with one foot on the bed bench, Bill Senior appeared very calm, but was wondering if this lad had noticed the gun-shake. Had anyone else?

'Could be worse, Tony. You could have cancer.'

Rice stopped pacing and looked at the detective, then looked at the door, his mouth suddenly going very dry as he said, 'What's the chance of doing a bit of business? Me getting out of here?'

Asking a detective that always involved a risk, especially in the current climate, Tony Rice realised, but he felt he owed it to himself to try. His apprehension didn't slacken until he saw the DI step over to the door and push it to.

'I think there are probably too many involved to do much, Tony,' Senior said, not wanting to close off that avenue entirely but recognizing the risks involved. 'Too many CID from other forces looking at what we're all doing these days. S'fucking everything for everyone.' Having less direct contact with villains at the point of arrest in Criminal Intelligence, Bill Senior had less opportunity to earn, and the presence of the Wiltshire lot seemed to diminish what opportunity there was even further.

'Can't say I'm surprised. There's more than enough Old Bill at it. Some of them make our enterprise look like a bit of hoisting from Woolworth's.'

Bill Senior waited, sensing something else was going on with this villain. He might not go and earn anything with him, but he might get some other sort of result.

'What if I was to put you into the firm I was getting the guns for? That's got to be worth some help.'

75

'My governor might go along with that. I'll give him a bell.'

DCI Burroughs was very keen to go along with the scheme Bill Senior worked out with the villain – letting him out with the guns to meet the firm of blaggers – but he couldn't sanction such a move without clearing it with the DCS. Jack Bentham was less keen when the proposition was put to him, and not simply because in theory he should have gone to his governor, Commander Ernie Wiseman. Often he took such decisions upon his own head.

'There's a lot at risk if it goes wrong, Frank,' Bentham said, stating the obvious. 'If you let that villain back out with those shooters, it means putting policemen more at risk than they need be.'

'I know,' Burroughs said solemnly. 'But it's less of a go without the guns – if we want to make sure they stay nicked.'

'Who do you plan to use? The Robbery Squad or Reading?' That was the dilemma as Bentham saw it. He wasn't sure that by using either lot of policemen they could keep it well enough closed up for some worthwhile arrests to result. Reading CID might bell any one of the would-be blaggers if they were a local firm. If they weren't, the same move might come from the Squad. Perhaps he was over-reacting to what was going on because of the internal investigations that were under way. That was the real danger of the Wiltshire operation. It sowed the seeds of doubt, and regardless of whether there was substance enough to support those seeds, some inevitably germinated. He had heard from his governor that Wiltshire wanted to interview him at some point, along with some of his men. Bentham hadn't responded with an offer of availability, and the Turnip Squad, as they had come to be known, were probably too overworked ever to get to him.

'Bill Senior wants to go in with some of the lads from out at Reading. He thinks he can contain it.'

'Let's take a chance then,' Bentham said. 'But make sure they have enough men to cover it properly.'

With the seven detectives he had and nine more from Reading, Bill Senior felt he had plenty of cover for the job and for the Reading CID to make some arrests. It was the same multi-storey car park that was chosen to pass over the guns. Only this time the police had chosen it on Tony Rice's behalf.

Seventeen detectives were spread out between six police vehicles: five were on the top deck of the car park, the other one, with two DCs in reserve, was on the lower floor. Some of them took up their positions before Tony Rice contacted the prospective buyer, and all but the reserve car were there to watch the Mars Bar kid arrive. What they hadn't realised was that the would-be blaggers had arrived ahead of Rice and had parked in a similar way to the police. A Vauxhall Cavalier had pulled into a space on the top deck, parked, and the driver had got out and gone off to the lifts and apparently away. In fact he had gone no further than to a car opposite the entrance to watch the gundealer's arrival.

The three men in the car kept as well out of sight as the detectives, who, had they been less than careful, might have been seen and alerted the blaggers.

Three men waiting out of sight in a car was a cramped and difficult exercise, no less so for the police than the robbers. The detectives used trench periscopes to keep obo, one whispering developments to the others. A full five minutes passed following the arrival of Tony Rice before anything happened, and then DI Senior was quite shocked to see those three men appear in that harmless, passed-over Cavalier. Two climbed from the car and approached the Ford Escort Tony Rice was sitting in, the third slid behind the steering wheel.

The exchange between Tony Rice and one of the villains was brief and familiar. A parcel of money went in, while the second villain went to the boot to check the guns.

'Check the money, you cunt,' Senior said quietly, urging Rice to do what tension had obviously made him forget to do. Possibly the villain was as tense and unobservant as Rice, for it didn't alert him to do anything, and he was diverted by the man at the boot of the car, who now hefted out the bag and slammed the lid.

Tension mounted in each of the other police cars as the whispered commentary continued. DS Kingham watched the villains approach their own car with the bag. The third man started the engine.

'Why the fuck doesn't he give the signal,' Kingham said to no one in particular. 'They've got the shooters.' He couldn't make out Bill Senior's delay, and didn't until he saw the villain with the bag open the boot, drop it in and close the boot again. It was a gamble on the DI's part. The villains may have kept the guns close by them.

'Now! Move,' Senior said through his radiophone.

Two of the police vehicles started almost instantly while six Reading detectives from the two nearer cars sprang out and raced at the startled villains. Tony Rice let in the clutch on the hired Escort and screeched away towards the exit. One of the moving police cars tried to head him off, and just clipped the back of the car as it nosed into the ramp. The bump sent it out of control briefly, causing a rear wing to scrape the parapet wall before Rice managed to straighted up. The detective's car reversed and swung down into the ramp in pursuit.

The reserve car from the lower floor entered the chase ahead of the pursuit car, following the developments through the open radio as near-hysterical instructions were screamed from the other cars.

'Get the cunts, get them!' was the prevailing instruction, no one observing the formality of r/t procedure.

The Escort burst off the ramp with too much speed to brake. The boarded arm was smashed from its hinge and the three cars sped through, entering the traffic without braking and causing other cars to screech and swerve, giving the would-be blagger in the fourth car the opportunity to join the traffic unnoticed and drive calmly away; there was nothing he could now do for his partners.

Tony Rice, his mind in total confusion, unable to understand for a moment why he was being chased like this, entered a new experimental roundabout at speed, adding chaos to an already confused situation. He sped off along a busy shopping precinct, where traffic lights, lorries, buses and shoppers all endeavoured, it seemed, to impede his progress.

It seemed a curious irony that at the precice moment when he was thinking about a Mars Bar, a Mars delivery lorry brought him up sharply. He trod on the brake, but the car wasn't going to stop and Tony Rice didn't hesitate in swinging hard right across the traffic to enter a narrow one-way street from the wrong end. The detectives' cars didn't try the same move, but stopped and tried to force their way through the oncoming traffic.

But for a flat-bedded builder's truck, Rice might have got away with his audacious manoeuvre. The truck was temporarily blocking the street where it had drawn up alongside a skip, into which the driver was throwing empty paint cans.

The Escort was travelling too fast to avoid impact with the truck, and even if he had mounted the narrow pavement at the side, Tony Rice judged that he would not have got through, and possibly stood to kill pedestrians in the attempt. His last minute decision as he stood on the brake was to swing the wheel hard over to the left and shut his eyes. The car mounted the double set of barrow boards on the end of the builder's skip, the bonnet rearing into the air as if, with a will of its own, it was about to leap right over the obstacle in its path. It rose two feet and flopped onto the building rubble, the nose smacking into the end of the skip and tipping it up, jarring Tony Rice against the steering wheel in the process; the back end of the car settled with a crash and kicked the skip back up onto its base as the engine stalled.

Unable to open his door, the stunned driver eventually wound down the window. Five armed detectives ran up to him, all laughing, which only served to make him more angry.

'You cunts. I was s'pose to get away. I was, you cunts.'

When they eventually stopped laughing, one of the detectives said, 'I don't think so, Tony.' Whatever C11 may have promised Rice, he wasn't a party to the deal.

With three would-be armed robbers safely tucked up in cells and a clear description of the fourth now circulating, Reading CID were feeling both bullish and bouncy, and would have granted Bill Senior and their men anything that was within their power to grant. If the DI had said he wanted to let the Mars Bar kid walk, no one would have objected, just as no one had objected to Bill Senior taking charge of the money that the villains had paid over for the shooters or questioned that it was now lighter by five hundred pounds. None of those in police cells would challenge this for fear of needling the detectives unnecessarily.

Tony Rice was left to Bill Senior to deal with as he saw fit, but he wasn't about to let him go. Instead he sat patiently on the edge of a desk in the squad room at Reading and watched Rice pace angrily up and down, the range of his pacing limited by the expansive movements of other detectives as they careered about the office splashing scotch into polystyrene cups and congratulating each other. Their jubilation only made Tony Rice feel worse.

'Fuck me,' he complained, 'I did the fucking business all right. You lot took a right fucking liberty with me. You could have got me killed. I could've been killed stone dead. I mean, we had a fucking deal. Did we have a deal or didn't we?'

'If you had got away, Tony,' Senior reasoned with him, 'those blaggers would have known right off that it was you who had tucked them up.'

Tony Rice understood the logic of that, but didn't like the consequences. 'So what am I s'posed to do? Go and pull a twenty with them just to prove I'm not? What about giving me a new identity and a ticket to Marbella?'

'That's the five-star treatment, Tony. A few bodies with shooters doesn't rate that sort of treatment.'

A cold shiver ran along Tony Rice's spine. He stopped pacing and looked at the policeman. He knew this was the price of being a grass. Once the police had their hooks in they wouldn't let go; liberty was only ever purchased in inches and always the price was an upwards spiral.

'What if I come up with more? A lot more?'

Suddenly feeling irritated at villains in general rather than this one in particular – villains who believed that all they needed to do was to put up others who were working to secure their liberty in luxury – and more irritated by the fact that it all too often worked, Senior said, 'I'd like someone to give me a new fucking identity and a luxurious lifestyle in Spain.'

'What if the information's about corrupt policemen.'

'Someone'll probably make you assistant chief constable of Wiltshire,' Bill Senior said drily. 'I'll have to put it up to my governor.'

Rather than deal with this situation at a distance, Frank Burroughs told Senior to bring the informant to Rochester Row police station, where he interviewed himself. It wasn't a short interview. Tony Rice had a lot to say for himself, and had a good memory for details, especially where policemen were allegedly involved in crime. The villainy he detailed ranged all over South East England, but largely in London; he had mostly supplied the guns, but had been on one or two jobs made doubly safe because policemen were not only earning money, but had actually put the villains into them in the first place. Everything was taken down slowly and carefully by Frank Burroughs, and at the end of it Tony Rice was no nearer being turned loose than he was at the beginning. For his part, Frank Burroughs wasn't sure that Rice should ever go free. It was possibly best that he stayed nicked for dabbling, and that his statement was shredded. But the same wouldn't happen to Rice's memory, and one day the villain might find himself confronted by a situation similar to this one. So Burroughs found himself staying on until the small hours of the morning typing the forty-nine page statement, and leaving it in a sealed envelope on his governor's desk.

'I don't know about a new identity for Tony Rice,' Jack Bentham said when he had read the report. 'We might drop the fucker out of the plane on the way to Spain.'

'To be honest, guv,' Frank Buroughs said, 'I'm inclined to ring up those detectives he's named and put it to them. I mean, fuck it, I've worked with some of them, they got to have half a chance.'

'All that gets us is those lads from Wiltshire looking at us a bit harder.'

'We've got that anyway.' Burroughs stabbed at the lift button with a thick finger, not looking forward to the hastily called meeting he was going to with the DCS.

'I feel the same way, Frank. No one minds policemen having a few earners, or being a bit swift with villains when they won't go any other way. But actually putting robberies up to villains, that's something else.'

They stepped out of the lift at the fifth floor and crossed the wide bridge that connected Victoria Block, where their offices were, with Tower Block. They entered one of the four lifts there and pressed for the seventeenth floor.

After Bentham had finished reading the report for the second time and had discussed its contents with Burroughs, he had gone as a matter of courtesy to see DAC Doc Holliday with it, but at the same time had sent a Xerox, via one of the civilian messengers who trudged the corridors, to Deputy Commissioner Harry Streeter. He had guessed that the immediate outcome would be this afternoon's hastily-arranged meeting in the commissioner's conference room.

Denis Whites, the commissioner, chaired the meeting and sat at the top of the long, brightly-varnished table. He was ascetic-looking, wore large glasses and had the sobriquet 'The Head' on account of his long forehead. He was evidently not pleased by what he had read in the report, especially because of the presence at the meeting of the assistant chief constable of the Wiltshire Constabulary. Assistant Chief Constable Alan Leeper, who was fifty, was the only one present in uniform; he had with him a detective inspector who wasn't exactly noted for his humour. DCI Humpfress had had no sense of levity while on his home ground, where he managed to cope; however, away from home – as he had been apart from at weekends – he had been under constant pressure to produce results, and had produced precious few in the face of persistent hostility and resentment from Met officers. Of the seven other senior Met officers brought to deliberate on the 'Rice statement', of which each had a copy, Assistant Commissioner Peter Vyvyan was the only one who was coping with its connotations. He did so by emphatically dismissing it.

'No disrespect intended to you personally, Jack,' he said, glancing from Bentham to Burroughs, who he knew to be the real author of the piece, 'but I don't believe a single fucking word of what Rice has said. It has all the hallmarks of a villain desperate to save himself whatever the cost. It looks like he's grabbing at anything. Look at this.' He found a passage in the statement, heavily underscored. 'Waitrose in Richmond. "Detective Sergeant Bruce Fell told us how much was going to be involved almost to the pound, twenty-eight and a half grand, and that one of the security guards collecting the takings would be off sick on the afternoon concerned. It was a doddle." I checked back on this one. DS Fell has a hitherto unblemished record. There was a lad convicted for that robbery. I don't think the majority of this will bear examination.' He couldn't think what these two detectives were up to, especially not with the Wiltshire lot on the manor. If he had taken this statement he would simply have torn it up.

'There's no doubt about Rice trying to spare himself a long prison sentence,' Bentham said equitably.

'Instead he expects to languish in the sunshine in Spain at the taxpayers' expense.' There was a sense of self-righteous piety in Peter Vyvyan, often appearing when his ground was shaky. 'These people think all they have to do is throw a bit of mud at coppers.'

'What's important to establish, Peter, and the sooner the better, is how much of this can be substantiated.' The commissioner paused and stared owl-like along the table. 'For my part I'd be happy if none of it could be substantiated, very happy.' He would be equally happy if nothing of what the Wiltshire Constabulary were investigating could be substantiated. But he didn't say as much with their officers present.

'I'd be very surprised if any of it can be,' Vyvyan added.

Denis Whites looked across at Jack Bentham.

'Some of it's bound to be rumour, thrown in to make the picture look blacker. It's not for C11 to investigate. It's CIB2's bag, or the Wiltshire Constabulary's.' He looked across at Commander Rex Parker, who ran the Met's internal complaints investigation bureau, a short, thickset Scotsman with dark bushy eyebrows that met in the middle to form one continuous line. He had followed Assistant Chief Constable Leeper into the conference room and had taken a chair as far away from him as possible, still feeling great animosity towards this outsider who had come in to do his job. Bentham had been asked to go to the ever-expanding CIB2 as its operational head when the reorganization took place, but not only did he not like the idea of policing policemen, he wasn't enamoured of working under Rex Parker. He suspected Parker felt a similar hostility to him now for having taken on the inquiry into the death of Paul Bailey out at Hackney.

'A lot of this does cut across lines of investigation C11 is running.'

'It might be sensible if this was simply pushed sideways to Mr Leeper,' Deputy Commissioner Harry Streeter said. He suspected that Jack Bentham had presented this statement in the way he had, rather than passing it to CIB2 or Wiltshire, in the hope that the commissioner would sit on it and so allow his own investigations to continue at a fast enough pace for all the evidence to be found in place. The alternative was usually to cobble together a compromise, such as quiet retirement with pension intact – a move the Met was fond of.

'That means extending their original brief yet further, Harry,' the commissioner pointed out. He wanted these people to finish their investigations and go home.

'There really is no other choice.'

'Whatever the outcome, Harry, we get a hammering,' ACC

Vyvyan said. 'As of this moment morale in the Met is about as low as it can get. There's no way it's going to get off the floor until Wiltshire has completed its investigation and it's shown to be a waste of time. Corruption isn't endemic, it never was. The lads in the job care too much about what they do for that.' Peter Vyvyan was adamant in his belief, and the money that was brought to him on a monthly basis in no way affected that belief. He was very adept at compartmentalizing his own actions. 'No disrespect is intended to you personally, Alan, but you and your men should never have been brought in like you were. I don't care how often I have to say it: you're wasting your time, and everyone else's.'

With the exception of Detective Chief Inspector Brian Humpfress, no one around that table took ACC Vyvyan's words as other than an indictment against the commissioner, Denis Whites, for allowing the situation to develop to this point. Humpfress took it personally, and was left smarting with frustration through the brief silence that followed. His face reddened as his anger deepened. He wanted to say how they had been hindered and ridiculed at every turn, but didn't dare to.

'With respect, sir,' Alan Leeper said, offering the standard apology that prefaced anything that was thought might give offence to a senior officer, 'we can't expand our investigation to the size indicated by this statement. Not without bringing in a lot more men.'

'This is fucking ridiculous,' Commander Parker said angrily. 'What's the fucking point of my department if every time there's an allegation of major corruption we get passed over? If more detectives are to be brought in on this they ought to be Met men, out of CIB2. We might get some fucking results then, assuming there are results to be got.'

'You'd have your results all right if policemen up here would be more co-operative, instead of openly obstructive,' Alan Leeper said firmly, trying not to get angry.

Humpfress felt some of his frustration ease now that his boss was saying what needed to be said.

The commissioner knew there was no way he could please everyone around this table, and if they sat there until midnight they wouldn't find an equitable compromise. He wondered briefly about pleasing himself and closing the whole investigation down. The solutions, like the problems themselves, had been so much simpler when he had been a working policeman with a warrant card; they had been a great deal simpler when he had been chief constable of Greater Manchester. When there had been a problem without an arrestable offence, his answer was always to have whoever he wanted out of the way picked up and put on a train to London. That was how he had dealt with the homosexual problem in Central Manchester. But now he was in London there was nowhere he could send the problems to.

'Bring in what extra men you need, Mr Leeper,' Denis Whites said irritably. 'Arrange the details with the central office. You'll get all the co-operation you need. I want this investigation done with as soon as possible. Finished. The whole messy business cleared up. There are more important issues to contend with. Public order issues. This is distracting us. So let's get it done.'

'With the greatest respect, sir,' Peter Vyvyan said ironically, 'it's absolutely fucking daft to allow this investigation to continue, much less get any bigger. It's getting completely out of hand.'

'Everyone knows your views, Peter, and I'm sure a lot of the men in the job respect you for the support you give them. But I have to walk a tightrope, balancing thirty-six thousand employees on the one hand, so to speak, and the whole political spectrum on the other. Your complaining about the situation in public doesn't help one little bit.'

'Do you want my resignation?' Peter Vyvyan asked impulsively, his heart racing in case the commissioner accepted his challenge.

'I'll let you know if ever I do. But you know what pressures are on us. They're not going to go away until the Met is either seen to have a clean bill of health, or is under the direct control of the politicians.'

A smile almost crept across Jack Bentham's face when the meeting broke up and he remembered the conversation he had had with Julian Brind, an ex-university chum in the Home Office, about police strategy. He wondered who was kidding who with all this concern for police morale and anxiety about political takeover. There was a high degree of political naivety in the upper echelons of the police force, amongst those good old practical coppers who kept the respect of the lower ranks because they knew how to feel a collar. They would, in the not-too-distant future, be an anachronism, not because there would be any less collars to feel, but rather because they seemed not to understand the political ramifications of what they were doing. Certainly none of them seemed to share Brind's understanding that the development and escalation of the internal investigation into police corruption was little more than occupational therapy for the media and these anachronistic policemen; it distracted them from the new wave of men who were being carefully selected and put in position – those who could cope with the political implications of what they were doing and see them as being as viable as any other aspect of the job. Jack Bentham assumed that because of his educational background he was expected to be part of the new wave, capable and willing to go along that path. Although Jack Bentham didn't doubt that he would be able to cope with that new direction, he hadn't decided if he was prepared to take it. He felt he wanted to reach a certain point, where he could make a free choice, but deep inside he knew things didn't happen like that; in his job he was subject to both subtle and unsubtle conditioning processes, and almost without realising it often found himself doing, saying or thinking things which were somehow out of character. That was how policemen became corrupt and bigoted, sexist and racist. The majority didn't start out that way. All he could do was try and check the process whenever he found it taking him in an unchosen direction.

8

Detectives from Criminal Intelligence kept observation on Frank Howie's house in Sidcup in Kent for over a week, and were about ready to give up on him when he arrived home by car at around four o'clock in the afternoon, slightly drunk – as from a two or three bottle lunch – but behaving in no way to suggest he'd been out for any other reason.

The moment Howie's car stopped on the parking space that had been hacked into the small front garden, their car drew across the path and the two detectives sprang out, drawing the guns which had been issued to them for this observation.

'What the fuck's going on?' Howie demanded as he was pressed against his car and handcuffed.

'You're nicked, Frank.' Policemen had a habit of stating the obvious.

'What d'you want to do, breathalyse me? Why not do it a bit sensible, in the house, away from the neighbours? I got to live here.'

'Saves splintering the door, alarming the old woman.'

When he was taken to Rochester Row police station, where suspects who were picked up by squads operating out of Scotland Yard were frequently taken, Frank Howie seemed determined to hold out under interrogation, even when it was put to him that he had been grassed by those involved in the King's Road robbery. That was only conjecture on the part of the detectives, based on information received; they had no corroborative evidence to back it up. What these detectives did have was time. It would be some five days before he would crack. Five days of mostly sitting in a police cell, seeing only the gaoler, and occasionally the detectives who came to interview him, and not being allowed to see anyone resembling the solicitor he repeatedly asked for. Howie accepted that he had been grassed, believing there was no other way the police ever arrested anyone. What he didn't want to believe was that it was done by one of his firm, even though he had never worked with them before. He believed that Ronnie Letts, the man who had offered him the work, was a diamond. He had bent more than enough Old Bill, and Howie knew he had done so on this robbery, having mentioned the names of a few detectives he knew himself to be well bent. They weren't the names of any who had arrested him. These detectives were all completely unknown to him, which, he assumed, was why he hadn't received any sort of warning about his arrest from the local CID. He had been given a straight knockback when he had suggested some kind of deal to these detectives. The only deal they seemed interested in was him putting his hand up to that one across the pavement.

Five days in a police cell with nothing to do and no one to talk to was enough to weaken the firmest resolve, especially when those five days began to look like being stretched endlessly. For all he knew he was lost within the system. There was no way he could communicate with anyone; his wife obviously didn't know where he was or she would have had a solicitor hammering on the door.

'Aren't you supposed to produce me in court or something after all this time?' Howie asked when one of the detectives visited him.

'I don't think so, Frank. Why would we? You haven't done anything, have you?'

'You know that. I know that. You have to get up in court and prove it.'

'Any time you feel like making a statement – 'you have anything to state, that is.'

The detective left him, only to be summoned back by Frank Howie within ten minutes of his leaving the cell. The gaoler conveyed the message, only the detectives on C11 didn't respond. Ten minutes later Howie asked again, and then again a short while after that; finally the gaoler didn't even respond to his ringing on the bell. When later that evening the door opened and Detective Sergeant Kingham stepped into the cell, Frank Howie started to talk out of sheer relief, and fearing his visitor would simply go away unless he gave him something.

'I was grassed right. 'Course I was. That's the only way you ever nick anyone. Well I can play that fucking game. I know more than enough who are at it. Old Bill as well. More than enough of them at it. What about those cunts on the Robbery Squad. D'you know DCI Sneed?'

'I heard he was well bent,' Kingham said obligingly, having heard no such thing. 'Did you do business with them?'

'How can you trust those bastards? Specially not that filth. No matter what they promise you, you end up just the same.'

There was no sense of irony in his words, he may have been talking to a friend in a pub rather than a detective who was going to take a long and detailed statement from him.

Getting forty protesters out on a weekday morning was a feat of organization, even with unemployment so high. Somehow people weren't mentally geared to weekday demos, and to find that many who would not only protest but were prepared to be arrested was even more of an achievement. Helen Daniels wasn't sure about the 'being arrested' part when she was phoned up to go on the demo, but supposed she would be released in time to get to the theatre if she were. It might have provided some welcome publicity, both for the play and for the movement, had the curtain not been able to go up for that reason.

The protesters continually crossed and recrossed the road in front of Hackney police station, managing to hold up the traffic for fairly long periods before the police stepped in to let vehicles through, or drivers became so impatient as to force a passage, defying the protesters to remain in their way.

There were enough policemen present to forcibly remove all those people causing the obstruction; only they weren't technically obstructing the highway, merely going from one side to the other. When the television news camera arrived in addition to radio news reporters, the police reduced their numbers on the street, pulling some of the sixty policemen present back into the station.

'Why are the police covering up Paul Bailey's death?' someone cried.

'Because they murdered him,' came the chanted response. 'Murderers, murderers, murderers.'

The police didn't enjoy these taunts, especially as most of them had been on that earlier demo and hadn't entirely resolved their own feelings of culpability over the death of the young medical student.

Superintendent Mike Regan smarted as he watched this untidy rabble from the steps of his police station. They wouldn't have been allowed to get away with this offensive behaviour had he not been told to keep a fairly low profile. He had done that, and traffic had been disrupted for over an hour. How much longer they would go on for if left to their own devices he couldn't guess. The possibility of withdrawing his men entirely had occurred to him. But having experienced the Brixton riots, when the police had for a short time lost control of the streets, and having seen the effect on the morale of his men and the anarchy that had swiftly followed, Mike Regan had determined that such a situation – whether tactically or accidentally brought about – would never occur again in any policing situation where he had influence. It looked as though there were one or two of what he called 'respectables' among these protesters, and that always worried him. How they got involved he couldn't imagine. He turned his gaze along the street to the queues of vehicles, the damp air thick with exhaust. A number of cars were making U-turns to take alternative routes. It was time to do something. He turned away angrily and went into the station.

The four reserve squads of eight policemen each sat around the disused muster room, looking bored; having run out of conversation, they were waiting for something to happen. That something looked in prospect when Superintendent Regan entered, and they became alert as if from a jolt of electricity.

'Right,' Superintendent Regan said decisively. 'It's time we cleared the street.'

That brought a cheer from the policemen.

'The television and radio people are here. Now you know there is nothing they like more than a bit of violence to show their viewers. But we've been instructed to keep a fairly low profile, so what I'm going out there to do now is ask them to remove themselves to the far pavement. If they refuse to do this, form yourselves into four-men snatch squads and remove them.'

'All of them, sir?' a sergeant asked.

'As many as it takes to make those who are left ineffective. I suspect we'll probably only have to pick up half a dozen or so and the rest will pack up.'

He was entirely wrong about the number. The snatch squads started work after the protesters refused to heed the superintendent's advice to clear the street. They arrested twenty-seven people before the other fourteen dispersed, having been rendered less than effective.

Helen Daniels was one of the first to be arrested, and protested loudly at both her arrest and the unnecessary force she believed the police were using. She ended up in a cell with nine other women.

They hadn't been there but a few minutes when suddenly Helen felt an overwhelming sense of despair at the apparent hopelessness of it all. They were so few; the animal torturers were so many and so wealthy and such powerful propagandists, and those whose hearts and minds the movement had to win for any lasting change were even more. Standing between them and us, she realised, were those powerful institutions of police, medicine and a government, each of them equally dedicated to supporting the status quo.

One of the women started to hum, and others joined her. After a few moments Helen found her spirits lifting and she joined in also. Humming was so powerful and effective, she thought, because it was so close to the 'ohm', which was one of the basic sounds man made. They went on to sing, then chant, and finally, after about an hour, fell silent. They were given nothing to eat or drink. And when one woman rang the bell and asked for water she was politely smiled at and told she would only then need to pee.

There was a flushing toilet in the corner, but feelings of delicacy prevented any of the women from using it for a long time. They expected not to be in there that long.

'Look, do you think I could have some water, young man,' one of the older women said to the young policeman who responded to the bell. 'I'm not feeling well.'

'Then you shouldn't have been out protesting, should you,' was the response. 'The doctor'll be round to see you soon.'

'I won't be talked to like that, not by you or anyone else,' Marjorie Lodge retorted, 'you should have some manners.'

'Do you want to give your antecedents and have your photograph took?' the policeman asked.

They had given all the information they intended giving – their names and addresses.

It was mid-afternoon before the doctor got there, a smooth-looking individual in blazer, grey trousers and brown suede shoes, with the slightly glassy-eyed look of a drinker, confirmed by the brown stains in the corners of his mouth. He introduced himself as Dr Spink, the police surgeon, and asked if anyone had any particular medical problem that being in a cell exacerbated. That was the extent of his examination.

No one else came to see them for the rest of the afternoon, apart from the unhelpful gaoler, who didn't respond to any of their requests.

By seven o'clock Helen was wondering if she would get to the theatre in time. Her telling the gaoler about her problem only brought the now familiar response: that she shouldn't have been on such a demonstration. They were told the delay of their release was due to the police having difficulty in establishing who they were, since they had offered no antecedents and refused to have their photographs taken. In fact the police had several times tried to photograph them when they had arrived, only Sheila Weymouth had alerted them and they had all avoided the lens.

When Jack Bentham arrived at Hackney police station to interview the policemen involved with Paul Bailey's death, only the chief inspector was on duty, but someone had made sure that the policemen on Bentham's list were there.

'Do you still have Helen Daniels in the cells?' Bentham asked.

'If she's one of those protesters from this morning, yes. They're all here still.'

'When are they going to be released?'

'They can go anytime now. We'll bail them in their own recognizance to appear before the local magistrate in the morning.'

It wasn't much of a favour that he asked of the chief inspector – having Helen Daniels released ahead of the others. Bentham didn't tell her that as he led her out through the back of the station to where his car was parked in the yard.

'How can I remain impartial in my inquiry now I've sprung you?' he said humorously.

'How could you be impartial anyway? You're a policeman.'

Bentham considered her. He had hoped for a sign of gratitude. 'Get in the car. He'll take you to the theatre.'

'Thanks. I do appreciate your doing this. But what about the others? The police won't be able to deal with that many corpses.' The words were regretted as soon as she had said them. She realised this was an antidote to her feelings; she felt embarrassed about feeling anything positive or nice towards a policeman. There was no expression on his face.

'There's a dog pound here – they'll cut them up and feed them to the dogs, as they all love animals so much.'

The words were distant and defensive and didn't match the way he reached out and protectively tied her scarf about her neck. Helen felt confused.

'I have to interview some of the policemen who were there when your friend died. But I wondered if I could buy you a cup of mint tea when the play ends.'

Helen hesitated, feeling both uneasy about allowing this policeman near her, yet also curiously attracted.

'If you know where we can get mint tea at that time. The play ends about ten fifteen.'

'I'll find somewhere.' He closed the door after her and turned away towards the steps into the building.

Ringing up and arranging for those policemen who Mr Bentham wished to interview to be available at his convenience was something DI Joe Russell did matter-of-factly, brooking no argument. The interviews he had arranged for this evening involved two of the policemen who were in the first District Support Unit van to arrive at the scene of Paul Bailey's death. To pick out just two at a time was a move to divide them. The other policemen in Uniform Carrier G/60 would worry no less than the two who were being interviewed again; they would be anxious over what might be said about them.

PC Phil Westbrook was overweight, overanxious and sweating under his uniform. He sat in the interview room opposite the small table. Folders were spread out and Bentham was glancing over the contents of one, leaving the constable to his thoughts in the long silence.

Finally he separated a xeroxed sheet and passed it to PC Westbrook. 'That's a copy of your duty log covering the entire tour of duty up to and including the time Paul Bailey died. Any dispute with what's on it?'

'No, sir,' Westbrook responded, hardly glancing at the sheet.

'You set out clearly what happened when you arrived in Uniform Carrier G/59 just below Tudor Grove. Your vehicle, in conjunction with DSU G/60, formed a roadblock. You waited there for four minutes, during which time the demonstrators turned into Tudor Grove away from you; you then drew truncheons and proceeded to disperse them.'

'Yes, sir.' PC Westbrook swallowed several times, knowing what was coming next.

'This is a copy of the statement taken from you earlier today by Superintendent Pitt.' Pitt was one of the nine-man investigation team. Bentham pushed the sheets across the desk and let the constable identify them. 'There's a serious contradiction between the two. In your statement they were coming at you along Tudor Grove, throwing stones at the police.'

Anxiety leaped through Phil Westbrook. 'They did attack us, sir,' he said, keeping to his second statement. 'They were throwing stones. They were throwing stones at us when they were coming along Well Street.'

'I'm not saying they weren't. You're saying that in your duty log. Why did you wait for three or four minutes before getting out of the van?'

'I don't know, sir. We waited for Inspector Hern's order to draw truncheons.'

'You received that order, did you?'

'Yes, sir, of course sir.'

'You're quite sure, are you? Because none of your colleagues are. You certainly omitted that detail in your report attached to your duty log.'

Anxiety tugged again at PC Westbrook. He was sure they had agreed among themselves about the order to draw truncheons, and he couldn't believe they had gone back on it, knowing what that could mean: unlawful killing. He assumed this detective was trying to trick him, and he felt sick for being the one singled out in this way. Policemen were supposed to stick together, just as they did in the DSUs.

'I think we received the order to draw our truncheons. Inspector Hern said, "Let's get the fuckers ..."' He suddenly stopped, then added, as if trying to retrieve his words, '"Let's get them off the streets."'

'But he didn't say draw truncheons,' Bentham challenged.

'I believe he did, sir,' a note of uncertainty in his voice.

Jack Bentham looked at him a long while, then pushed up from the desk. 'I'm going up to the canteen to have a word with a colleague.' He had heard that David Evans had arrived and needed to see him. 'Meanwhile you have another think about what happened from the moment your van stopped below the junction of Tudor Grove, up until Paul Bailey's death, and then

94

make another statement. This time without reference to your colleagues. Inspector Russell will give you any assistance you need.'

The police constable looked haunted as Bentham left the room.

DCI David Evans was on the top floor of the station drinking tea like he would have preferred something stronger when Bentham found him. Without a word, Evans passed over a copy of a long, typed statement that Frank Howie had given. The DCI's silence, along with his presence here, suggested to Bentham what he would find in the statement.

'Do you want some tea, guv?' Evans said as Bentham opened the folder and started to read.

He didn't, and Evans went and made more tea for himself. There were facilities but no staff around to cook for those on the late shifts. Policemen on any relief later than four in the afternoon tended to eat eggs and beans, or take-away.

Bentham read very quickly. He needed to in order to keep up with the volume of reports. What he read here he didn't enjoy particularly, but none of it surprised him. Details of police corruption never surprised him, and he always found the public reaction of 'shock horror' a little naive. To ask a man to deal with thieves on a daily basis and not succumb to temptation in any way was, he felt, expecting superhuman qualities. He had met no superhuman policemen, but a lot of corrupt policemen, who mostly tried to keep a sense of proportion in their illicit exploits. Things had been getting out of hand these past few years, and what did surprise him was that the level of corruption had gone unchecked for so long.

'It's getting to be open season on policemen,' he said, without lifting his eyes from the page.

'A lot of what Frank Howie put up ties in with Tony Rice's statement.'

'I'll keep it in mind, Dave.' He looked at the DCI. 'Who else has seen this?'

'I typed it. I thought you'd want first look.'

Bentham nodded. 'Pull all the references to corrupt policemen. Then pass it on to the Squad, let them pursue the regular villains for now.'

'You going to pass the names of those policemen to the Wiltshire lot, guv?'

'I'm not sure.'

'You might get your collar felt, 'it comes out,' Evans warned. 'We've got the Wiltshire CID looking at us tomorrow.'

He hadn't forgotten them. They would certainly think the worst of his not passing on the names of the policemen named in corruption allegations either to them or to CIB2. Jack decided he would live with that for now. Despite himself he felt some sense of loyalty to brother officers, and recognized that too much was asked of these men too often, and that simply weeding out the bent ones as their names were thrown up provided no real answer. He suspected the solution was bigger than anything that could be tackled from within the force. Policemen, after all, only reflected the values of society, and there was no way they could be isolated from them.

'Come on, I'll buy you a drink,' Bentham said, glancing at his watch. He had time before going to the theatre. 'Stop worrying, s'my problem.'

Even police drivers misjudged traffic at times. This was one such time and Bentham was late getting across London to Sloane Square. The theatre was empty, the front doors barred. Bentham went briskly along the alleyway to the stage-door.

'Is Helen Daniels around?' he asked the lad behind the glass.

'She's gone. She was here a short while ago.' The doorkeeper paused from pulling on his jacket and looked at Bentham. 'Have you tried the pub next door?'

Swiftly checking both bars, Bentham could see no sign of her red hair. He stepped out, feeling annoyed with himself. He wondered briefly about the tube train, and ran through the barrier and down the steps. A train was braking out of the tunnel as he searched quickly along the platform. He saw what he believed was Helen step into the last carriage but one. There was no way he could get to her before the door closed, so he stepped into the nearest carriage and out at the next station, and hurried along to the back of the train. It was her and he felt pleased. She was sitting on her own reading a script and didn't look up when he sat next to her. He tried not to show what he was feeling, as if believing it would somehow weaken his position.

'You didn't wait,' he said, sounding a little cross.

'I assumed you had got involved with something more important,' she said.

'Oh I had, much more important,' he said, watching closely as her eyes flicked back to the page in a dismissive gesture. 'I was given some information on a whole gang of corrupt policemen, and I don't quite know how to handle it.'

Helen closed her script and looked up at him. He had her attention now.

'I thought there was a whole department to investigate police corruption.'

'CIB2. Don't tell me you have faith in internal police inquiries?'

'You don't?' she said, a little surprised.

'I'm supposed to. Here I am hanging onto all this information and I've got policemen from an outside force coming to investigate me tomorrow.'

'It's not surprising there aren't many criminals caught these days.'

Bentham smiled, having decided he had given enough. 'Where are we going?'

'I was going home.'

'Well what about that mint tea?' he offered.

'I have to get this script read. It was left at the theatre. They want an answer by tomorrow.'

'Then you should say no,' he told her. 'If it's important, you need more time than that to decide. Why not come and have some Chinese food? It's vegetarian.' He rose decisively as the train pulled into Notting Hill Gate station and, to his surprise, so did she, without protest.

There wasn't a Chinese restaurant on the Gate, vegetarian or otherwise. Helen suggested Tootsies, a hamburger restaurant which had two vegetarian dishes on the menu. It wasn't an ideal choice: the tables were cramped together and the place was noisy with people trying to talk over the constant loud music. His best jokes didn't stand being shouted. He wondered if he should confess to not being vegetarian, go for a steak and risk alienating her, or put up with limp lettuce and grated carrot.

'The vegetable pie is very good if you're still a vegetarian who eats cheese,' she said leaning over and indicating it on the menu.

What else do they eat? he almost said. The warmth and smell that came off her decided him. It was a long time since he had had any sort of relationship with a woman and he felt a strong need just to be held, not necessarily to have made love; he didn't want his gross eating habits to come between them. He took the vegetable pie, and noted she had a salad without the eggs or cheese.

'I think I'd like a drink,' Helen said.

Bentham felt grateful for that. He ordered a bottle of wine.

The prejudice he felt about vegetarian food was entirely unfounded. The pie and the salad that came with it were as good as any he'd had with meat in.

'Are you a vegetarian for the sake of your health?' he asked as they were eating.

'It's more for the health of the animal,' she said. 'It doesn't do a chicken's health one bit of good when it's put in the scalding tank to have its feathers removed – alive.'

Bentham wanted to get into her knickers and was prepared to go along with his pretence to do so, though he wasn't sure how far he could go if she regaled him with too much horror over what he had been eating up until this evening.

'I thought the chickens were stunned first.'

'They're supposed to be. But often their heads don't go into the stunning bath, and the automatic throat cutting is botched so that some go into the scalding tank fully conscious.' She smiled grimly, thinking she might be getting too heavy, but also knowing she was testing him. Helen didn't think she could have a relationship with a non-vegetarian. 'I think not eating dead animals is better for my health as well – most illness comes from what we eat. Animal fats cause a build-up of toxins in the body. Almost all food poisoning comes from meat and fish. Why are you vegetarian?'

He avoided saying, 'Because I thought it the easiest way into your knickers,' and said instead, 'Laziness, I suppose. I eat at such odd hours most times that it's somehow easier to eat a carrot or an apple and a piece of cheese than cook a piece of meat.'

Their conversation moved from vegetarianism to the inevitable animal rights, and, almost as inevitably, to the police reaction to those who championed them.

'Why are the police so heavy towards us?' Helen wanted to know.

'Because of the movement's commitment. They're interested in maintaining law and order on the streets.'

'They're such loving, well-meaning people – the majority of

animal rightists.' She thought about all the jealousies and in-fighting that were currently splitting the movement.

'They physically attack scientists who experiment on animals.'

'That's not logical or reasonable. They care about all animal rights, including human animals. Vivisectors are no different from the Nazi scientists who experimented in Auchwitz and Belsen during the war. All they ever do is attack their property and try to liberate the animals.' She felt her emotions rising.

'Policemen are often fairly limited. All they can do is enforce the law. They don't know any better. An act of violence against property is breaking the law.'

'Yes, but how do we change the law? By acting outside it to bring attention to what those Nazi-like scientists are doing.'

'You're doing that all right. A lot of people are aware of your case now. What you have to be careful not to do is alienate them by letting someone get hurt.'

Helen considered him for a few moments, her feelings quite confused. 'You seem to care about the issues.'

'I'd prefer the law not to be broken. It would be better if it was changed so that people in these situations didn't feel the need. But if it isn't going to be changed just yet then you should find a way round it.'

The restaurant was almost empty by the time they had finished talking. Chairs were being put up on tables; it was time to go, only Bentham wasn't sure where. He hadn't exactly spent his time advancing his romantic intentions, he reflected gloomily, it had been animal rights all the way. Helen arguing with him over splitting the bill wasn't encouraging either. Finally he wearied of it and insisted on paying. A mistake, but one that he felt now made no appreciable difference to his position.

On leaving the restaurant he turned down the hill of Holland Park Avenue towards Shepherd's Bush with her. He no longer had his car in tow.

'Where are we going?' Helen asked directly.

He laughed as if being caught out on a lie. 'I was planning to take you back to my place for some mint tea. If you don't mind.' He experienced a stab of anxiety, fearing rejection, but added regardlessly, 'Perhaps make love to you.'

It was her turn to laugh nervously. 'I'll have to think about that.' She thought immediately how stupid such a response was, deciding it made her appear foolish.

They continued in the same direction, each anxious that the other shouldn't do something to prevent the contact, the comfort they each wanted, yet each unable adequately to communicate that need, for fear of giving too much. Bentham glanced around, then hailed a cab. He opened the door for her, gave the driver his address in Hammersmith and climbed in himself in silence. After a few moments Helen put her hand in his, and Bentham decided it was going to be all right.

It wasn't. Their attempt at love-making was a disaster. Getting undressed and into the double bed in his untidy bedroom overlooking the Thames was businesslike enough – she even borrowed his toothbrush. She was thirty-seven and slightly crêpy, while he was forty-three and slightly overweight, which didn't go with his five feet eight. They were like an old married couple. There was no passion, only need combined with anxiety, which made Bentham try too hard and Helen hesitate too often. He got an erection immediately they were in bed together, holding each other, but she wasn't ready for him and he feared he wouldn't sustain it. Fear created its own reality, and no matter what he did to stimulate her his erection wouldn't return. She fondled him to semi-stiffness and helped him achieve penetration, but that was far from satisfactory. His abstinence caused him to come too swiftly, which only added to his embarrassment; hers made the triggers of response seem so far away and forgotten, and she felt disappointed when he asked if he could come inside her, but pleased that he was considerate enough to ask. She was starting her period and told him it was all right.

After orgasm he quickly withdrew and pushed himself down the bed under the duvet to avoid what he imagined to be her unspoken censure and assuage his feeling of inadequacy by stimulating her to orgasm with his mouth. It took a long time, and his feeling didn't abate. Thoughts about work started to intrude, and the more he tried to push them out the more they forced in between him and Helen: the information about corrupt policemen that David Evans had given him, some of whom he knew personally – what was he to do about them? The visit he was expecting tomorrow from Wiltshire CID – what did they want? How would he handle that interview? What corruption had he in some way been involved with that might be out-standing? He hardly noticed Helen achieve orgasm, she was so quiet, and for a moment he wasn't sure that she had. Then he felt the tension go out of her body. She was like someone who was used to considering other people. Once he had had an affair with a mother of three children who had been like that, anxious about disturbing her children, always alert for their needs. He knew from the police intelligence computer record that Helen Daniels was divorced but without children. He wondered if she knew she had a record, like so many other animal rightists, CND supporters, protesters of all sorts; they no longer had to have a criminal conviction to be listed. Anyone who the police knew about and thought likely to commit an offence or a disturbance gained a place on the computer; there was lots of space.

'Helen?' he said quietly. But she was gone, having drifted off to sleep. He was left with his thoughts of failure, his feelings of guilt.

Bentham slept fitfully, haunted by both his sexual failure and diminishing power at work. The Wiltshire police entered his dreams. They were driving him up a rickety staircase that led nowhere, it had no handrails and was dangerous to climb. He woke himself up out of a similar dream about Terry Sneed, who he had to rely on to pull him out of a deep pit. He got up out of bed, trying not to disturb Helen, tucking her arm and shoulder under the duvet.

The flat was warm and he didn't bother to put anything on. He went and made some instant coffee and took it through into the sitting room, leaving on the kitchen light but standing in darkness in front of the window that overlooked the river. He had come to like the dead hours of morning, perhaps because from a police viewpoint there was very little going on.

He heard Helen get up but didn't stir as she padded softly out to the kitchen. She moved well, with a gracefulness which might have been natural, or the result of training as an actress; or perhaps she had done ballet as a child. The image of young girls going through ballet exercises popped into his head. The sound of the fridge opening reached his ears and a vague, dissociated alarm bell started in a distant part of his mind, only he couldn't identify its cause.

Helen had put on a King George V crested sauna robe, that

also swamped Bentham when he wore it. He had packed it after a brief stay in that hotel in Paris a few years ago. She came through to the sitting room and stood behind him, feeling a little depressed – she had thought him a strong man, one who had withstood life's cruelties and yet remained fairly sensitive, but believed that instead she had found a liar.

'What are you doing?' she asked.

'Pissing into the river,' he said, without explaining his cryptic statement. 'S'what it seems like.'

The feeling was very familiar to Helen, but she didn't know if the remark was for her benefit or his own. She didn't respond when he reached out and put his arm around her, and certainly didn't say what she wanted to say.

'I couldn't remember where I was. Couldn't you sleep?'

'It happens.'

'Conscience?' Helen asked.

That wasn't what she had wanted to say. And he easily deflected her with a 'Probably.' She didn't know why she held back as she did over her discovery in his fridge.

'We have over eighty detectives here from Wiltshire looking over our shoulders.'

'You included?' she asked. She knew that policemen suffered the frailties of other humans, but it had always been easier not to acknowledge it. Now that she had first-hand experience of that frailty she wasn't sure if she was pleased or disappointed.

'They'll run over us, looking at everything we've done, wanting to know what we had for breakfast. It's seriously affecting results.'

Helen realised she had missed her opportunity to challenge him about the packet of bacon in his fridge when she said, 'Criminals who have been put away by corrupt policemen – and some who aren't criminals.'

'Corruption is the price of an effective police force,' he told her.

'That's a contradiction, Jack.'

He laughed, not unkindly. 'In your world someone sits down and writes the answers before the questions are put, and if the questions don't bring about the right answers the playwright changes them. I have to decide what level of corruption is acceptable.'

Frustration and betrayal suddenly assailed Helen. 'That's

beginning to sound like those policemen out in Hackney didn't kill Paul,' she said.

He looked at her. 'I'm talking about seriously corrupt policemen, not one-off events, no matter how tragic. I wonder if I shouldn't just turn all that information over to the Wiltshire detectives tomorrow.'

'You might end up with a less corrupt police force.'

'I wouldn't count on it. More likely we'll have one that's looked at less closely. That is what this whole investigation has become, really, a public relations exercise. At the end of the day the public are supposed to believe that all is well within the police again. Perhaps if they believe it ...'

There was a moment between them when neither was sure of the way forward. He didn't want to say any more about the situation within the police. She didn't want now to bring up the bacon in the fridge. Instead she wanted it to be all right.

Despite herself Helen said, 'There's a packet of bacon in your fridge. I always go to the fridge if I wake in the night.'

'Is that all?' he said casually. 'I'm surprised. It's probably out of date, isn't it? A friend stayed here a couple of weeks ago. I find it difficult to impose my will, telling him not to smoke, not to eat meat.'

'I do it all the time – is it awfully boring?' Helen asked feeling foolish and anxious.

At once he knew he was out of trouble. 'You can get away with it. I don't have your conviction. But I'm trying, honest.'

Helen felt hugely relieved, that things were going to be all right, that she wouldn't have to compromise her principles for the sake of a relationship – any more than she had already by going with a policeman. She laughed and leaned her head against his naked chest. She saw in the pale, pre-dawn light that he had an erection and she let out a little surprised 'Oh' as she took hold of it.

'Nervous tension,' he said.

The love-making was much better on the second attempt, each being a little more sure of the other, a little more secure in themselves.

9

Having solved his immediate sexual problem, Jack Bentham was able to bring his attention to focus on the work problem that was yawning before him like a flint-filled chasm. His dilemma over the revelations of corruption remained the same, only he felt more comfortable with himself for what had taken place last night. He had left Helen at his flat reading her script over elderflower tea that he had managed to buy at the Indian grocer's around the corner before his driver collected him. He wondered what other nasty surprises she might find there – like the bacon – but wasn't particularly worried. The same non-existent guest could be blamed.

'Morning, Jack. You've got visitors,' Commander Wiseman said as Bentham stepped from the lift on the fourth floor to find his acting boss popping a mint into his mouth – C11 currently had no commander of its own. Ernie Wiseman was large, baldish and in his early fifties, but what made him notice-able was his weight – not especially his size, but the fact that it continually went up and down. Wiseman was a serious believer in dieting, but found difficulty keeping to his latest, and often most effective diet, and when breaking it he would eat double the normal amount to compensate for what he had missed. As a result he went up and down like a leaky tyre. Currently he was eating anything in sight and his clothes strained at the seams. Polo mints sustained him between between-meal snacks.

'They're clocking us in are they?' Bentham glanced along the corridor to where Brian Humpfress and his boss, Detective Chief Superintendent Bulmer, were waiting outside his door. They were early; Bentham had expected to get in ahead of them and at least have the advantage of placing his desk between them.

'I doubt if they'll find anything more serious with your lot, Jack.'

Being an acolyte of Peter Vyvyan's, the commander took the defensive line about all Met policemen who were under investigation. He sounded at times like a lesser version of the ACC.

'Don't put up with any nonsense from them, Jack. You need

any help, give me a shout. You outrank that Wiltshire DCS anyway, he's only a jumped-up superintendent.' Wiseman spoke loud enough for Bulmer to hear, but if he did hear he didn't respond. The commander stepped into the lift, scrunching another mint as he went.

'Good morning. I'm Chief Superintendent Bulmer. This is Chief Inspector Humpfress.' The lean, sharp-featured man dressed in a cheap high-street suit extended his hand. Bentham shook it, then Humpfress's, surprising him.

'Wouldn't say much for our intelligence if I didn't know who you were by now,' Bentham said. He opened his door and showed them into his office. 'I can't say I welcome your presence. But I won't obstruct you.'

'Fair enough,' Tony Bulmer said, having to stop himself calling this senior policeman sir for the second time.

Bentham got them chairs and made a space on his desk for Humpfress to put the armful of files he had brought. It looked like being a long morning.

It was, but Bentham only gave them half of his attention once he had established that they had little that was concrete and were fishing, hoping he would offer something. He had no such intention, and the part of his brain that wasn't coping with these two visitors he casually put to work on the reports that had arrived on his desk overnight.

Only occasionally did items command his full attention, such as mention of the armed robbery that had taken place in Faversham in Kent fifteen months ago, when the robbers had cut open the truck with a chainsaw. Bentham tried not to signal the mental change of gear.

'You conducted the investigation jointly with the Robbery Squad, and followed it through to the point of arrest. It's unusual for Criminal Intelligence detectives to make arrests.'

Bentham shuffled some papers across the desk in front of him, no longer seeing what was on them. 'It depends how involved the case is. We try not to put ourselves on offer. The lads here are policemen, they do occasionally like to feel a collar. I expect your lot must get to feel a bit like that,' he added, unable to resist that mean observation. The Wiltshire detectives had been a long time on this investigation without making any arrests at all. 'We did put someone away for that. Peter Forster?' He wasn't entirely sure of the name now. 'And a security guard . . .' whose name ne couldn't remember. 'The others involved wouldn't come.' He glanced over at the sour-looking Brian Humpfress, who was checking these points of reference in a file. This detective troubled Bentham for a reason he couldn't quite get to.

Bulmer glanced at his colleague, not sharing Bentham's reservations. 'One of the suspects was David Lane.'

Here we go! Bentham thought. He remembered David Lane's phone call from Spain, when he had tried to make a deal about coming back. Bentham had heard rumours about the Wiltshire police putting more illegal taps on CID phones than C11 did on suspects' phones. He assumed it was only a rumour or they would have found out more than they currently seemed to have, unless they were being very close; but then he had also heard that Met officers were simply undoing the taps, something Wiltshire didn't dare complain about.

'David Lane disappeared to Spain, as I recall, before we could pick him up. The evidence wasn't that good, but we might have given it a go if we had him tucked up in a cell somewhere.'

'Chief Inspector Sneed was involved in that case, even though the robbery didn't happen in the Districts covered by his squad.' Bulmer made it sound like an indictment.

'We had information that it was connected to other blags, that's why we passed it to Terry Sneed's squad. I think the Kent police welcomed their help.'

'Did you exchange information with him about David Lane?'

'I expect so,' Bentham said casually, being two or three jumps ahead of Bulmer and anticipating where he was going. 'We usually pass on whatever information we get to the policemen on the ground. But my DCIs handle the daily flow. They'd know better what was passed to who and when.'

'What was Chief Inspector Sneed's relationship with David Lane?'

Just because he saw where this DCS was going, didn't mean he was enjoying the route, and an edge came into Jack Bentham's voice. 'You'd better ask him.'

'Was Lane warned about his imminent arrest?'

Bentham laughed, both at the audacity and the naivety of the question, but went on to admit that it was a possibility.

'By someone on the Robbery Squad?' Humpfress asked.

That question merely drew a disdainful look from Bentham, and left an embarrassed silence.

'When the Robbery Squad arrested Peter Forster,' Bulmer asked, 'did you get any sense that this was a body that had been put up to satisfy the record?'

'Not in view of the amount of work that some of my detectives put in.'

'Did Sneed's squad put in as much work?'

'More, I'd say,' Bentham said generously. He didn't think anyone worked as hard as his men for such little thanks or show of results on their record. Results were important to a policeman's career, regardless of the squad they were on. There was, always had been and likely always would be, an official denial that such a situation existed. But results usually meant a policeman was hard-working; convictions in court confirmed it and promotion was the just reward.

'Just a couple more questions, chief superintendent. Have you had any contact with David Lane since you investigated the Faversham security truck robbery?'

Bentham stared across the desk directly at this man. The easiest way to tell a lie, he found, was to make eye contact with the subject. The least effective way was to look elsewhere or try to be busy. 'No. Then nor did we have any when we investigated him.'

'You did recommend to the DPP that Lane's brother Charlie shouldn't be prosecuted over a warehouse robbery he was involved in,' Brian Humpfress said. 'The two incidents weren't connected?' Humpfress thought possibly they were, which was why he raised the matter.

'Charlie was a body on that. That's why he was taken along.'

'So that the policemen involved in the case could arrest someone, have a result, take the pressure off the investigation?'

'That's what you're here to try and find out. Charlie is a bit subnormal. There would have been no point in prosecuting him. He went into a mental hospital as part of the deal.'

'You've had subsequent contact?' Humpfress said, as if knowing he had.

Bentham was too experienced an interrogator himself to go for that technique. 'I heard that he was out of hospital and holding down a job. One of my successes.' He smiled, avoiding mockery, and looked at his watch. 'If you've about finished, I've got a briefing at eleven-thirty.'

Bulmer glanced at his colleague, seeking more points, but Brian Humpfress shook his head, his teeth clamped shut, his lips pulled tight and bloodless in anger at the polite stonewalling by this senior officer. He had hoped that Bentham wouldn't show unswerving loyalty to Met officers as running the RCS for so long should have made him an outsider. There was one more tack to make, one that wasn't generous and was possibly impertinent, but then Brian Humpfress was getting more and more desperate and felt under particular pressure. He had come onto this investigation over a year ago with a sense of optimism, expecting some fairly swift results; it had also been a way of resolving some domestic problems which he had hoped a brief separation would help. But its continuing for over a year had exacerbated them. At forty-two Brian Humpfress was in a deep emotional crisis, only he was the last person to recognize this, and would have been reluctant even to acknowledge it.

Having collected all his files and got out of the chair, he said, 'One more thing you might be able to help with, sir.' He used the 'sir' almost as an insult. 'Detective Sergeant Leonard Feast was on that investigation at Faversham.'

'I'll take your word for that. I don't handle operational details such as the make-up of squads.'

'He was on the Robbery Squad up until a year ago,' Humpfress persisted. 'You heard none of the rumours about it being him who alerted David Lane?' They had heard several stories about DS Feast, but alerting David Lane was an invention that he hoped would lead Bentham to offer them something.

'I didn't say Lane was alerted,' Jack Bentham pointed out. 'I merely said it was a possibility. Perhaps you should put that question to DS Feast.' There were a few questions he wouldn't have minded asking Feast himself.

The interview was finally over and Bentham sanctioned their going on to talk to the rest of the detectives in C11, doubting they'd get any further with any of them. One or two, like Frank Burroughs, would be openly hostile and they'd regret the encounter.

Jack Bentham couldn't ordinarily drink at lunchtime, unlike a lot of his colleagues. Alcohol during the day gave him a fogged brain and a tendency to sleep; this he found to be a distinct professional handicap, for a lot of good police work went on in pubs and clubs. Having done a lot of talking this morning, Bentham felt in need of a drink, and as he wasn't going to have time to eat lunch he decided to get a drink in the Tank, a bar-room without any style or comfort on the ground floor at Scotland Yard. It was exclusively for policemen, and all ranks drank there, mostly on a top-up basis between watering holes.

Terry Sneed was at the bar getting some drinks when Bentham approached. He turned and acknowledged him.

'What are you drinking, Jack? Scotch?' It was glasses of scotch he had in his hand. He signalled to the barman, permitting no refusal. Bentham asked for a pint of bitter. 'How's it going?'

'I had the Wiltshire lot in this morning, wasting my time.'

'Been at it again, Jack, have you?' Sneed said with a smile, and nodded across the bar-room. 'There's a bunch of them in the corner there. No one wants to drink with them. You'd think they'd all got AIDS.'

Bentham followed the direction of Sneed's nod. There were four Wiltshire detectives completely isolated in the corner, nursing their drinks as if each was reluctant to finish and venture out for more, but all determined not to be intimidated and driven out of the place. Brian Humpfress was one of them. A feeling of compassion rose momentarily in Bentham, and he wondered how these men functioned at all in such an atmosphere of hostility. He squashed an impulse to go over and offer them a drink, but instead found himself saying to Terry Sneed, 'They were asking about our joint effort on that one in Faversham – whether David Lane was given a bell and warned off.'

Sneed laughed out loud. 'Some fucking chance. They asked me more or less the same thing when they interviewed us. They must be going through everything, whether they've had complaints or not. They hinted to me that you had a deal with Lane.'

There was no expression at all on Sneed's face, and those eyes, at once cold and smiling, revealed absolutely nothing. Sneed was one of the few people Bentham found he couldn't read.

'They showed an uncommon interest in a DS you had on the Squad. Lenny Feast,' Bentham said. 'I thought you might want to mark his card.'

'I don't think so, Jack. It's about time they nicked someone.

109

Though I can't think why Lenny Feast should've been elected, if he has.' He gathered up his drinks. 'It's the old divide and rule tactic, the cunts! The sooner they go back to fucking sheep the better. Good luck, Jack.'

Bentham raised his glass and watched Sneed cross the bar. His gaze then found the four isolated Wiltshire detectives in the corner. Brian Humpfress met his look briefly, then turned away. The unease Bentham felt about that man remained with him, and he didn't think it was to do with the fact that Humpfress would probably like to nick him if given the opportunity.

10

The heating had yet to go on in the stone-built, corrugated-roofed Baptist chapel. It was only early October and there were insufficient funds, despite a belief that God would provide. With a congregation of ten in this spartan house of worship, the atmosphere was cold; condensed breath streamed out of mouths that at one moment led, the next followed Brian Humpfress's organ accompaniment of *Rock of Ages Cleft For Me*. Brian Humpfress's organ repertoire was adequate rather than inspired and lit no fire in the familiar congregation, any more than the sermon that was offered by the preacher. The problem was that they had heard it all before, many times: if they led the good life they would find God's reward. They would hear it all again at the six o'clock service, when most of these people would turn up again, out of loyalty, along with two or three other loyal worshippers. They all seemed to be trying to deny to themselves that their church was dying on its feet. They had failed to attract any young blood, or any new blood at all, come to that, young or old. They had hoped that the black Fundamentalist community of Devizes, which wasn't exactly large, would join them, but they worshipped elsewhere, possibly a more potent God.

'That was a very uplifting accompaniment, Brian,' the minister said as Brian Humpfress shuffled out with the others. 'Pity we don't see more of your family, especially the young ones. God needs them, Brian, more than ever. While you're away dealing with those devils in London, the devil's workers undermine us at home.'

Embarrassment seared Brian Humpfress's face and he felt oppressive guilt at not being more insistent about getting his two boys up for chapel this morning. He was trying to find the conciliatory way with his wife. The flush he felt at the minister's censure cut through the chill air and made his cheeks bright pink.

Embarrassment had turned to anger by the time he had made the ten-minute journey home by car, and he was determined to have it out with her. He couldn't let his family slip from the fold, whatever Carol's current problem. God would help her, just as

He would help him reunite his own family with the Church. But God couldn't do everything on His own, He needed Man's help to punish so much wickedness and sin in the world. That was why he had joined the police force; it was a part of God's design, he believed, for combating evil. As a child he had had a vision in which he saw himself as an instrument of God, fighting evil on Earth. That was why he had put himself forward for the investigations into corruption in London – not that he imagined sin in Wiltshire had been defeated.

Brian Humpfress found his wife in the kitchen at the end of the narrow hallway of their pre-war terraced house. She was at the sink with her back to him; he could see the outline of her thickening hips under her dressing gown and he felt a stir inside himself. He had no memory of the last time they had made love and he prevented his mind from seeking out the answer, as if fearful of being caught with such thoughts.

'Why didn't you get the boys up for chapel this morning?' he demanded, without prelusive nicety. His words came out as an accusation, partly disguising his own failure to have done so; his rationale was that he had to get to the church early and unlock the organ.

Having heard him enter the house, Carol Humpfress had felt trapped in the kitchen. She would have preferred to have slipped upstairs to the bedroom and simply avoided him as much as possible until he returned to London the next morning. She was worn down by his constant accusations and interrogations over every action she took and whatever Luke and John did.

'Brian, you're away weeks on end. The weekends when you are home you start getting heavy with them straight away. Why haven't they done this, why haven't they done that. They're getting worn down by it. I'm getting worn down. I can't take it much more.'

She was a large lady, with red fleshy cheeks and grey eyes set in deep sockets; the bruising around her left eye accentuated the weariness her face showed. She no longer laughed or smiled much. But Brian Humpfress didn't notice. There was so little to laugh or smile about in the world today.

Anger flashed, the same anger that had caused him to strike out at her on Friday night on his return from London. But she was across the kitchen from him.

'I tolerate your not going, Carol. You're no better than you should be. But I won't accept that from them.'

'They're old enough to please themselves,' Carol Humpfress found herself saying, a little to her surprise. She knew it was better not to argue with her husband, but sensed a change coming about in her, as if she was about to commit a last, desperate act before breaking point.

'When they leave my home and I no longer support them they can decide for themselves, and no doubt will under your influence. But now get them down here. I won't have them wasting their time in bed. They can go and weed the chapel garden to make up for missing the service.'

'I can't,' Carol Humpfress said quietly and shook her head. She had wanted to say she couldn't go on.

'I'm not prepared to argue with you. I want them down here instantly.'

At first he was shocked when his wife didn't respond, then confusion took over and he didn't know whether to rush across the kitchen and strike her, or charge up the stairs and punish Luke and John for their disobedience. He chose the latter.

There was a further shock in store for Brian Humpfress when he crashed open the first door on the landing and discovered that the bed in this stark, unadorned room hadn't been slept in. He swung around the door jamb and along to the next room, only to find that bed hadn't been slept in either.

'Where are they?' he demanded as he burst back into the kitchen with a rush of furious energy.

Carol Humpfress's hands tensed on the teapot she had just filled; it burned her, but she hardly noticed. 'Brian, I can't stand this any more. I want a divorce.' She turned away, set the teapot down and waited for the explosion from her husband, trying to think out her next move. The wait was unbearable.

Disbelief assaulted all Brian Humpfress's senses at once as he hung there for a moment, not knowing what to do. Thoughts of failure assailed him: how would he face the congregation with the stigma of divorce?

As a child he had managed to shut out the things he disliked most and pretend they didn't exist – the rows between his parents, for example; now he believed they had been ideally suited and had led a happy life. Now he shut out what Carol had said and pretended her intention didn't exist.

113

Stepping across the room to her he wrenched her about, demanding to know where his children were. 'I will be obeyed. I will be obeyed.'

'They can't stand you either,' Carol screamed at him. 'You drive us all round the bend. They spent the night at a friend's. I do want a divorce, Brian.'

Unable to internalize this emotional affront any longer, Brian Humpfress let out an anguished cry and punched his wife in the face, splitting her nose, breaking it.

An assault charge was talked about at the hospital, though not by either Carol or Brian Humpfress. One of the nursing staff called the police on Carol's behalf, having seen the older bruising around the eye.

Even if her husband hadn't known the policeman who came to the hospital, Carol Humpfress knew there was no point in proceeding with such a charge – it would be lost somewhere in the system – and so said nothing more about her accident, either to the police or the hospital staff.

It was an accident. That was Brian Humpfress's story and quite soon he believed it, just as he eventually dealt with Carol's request for a divorce by denying the possibility existed.

He returned to London early, the Sunday-evening drive from the West Country serving as a barrier between him and his troubles at home. He was back doing God's work.

The devil had been working even harder in his absence, Humpfress discovered when he got to the dark, deserted offices they had been assigned in Camberwell Green police station. During the weekend someone had been into their locked offices and ransacked their locked filing cabinets, which contained all the strands of information on all the corrupt policemen they were pursuing. Furthermore, the intruder evidently had no care about their knowing it. The whole episode was designed not only to gather information, but also to show what utter contempt the Met felt for them and their efforts, Brian Humpfress decided. Had he something to go home to, he might have quit right them. Instead it only hardened his resolve to see this investigation through to the bitter end.

In the quiet of the office he knelt and prayed for God's hand to guide all his actions. Then, as he rose, self-righteous anger flooded him, God's wrath. It carried him down to a confrontation with the duty sergeant – in the absence of the duty officer.

'That is the end,' he said, entering the duty office where the sergeant was checking reports in the beat crime book. 'We've put up with all we intend from you corrupt bastards. I'll be happy to see every one of you disciplined if not prosecuted for theft.'

'What's the problem, chief?' The sergeant, who was twenty-four, managed to make an innocent inquiry sound like an insult.

'If we didn't have proof before how widespread police corruption is, we have it now – breaking into our offices and stealing confidential files. We'll have the lot of you.'

A satisfied smile stretched tightly over his face and he wheeled out.

Fortunately Detective Chief Superintendent Tony Bulmer was in town. Being a single man he had no reason to go back to Wiltshire, and preferred to spend his weekends in London, where it was generally believed he led a fairly debauched existence. The reputation had by far exceeded the deeds, but Tony Bulmer enjoyed the reputation almost as much. Brian Humpfress found him watching television in his hotel room.

'The situation's getting to be fucking ridiculous, Brian, when we can't leave files under lock and key at a police station.' Bulmer sat on the edge of the bed with a drink in his hand and watched his colleague pace up and down the orange and yellow carpet. He wished he would sit down and have a drink, but knew he drank rarely and relaxed never. 'We did lock up on Friday?'

'What difference does it make? They wanted us to know. They're mocking us, the corrupt bastards. I've had just about enough of them and their evil ways. Most of the lads feel the same way.'

'We'll see it through, Brian. The commissioner here promised full co-operation in everything we do. I'll have Alan Leeper speak to the DPP and make sure we get it.'

'Either they've all gone scared on this or they're deeply involved themselves. No one's going to suddenly start to co-operate. We have to take a different approach.'

Bulmer arched his eyebrows in question as he raised the telephone and started to dial the assistant chief constable's home number.

'We've got to start pulling in some of these policemen and treating them no differently from the way we treat animals. It's what they are. Hold them in isolation until they give us what we want.'

'But where, Brian?'

One of the Director of Public Prosecution's deputies, Colin Wells, a large young man with mutton-chop sideboards and curly hair, made a suggestion at the meeting in the DPP's office which had been arranged for the Monday morning.

'The solution might be to have the Wiltshire force based outside the Metropolitan District, Sir Trevor,' he said, addressing his boss who was chairing the meeting.

'Where do you suggest we're based?' Bulmer asked tartly, addressing the previous speaker directly, seeking to admonish him. 'Wiltshire?'

Acknowledging the chair the whole time took the heat out of meetings such as this and avoided personal recriminations. Assistant Chief Constable Leeper understood this.

'Either we were brought here to do this job, Sir Trevor,' he said, 'and if so we should be aided in our task, or we're not wanted, and should go home.'

'There's no doubt about your being wanted to continue this very important job,' Sir Trevor Rump said in a conciliatory tone. 'If the Met is as corrupt as it has been suggested, then something must be done about it. But just because we have the desire and the means to do something, does not mean that long traditions and entrenched attitudes will change overnight.'

'That's understandable, sir,' said Sydney Phillips, Wiltshire's chief constable, who had come down for the meeting. 'But these are criminal acts being used to prevent my men doing their job.'

The DPP nodded and turned to Colin Wells. 'I think perhaps you have hit on the solution, Colin. A different police force might be more welcoming. What had you in mind?'

'I was thinking of somewhere closer than where Mr Bulmer was suggesting, Sir Trevor,' he said undermining the DCS. He had no wish to see this investigation prosper – not because he wasn't concerned about police corruption, but because he didn't believe that allowing one specific inquiry to grow unchecked was the right way to tackle it. He and other deputies had to work with Metropolitan police officers on a day-to-day basis, and this wide-scale inquiry was making that relationship difficult, especially as the Wiltshire police had continually to bring them their evidence to see if it amounted to a prima facie case. The deputies in the DPP's office were being identified with the Turnip Squad, and they didn't enjoy that nickname.

'Possibly the Kent Constabulary could provide a base. Swanley police station might play host. It has a lot of accommodation. I'm sure they could be fitted in somewhere.'

The objections Alan Leeper made to the proposal were in principle rather than detail. He knew his men would expect him to protest and he focussed on the logistical argument, but at the end of the day he knew such a move made sense. To be out of the arms of the Met but within easy striking distance would suit him perfectly well, his men also, especially if they found a kindred spirit in another county police force. He only wished he had thought of it earlier, but the fact that one of the DPP's deputies, an obvious Met stooge, came up with it made him a bit suspicious.

'In order to overcome any logistical difficulties and to show that we are doing our utmost to facilitate this investigation, perhaps you would base yourself out in Kent with them, Colin. So you'll be on hand to answer all the legal questions.'

'Yes, of course, gladly, Sir Trevor,' Colin Wells responded as if it were a promotion, but the proposal came as a shock to him. Even though he lived in Sevenoaks and the journey to Swanley each morning would be far easier than commuting to London, he saw Queen Anne's Gate as his true place, and he would feel displaced for a while. But then being the legal centre of that investigation would enable him to keep his finger on every pulse, his eye on all developments – and to give help where help was needed, to whoever needed it.

11

Coinciding with the Wiltshire detectives' move to Swanley in Kent was a series of raids and arrests of Met policemen, organized by Detective Chief Inspector Humpfress. Most of those picked up were detectives, who drew a lot of adverse publicity but gave too little information to take Wiltshire's inquiry much further. Instead they tended to frustrate those detectives who did the arresting and further alienate those who were arrested.

The two Wiltshire detectives sitting in the back of an un-marked car in a street in Croydon in the dead hours of that cold October morning, waiting for a raid to go off, weren't feeling particularly pleased with their lot; nor were they optimistic about the raid producing anything worthwhile. They'd have felt happier if they could have had the car engine running and the heater on, but that might have attracted too much attention.

The street lamps clicked off, leaving the darkness pressed in around the car. The three men inside shifted positions, bored and restless, their small movements showing their irritability. Their bodies weren't designed for seemingly interminable waits in cars, and they didn't know why their boss didn't give the signal to crash the door. They were waiting because they were being co-ordinated with other raids that were also taking place this morning.

The driver flexed himself inside his heavy quilted parka and yawned. 'I wouldn't have thought much was going to happen again tonight, skip,' he said in a Cockney accent. 'I wouldn't be surprised if someone ain't marked this villain's card and he's legged it. Know what I mean?'

Neither detective responded. Detective Sergeant Del Preece smiled to himself. The fact that this driver, who – like most of their drivers – worked for the Metropolitan Police and had been assigned to them on account of his knowledge of London, believed they were raiding a villain and not a Met detective was something of a triumph. It cheered him a little.

'S'bin a poxy month for you,' the driver continued, casually riding them. 'Ain't nicked fuck all, have you, apart from your throat, shaving. Nor last month, did you.' He glanced at them through the driving mirror, felt anxious when he saw them bristle, and wondered if he had gone too far. 'Still, s'another mortgage payment gone,' he said, trying to retrieve the situation. The atmosphere remained icy, and the driver slid further down in his seat, as if to shrink from their sight.

After a few moments he tried once more to leaven the situation. 'D'you hear about the Old Bill who caught two lovers bang to rights in the back of a car? He says to them, "All right, either it's my turn next or you're nicked." So he's waiting there at the car door, with the raving popcorn, after a couple a minutes the fella comes, then gets out of the car trembling like a leaf. The officer says, "What's the matter with you, what you shaking for?" "I'm scared," the fella says, "I've never fucked a policeman before."'

It fell like a lead balloon on the two detectives. The driver wondered if they'd ask the name of the policeman involved so that they could go and nick him. That would be about all these clowns could nick, he thought, and glanced at his watch.

'All right if I slip down the road and have a shit, skip. I got a touch of diarrhoea. There's a public karsey down there by the park.' He had noticed there was a phone box too.

DS Preece was uncertain what to do. A man taken short with diarrhoea was of no use to anyone, but they had been warned about keeping an eye on their drivers less they alert the Met officers they were raiding. But then their driver believed they were waiting to raid a villain's home, and the thought of being trapped in a car with this man shitting himself didn't appeal to him.

'Well, if you must,' he said tersely. 'But don't be too long, case we get a shout.'

'The only shout you'll hear is mothers calling their kids for school.'

The driver slid out of the car quietly and scurried back along the street into the darkness.

Silence followed his departure. After a few moments the second detective, who was marginally younger, slimmer and more smartly dressed, said, 'The driver could be right about this one. He often is.'

'Let's hope he's wrong.' Preece looked at his watch. 'I'm getting poxed off with this job.'

DC Horne nodded. 'This is the third fucking night on the spin we've been up.'

'The whole fucking operation,' Preece complained, taking his opportunity now they were on their own and the Met driver couldn't see how the work was grinding them down, 'being up in London away from the family so much. Away from the kind of villains you know.'

'I can't say I'm that bothered myself,' Roy Horne said. 'There's plenty of fiddle on overtime and expenses.' He knew a lot of detectives up from Wiltshire who were making fifty or sixty pounds a week on their overtime and expenses, and he assumed they were all doing the same. As if by way of compensation for being here, no one was looking closely at the duty log sheets.

'I was going home at the weekend to buy a new car. These fucking raids put a stop to that.'

'What kind of motor are you getting?'

'Montego. There's a dealer in Devizes who's giving me a bit of a discount.' He glanced round and met DC Horne's look. 'Almost fifty per cent off the list price. I overlooked a couple of things for him. It's a lovely car. Does very nearly forty to the gallon. I hardly got to bed last weekend, much less get home for my new motor.'

'Oh yeah?' Horne challenged with a smile. 'Where d'you do that ol' WPC then? Against the station wall?'

The memory, along with the acknowledgement of his prowess, caused Preece to glow with pleasure.

It was cut short when his colleague said, 'I'd sooner the ten-quid whore I had in Old Compton Street.'

'You never gave any of that rubbish ten pounds?' the detective sergeant said disdainfully.

'Did I, fuck. I shoved my warrant card under her nose and told her I was investigating police corruption.'

'I know this, Roy,' a sombre note entered Preece's voice, 'some know a lot more than we. The owner of that video shop the other week – he reckoned most of the Robbery Squad are taking money, and most of the uniform branch handling pornography.'

'Didn't give us fuck all though, did he. S'just rumours.'

'I'm not so sure. I mean, a bit of fiddle is all right, no harm in that. We all do it. That's not getting a living at it like a lot of these ponces in the Met. I mean, look how many times Commander Wiseman's name's come up in connection with corruption. That's got to be more than just a rumour. There'll be no one brave enough to lay a hand on his collar. I tell you, enough senior officers' names have been coughed for some sort of action if it was ever going to be taken. They're making monkeys out of us. Especially that ponce from the DPP's office who they've put down with us. I'm sure most of what he sees goes right back to these corrupt sods.'

'You've been up here too long, Del, that's your trouble. You're starting to think like them. Just because you got a suspect's name, a rumour, it's not enough.' Roy Horne thought about the situation he found himself in and decided that, despite his present discomfort, it was very enjoyable. 'This'll do I for another year. I must have screwed more women up here than I knew existed.'

DS Preece fell silent, thinking about his half-price car. Their driver slid across his thoughts and he wondered if he should go and find him.

A similar thought sped across the driver's mind as he listened to the ringing tone inside the darkened telephone booth – he had broken the bulb. He glanced round in case one of the detectives came looking for him, then worried in case other detectives on the raid were close enough to the target's house to hear the phone ringing. He was about to put the phone down when it was answered.

'Lenny Feast?' he said quietly, fearing his voice would carry through the still morning, yet trying to make his tone urgent. 'It's off – you're about to be nicked.' The sleepy voice suddenly demanded to know who it was, but the driver put the phone down and dived out of the box.

He didn't get back to the car before the shout was off. Seeing lights go on in Feast's house, DI Pritchard jumped the gun and ordered his men in.

As if to redeem themselves for their error in letting their driver out of their sight – even though they assumed nothing was to come of it – Preece and Horne raced on foot to the front of the modern Wates house, getting there before the two detectives from the opposite direction, and kicking the imitation Georgian door with such ferocity that it broke in half.

They found the overweight, balding forty-three-year-old

Detective Sergeant Lenny Feast in the bathroom in his underwear, straddling the lavatory with his pants down. As the detectives burst in he reached round to try and flush the cistern that was still filling from a previous flush. His action galvanized the detectives, two of whom sprang forward and thrust him off the loo.

'What is this? What's your fucking game?' Feast demanded, pulling up his pants as he picked himself off the floor.

'Got the runs have you, sergeant?' Detective Inspector Pritchard said, stepping into the now crowded bathroom. I think you know who we are.'

Preece prickled with embarrassment, believing the DI was getting at him over letting his driver answer his call of nature.

'You no-good sheep-fuckers,' Feast protested. 'Coming in here like this. It's out of order.'

DC Horne had his hand down the lavatory bowl and was fishing out ten-pound notes.

'Perhaps you should have tried eating it,' the DI said.

'Or a less rich diet, boss,' one of the other detectives quipped. Everyone but Feast laughed.

The dog barked. The children cried. Mrs Feast stood on the landing looking resigned, as if she had expected something like this for a long while.

'There's a few more stuck round the bend, boss,' Horne said, stretching his fingers for them.

'Out the way.' Pritchard took an axe from one of the detectives and swung it against the loo, smashing the bend, causing water to flood onto the pink, tufted carpet.

'Fuck off,' Feast said, despite his protests having no effect, 'that suite cost two hundred fucking sovs. S'fucking ruined now, look at it. And the carpet.'

There were three tenners freed from the bend, and a whole packet in the soil pipe going through the wall. All the Wiltshire detectives present felt as if they had won the pools.

'OK,' Pritchard said decisively, 'let's do it the proper way.'

They searched the house neatly and thoroughly in the presence of either Feast, who they allowed to dress, or Mrs Feast, who remained silent and gave what comfort she could to her six children.

Apart from the money from the lavatory, they took away pieces of jewellery, a television set and stereo equipment, ignoring Feast's declaration that everything here was straight. They also took bank statements, and Feast himself, who they didn't inform of his destination.

'You cunts are well out of order,' Feast persisted as he paced the interview room in an increasingly agitated manner, failing to notice how dangerous his continual insults were making the situation. 'I've never heard of anything so fucking outrageous as what you done. Who do you cunts think I am, a villain? I've been a detective twenty years. Twenty fucking years. You fucking yokels must have got the wrong address. S'fucking outrageous.'

Detective Sergeant Preece had listened to this all the way from Thornton Heath by car, and for the last twenty minutes in the interview room, and was about to flatten him when Feast changed tack.

'Look, I'd better give my governor a bell. I mean, this is not on, is it? I'm s'posed to be in court this morning. Here I am, I don't even know why I'm nicked. I mean, let's be sensible, friend. You could at least give me half a chance. You can be half decent to a brother officer, can't you?' He waited, hoping his appeal would find a sympathetic response. When it got none, Feast said, 'You no-good sheep-fuckers. There's not one of you worth a toss compared to Met officers – you could put fuck all away, not even if we put our hands up to it, you cunts.'

Preece glanced at his colleague across the room. It was an unspoken signal, which Feast read clearly for he backed away with a nervous laugh. The arrival of Brian Humpfress didn't guarantee his safety, but it forestalled any immediate action.

The DCI brought with him a clear plastic bag of water-sodden banknotes, which he dropped on the table with an air of disgust, as though believing they were wet with piss.

'There's nearly two thousand pounds here,' he said, as though the mere presence of the money was a crime. A cloud had lifted from Brian Humpfress, he was like a holiday-maker at a strike-bound airport who had just heard his flight called: he wasn't yet airborne, but believed he was on his way; they hadn't yet convicted Feast, but he was almost in the prison van on his way to court.

'These cunts crashed my door in the middle of the night, sir,' Lenny Feast said, his manner more whingeing now. 'It's fucking outrageous, that sort of behaviour, sir. I mean, I am a police-man.'

'But what did they find?' Humpfress asked reasonably. 'You stuffing banknotes down the loo.'

'Me?' Feast tried, incredulously. He knew he had to try, as there would be no help if he put his hand up. 'Don't talk silly, guv. I mean I was in the bathroom – a bit of diarrhoea.'

'You're denying this was in your possession?' Humpfress didn't mind what hoops this man tried jumping through. They had him and weren't going to let him go, unlike the other three detectives they had picked up earlier that morning. Eventually they would have to let them go – a provisional look at them had made that clear – unless Feast could be persuaded to incrimin-ate them. He had been their lucky break, and Humpfress was determined to exploit that for all it was worth.

'I don't know anything about it. If it was in my lavatory, then what most likely happened was these clods brought it with them.'

That did it for the overweight detective sergeant. 'You lying fucker . . .' He moved forward, shifted his heavy weight onto the balls of his feet like a boxer, and slammed two punches across Feast's kidneys.

Feast hung breathlessly in the air, not daring to move for the searing pain. Finally DC Horne slid a chair behind him and guided him onto it.

Humpfress smiled, believing that was no less than this foul-mouthed policeman deserved. 'Why don't you stay calm and try to remember how that money came into your possession.' He waited through Feast's first breathless attempt to speak, enjoy-ing this dominant position. 'Take your time, sergeant. We've only been on this investigation a year and a half.'

'S'my old woman's money,' Feast managed at last.

'She won it on the horses, I dare say?' Humpfress mocked, having heard similar stories from villains a hundred times before. The conviction in Feast's response slightly undermined him.

'I don't think so, guv. Bingo.'

'Why were you putting it down the lavvy when my men raided your house?'

'I'm tryin'a stop her going to bingo,' Feast said spontan-eously. 'I told her 'she brought her winnings home any more

I'd burn them – only our house don't have a fireplace.'

This man's mockery made the DCI angry. He wasn't going to let him get away with it, but was having difficulty staying in control. He glanced at the typed sheets in the open folder before him, looking for a stick to beat Feast with. 'The money in your possession was part of the proceeds of a robbery that took place at Coutts Bank just over a year ago when you were on the Robbery Squad.' He had combined two separate items, but it proved effective.

'You're a fucking liar, pal,' Feast said, his mirth having evaporated.

Humpfress glanced at DC Preece, who was wound up ready to spring.

Feast was prepared to throw a few punches back. 'That cunt tries another stroke like that,' he warned, 'I'll knock him spark fucking out.'

No one moved in the small interview room. A door opened and shut somewhere nearby, taking with it the laughter of two men sharing a joke. The sense of freedom contained in it made Lenny Feast feel sick with regret, and he wondered if his freedom would ever prove retrievable, or whether he shouldn't just put his hand up and try and get himself some help. Sweat trickled out of his armpits and ran down his fleshy ribcage – it was cold and clammy and left him feeling uncomfortable. He didn't want to be there and would have given anything to be back home with his missus, stealing another five minutes in bed before getting up for work.

'Just because we're on opposite sides of the fence,' Humpfress said, 'nothing says we can't behave decently towards each other. Like brother officers.'

'I was dragged out of my fucking bed.'

'You were in the bathroom,' Preece reminded him.

'Bathroom – for all the fucking dif' it makes.'

'Yes, yes,' Humpfress said. 'I dare say we could have behaved in a more civilized fashion. Perhaps telephoned beforehand.'

Feast went for it. 'You'd have found me co-operative.' Then he saw the smile in the corner of the DCI's sour-looking mouth. 'You cunts,' he said.

'Your name was given us by three criminals who have so far been charged with no less than eighteen robberies, one of them on Coutts Bank fourteen months ago. As a result of their statements implicating you, along with four other Robbery Squad detectives, and the money found at your premises, I am now going to charge you that on or about the twentieth of July you did conspire with others to rob Coutts Bank. You're familiar with the caution.'

Panic swelled in Lenny Feast. Because of his experience as a policeman, he knew what could happen. Someone at some point had to end up in the frame. The amount of time and expenditure that had gone into this investigation dictated as much. It would mean that justice would be seen to be done, that the Met was clean once again, and business could get back to normal. What Feast also knew was that he could easily prove to be one of the bodies, if not *the* body, in the frame. He had no such plan for himself, especially not when there were so many others more deserving: others more junior who hadn't got as many years invested; others more senior who had far more than he and who wouldn't now lift a finger to help him. In his time, Lenny Feast had seen many villains in these circumstances, and when they had reached out for a bit of help he had given it to them. A lot of them had walked away. He had some expectation of doing the same for, reluctant as he was to sell brother officers, there seemed no alternative.

'You don't want to nick me,' Feast suggested. 'I don't know fuck all, I mean, what am I? I get fuck all. You nick anyone, nick someone what takes the lion's share. They're the cunts that need nicking, not me, pal ... I mean, they're all at it. They are.'

The three Wiltshire detectives remained expectantly silent, each realising how momentous this was. They had been waiting for this for almost a year and a half. They didn't dare breathe for fear of fracturing the moment and perhaps discovering somehow that what they had before them was an illusion.

Having first overcome his shock, then his instinctive objections, Feast said tentatively, 'The thing is, guv, if I'm expected to give you a few names, what good is it gonna do me? I mean, can I go and get myself a bit of help?'

'Oh, I imagine something could be arranged,' Humpfress said calmly, but without any intention of honouring whatever promises this man was made. This was a policeman who had betrayed his trust and had to be punished; Brian Humpfress was determined he would be. So far they had promised a number of robbers help of one kind or another for turning supergrass, and although they were living in unusual style in police cells, none had their freedom, nor would they get it this side of a trial.

Tony Bulmer and the Assistant Chief Constable Alan Leeper were keen to promise Feast anything, as was Chief Constable Sydney Phillips, who even seemed prepared to fulfil their promises if it led to the arrest and conviction of other policemen, especially senior policemen.

'They're hungry bastards up here,' Alan Leeper observed to the DCS and Brian Humpfress who were in his office at Swanley police station. He was a short, hairy man with high blood pressure that wasn't helped by the frustrations of this investigation. He lived on beta blocking drugs. But even though the prospect before him was attractive, and might even help reduce his blood pressure, he still had reservations. 'Feast's price might not be cheap.'

'He gets nothing until we do,' Bulmer said. He didn't understand his boss's sudden reservation. They had absolutely nothing to lose. 'He wants to keep his pension. It's not unreasonable.'

'He's offering us the most corrupt policemen in London?' Alan Leeper speculated.

'That's what he said, sir,' Humpfress put in quickly, slightly resenting the way the chief superintendent had taken over since he had broken Feast.

'Sounds very attractive, Tony, especially after all the foot slogging we've done. Not that I want to see brother officers fall, least of all senior officers. But I suppose it's what we're here for. What does our resident DPP feel about this?'

'Not much,' Bulmer said. 'I didn't go into it with him in detail, but I did indicate the nature of the move. He thought we wouldn't be on very firm ground having a self-confessed corrupt detective to give against other corrupt policemen, especially if his freedom was used as an inducement to make him talk.'

'Bugger me!' Leeper exclaimed. 'They do it all the time with regular criminals.'

'It might be best to by-pass Mr Wells on this until we get it firmed up.'

'I can't promise that Feast will keep his pension,' Alan Leeper said with a smile. 'But there's no need to tell him that.'

A sense of satisfaction enveloped Brian Humpfress; it would have been a bitter pill indeed if a real commitment had been made to honour any deal with Detective Sergeant Feast.

However the feeling was short-lived, because Bulmer continued to involve himself closely in the details. Humpfress had expected to discuss the overall plan with his boss, then be left to put it into effect. After the noises the DPP's deputy had made, he knew that the only certain way to secure convictions was for Feast to go back into his community of corrupt policemen with a wire and a tape recorder. It was his idea, but Bulmer took it over as if he had thought of it.

'Are we on then?' Lenny Feast asked when Humpfress entered the interview room. He had been in custody for two days and had still had no contact with the outside world. His wife had phoned Swanley police station twice, and had spoken to Humpfress, but he had refused to confirm that her husband was there, only that he was still being held.

The DCI considered this sweating, unshaven wretch. 'Forgotten something, sergeant, haven't you?'

A puzzled frown creased Feast's broad forehead. If he forgot to make the right moves it might jeopardize his deal. Suddenly he knew. 'Sir. Yes, sir.'

The correct form of address made little visible difference to the senior policeman. 'If it was up to me, sergeant, you'd be in Brixton prison on remand by now. We've got so much evidence on you. But that's what makes my boss interested in your nasty, neck-saving schemes.'

A nervous laugh emerged from Feast, and he was relieved when the door opened and Tony Bulmer stepped briskly in.

'Right, Mr Feast,' he said, slapping his bony hands together. 'You want to do a little horse trading.'

'It would be useful, sir,' Feast said, with an apprehensive glance at Humpfress. 'After all, I put up a lot of useful information, sir.'

Bulmer slid the folder from under Humpfress's arm and opened it. 'A lot of senior detectives, is all.'

'But I gave you details of what some of them have been having.' Feast felt decidedly unsure of his future just then. His insecurity made his stomach churn and his mouth go dry.

'No evidence to support it. As my good friend the DPP pointed out, there's nothing here that gives anything like a fifty-one per cent chance of conviction if we were to arrest these officers.'

'Fuck me! What does he want, signed confessions? We've stuck villains up on a lot less, and got a result.'

'But we'd be dealing with police officers, men with hitherto unblemished records. Villains are half-way to gaol anyway by the time they reach court.' He glanced over the sheets in the folder, knowing he'd be happy to pull in any one of the policemen named there if the assistant chief constable gave him the go-ahead. 'Take this man, for instance, Chief Inspector Sneed. He has twelve commendations. One from the Queen, no less.' Bulmer knew what the media would make of that.

'Cor, fuck me, Terry Sneed invented corruption!' Feast exclaimed.

'On what you've given us, he'd only have to stand by his record. That sort of result would set us back even further. You know well enough what the problem is, with your experience as a policeman.'

'The DPP did say things might be different if he agreed to go into the witness-box, boss,' Humpfress lied helpfully. He had put that to Feast earlier, but had been turned down.

'There's no way I'm going to stay in the job and keep my pension, 'I do that,' Feast said.

'Well, unless we find some other way, that prospect is less than realistic.'

'I've got half a chance. I mean, I've got that if I go to court.'

'If that's what you want.' Bulmer passed the folder back to the DCI and turned to leave.

'What is this, a fucking get-up? I gave you more than enough for you to nick any of them. I mean, I didn't want to be involved. They put a gun to your head, you're either on the firm or out of work. Let's be sensible. We gotta be able to work something out.'

'We can. All you need do is go into the witness-box,' Bulmer told him.

Feast was adamant. Naming names was only all right as long as he wasn't identified, so that he could go back to work afterwards with no one the wiser. However unrealistic that might be, he believed it possible. 'I like being a policeman too much.'

'An alternative would be for him to get us some new evidence, boss?' Humpfress said tentatively, as if the thought had only just occurred to him.

Instantly Feast saw a gap in the fence and made a dash for it. 'I'll do that all right. Anything. Just tell me how.'

'The easiest way would be with a wire,' Humpfress said, with a glance at his boss in case he was thought to be speaking out of turn. 'You arrange to meet these policemen, get them to talk about their criminal activities, all of which you record.'

Mind-boggling disbelief stunned Lenny Feast, and it was all he could do to stop himself abusing this detective. He wondered how they had ever got to be senior policemen, and what sort of villain they dealt with in Wiltshire. Most villains were pretty stupid, as any policeman would confirm, but this lot must have been used to dealing with subnormals. There was no longer any mystery about why they hadn't nicked anyone during their time in London – his own arrest was just a bit of bad luck. Realising just what he was up against, the prospects suddenly appeared less daunting.

'Just like that?' Feast said. 'That's all you want me to do? I mean, that shouldn't be difficult; after all, they've only just got off the boat, this lot.'

'That's your problem,' Bulmer said, slightly irritated. 'If you're not up to it, then say so. But there'll be no help for you.'

'Oh I'll give it a go, guv,' Feast declared. 'Fuck me, I've got to. I'll get you everything you want.' He considered how he might double-cross them by switching the microphone off at strategic moments so that it appeared that he had tried but got nothing. 'It might take a little time, sir, to collect the sort of information you'll want. I mean, I can't simply approach those Ds and stick a mike under their noses and ask what they've had lately.'

Bulmer nodded. Then, as if anticipating Feast, he said, 'Understand this. Any agreement the DPP, you and me enter into is entirely dependent upon results. I don't want you coming back with nothing and still expecting to walk. Is that clear?'

'Oh, perfectly, sir,' Feast agreed with alacrity. He anticipated no difficulty at all conning these detectives. He began to breathe easily for the first time since his arrest.

12

'They pull some fucking strokes with their overtime and expenses,' Terry Sneed said, half to himself, as he checked through the weekly duty log sheets of the men on the Squad. The detective inspector who was in the office with him glanced up.

'S'pect they think it's the Squad of old, guv.'

'Even there they didn't pull strokes like this,' Sneed said, angry at the audacity of the detective involved. 'Or if they did they knew how to conceal them better.' That was the truth. Realism told him that people fiddled, all people. He had built his entire working life around that assumption – it would have been a shock to find someone who was completely honest. He believed no such person existed; pragmatism dictated that fiddling, especially where detectives on the Robbery Squad were involved, should be done with skill and discretion. 'I'd better have DC Squires in and rap his knuckles, the prick. Is he around?'

'He's gone on leave for four days. He's worked too much overtime this month.'

'Not if he's pulling strokes like this.' Sneed scoffed, putting the duty log sheet aside. He would speak to Colin Squires about that on his return. He was the newest recruit to the Squad, and the way he was shaping, he wasn't going to be around long. If he wasn't a lot more careful, Sneed would recommend that he went back to District.

Two of the office phones started to ring at almost the same time. Sneed answered one.

'DCI's office,' he said briskly, and was surprised to find Lenny Feast on the line. He had a soft spot for the DS, having prospered under his wing as a detective constable. Feast had educated him in the ways of surviving and getting a living. He had suggested he joined the Freemasons as a means of advancing; they shared the same lodge. He trusted Feast more than most and missed not having him around on the Squad.

'Any chance we might have a meet, Terry?' Feast said. 'Something's come up.'

Reaching for his diary to see what his afternoon looked like, he asked, 'How urgent is it?' He had heard Lenny Feast had had

131

a bit of bad luck, and wondered if he was looking for help. Perhaps the wisest thing would have been to give him a miss.

Neither old time's sake nor curiosity brought Terry Sneed onto the District Line underground train heading into Hammersmith with Lenny Feast, but a personal sense of his indestructible security.

There were few people in the carriage, so identifying any detectives with an interest in their meeting would have been easy. Sneed checked the two adjoining cars – not because he didn't trust Lenny Feast, but because he was cautious and expected to get old by being so.

'Nicking plenty of bodies, Lenny?' Sneed said casually when finally he sat next to Feast. He glanced across the aisle at a punk girl in so short a leather skirt that it allowed him to see her pants. He would have given her one in the right circumstances; she looked quite pretty under her weird get-up.

Feast followed the glance to the girl, but sex was about the last thing on his mind. In fact, he hadn't been able to get it up since his arrest. His wife had suggested he see a doctor, but he knew there was only one thing that would make any difference.

'S'not like being on the Squad, Terry.'

'You do your three years, then spew out on the computer. Fucking computers run everything now. Soon they'll be telling us how to feel a collar. They already tell us what collar.'

'I ought to have pulled better than I did. S'fuck all where I am now. Blacks have fuck all. Even the overtime's not worth a toss. I've had so many days off because I'm over my limit.'

'You're too active, Lenny. The Squad's not what it was, not since the reorganization. Too many controls. S'all policy meetings. S'even worse with those cunts from Wiltshire looking at everything.'

There was a pause between them as each shared the same thought. Feast got to it first and Terry Sneed was glad.

'I got a spin, didn't I. The cunts.'

'I heard you had a bit of bad luck.'

'What did you hear, Terry?' Feast asked jumpily. If he was known as a grass anyway, then he may as well have gone into the witness-box and spared himself all this. 'There ain't no stories going around about me, are there?'

'What did you have in mind, Lenny?' Sneed asked, glancing at his watch.

That response did nothing to ease Feast's anxiety. 'The cunts had to wipe their mouths.' He felt a need to explain the situation fully, but saw Sneed's impatient look. 'There's a lad called Peter Rodgers from off my manor who's been nicked by the Fraud Squad for credit-card offences. Superintendent Stern's dealing with it. S'worth a grand, 'he can be dropped out.'

The train pulled into a station and Sneed waited for the doors to open and close and the train to start off again. 'I can't think that anyone'll put themselves on offer for that. You'd be looking at about three at least.'

'That won't be a problem, three grand won't,' Feast said quickly.

'He must have earned plenty off those credit cards, your friend Rodgers.' He waited to hear what figure was involved, as that determined the final price. Feast volunteered nothing, so Sneed assumed he didn't know. It wasn't important. Harry Stern would have all the figures. 'How involved is Harry Stern?'

'Well involved. Rodgers fronted him up when it came on top. He wanted to do the business, but he didn't know Peter, and like everyone else he's shit-scared with them other cunts around.'

Sneed gave him a look, showing no feeling whatsoever but not enjoying being placed in that category. 'They've nicked fuck all, have they,' he said disparagingly.

'There are a few in the frame, is what I heard, Terry.'

'They couldn't capture ducks off the village pond. The cunts will have to go back to sheep-fucking.' He waited while the train disgorged a few passengers at the next station, and started off again. 'I'll have a word with Harry Stern, see how things are looking for your friend. You acting as the go-be, Lenny? Or how is he planning to deal?'

'He wants me to handle the money.'

'Is he settling up with you?'

'It's a favour,' Feast said impulsively. He hadn't thought that through, not expecting the question.

His answer made Sneed wonder, never having known Lenny Feast to give anyone a free ride when there was a reasonable prospect of earning something.

Doubt led him to proceed cautiously, not only in his approach to Superintendent Stern, whom he knew quite well, and who confirmed that he had arrested Rodgers. Sneed laid some ground cover by phoning Jack Bentham to ask if he could check Peter Rodgers out on the Criminal Intelligence computer. The only space he had on the Criminal Records office computer started with his recent arrest by the Fraud Squad.

Disappointment was the common experience among the senior Wiltshire policemen when Feast despatched his first tape to them. It was full of train rattle and indecipherable voices, of which only the odd words had any recognizable shape – and most of those were Feast's. They were disappointed but not daunted by this, and urged Feast to arrange a quieter location for the next meeting.

After his fortnightly DCI's meeting at Scotland Yard, Terry Sneed called along to see Jack Bentham, still with the prospect of selling some help to Peter Rodgers.

'There's a fair bit in our computer on him, Terry,' Bentham said, passing him the print-out sheet as he rose and went to a filing cabinet for a bottle of scotch and a couple of styrofoam cups. 'It's too early in the afternoon, of course. Can I twist your arm?'

'It's far too early, guv,' Sneed said with a smile, taking one of the cups. 'He's earned a fair bit, if all this is down to him.' Sneed glanced over the sheet again. Although interested in the amounts Rodgers might have earned from fraud, he was more interested in the company he kept. He seemed genuine enough, judging by the list of would-be fraudsters he knew. 'Did you hear what the word was on Lenny Feast being turned over by the Wiltshire lot?'

'A villain who was arrested offered a sackful of names for a bit of help. I don't think it did him much good. Feast was one of the names.'

'Nothing more?' Sneed said, without showing his relief.

'I don't think so,' Bentham lied evenly. He guessed this DCI hadn't come in to idly pass the time of day, that there was something going on. According to the information he was holding, Feast had been actively involved when on the Flying Squad with Sneed. 'What's the SP, Terry?'

'He was looking to do some biz for that lad Harry Stern nicked,' Sneed explained truthfully. He had always found that when seeking an alibi or ground cover it was best to use at least a part of the truth. Although having no levers under Jack Bentham, he believed he wasn't so straight that this conversation would result in any sort of problem.

'You think he's setting you up?' Bentham knew it was a possibility that Wiltshire would get to Sneed before any move he might decide to make himself, in which case he could be left in a difficult position.

'Lenny Feast never had that much arsehole, Jack. But these are dangerous times. Someone puts a gun to his head, there's no telling what he might do.'

'I'll make a note of this conversation in my diary.' He wondered if perhaps he should have another conversation with the deputy commissioner about the information he was holding on corrupt policemen. But if he did there was the possibility that he would now be advised to pass on what he had.

Sneed finished his drink. 'Thanks, Jack. I don't want to put myself on offer.' He went out as Bentham's phone rang.

It was Julian Brind from the Home Office, reminding him about the policy meeting he had been invited to the following afternoon. Bentham didn't need the reminder; it was unusual for a DCS to be invited to a meeting at that level.

'Can we meet earlier, say two-thirty, Jack, at Horseferry House?' Brind suggested. 'I'd like to take your mind on a couple of matters.'

'I'm supposed to be at Gatwick at eleven. I should spend some time with the party I'm meeting.'

'If you can't, then perhaps we'll have a word afterwards, depending how the meeting goes.'

'That'll be fine, Julian. I'll make two-thirty, at Horseferry House.'

Sneed arrived back at his office to find DC Colin Squires waiting, having got the message that the DCI wanted to see him when he got back off leave.

Colin Squires was young and bright and a good thief-taker, but not as educated as he should have been, or would be by the time Sneed was through. He looked anxious as he stood before the DCI's desk, trying to read his governor's totally blank face.

'You're bang in trouble, uncle,' Sneed said. 'You're a hard-working copper and I'll be sorry to lose you.'

'Guv?' The bottom suddenly dropped out of the DC's world. He enjoyed being on the Squad that much.

'Even sorrier to have to nick you,' Sneed continued.

The young man stammered in his confusion, 'Nick me, guv? What for?'

'D'you think I am thick, uncle? You've been fiddling your overtime and expenses.' He passed Squires a Xerox of his duty log. 'This overtime and the meals allowance you're claiming, it's a get-up. Unless you were on a job I don't know about?' He turned and picked up the phone on its second ring, leaving Squires to puzzle over his predicament. 'DCI's office. Sneed.'

'Terry, s'Lenny,' Feast said down the phone. 'Could we meet tonight on that other thing?'

'What thing's that, Lenny?' Sneed asked. He had no intention of meeting tonight. He was taking out the DAC's secretary, besides which he rarely walked into situations suggested by a third party.

There was silence down the phone. Sneed glanced across at the shamefaced Squires and remembered his own education with detectives like Feast. The cardinal rule was never to admit your guilt, even when bang to rights. He wondered if Squires would observe it. If he didn't, Sneed would find a reason for terminating his time on the Squad.

'Terry, when do you think?'

'I'll give you a bell when I've got some information for you. All right?' He replaced the phone and smiled a cold, unremitting smile at the DC. 'Such a waste, Colin, being nicked over a poxy few quid. All that training; all that talent.'

'It's a mistake, guv,' Squires tried. 'I wasn't fiddling. DS Munday missed it, too.'

It was a nod in the right direction, but Sneed believed he could crack him. He opted for the warm, matey approach. 'Come on, Colin, don't take me for a prick, mate. I've pulled more strokes than you ever imagined existed.' Sneed smiled, as if sharing a joke with him. 'You were at it – unless you're the first fucking policeman who doesn't fiddle. I see everyone's duty log on the Squad. I know what this one reads like.' He stopped smiling when Colin Squires raised his shoulders in a shrug of admission and nodded. Sneed made his decision about this man's future. 'I ought to give you to Wiltshire. Then at least they'd have someone to nick. But I'm not going to nick you, uncle. A ruined career, especially one so promising, s'going to do neither one of us any good. Take a clean sheet, start again; then bring it back to me. Make sure what you put down bears some passing resemblance to what others on the Squad have got. 'You need a few quid, come and see me. Now make yourself busy, show me I've made the right decision.'

With his hand on the grateful DC's shoulder, Sneed shepherded him out. But he wouldn't change his mind about moving him off the Squad.

Meanwhile he would file the copy of Squire's bent duty log along with the substituted one for future reference. He might be able to find a use for a lad with such susceptibility to corruption.

13

DCI Frank Burroughs had put away as many scotches in as many minutes as they had been in the bar at Gatwick airport. Jack Bentham finished his single beer, glanced at the arrivals monitor, then signalled to Burroughs to finish his drink. The Iberia scheduled flight from Malaga had landed on time. He looked at his watch, concerned about his meeting this afternoon at the Home Office, but wanting at least to get started with the passenger they had coming in from Spain.

'We'd better see if he's on the plane,' Bentham said. He hadn't checked to see if David Lane was on the computer passenger list, but knew he would be.

The two detectives waited by the barrier outside the customs hall and watched as tanned and smiling holiday-makers struggled through with too much luggage, the anxiety of flying leaving their faces as they were met by family and friends.

David Lane had no expression of relief on his face as he strolled through with just one small shoulder bag. Dressed in faded clothes, he was lean and tanned and looked like a man who knew he was walking into a prison sentence. The fact that, as he kept telling himself, he was also walking away from the prison sentence Spain had become over the past year didn't much cheer him. He had heard lots of stories about reasonable deals that could be made with Old Bill for the right sort of information, and it was on this that he was pinning his future. Lane knew it was better to take the initiative as he had, that the terms were likely to be more generous.

It gave David Lane a fleeting sense of pride to know that he could still pick out detectives in a crowd, and he knew as he moved towards them that they had clocked him too. DCS Bentham was only vaguely familiar to him, and he was surprised to see him there in person, having expected a couple of DC's instead.

'Welcome back to Britain,' Bentham said.

'Never thought I'd see the day. S'not all that great, Spain, take it from me. All right for a holiday with the wife and kids, but when it's a lifetime and you're broke and can't get no work even if you want to ... I put all my money into an English restaurant, thought it would do well with all the tourists. Nothing they like better than a bit of home, they flock to the English bars. It turned out my partner was a right fucking con artist. Took a runner with my bit of dough, I was left with the bills. Lucky not to have ended up inside. I mean, what else could I do? Doesn't do, bumming around. I always like to dress a bit near the mark, s'how I came to get started. It's really demoralizing having to beg like some fucking tramp. I had to borrow the plane fare from my ex. I'm better off back here doing my time, least that's what I convinced myself. Might not be so bad – get some help.'

Not only had David Lane been short of money in Spain, but also company. He had an implacable need to talk, which he did all the way to Croydon police station.

They took him there because it was out of the way, and Bentham was on good terms with the governor of the nick – an ex-RCS man who wouldn't carry tales about who was brought there or how long they stayed or who visited them.

'This bad is it?' David Lane said when he was booked under the name Marc Kenwick, a minor villain whom no one was likely to know out there.

'I don't want anything you tell me passed to bent detectives and see villains pulled clear before we can put them in the frame,' Bentham said. 'Mr Burroughs is going to take down everything you say. It'll only be Frank or myself dealing with you at this stage. No one else. If any other policemen turn up to question you, no matter who they are, just keep closed up.'

'I just hope it's worth it, Mr Bentham,' Lane said, impressed by all the secrecy. 'I end up with a nice deal for myself.

'There's a chance you'll end up with a bit of money and the Queen's award for industry, if you've got the right information,' Bentham told him. 'Let's start with the last thing you were involved on, the blag out at Faversham.'

With only a slight hesitation, David Lane said, 'You nicked Peter Forster. He was grassed right. He was the body we put up to keep everyone happy. Everyone 'cept Peter, that is. But he was as good as gold, didn't say a word, did he. Shame, isn't it, but what can you do? The Robbery Squad had a gun to our head.'

'How involved were they?' Bentham asked.

139

'Oh, well involved, right from the off. That's why I had my ex-missus contact you about my coming back, Mr Bentham. There are so many firms within firms, you don't know who's involved or who you can trust. I mean, I've even heard stories out in Spain about this other little mob you've got here looking at you, how they've been selling bodies to other villains. Where do you go? Who do you talk to?'

A grim smile fell over Bentham's face. 'How do you know I'm not involved then?'

That caused David Lane an uneasy smile. He looked between the two detectives, not knowing whether to laugh. Neither of them were laughing.

'You both probably earned more than enough, I mean, show me a detective who hasn't. But after the way you helped my Charlie, I decided you'd probably keep your word.'

'I didn't give your brother any guarantees. I can't give you any. All I can do is try.'

David Lane closed his eyes, offered up a prayer to a God who he had some belief in when things were going well for him, and nodded. 'I don't have much option now.'

He talked at a speed that made Frank Burroughs' hand ache from trying to keep up, and seemed determined to talk himself right out of a gaol sentence if possible. No matter what Bentham put to him, the villain had something to say about it. At one point, before leaving for the Home Office, he wondered if Lane wasn't saying the first thing that came into his head in order to ingratiate himself and earn his freedom. What he did say confirmed a lot of what Frank Howie had told them, and spelt out police involvement in three major robberies before they were committed.

Taking a Xerox of the pages Frank Burroughs had so far written to read over in the car, Jack Bentham left the DCI still writing. Lane had a wonderfully clear memory and all that he had to tell was fleshed out in vivid detail. He might almost have invented it. In some ways Bentham wished he had. Terry Sneed was a name that recurred, and at one point Lane had even described what the DCI had been wearing. Bentham smiled at that, knowing Sneed to be a stylish dresser; he not only had a good shape, one which off-the-peg clothes fitted well, but if Lane was to be believed, an income that enabled him to dress as he wanted. Much as he enjoyed Lane's description of Terry

Sneed, it didn't in any way help him resolve his dilemma over what to do about the DCI, or those other senior detectives mentioned.

'Julian Brind,' Bentham said to the security officer inside the west entrance of the seedy post-war Home Office building in Dean Ryle Street, opposite the equally seedy Westminster Hospital. This was F7 Division, the department which Brind oversaw. Bentham gave his name but not his rank.

The assistant secretary obviously identified Bentham to the security officer – his manner was much brisker when he came off the phone and he directed Bentham to the lifts, telling him Mr Brind would be waiting for him on the sixth floor.

Bentham knew the procedure from previous visits. The assistant secretary wasn't in fact there when he stepped out of the lift, but was getting hot water for tea from the urn room. Two urns were kept boiling for civil servants to get their own tea. The arrangement had less to do with democracy than with cutbacks. The traditional tea lady had all but disappeared from the corridors of power.

'Thought you might like tea, Jack,' Brind said, extending his free hand to shake Bentham's. 'How are you?' He ushered him along the uncarpeted corridor.

His own office, which was the regulation ten by twelve, did have a carpet, as befitted his rank. Within the civil service, window-space, curtains, carpets, type of furniture, even pictures on the walls, were granted according to status, and were closely controlled. Brind had a wooden desk, a cloth-covered, padded swivel chair, a small conference table and a secretary, whose office was situated between his and the deputy chief scientific officer's. He also had two quite good watercolours on the wall, obtained by effort and knowledge of paintings rather than bald entitlement. There was an entire civil service department to issue paintings and furnishings and rearrange office decor to suit the tastes of incoming ministers.

'I don't have any milk,' Brind said, his long elegant hand indicating a chair to Bentham.

At university, Jack Bentham remembered, he had played the piano; perhaps he still did. Certainly those hands didn't do anything more physical – they weren't spare-time gardening, motor mechanicking or carpentering hands.

'You're not a vegetarian by any chance, Julian?' Bentham said with a smile.

'It's too boring having to cope with milk and sugar. They are messy things to have around.' The office was very tidy, like the man who occupied it. His grey suit, white shirt, maroon tie and black shoes all looked as if they had just been pressed and polished, as did Brind himself. Bentham envied such men their appearance, feeling himself always a little under the mark, under-brushed and under-pressed, even when first starting out in the morning. His clothes were regularly laundered and frequently changed, but he seemed to have one of those bodies that collected dross and ruckles.

'Who's coming to the meeting this afternoon?' Bentham wanted to know, curious as to why he had been invited to a senior policemen's policy meeting. He was a senior policeman, but didn't carry the weight of the assistant commissioners and chief constables who had been at other Home Office meetings he'd been invited to without explanation. Now he decided it was time for an explanation: if he was there on the whim of an old acquaintance from university, he wanted to know.

Brind came around the desk, proffering a stapled agenda. Along the top of page one he saw 'Co-ordinating Policy Meeting on the Police use of Computers'. On page two were sixteen names of officers invited to the meeting. Besides his own, Bentham saw those of Deputy Commissioner Harry Streeter, ACC Peter Vyvyan, the assistant commissioner with overall responsibility for traffic, the one who looked after public relations, the chief constables of Humberside, Merseyside and Kent with their assistants, and Home Office officials and technical staff – under the chair of an assistant under-secretary of state, who was hosting the meeting in his office up at Queen Anne's Gate. There was a Home Office discussion document entitled 'Police, Computers and the Future'. Its author was Brind.

'No one's had this agenda yet, Jack. Everyone apart from Martin Walker, the assistant under-secretary, and myself is coming into the meeting in the dark the same as you. They know the area, of course.'

'I wondered why you invited me, Julian. It's not that I'm not interested. I'm not sure that anyone would take much notice of me.'

'You undersell yourself, Jack. Yours is perhaps the most

important area of police work as far as computers are concerned. They have, after all, made a lot of criminal intelligence possible. Stopping crime before it's committed is the future as far as your department and my department are concerned. I want to give you the capacity to do that.'

'A bigger computer?' Bentham speculated.

'Oh, a much bigger computer,' Brind said with glee. 'Until now the police have been using computers on an experimental basis. A system here, a different system there; limited capacity, no coherent overall strategy. On the whole, computers have been a success. They've created efficiency, and there's no way we can now go back to manual files and searches. But the next stage is what I call in my discussion paper "The Master Computer Syndrome". The police need a master computer that can collate and extract from all police computers throughout the British Isles ...' He stopped abruptly, expecting a reaction from Bentham.

'And all the other computers, Julian?' Bentham said obligingly.

Brind laughed, delighted by the notion. 'Of course. It has to be a two-way process. Consider for a moment what a boon that would be to you in your investigations, Jack. You have a suspect who you believe is living off the proceeds of crime. How much simpler it would be if you could merely access bank computers to examine accounts.'

'The mind boggles,' Bentham said. He didn't point out that blaggers rarely used banks to hold their money.

'Capability isn't beyond us. What is needed is legislation to make all that possible.'

'I can see one or two problems.'

'I suspect there would be fewer objections in Parliament, curiously enough, than there would be here in the Home Office.'

'I hadn't noticed much championing of civil liberties from this ministry, Julian.'

'Oh it wouldn't be resistance on account of the infringement of civil liberties, but more a case of toes being stepped on, territory being taken over by my department. That's where the real objection will come from. But it's not something that can't be overcome, I'm sure.'

'I wish I shared your confidence about Parliament. Look at

the way they fucked over our last piece of legislation. The new White Paper proposals still won't give us all of the powers we need. Getting new powers piecemeal, as we do, all that happens in Parliament regularizes what is already being done out of necessity. But in the meantime it hampers us with things like the local authority consultative procedure.' It affected Bentham's area of work at the Yard far less than the Intelligence Support Units at District level who dealt with local criminal intelligence and the regular CID. Any District which held suspects for days on end while they were being interrogated was likely to run foul of a visit from the lay consultative body, made up of local councillors, clergy, solicitors and goodbodies who could drop in at a station at a moment's notice to check that everything was as it should be. Suspects being held for longer than prescribed under the law were either released then immediately re-arrested, rushed in front of a magistrate, or charged quickly. The problem was often no more than a distraction, but one police officers could do without. That was the sort of problem they might run into with David Lane being held out at Croydon, as Bentham anticipated him being around a long time before he was charged. Presenting him to a magistrate might prove strategically unsound.

'We're becoming a little more sophisticated, Jack. Parliament is now terribly malleable, especially where law and order issues are concerned. You went some way in that direction with your speech to the ACPO Conference in Brighton last month. There is a growing fear of lawlessness among members on both sides of the House. It's fear of the haves losing what they have to the have-nots. It's right and proper that left-wing MPs espouse the cause of the have-nots, but you'll find they're not keen to let go what they have either. When the police need resources for more SPG units or District Support Units, what happens? The commissioner emphasises the value of those units in nipping riots in the bud. Lawlessness, anarchy, the potential breakdown of society as we know and enjoy it, they are the sticks to beat Parliament with.' He was smiling, knowing all this was possible. 'The commissioner says in his last report that there are no longer adequate resources to police crime in London. By implication, too much is being spent on public order.'

'Public order has become the priority – we're into a very new kind of policing.'

'The Home Secretary's asking for increased powers for the police in this area. One complements the other, Jack. One doesn't follow the other by mere coincidence. The public order issues will increasingly affect your department. The emphasis of C11 has been intelligence involving major crime against property. But an area that is going to require your sharpest concentration is the criminal element entering public order issues. It would be naive to think that all demonstrations are made up of well-intentioned citizens who merely wish to influence public opinion. There are elements among all those organizations who will act outside the law against both property and persons in the furtherance of their aims. That element is not only increasing in size, but also in what it's prepared to do to achieve its ends. The criminal who is prepared to destroy a nuclear power station site or burn an animal research laboratory is different from the armed robber in so far as the former is more highly motivated.'

'But often the motivation of the former is a moral position,' Bentham argued uneasily, hearing echoes of Helen Daniels.

'Oh, come on, Jack. We're a democracy.'

It was Bentham's turn to laugh. 'You've just demonstrated how the democratic process is open to manipulation through fear.'

'Nonsense. It's called lobbying. The process is equally available to the criminal element, if they chose that route. But unfortunately they're not as principled as you imagine.'

'Consider the two areas you mentioned, Julian. The current thinking is ruled by fear. Fear of energy running out; the nuclear threat; fear of disease.'

'But what are you saying – that as a result they are justified in going outside the law?'

'I'm an old fashioned copper. If I see someone operating outside the law I have to do something. What I'm saying is, I can understand the sense of frustration that leads in the direction we've been talking about.'

'That makes you a thinking policeman, Jack. Which makes you an ideal candidate for running the department I believe C11 should develop into.'

'What can I say?' Bentham ventured, as an excuse to give himself time to think. He wasn't sure what his feelings would be if this were to represent an offer. He was unsure about a lot of the political areas the police were being pushed into; some were going into those areas unwillingly, the majority unknowingly, but some were eager for the imposition of a wider order in the political sphere – not realising that they were merely projecting their own inner conflicts and unresolved emotions onto the outside world, seeking a solution for the symptom rather than a resolution of the cause. 'Know thyself' was not a philosophy they could entertain, let alone understand.

'I'm not making you an offer, Jack. I'm not in a position to make one. First we have to develop our computer network and create the master computer syndrome. But it's good that you're in on these meetings. Certainly I wouldn't have thought your boss, Wiseman, would be a candidate. And the DAC, he's the old-fashioned type of policeman if ever there was one – this is a private conversation, by the way.'

Bentham suddenly felt angry, mostly at himself for having been manoeuvred into this position. He wasn't likely to talk to Ernie Wiseman or anyone else about this, but disliked the presumption that he could be pledged to secrecy. He felt worse for not saying anything about his feelings, knowing that he hadn't made up his own mind. Recognizing that this would be the level he would have to deal at if he became part of Julian Brind's scheme, and seeing the complete set of mental hoops he'd have to climb through, he wished it were possible to go back to being that simple copper imposing order on simple chaos.

'We should get going,' Brind said looking at his watch. Queen Anne's Gate was a ten-minute walk.

'I have my car outside,' Bentham informed him.

'Ah,' said Brind, as if he'd forgotten senior policemen had such perks. Civil servants at Brind's level had to take taxis. He gathered up the xeroxed agendas for the meeting.

In the back of the car Bentham intuited that this man had yet to get to the main point of their pre-meeting chat. Brind's approach to what was on his mind was so casual that Bentham might have missed its significance had he been less alert.

'How goes your investigation into the death of that animal rights demonstrator out at Hackney, Jack? Are you getting all the co-operation you need?'

'As much as can be expected. The men in the job aren't very

pleased. They keep trying to call foul, or accuse me of changing the ground rules.'

'One can understand: they must feel the rug is rather being pulled from under them.'

'It shouldn't really have been under them in the first place. The impression I get is that they were trying to save face after having fled from the protesters earlier in the demo.'

'You think perhaps the commander of A8 ought to be disciplined?'

Bentham shrugged. 'I'm trying not to have an opinion, Julian.'

'That's commendable. Though it would be fairly disastrous if this chap who died became a martyr to the animal rights cause. There are indications of that. At present the different animal rights factions are divided. The last thing the minister wants is for Paul Bailey's death to unite them.'

'I can see the problem politically, but there's little I can do about it. My findings aren't likely to influence the needs of the movement one way or another. Either they'll take this opportunity or they won't. My feeling is that if they're that divided and haven't done so already, then they won't.'

'Perhaps you're right,' Brind said and fell silent as they inched out into Victoria Street. Bentham felt irritated that his driver had taken them into this sort of traffic.

The silence in the car didn't help to dispel Jack Bentham's unease. He wondered if Julian Brind knew of his relationship with Helen Daniels and considered whether he ought to find some way of declaring it. She was a fairly prominent animal rightist and Brind was obviously well informed. Possibly he was trying to draw him out, provide him with an opportunity to declare himself, only Bentham couldn't work out the purpose of that. Deciding he was just being slightly paranoid, especially as his relationship in no way compromised what he was doing, he had made up his mind to say something when Brind said, 'The animal rights movement is potentially one of the most dangerous in existence, Jack.'

Bentham said nothing.

'Far more so than say CND. They tend to defeat their own argument by being perfectly happy with the retention of conventional weapons, which is totally illogical to a lot of people. But on the other hand, the animal rights movement has the

147

moral high ground and is voicing both the hearts and the minds of the people. The minister isn't worried about the minds, because anyone persuaded by intellectual argument can be swayed by intellectual argument, but once they've committed their hearts, so to speak . . .'

'Perhaps ground should be given to them, the law arranged to bring them inside,' Bentham pointed out. 'Back on that democratic argument.'

'Now you're being slightly naive, Jack. Can you imagine how the country would be run if it were to legislate at the whim of the people. Having what appears to be the moral high ground,' Brind said, slightly changing tack, 'isn't enough. There are other considerations, not least of all economic. Animals are part of our economy; if the minister gave way on experimentation – and he does have a responsibility to the public to try and ensure that drugs and consumer products are safer – how long do you think it would be before ground had to be given on farm animals, wildlife, animals for clothes? Giving animals some sort of rights isn't really on, and the sooner the animal rights movement is alienated from the public, the sooner it will wither and die. Ideally, they should be stripped of that romantic image as rescuers of helpless animals from the clutches of cruel experimenters. All the time they have it they'll continue to attract public sympathy. They're criminals, after all, a lot of them.'

'I can see the dilemma the Home Office faces, Julian, but I can't immediately see a way of resolving it,' Bentham said, being purposely obtuse, though he saw all the while where this influential assistant secretary was leading.

'There are certain people in the Home Office, people with the ear of the minister, who would like to see the more volatile factions of the animal rights movement totally frustrated and driven to desperate acts, things that would detach them from public sympathy. That minority would, of course, be seen to speak for the majority. No one identifies separate factions.'

Again, paranoia reared up in Bentham, and again he questioned whether this man was warning him about his personal relationship for fear of its jeopardizing his future career. This momentary aberration caused him to lose sight of the path and the point to which Brind was leading him.

'Depending on how things turned out at Hackney for those policemen, there's a section of the more militant animal rights people who would feel very frustrated and might stop at nothing to avenge a fellow traveller. The government can't give in to them, not with so much at stake. Of course, there is no reason they should give in to criminals. No reason at all.'

There he had it. Brind was pushing him in a clear direction. Straight down the middle with a set objective that would almost certainly result in irredeemable consequences for those elements of the animal rights movement who would be unable to contain their anger and frustration. It was a calculated risk on the part of someone in the Home Office, in their expectation both that he would go along with this scheme and find in favour of the policemen at Hackney, and that if he did the animal rights activists would respond. Bentham didn't comment. He didn't know what he'd do, and consoled himself with the belief that he couldn't do anything until his inquiry was complete. He found no consolation over his uncertainty about warning Helen of this. He tried to tell himself that none of it might come to pass, but that reassurance lay like a thin film of oil over a raging sea of thoughts as he went gloomily into the Home Office meeting.

14

Setting aside time to do the bidding of the Wiltshire CID was difficult, Lenny Feast found, even though their demands weren't excessive, and meeting them was a lot better than being inside or suspended on a major corruption charge; that prospect didn't in any way alter his lack of enthusiasm for the entire enterprise. He had tried to explain to Brian Humpfress that he ran a busy CID office, but whether he knew Penge or simply wasn't interested in his troubles, Feast couldn't tell. He was pretty busy with the three books to run – burglary, beat crime and theft from motor vehicles. There was plenty in all three categories that the uniformed branch got lucky with or had reported during the night, and which the CID had to follow up on the next morning, assuming the crime had enough points to warrant CID action. Often it didn't – if no one had been hurt, nothing of enough value stolen, or if there was no immediate prospect of a collar in sight. Those country coppers wouldn't understand about the pressures in policing in the Met, Feast thought, as he stood naked to the waist in Humpfress's office out at Swanley. They had but one thing in mind, nicking a senior detective, and thought everything else could stop while they went about it.

Rolls of fat around Lenny Feast's waist almost swamped the small transmitter that DS Preece was taping to him. Twice before he had gone into Tery Sneed with a wire, but on both occasions the recording had been an abysmal failure. The first time because of train noise; the second time because he had gone with only a transmitter, but they had jumped out of the train as the doors were closing and had lost the Wiltshire detectives who were receiving the signal in the next car but one. Feast had no expectation of being any more successful this time. He carried both a tape recorder and a transmitter, and was to meet Terry Sneed to give him some money.

'What if he finds this?' Feast asked, his anxiety emerging as a reedy whine.

'Tell him it's a pacemaker for your heart, Lenny,' Humpfress responded, despising this man more for seeing him like this with his visibly dripping fat. 'You'll need one soon enough, I'd say.'

He opened a buff envelope. 'Here's fifteen hundred pounds for your greedy friend, make sure ...'

'Not fifteen!' Alarm swept through Feast. 'He wants three and a half. That's what's agreed.'

'This is as much as we can raise,' Humpfress informed him.

'I don't fucking well believe this. What d'you do, take a hat round?'

'Tell him the rest is coming.' Humpfress's embarrassment was increasing.

'That's cuntish. He's not just off the farm – fuck you!' he screamed at Preece, who suddenly ripped the tape off his stomach, pulling the hairs. It stopped Feast's tirade.

'Needs a longer piece,' Preece explained with a smile. 'You don't want it slipping and dropping out of your pants like a turd.' He knew about the problem over the money. It resulted from lack of co-operation. When they had asked the Met Receiver for money to entrap this corrupt policeman, that was all they had been allowed, as if they couldn't be trusted with more.

'You do it our way. We know you can make it work,' Humpfress assured him. 'If we don't get Mr Sneed and soon, you'll have to come back inside.'

That was a threat Lenny Feast liked not one bit. He remained silent as the equally fat DS Preece wound sticking plaster about him; he then helped Feast to dress, carefully threading the wires through his sleeve and fixing them to the microphone just inside the cuff of his shirt.

'Just make sure he takes the money. He must have it on his person when we arrest him.' This came as an ominous warning from Humpfress. He knew that with the money in his possession Sneed would be in grave difficulty.

Despite his own predicament, Lenny Feast vaguely hoped that his ex-governor wouldn't show up, that he wouldn't bother to make the call to the phone box he was now heading for. That would leave him up shit creek without a paddle, he mused, somewhere he had been a few times before and yet had somehow managed to survive. Perhaps he could again. He doubted it. There was too much at stake, now. Those CID from Wiltshire were desperate; without Terry Sneed in the frame, they would collar him instead, notwithstanding how hard he had tried for them. There was but one way he could go on being a policeman.

Even so, a little part of him kept hoping the telephone wouldn't ring as he sat outside the box at the bottom of Berkeley Square. When it did, it startled Feast. He hurried to pick it up. Terry Sneed gave him the location of their meet – a pub at the top of Mount Street. Feast repeated the name for those at the receiving end. Sneed had given him five minutes to get there, which meant he was probably phoning from the pub. Possibly he could get there quickly, do the business and get away before Humpfress and his clowns got there. If Terry Sneed got clear and disposed of the money before they managed to feel his collar, that would be their problem. The thought of Humpfress having to explain to the Met Receiver how he had come to lose this money amused Feast as he drove up the west side of Berkeley Square and turned left into Mount Street. His mirth was short-lived. Sneed was in neither bar, so all Lenny Feast could do was buy a drink and wait.

From his car parked beyond the lights at the junction of Mount and South Audley Streets, Sneed watched Lenny Feast arrive, and continued to watch to make sure that none of the vehicles that appeared along Mount Street with Lenny Feast stayed around, or came around again too soon. There were none that he noticed. The streets were fairly quiet, most of the commuters having gone home and the Mayfair dinner set still at dinner. Even though he couldn't see any tail on Feast, Terry Sneed still wasn't convinced it was safe and had his driver cruise down Mount Street past the Audley and on round the block. There were cars parked in the street but they were empty. An unmarked van was parked outside a carpet shop in South Audley Street, but it was gone when his car came back round. Finally Sneed decided it was safe for him to approach the pub. The bar-room itself would be the only unsafe place, but he reasoned that no one could have got in there to stake it out as no one but himself knew the meet, and he had seen no one who remotely looked like a detective go into the bar after Feast.

As he joined Lenny Feast in the near-deserted bar-room, Sneed glanced over the other four customers – an old man at the far end of the bar, a middle-aged woman with a small dog that she was feeding peanuts to, and two pink-faced, bright-eyed young men in striped shirts and suits, both looking like they sold antiques.

'Scotch,' Sneed said to the barman, and indicated Feast's glass. 'And here.'

'Fuck I, Terry,' Feast said in a low, urgent voice that seemed to express exactly his ambivalence. 'I thought you wasn't going to show. I thought you were turning it down.' His voice grew clearer as his need outweighed the dictates of conscience. 'Rodgers could go up the steps any time. We'd have fuck all chance then. I mean, unless you can go into a judge. Come to think of it, you go sailing with that judge – unless you went into him,' he said, trying hard now. The Wiltshire CID had been particularly interested in Sneed's relationship with the circuit judge. All Lenny Feast knew about it was rumour.

'Inflation affects them like everyone else, Lenny.'

''s he earning?' Feast asked. Perspiration was pouring down his back and he was afraid it would cause his transmitter to short.

'A fucking fortune.' Sneed put a fiver on the bar for the drinks, then glanced at Feast. 'And it's all pensionable.'

Unable to bear the tension of this exchange any longer, Feast patted the inside pocket of his coat. 'I've got the money, guv. Fifteen hundred sovs. D'you wanna shoot into the karsey for it?'

Sneed smiled, a far from inviting smile, and shook his head. He tilted his glass and finished his drink as if preparing to leave, all of which visibly increased Feast's anxiety. The fat DS was pulling a right fucking stroke, and Sneed realised now why he was sweating. Certainly Rodgers wouldn't draw any help for that sort of money; Sneed wondered about taking the fifteen hundred pounds anyway for his trouble.

'Rodgers wants to see what sort of help he gets before he weighs on the rest, Terry.' The lack of response from Sneed caused Lenny Feast to panic. Seeing Sneed was about to leave, he remembered his instructions concerning the money. He had to give it to Sneed or Wiltshire CID would come bursting through the door and he'd be nowhere. 'He's as good as gold, Terry. I promise you. Look, take the one and a half, Terry, for yourself, for your trouble.'

'I don't think so,' Sneed said, instinctively suspicious but not wanting to believe that Lenny Feast would set him up. He remembered Feast's trouble with the Wiltshire CID and decided to leave quickly, but as he turned to go Feast's sweaty hand reached out to restrain him. At the same time Feast clumsily produced the package of money and tried without success to stuff it into Sneed's coat.

'Take it, Terry. Take it for yourself.'

'What's your fucking game?' Sneed demanded angrily, pushing away the restraining hand. As he did so alarm bells rang in his head. He had felt something hard the size of an acorn in Feast's sleeve, and knew at once he had been set up.

'You cunt,' he bellowed, causing the customers in the bar to turn. 'You dirty cunt – you got a wire.' He ripped desperately at Feast's clothes, sensing his world suddenly collapsing about him, and hating his own response to this. 'How much you got – switch it off.' Sneed tore with the fury of hatred and betrayal and fear at the other man's clothes. As Feast fought to protect his own interests the two men crashed to the floor.

'Don't be angry, Tel,' Feast screamed breathlessly, 'they got me by the balls.'

His plea in mitigation did nothing to assuage Sneed's anger. He heard the words but wasn't about to understand the argument, despite the numerous occasions he had tricked villains the same way and demanded they do his bidding. Often their co-operation hadn't bought their freedom; he imagined Feast's move wouldn't, either.

'Switch it off.' Sneed struggled to penetrate the clothing and so destroy the recording; but realising he wasn't making sufficient progress as Feast writhed on the floor, he tried another tack. 'You're nicked, you bent bastard,' he said loudly for the microphone. 'You're nicked. I'm arresting you for trying to pervert the course of justice.'

Feast looked in vain for the Wiltshire CID coming to his aid. Instead there was only the barman threatening to call the police.

'I am a policeman,' he said. 'I'm arresting this man. Please help me. I'm arresting him.' Where the fuck was his help, he thought fleetingly in the confusion.

'You're nicked,' Sneed said firmly, as if saying the words exculpated him. 'You're fucking well nicked.' He was stronger and fitter than Feast and was gaining the upper hand.

The members of the Wiltshire CID, who had been within

striking distance in the van that had been parked outside the carpet shop in South Audley Street, had driven away when Sneed's car had gone round the block – only to find themselves on Park Lane, three sets of traffic lights away from the Audley. At each successive red traffic light, they listened with increasing alarm to the altercation in the pub. Finally they jumped the lights at the junction of Mount and South Audley Streets, just missing a cab as they bounced up the kerb outside the bar, hitting a post carrying a waiting restriction notice. Four Wiltshire detectives spilled from the van.

Inside the pub they didn't stop to ask questions, but threw themselves at the two detectives on the floor, pulling them apart, landing punches on Sneed as they separated them.

'Leave off!' Sneed demanded. 'I've just arrested him.'

This impressed no one and so Sneed threw a couple of punches himself instead. If startled, the Wiltshire detectives weren't deterred. They were determined to make good after their bad start. However, neither Humpfress nor Feast wanted any part of this and drew back as the three detectives endeavoured to subdue Sneed; a knee drop finally did it, and they had him back down on the floor.

Fighting for breath, sitting on Sneed's back and twisting his arm, with another detective holding his legs and a third on his head, DS Preece said, 'Where are the cuffs?'

There was a moment's confusion.

'I thought you had some, skip,' DC Horne said. Someone had had some in the van. He looked at the other detective, who shook his head.

'Give us a chance, for fucksake,' Sneed said, trying to get free of them.

'Hold him, can't you.' He turned to Feast and his boss, who was speaking to the other unit through his personal radio. 'Got any cuffs?'

Sheepishly Lenny Feast fished a pair of handcuffs from his deep pocket and passed them over. These were snapped on Sneed's wrists and he was brought to his feet.

'There's no need for this,' Sneed protested. 'I'm a policeman, not a villain. I'm entitled to an explanation for this outrageous behaviour.' His gaze fell on Lenny Feast, skulking in the background, avoiding his look. 'You're nicked, uncle. I guarantee you'll stay nicked. You're finished in the job, I don't care what these cunts have promised you,' he said authoritatively. 'There's no place for you among decent policemen.'

Feast turned away, but there was nowhere for him to hide.

'Glad you've kept a sense of humour,' Humpfress said, flexing his shoulders as if to re-establish his own authority. He didn't enjoy the sort of confidence Sneed displayed. 'Take him out to the van.'

As Sneed was taken out Humpfress apologised to the manager who had been summoned by the barman. 'The excitement's all over now.'

'Well, I don't think there was much harm done. Fortunately we weren't very busy.' He turned away to discuss the disturbance with his customers.

'That was close,' Humpfress told Feast. 'We almost didn't get here.'

'He will stay nicked, will he?' Feast asked, his confidence severely dented.

'I wouldn't lose any sleep over it.'

'I mean, I'm finished in the job otherwise, word goes around I'm not only a grass, but I fitted him.'

Humpfress laughed at the irony of that. 'You'll probably get a commissioner's commendation. After all, that bent bastard got eleven of them. He's got the money for Superintendent Stern?'

'No,' Feast said reluctantly and closed his eyes as if expecting the world to fall in on him. When it didn't he said, 'I should have had the full amount, he'd have taken it then all right.'

Retrieving the package from the floor, Humpfress said, 'It's not the end of the world. We'll give it to him at the station. That'll do just as well.'

In order to show how relaxed and unconcerned he was over his arrest, Terry Sneed engaged DS Preece in a conversation about football as they drove to Swanley. He didn't follow the game, but knew enough from glancing across the sports pages of the *Telegraph* to have a conversation with someone from the West Country, where they had no football teams to speak of.

The exercise took very little of Sneed's thinking capacity and with the rest of his brain he ran forwards and backwards over his predicament. Forwards, planning with some satisfaction how he was going to make sure the treacherous Lenny Feast ended up on the scrap heap; backwards, trying to penetrate the shroud of disbelief that had fallen over the whole incident, yet at the same time decide what evidence they might have against him. Apart from circumstantial evidence, his meeting a corrupt detective sergeant in a pub, what could Feast have got? What had he said to him? Sneed ran their conversation over in his thoughts until finally convinced that he hadn't put himself on offer. Those previous conversations were where the danger lay, as he had to assume that they had also been taped. The two meetings on the tube train he thought were safe – a recording engineer whom he had once consulted on a case had told him that nothing much would be picked up with such background noise. There were the telephone calls Feast had made to him, but no one ever said anything on the telephone, certainly not on the phones from police stations. Regardless of whether anyone was under suspicion, policemen's telephone calls were often listened in to to make sure they weren't misusing the phones for their own private purposes. Feast obviously had no hard evidence against him or he wouldn't have been pursuing him this way.

Having convinced himself that he was safe, that he had covered himself as usual and the trouble he was in here was temporary aggravation that he would walk away from, it came as a shock to Terry Sneed – on being taken to the reserve room at Swanley and searched – to suddenly have Feast's package of money appear on the table with his possessions. He knew how it had got there. What shocked him was the realisation that they wanted him so badly that they were prepared to fit him, and none of the other policemen in the room, witnesses to the money being found in his possession, would say anything. This move was ironical, Sneed found, considering all the villains he had fitted, dangerous men who were a menace to society, villains who would go no other way; it was almost funny, only he didn't laugh. The situation made him angry, and it took all his powers of restraint not to show his feelings. If he did he believed he wouldn't walk away from this, he believed that like a deeply-entrenched superstition.

'You slippery cunt,' Sneed said evenly, pushing his face close to Humpfress's. 'You've got to be in real trouble. You pull a stroke like that. Planting that money on me. And you lot for going along with it. Either you put your hands up now and disown this bent cunt, or I'll see you're all done for conspiracy.'

That left an uneasy silence in the room. Eyes turned on Humpfress, waiting for him to make a move. The left-hand side of his face started to twitch – he was unable to control the tics.

'We'll see about that,' Humpfress said finally. 'If you want to make that the substance of a complaint, you know the procedure.'

'I certainly do,' Terry Sneed said with a confident smile. 'First I'll beat you at your own game, uncle. Then I'll make my complaint. You've set the ground rules, you'll have to take the consequences when you find how far they put you out of step with the rest of us.' It was worth a try. He knew that he had to try.

In view of their lack of response, Terry Sneed wondered if it wasn't a tactical error collectively threatening these policemen. He knew the police and knew that under threat they, like most other institutional bodies, closed ranks. They now had a vested interest in his staying nicked.

'Would you sign for your property, sir,' the uniformed reserve inspector asked, pushing the list of Sneed's personal effects in front of him. Everything he had on him, apart from the manilla envelope containing the fifteen hundred pounds, had been put into a plastic bag with a sealing tag that couldn't be resealed.

Sneed glanced over the sheet and then waved it away. 'You've made a mistake, uncle. The only money that was found on me was the thirty-six pounds and change you have down there.'

'You don't wish to sign for your effects?'

'Too fucking right,' Sneed said, the smile back on his face. 'Ask that cunt to sign, it's his money.'

Humpfress twitched some more, having greater difficulty than Sneed staying in control.

'You're not going to be charged yet, chief inspector,' he said. 'We're going up to the CID office where one or two things will be put to you about your past activities.' He picked up the packet of money. 'We'll take charge of this, inspector.'

'You mean take it back,' Sneed rejoindered.

Despite the fact that it was standard that whenever a policeman was interviewed on corruption charges, the interview was conducted by an officer at least two ranks his senior, Humpfress resented the presence of Detective Chief Superintendent Tony Bulmer, seeing Sneed as his prize. He was the one to find him, he was the one to arrest him; it was he who had suddenly got their whole investigation out of the doldrums, and now the DCS was conducting the questioning as if it had all come about because of his personal intervention. Much as he loathed Terry Sneed, Humpfress took some comfort from his attitude, in that he was both mocking and unforthcoming; a worm of an idea at the back of his brain even began to hope that this policeman would wriggle free as a result of Bulmer's handling of him.

'Why don't you sit down, Terry,' Bulmer said from the desk where a number of files relating to some of Sneed's previous cases were laid out. He appeared in control, but didn't enjoy this man standing over him as if he was about to leave at any moment.

Truth to tell, Bulmer knew that might prove to be the situation at the end of the day. Their resident deputy DPP didn't think much of the case so far against Sneed, and he probably wouldn't be happy about the money found in his possession, especially not if he learned how it got there. The trick was to convey none of this to Sneed, but he was obviously no fool. 'Do you mind if I call you Terry? Seems silly to be on rigid formal terms, especially as we're going to be talking for a long while. I'm Tony. You know Brian Humpfress. And that's Dennis Preece.' He turned to the DS who was across the room, causing him to straighten off the wall.

'Del, sir,' Preece said correcting him. 'It's Derek.'

'Of course,' Bulmer said without missing a beat, as if he'd simply been testing his alertness. 'How's your wife, Del. Had her baby yet?' Retrieving the situation, or so he believed.

Preece didn't answer as his only child was fifteen. He assumed the DCS was getting him mixed up with Roy Horne, whose wife had recently given birth.

'Some of your past cases make interesting reading, Terry,' Bulmer said, looking over the array of papers. 'One might almost believe you paid criminals to plead guilty. Very impressive.'

'Treat suspects decently,' Sneed mocked, 'they'll put their hands up.'

'You'll find us very fair. I see no point in sending people to prison without good cause.'

'Amazing. Absolutely fucking amazing. It's very reassuring knowing I'm dealing with straight policemen.'

'We could get this wrapped up in no time.' He glanced at

Humpfress who had paused from reading a file. 'You might like to make a statement.'

'About anything in particular? I've got nothing to state, uncle, only that I want to contact my brief, or my governor. I don't mind which.'

'I daresay we'll find something to talk about in this lot,' Humpfress put in, fanning the edge of a file.

'Might take a long time.'

'Oh, we're not short of time. It's only our children who are growing old without us and our marriages going to pot.' Humpfress couldn't keep the bitterness out of his words. This detective might have been solely responsible for what was going on back at home.

'S'all part of the job,' Sneed reminded him. 'S'not exactly a lot to show for it, is there? A couple of low-ranking detectives. Have you got enough to put them away?'

'You're not exactly low-ranking, Terry,' Bulmer pointed out. 'You're a senior policeman. You lead us on to other more senior policemen, we'll start making up for lost time.'

'I've got about ten years yet. I'm not planning on taking early retirement.'

'Come on, old son,' Humpfress said in a suddenly matey fashion, as if expecting to appeal to Terry Sneed's sense of what was right. 'Make a clean breast of things. You know it'll make you feel better.'

He felt let down when Sneed quipped, 'Like having a good shit?'

'There's no better time, chief inspector,' Bulmer said on a deadly serious note. 'Patience has run out. Everyone wants this cleared up with the minimum of fuss so we can all get back to some proper police work.'

'You putting some sort of deal on offer?'

'The DPP suggested that, for the right information.'

'It's senior policemen you want?'

There was an expectant air among the three Wiltshire detectives as they waited for Sneed.

'Let's suppose I'm agreeable. How about if I go into your assistant chief constable wired up like that plant you put into me and get him to put his hands up to unlawful intercourse with sheep? Will that do it?' Sneed found his proposition amusing, but no one else did.

160

'Is that what you're saying happened?'

Terry Sneed chose to misconstrue the DCS's question. 'Isn't that why country coppers are issued with Wellington boots?'

Almost without realising the hole he was falling into in his anger, Bulmer retorted, 'I doubt the crimes of country coppers ever amount to anything more serious.' He believed the minor peccadilloes of public employees were acceptable. 'What about it, chief inspector?'

'This is ballocks. What you've done, uncle, is made a very serious error.'

'What we have on those tapes is enough, Terry.'

A chink appeared in Sneed's confidence.

'You're talking to me like I'm a fucking wally,' he protested, as if suddenly wearying of this. 'I've been in the job too long, I know how it works. 'You had enough to charge me, you'd have put it to me.'

'I admire your confidence, Terry. I'd sooner deal with that than have them whimpering. Friend Feast's a wimp. Cried like a baby, did he not, Brian?'

'We had to fetch a mop in here,' Humpfress confirmed sullenly.

Sneed nodded, trying to resist his creeping anxiety. 'I've known some of the hardest villains who'd've let me fuck them up the arse for a bit of help.'

'Be interesting to see which way you go.'

'I don't know how many conversations Feast recorded, but none of it's worth a toss, Tony. If you put a corrupt policeman in the witness-box to give evidence against me, he'll have to put himself in it to gain any credibility. That'll be laughed at. I'll let my record speak for me.'

'It's impressive,' Bulmer said, refusing to be rattled. He glanced at the record folder. 'Makes this all the more tragic. Risking such a fine career for a few measly pounds.'

'Don't talk like a cunt,' Sneed said disparagingly. 'What you did is outrageous, putting Feast into me like that. A bit fucking swift.'

'You're the fit-up specialist, so rumour has it.'

'The only way some professional villains will go. I've had more than a few I've let go up on the evidence as it stood only to have them get a throw.'

Bulmer conceded this with a nod, giving something of himself in expectation of getting something back. 'If we were left to our own devices there'd be a lot more bad lads behind bars.'

He waited, but in vain. Finally he turned to Preece. 'See if you can rustle up some sandwiches and some beer, Del. It looks like being a long night.' He glanced across at Terry Sneed as the DS went out. 'Will you sit down now? It'll be easier.' Opening another folder as Sneed sat on the chair opposite the desk, he said, 'Brian Cayman.'

Terry sneed didn't respond, but felt anxiety claw at him.

'To refresh your memory, as if it needed refreshing, he's an armed robber who comes from Bickley. Feast put him in touch with you when he was on the Robbery Squad. A detective out of Tooley Street had contacted Feast to get your help for Cayman, to get him dropped from a security office robbery out at London airport.'

'Sounds like Lenny's been busy. I'm surprised he put his hand up. You must have promised him an awful lot. Get Brian Cayman into the box to say the same. A self-confessed blagger.' Sneed wondered briefly if Brian Cayman had been nicked – it was possible; and if he was, he probably wouldn't see the other piece of money Cayman still owed him.

'Let's move on to Paul O'Roake.'

'He's waiting to go up the steps for robbing the Post Office in Wimbledon.'

'The fact is, you were given O'Roake by the other members of the gang, along with seven thousand pounds, which you planted on him. I hold no brief to O'Roake. Prison's where he belongs and I don't mind how he gets there.' It was said without any sense of irony, which didn't go past Sneed unnoticed. 'To be perfectly honest, Terry, I'm only interested in using him as a stick to beat you with.'

'It's what I would do in your position.'

'He's quite willing to be used in that way now it's been explained to him how he was set up. He feels very aggrieved at the way he was used by his friends and you. You're all a parcel of slippery turds.'

'What villain has ever felt less than hard done by at the hands of the CID?'

With an impatient gesture, Bulmer said, 'Let's talk about this latest piece of help you were prepared to sell to a villain. The week before last, on the seventeenth of October, you had a meeting on the underground with Detective Sergeant Feast, who was seeking help for a Peter Rodgers, a large-scale credit-card fraudster. You agreed to approach Superintendent Stern on the Fraud Squad, the price was three and a half thousand pounds.'

'You've got some front,' Sneed said, 'Using an agent provocateur to draw up a crime where none existed. We do things a bit differently in the Met.'

'I'd say that's exactly what you've been doing.'

'With villains, maybe. We're talking about allegations of police corruption now. The ground rules are different.'

'No one's told me.'

'I can't see the DPP taking the same line. Then he's a bit more sophisticated.'

'You invoke the DPP like he's a personal fucking talisman. Right now he's on my side.' Bulmer waited, expecting an argument. 'Subsequent to your meeting with DS Feast, you approached Superintendent Stern to ask for help for Rodgers, saying it would be worth three thousand to him.'

'Harry Stern said that?' Sneed asked, believing himself to be ahead of the game.

'He's agreed to give evidence against you, as distasteful as he says he will find that,' Bulmer said trying to keep his nerve in this bluff. He believed in his bones that Sneed was deeply involved in corruption, but getting him to admit it was another matter.

'I'd say Harry would find perjury more distasteful. He's about the straightest detective I know.' He wondered if they had any evidence against Harry Stern. What they certainly hadn't got was a statement from him saying how he had been approached – unless the superintendent's memory was going, for it was two grand he'd been offered for Rodgers, not three. These Wiltshire CID obviously didn't realise how high expenses were in London. 'If it's as good as you say, why not come to court?'

'It's not that simple, chief inspector. We could go to court; a conviction would look impressive. But having come this far, we want more, because we know there is more and we believe you've the key to it.'

'Ballocks. You'll get to court, but that's as far as it will go. You'll make a cunt of yourself.'

'There's a lot of witnesses who'll give evidence against you.'

'Corrupt detectives with a gun to their heads,' Sneed said. 'Villains with a vested interest in seeing a good thief-taker discredited.'

'There are the tape recordings of your conversations with DS Feast.'

'Let's have a listen to them, shall we?'

'How long has this investigation been going on?' Bulmer said, deflecting the challenge. 'Sixteen months. Can you imagine what that has done to police morale, and public confidence? There's an urgent need to restore both. What better way than by putting all the corrupt policemen on trial, showing that what is left is clean and sound?'

Sneed nodded, agreeing with that sentiment, but he wasn't being deflected. 'I suspect those tapes corroborate fuck all. Am I right?'

'Perhaps you'd care to tell us the purpose of your meetings with Feast.'

The naivety of that tack unnerved Terry Sneed, and he wondered if this man was leading him into some disadvantage. 'Twice I was approached by Feast. He asked about getting help for a villain awaiting trial. What I was doing was collating evidence on DS Feast to pass to C1B2.' Had he been told that story he would have laughed, Terry Sneed reflected, but the DCS simply smiled and glanced round at Humpfress.

'That might have been believable, Terry, but for the fifteen hundred pounds found in your possession when you were searched at the station here. Those were marked notes that we had previously supplied to Sergeant Feast.'

'You dirty no-good cunts,' Sneed said, his anger momentarily running away with him.

'It's the job we have to do, Terry,' the DCS said, as if in mitigation. 'So let's think about a statement, shall we?'

Having it confirmed how determined they were to nick him, Sneed almost put his hand up. But when he pulled back from his anger, he decided they would have to work a lot harder than they had. The beer and sandwiches came, and with them they pushed on into the dead hours of morning with their interrogation, growing weary and impatient at his repeated and persistent denials. They challenged him on rumour after rumour, referring to both high-ranking suspects and those of lower rank than Terry Sneed; they even dredged up cases where he had had real results, but still his position didn't change. Finally he was allowed to sleep. The following afternoon the process was repeated, and it went on late into the night. Another day came, but nothing changed; Terry Sneed remained incommunicado, being allowed to talk to neither his governor nor his solicitor. Commander Wiseman might have been useful – he could have applied some pressure to get him released. He continued to ask to be allowed to contact either one. But it was denying him access to a shower and a change of clothes that was most likely to crack Terry Sneed. Sneed showered at least twice a day and often changed his shirt three times a day, so found three days with an unwashed body and in the same clothes very trying. He wasn't encouraged either when, finally, they told him that they had contacted Commander Wiseman, but he hadn't been willing to talk to him. Sneed didn't believe them. He'd have to hear that from Ernie Wiseman himself.

It was standard practice for police to hold suspects without benefit of a phone call to solicitor, family or friends for as long as they chose – at least as long as there was a prospect that they would crack and be charged, and certainly longer than the old judges' rules ever allowed. Now that the rules for the protection of prisoners had been enshrined in law with the Police and Criminal Evidence Act, and the perimeters limiting what the police could do with a suspect had been extended – almost as if they were being rewarded for previously breaking the rules – they tended to use their discretion over extending the present perimeter quite freely. Sneed wasn't enjoying the experience. It was a wearying process and he was having more and more difficulty concealing its effect on him.

Had he not been equally tired from this process of attrition, Tony Bulmer might have noticed those hairline cracks in the suspect's defences. He wanted to try a different tack, haul in all the senior policemen who were rumoured to be involved in corruption, either with Sneed or independently, and see how they held up. He was sure panic would be rife as they tried to save themselves, but his immediate boss, Assistant Chief Constable Alan Leeper, was nervous even at the thought of it. Only at Tony Bulmer's insistence did he pursue the idea, but not officially. He took all he had to ACC Peter Vyvyan, leaving out the odd rumours that had been heard with regard to the ACC himself.

The word that came back via Alan Leeper, far from encouraging the DCS, made him angry. He knew how the men below him would take it, especially Brian Humpfress, who had invested so much in Sneed.

'How's Sneed shaping up, Brian?' he asked, having called the DCI into his office. 'Shut the door.'

'He's not proving any more forthcoming.' Humpfress said, with a sense of his own failure. Left to his own devices, he had expected to break Sneed. 'There isn't any sense of morality in the man.'

Bulmer looked at him. He knew Humpfress's religious views and felt uncomfortable whenever they came up in conversation.

'He's still complaining about not being allowed to shower and change his clothes.'

There was a long, awkward silence. Bulmer didn't want to say what was on his mind as it only accentuated his feeling of impotence. He wondered if his colleague knew. It would have been an easy guess, as it was nothing short of what they had come to expect up here.

'We're not going to get any help,' he said avoiding looking at him. 'In fact it looks like the Met are about to pull the rug from under us. ACC Vyvyan says they're thinking of asking us to wrap up and go home.'

Anger exploded in Humpfress like hundreds of tiny blood vessels popping simultaneously, but the angrier he felt the harder he tightened it down inside him. 'Can they do that?' he said, barely getting the words out. 'This is the closest we've come to something, Tony.'

'They invited us here,' Bulmer said non-committally. 'They would like to end it with Feast and the Met driver who tipped him off. And Sneed, if we can make it past the post with him. If he's going to be put away, we've got to make it good, Brian. He won't go easily even then.'

Humpfress stared at his boss without seeing him, without hearing what he was saying. The forces of evil were working against him, he knew, and they were very difficult to fight. Clearly Terry Sneed was one of their black knights. He had to be defeated and forced to give access to all those evil policemen above him who were bloated on corruption.

He passed up Tony Bulmer's offer to get drunk with him. The DCS knew he didn't drink to any state of intoxication, and

Brian Humpfress couldn't imagine why he thought this should be an occasion for him to abandon his principles.

Terry Sneed was left to stew for yet another night in his cell, without benefit of newspaper, television, or a shower and shave. That gave Brian Humpfress some small satisfaction. He would have preferred pursuing the interrogation. He didn't mind how often he went over the same ground, each time looking for discrepancies in the response. But instead he found himself on the streets of Soho. The initial intention had been to interview a potential witness – the owner of a video porn palace – about police corruption, at least that was what he had told himself, but he hadn't conveyed the intention to his colleagues, and had gone unaccompanied.

Walking the streets of Soho was a chastening experience for him. The degradation there made his flesh creep – this was the lowest form of human achievement, this was evil incarnate. Mindless youths not much older than his own children lurched out of a pub on Old Compton Street, reeling from the effects of alcohol. On the corner of Dean Street two black men and a white were dealing in a darkened doorway. It was a drugs exchange, and Brian Humpfress had to stop himself stepping up to them to make an arrest. He looked around in vain for uniformed policemen, but his expectation of their doing anything would have been equally fruitless. Some three-card tricksters in a shop doorway further along the street might have been deterred by the sight of a uniform, though it was doubtful whether any of the seedy homosexuals or pederasts who slid into the garishly-lit establishment selling uncensored hard-core porn videos and books for gays would have been concerned. As he stood on the corner of Dean Street and Old Compton Street, surveying this scene of what he believed to be abject human misery, he felt himself getting increasingly angry at the openness of such sin.

'Have you got a light?'

The young voice was at his side, claiming his attention. Brian Humpfress felt affronted, for he detested the smoking habit. That initial response made him miss the real purpose of this contact as he turned to the fresh-faced lad who was holding an unlit cigarette between his middle and third finger. He had make-up on, and the detective wasn't immediately certain that it was a boy, but thought it was.

'How old are you, son?' His question related to under-age

smoking, but as soon as the boy turned and fled, Humpfress realised that this had been a homosexual proposition. He could just about cope with all this filth as a detached observer, but not when he was approached as a punter. He determined to do something about it there and then and pursued the lad along Old Compton Street towards Charing Cross Road. He would find out who he was, who had put him into this, or at least return him home to his parents. No thought of the circumstances that might have forced the child onto these streets entered his head.

With a cautionary glance over his shoulder, the lad with the unlighted cigarette saw Brian Humpfress coming after him and put on speed. He was fleet of foot and had got to know Soho well in the two weeks he had been operating there. He ducked into Frith Street and then Romilly Street and was gone, heading across Cambridge Circus for Covent Garden.

Humpfress stopped in Frith Street, knowing he wouldn't find the lad, and felt more angry for having handled the incident so badly. He found himself on a pavement outside an open doorway leading into a dimly-lit, uninviting passageway. A man shuffled out, hesitated on seeing him, then hurried away. On the doorframe was a lighted bell-push bearing the legend 'Tina – attractive young model.' The light seemed to be mocking him. It might have represented all he most detested and feared. He screwed his anger down harder, intending to turn away, but knew this was what he was here for. He trembled slightly as he entered the narrow hallway and started up the uncarpeted stairs.

The lady who opened the door on the first-floor landing was neither attractive, in the conventional sense, nor young, but she did use the name Tina. She smiled a wan, resentful smile, and released the door chain, having decided that Brian Humpfress wasn't here to rob her. She ushered him in and closed the door. A red light in the small entrance to the flat bathed the tatty black and red wallpaper in the hallway in a tawdry glow. The woman smiled again, revealing that her incisor teeth were missing.

'What can I do for you?' she asked, trying to make this an invitation.

Humpfress stood and looked at her without hearing the words. There were tobacco stains where her remaining teeth met her gums. The stale cigarette smoke in the flat brought to mind the child who had accosted him, causing his frustration to recur; it might have been her fault. The fact that Terry Sneed might walk clear from his involvement in this sort of corruption seemed to be this woman's fault as well. So ran the jumble of ideas and associations in Brian Humpfress's throbbing head.

'Let me tell you what I can offer, what I charge. Then you can say what you want. It's twelve pounds for hand relief; fifteen if I undress while I'm doing it. Twenty pounds is what I charge for full intercourse; twenty for French with a rubber and the same for Swedish. You can have a full half hour for thirty pounds, and if you want something kinky like putting on my clothes it's forty pounds.'

The bill of fare was rattled out automatically, but she stopped when she realised there was no response. The punter just stared at her with cold, slightly bulging eyes. For a moment she thought he was suffering a stroke or some sort of fit. That was the last thing she wanted to have to cope with. 'Something wrong, is there?' she asked. Then a worse thought occurred to her. 'You're not a policeman are you?' She paid her insurance premiums regularly, but that didn't stop policemen coming in for freebies. The last had demanded she give him French without a condom. He had ejaculated in her mouth. 'You are, aren't you?'

'You're trash,' Brian Humpfress said in a hoarse whisper.

'You'd better get out of here, before I call some help. Go on, I pay my dues . . .'

'You're utter filth.' His vehemence was given edge by the realisation that he had an erection, and the shame which resulted from it.

Either his words weren't sufficient warning or she didn't choose to heed them, for she didn't try to ward off the attack that followed. He swung his fists one after the other into her face, the right catching her hard on the cheekbone just below the left eye, splitting it, the left knocking out three of the remaining front teeth in her upper jaw. Blows fell relentlessly on her head, her chest and shoulders as Tina went down, screaming and trying to cover her face.

The attack stopped as suddenly as it had started, and Brian Humpfress turned and hurried away, feeling both ashamed for what he had done and deeply relieved. He searched for his handkerchief to cover his stinging, cut knuckles as he clattered

169

down the stairs, but used it to hide his face from the equally confounded punter who was starting along the hall from the street. It wasn't until he was on the street and safely moving clear of Tina's door that he felt wet and uncomfortable in his underpants. The shame he felt hounded him right out of Soho.

It took him a good deal longer to bury the memory, but finally he managed to do so – in the deepest recess of his mind, to the place where he had consigned all his fears from childhood and the disappointment he had suffered from his wife, never to be dredged up or even acknowledged as having existed. The surface was left reasonably calm and in control; that was how Brian Humpfress was determined it should remain.

15

Hostility and strife among participants at animal rights meetings was nothing new, nor the emotional tirades of individuals who exhorted the rest to harmony and accord for the sake of the animals. The moral and spiritual arguments they could muster completely confounded the scientists and vivisectors, who knew the animal rightists held the high ground; and comparing them to their scientific forebears in Dachau, which Helen believed was justified, started them all but foaming at the mouth with rage. But harmony and accord and a little ordinary tolerance were hard to find with so many factions pursuing different objectives. The infighting was bad enough but fanned as it was by infiltrators to the movement it became highly destructive. That there were infiltrators at all levels was something most people acknowledged, but few came to terms with. Their infiltration of the scientific establishment didn't work in quite the same way, mostly because of the sensitivity of those involved, the concern which brought them to animal rights in the first place; it was too much to expect of them that they should connive in horrific experiments on animals. Their empathy with animals' suffering was too immediate. To be accused herself of working for the opposition, as she had now been, was something Helen Daniels found deeply shocking. The accusation left her both numb and angry beyond relief, even beyond speech initially.

'I am not going to be in a meeting with Helen knowing that anything I say will go straight back to the opposition via the police,' said the tight-mouthed blonde woman in tight blue jeans and a skimpy pale blue sweat shirt bearing a familiar animal rights legend. 'It's just ridiculous. We're playing right into their hands.'

'You're being ridiculous, Freddy,' said Sheila Weymouth, who spoke clearly in defence of Helen and was the unelected leader of the group. She, like Freda 'Freddy' Ransom, was a paid member of the movement.

'Well, look at that bloody raid last Friday. The police were waiting in force. They didn't just arrive after the raid when the animals were away. They were waiting to pick everyone up.'

'But that doesn't prove anything,' Brenda Hersey, another council member, said.

'I find the coincidence a bit hard to swallow. It doesn't need much figuring out.'

A sick feeling was rising in Helen; she felt the need to get up from the table and leave the room, but was afraid to, fearing it would look like an admission of guilt. She understood why Freddy was behaving like this, or thought she did. It was the result of the disappointment each of them felt at the failure of the raid on the primate research laboratory in Surrey. Not only had they failed to rescue any of the animals, but twenty-three activists had been arrested: some had convictions for similar acts of liberation; others had been previously bound over. Sentences that were getting increasingly heavy as the establishment became more panicky and more vindictive would be even worse for those. But she hadn't betrayed them, not to Jack Bentham or anyone else. That was why Freddy was accusing her – because of her relationship with Jack Bentham, who happened to be a senior policeman; perhaps it was partly to do with the fact that she had a relationship with a man at all.

'I think you should apologise to Helen,' said Ian Gittings, the chairman of the meeting, but with little prospect of being taken notice of. 'We should avoid personal attacks. They're counterproductive. We'll get so as councillors will be afraid to either give or receive information for fear of being put in the star chamber.'

'Well, I'll certainly be very careful about what I say in future,' Freddy Ransom declared, showing no intention of apologising, but attracting no more support than that which came from her own small, unquestioning following.

'What do you think, Sheila?' the chairman asked, not wanting to give a ruling himself.

'I think Freddy's over-reacting. It's fairly obvious we were infiltrated, but we can't rule out the possibility of the leak coming from someone in the activists' group, perhaps even unintentionally.'

'Oh, I don't say that Helen gave the information intentionally,' Freddy said. 'But that doesn't change the situation at all.'

'I didn't,' Helen managed to say at last, pressing back her tears. They were no more impressed by those than by emotional outbursts. 'I didn't tell my policeman friend about

172

the raid, of course I didn't. I wouldn't even though I don't believe he'd have done anything.'

Freddy Ransom dismissed the notion with raucous laughter.

'This is stupid. Absolutely stupid,' an older member of the council said. Majorie Lodge had been an animal rights worker all her life, and an impassioned one; the common sense of her arguments was often coloured by emotion. 'It's not getting us anywhere. We'll just have to live with another setback and try again. It's not the first time, it won't be the last. But I would like it, Mr Chairman, if we came back to the item on the agenda – Paul Bailey's death, and what our next move is going to be.'

'But we're back to the same problem,' Freddy Ransom said. 'How can we get an advantage over the police if it goes right back to them?'

'Freddy, that isn't proven,' the chairman said.

'Look, Ian, I'll leave if it'll help,' Helen said. 'Paul was a good friend. I'm very upset about his death, but I'm not prepared to sit here and squabble over his remains. I'm willing to do something tactically about his murder, I'm sure he'd want that. I think a petition to the Home Office to get the police to release his body for burial might be an idea.'

'Why don't you ask your friend,' Freddy Ransom put in.

'I did, Freddy. I thought he might be useful. He said the official position is that they can't release it because if there are any prosecutions the suspects have the right to an independent post-mortem.' She hesitated at revealing the unofficial reason, but felt she had to prove herself in some way. 'Unofficially it's because the Home Office want the incident to fade from memory, so there won't be too many demonstrators on the streets at his funeral.' Perhaps her revealing that here would get back and compromise Jack Bentham, but he hadn't told her not to tell anyone. For all the impression it made with the disaffected at the council meeting, she wished she had said nothing.

Freddy Ransom said, 'If he told you he must have had a reason.'

'I think our next move should be to call a press conference and release the post-mortem reported by Professor Kapleau,' Sheila Weymouth suggested. 'That might undermine any police cover-up.'

'I don't think Jack would cover anything up,' Helen said impulsively, unsure why she had such faith in this man she had known for such a short while and under such strange circumstances. Maybe it was nothing more than hope. Having committed herself to Jack Bentham, she wanted him to be different to how she believed all other policemen to be.

'I was driving home from a friend's the other night,' a quiet voice said from along the table, 'when I found a rabbit sitting in the lane near our house, just sitting there, blinded by myxomatosis. It didn't even try to run when I got out of the car and went up to it. I took it home and put it in a box of straw in my bedroom. There didn't seem to be much I could do for it. It just crouched in the corner of the box, not seeing the carrot I put in front of it. It woke the whole household in the night squealing. It had managed to get out of the box and was lying a foot or so away on its side, twitching, its eyes covered in pus. It stopped squealing when I touched it, and it died a few moments later.'

The young woman broke off and lapsed back into her usual silence. No one asked what this had to do with anything, or declared her out of order. Everyone knew what she was saying; her peculiar emotional tirade was her way of saying amidst the hostility, 'What about the animals?' A couple of the committee members had tears in their eyes at the end of the story, including Freddy Ransom. When Helen glanced over at her she averted her eyes and fished in her bag for a cigarette, then used the smoking prohibition as a reason to step outside. From Freddy it was the next best thing to an apology.

They took a ten-minute break, and afterwards agreed to release the report on Paul Bailey's injuries from the professor of forensic medicine at St Thomas's. Professor Kapleau, who was acting for this committee – as Paul Bailey had no family – was adamant that death had been caused by any one of three blows to the back of the head. There were no other injuries on the body apart from lacerated fingers, consistent with the hands being stamped on. He stated that the instrument was heavy yet soft, indicated by the absence of lacerations to the scalp which a hard-edged weapon such as a truncheon would have caused. He suggested a sandbag might have caused this extensive damage to the scull and internal haemorrhaging, which would have led to death within the hour. He had added in this report that 'to the inexperienced or less than thorough medical practitioner,

174

and certainly to paramedics among policemen, such injury, in the absence of outer damage, might easily pass examination without raising undue alarm'.

Those on the committee who wanted to pay the police back for the endless hassle they got from them wanted to leave off that last part of the statement, and another row flared up. It wasn't the last before the meeting finally broke up around seven-thirty, three and a half hours later than its schedule.

'What a way to spend a Sunday,' Sheila Weymouth said in her usual jokey manner, 'when we could be out on a demo!' Sheila's humour was her way of dealing with the nightmare they continually faced. 'Hopefully it'll do some good, releasing a press statement about Paul's injuries. We should think about tackling the Home Office and getting his body released.'

'It would be easier if we were family rather than just friends,' Helen said.

'We're not even just friends, are we. We're loony activists who are out to cause trouble.'

Helen smiled at Sheila Weymouth's description. Sheila was one of the few people in the movement who seemed capable of laughing at both herself and the way everyone took themselves so deadly seriously.

'You might talk to your friend, Helen. You shouldn't worry about who you use to get what you want, or what anyone here thinks of it. That's part of the trouble with most of our lot – unless you're ideologically sound they won't even talk to you. I'll talk to the Home Office officials, vivisectors or anyone else if it'll help to get animals out of laboratories. You just have to be careful not be be conned by their claptrap.'

Helen knew she was right, but still couldn't help caring about what people felt about her – even those who could not see what they were doing by their actions and had to stumble over obstacles of resentment and suspicion which were mostly of their own making, getting hurt along the way. She wasn't really any different, and knew the obstacle she continually stumbled into was her own ego.

Out of her soul-searching came the determination to use Jack Bentham shamelessly to help animals. The way that immediately came to mind was to ask him to help the activists who had been arrested in Surrey. She didn't know if he could help, but he was a senior policeman and wasn't without influence. She suffered a brief bout of conscience as she parked outside the mansion block in Hammersmith, telling herself that he wouldn't use her in a similar way to penetrate the animal rights movement. But then he didn't have the same objective or commitment to an ideal.

Jack Bentham wasn't in when she reached the flat, and she opened the door with the spare key from under the carpet that ran along the centre of the hallway. It amused her that, after all the police campaigning for people to make their property more secure, his should be so insecure.

She made herself some camomile tea, checked the fridge to make sure his bacon-eating friend hadn't slipped in to stock up, found some sticks of celery, and went through to the sitting room to make some phone calls. They were mostly to non-animal rights friends – actors and a couple of fringe directors – with whom she found it difficult to stay in touch, because of both her involvement with the movement and her relationship with Jack Bentham. The play at the Royal Court had finished, and she had since seen a couple of directors for some television work – one piece she wasn't interested in, the other she didn't think she would get. Again she thought about quitting acting, but knew she wasn't brave enough.

Starting awake as something touched her face, she saw Jack Bentham smiling at her. She wasn't sure how long she had been asleep. It was quite late. He apologised for being so long, adding, 'I'm glad you waited.'

'I didn't realise I was so tired. It's the hostility of our meetings, I suppose.'

'Difficult time?' He could take chapter and verse off the computer back in his department. Everything got reported back.

'It always is when you don't seem to be winning much.'

'I know the feeling. Do you want a drink?' He went into the kitchen and opened a bottle of wine.

His feeling of frustration wasn't unconnected to hers. The further he got into his investigation over the circumstances of Paul Bailey's death, the muddier the water became. One of the latest developments was a message he had received from Commander David Mitchell, who had overall responsibility for the selection, training and dispersion of the District Support Units, including Uniform Carriers G/59 and G/60. Commander

176

Mitchell had informed him that he had told all of his men who were involved on the animal rights demo in Hackney that they were protected by a lawful order to use truncheons. Mitchell had thus pre-empted his inquiry, and Bentham wondered if the commander had the support of the DAC or whether he was acting off his own bat. He could have gone to Deputy Commissioner Harry Street to find out, but decided that, if the rug was being pulled from beneath him, he would hear soon enough. He had found Commander Mitchell's statement strange in view of the report from the professor of forensic medicine at Guy's Hospital whose advice the police had sought. It had stated conclusively that a hard-edged truncheon couldn't have caused the death of Paul Bailey. He hadn't pointed this out to Commander Mitchell, but couldn't believe he hadn't seen the report. Adding to the confusion was the anonymous note he had received advising him to look in the lockers of those policemen who formed part of the DSU. That was what he had been doing on this Sunday, rather than watching television. He had found a staggering array of weapons in the men's lockers at Hackney police station, all of which could be classified as offensive and illegal if found in the possession of civilians. In one there had been a flat metal bar, a small metal cosh, a stock whip and a regulation long police truncheon issued to the mounted police; the owner of this locker was the driver of Uniform Carrier G/59. Sergeant Robert Wolf, who had been in charge of that vehicle, had an American police night stick, a Bowie knife, a flick knife and a brass knuckle duster; Inspector Hern, who was in command of those two DSU units, had three wooden pick-axe helves and three regulation police truncheons. PC Philip Westbrook had a sap, which had been a present from a policeman he had stayed with in America, and a length of fireman's hose filled with sand. Two other members of the DSU had similar lengths of sand-filled canvas hose. One had a replica .38 Smith and Wesson, another a set of knuckle dusters and a length of lead pipe, while another had a home-made mace – a pick-axe helve with nails driven into the end. None of them had been particularly concerned about these discoveries; only PC Westbrook had panicked slightly and tried to slip the cosh into his coat pocket. Having been seen by DI Joe Russell, he was asked to turn out his pockets. His explanation was that he hadn't wanted to lose this treasured present from an American colleague. It had all been carefully collected up and labelled, signed for and consigned to the forensic lab for examination. In order to avoid any more stonewalling, Bentham had had all those officers in Uniform Carriers G/59 and G/60 stood down from duty and made available at the station until further notice. He knew there was a lot more lengthy questioning to be done before something like the truth emerged.

The veiled warning from Julian Brind at the Home Office – about the outcome of this inquiry and how it might be used to provoke the animal rights movement into acts of lawnessness – echoed in his head. He considered Helen and her involvement, how she might be compromised if things went according to Julian Brind's scenario. Eventually he would need to resolve the dilemma her illegal activities caused him. All he was doing at the moment was avoiding it.

'What are you thinking, Jack?' she asked, disturbing him. He shook his head, dismissing the question, signalling he wouldn't say rather than it wasn't important. 'Work?' she concluded.

Later that evening, in bed, the animal rights issue came up again, when Helen broached the question of the raids out in Surrey.

'They did quite a lot of damage, didn't they?'

'I don't think so. The police were waiting for them. How do you think that was, Jack?'

'There's only one way. You've got a grass in your camp. That's how the police come by most of their intelligence information.'

'But why weren't they stopped before they got in?'

'That's a prevention. They might nick them for conspiracy, but that doesn't look as impressive as a collar in the commission of a crime.'

'They're not criminals,' Helen insisted.

'Helen, there's no Robin Hood – or Scarlet Pimpernel – law. They were breaking and entering with intent to steal or do criminal damage.'

'Do you know what experiments are done at that laboratory?'

'Only what I read in the newspaper – essential medical experiments.'

Helen laughed, but it rang hollow when she considered the medical propaganda that the media published and the public swallowed. 'Making the future safe for our children! It's

178

psychological and behavioural research. Monkeys are operated on to produce brain lesions. They are then observed for their responses to different stimuli, such as colour, light, noise, food. They remove sections of the monkey's brain to observe its behaviour patterns. Psychologists study the effects of deliberately-induced stress caused by social isolation. The list is endless, Jack.'

Helen listed other experiments that were essential to nothing but the scientists' intellectual curiosity, until she felt Jack Bentham understood enough of what went on there; then she fell silent. The silence went on for a long time, accentuated for Helen by her still unvoiced request and fear of being rejected. She wondered if he had gone to sleep, and a part of her hoped he had.

'Jack? Can you help them at all?' she asked. The silence continued a while longer. 'Jack?'

'I doubt it. Even if they were on my manor.'

'They're not criminals, Jack. They aren't.'

'I accept that they're well-meaning, Helen, just as you have to accept that they were acting outside the law. What they were doing is criminal.' He wanted to tell her to get out from under, not to let herself become more actively involved, but found himself hesitating.

'You should see how those poor creatures are treated. How they're kept is bad enough. The way they cry out when tortured. They're like children. They have the same principle of life, Jack, the same feelings. Human speech is all that separates us from animals. Would we dare commit these atrocities if they spoke our language, communicated to us in the same way? Of course we wouldn't.'

Glancing over at her, Jack Bentham saw she was crying, and he thought it might be easier to tell her to stop breathing as stop struggling to gain rights for animals. 'I'll do what I can,' he said quietly, and leaned over and kissed her on the eyes, tasting the salt of her tears. 'I'll have a word with the governor of the nick where they were charged.' He made no promise beyond that.

Helen put her arms around him and held him, feeling secure at that moment, as if believing this man could make everything safe in her world, just as she had once believed her father could. She no longer believed that.

In exchange for his offer of help, she told him about their

179

releasing the medical report on Paul Bailey, not because Jack Bentham had demanded this, but because she felt she owed it to him. Then he told her in confidence about the arms found in the policemen's lockers.

'So one of those bastards did murder Paul,' she declared sitting up in bed angrily.

'It doesn't mean that at all, Helen.'

'You saw the medical report, it suggested he was sand-bagged.'

'Just because they had illegal weapons in their lockers doesn't mean they took them on duty, or used them.'

'Come off it, Jack. What do you think they were for, decoration!'

'That's for me to find out. And I will, Helen, I promise you.'

Releasing the medical report was only important in that it slightly pre-empted him. He doubted if the press would take much notice of it without knowing about the locker weapons. Possibly policemen on the DSUs knew about the police forensic report and were so confident of Commander Mitchell's support that they didn't even feel the need to dump their weapons. Either that or this new breed of policeman was completely committed to thuggery, regardless of the consequences. He hoped Helen would keep quiet about what he told her in case he needed to leak this weapons information at some stage in the future, in order to create a crisis to effect his own end.

The chief superintendent at Guildford police station, where the raiders of the research lab had been charged, was surprised by Jack Bentham's arrival first thing on Monday morning, but cordial. Bentham had found difficulty making time to go out to Surrey and had put off a couple of meetings, but was pleased to be away from the Yard – and the visit from Commander Mitchell that he was certain would result from his search of those DSU policemen's lockers.

'What's your interest in these animal rights people, Jack?' Chief Superintendent Jim Sloman asked. 'I wouldn't have thought there was much in it for Criminal Intelligence.'

'Probably nothing. Our drugs intelligence unit had a rumour that primate stations were being used to import heroin,' Bentham told him. The information had come from Helen Daniels, but he wasn't convinced, and it didn't explain why a DCS would go out visiting rather than a DS. Jim Sloman waited for more.

'The animal rights movement is getting increasingly militant. The Home Office, without being seen to give in to them, would like to try and defuse the situation, bring them back from the brink, so to speak.' That was, in fact, the opposite of the true position if he had read Julian Brind aright.

'They haven't sent any smoke signals this way, Jack,' Chief Superintendent Sloman said.

'They're a pretty cagey lot. You don't know what signals they're putting up half the time. I suppose I'm it.' He didn't know if Sloman had any Home-Office contacts whom he might ring. Bentham could have found himself in trouble for what he was doing, and he wasn't even sure why he was doing it, other than his objecting to being manipulated by either the Home Office, media propaganda or Helen Daniels. He was determined to see for himself, make up his own mind. That was especially important in view of his investigation into the death of Paul Bailey. It was too easy to dismiss animal rightists as an unruly mob that needed to be contained or treated as law-breakers; the rightness of their cause, if it could be determined, had some bearing on the way they were dealt with, even when they broke the law. The unthinking way was simply to take the line that Parliament made the laws and all policemen had to do was enforce them, regardless.

'Any chance we could take a look at the research station they broke into?' Bentham asked.

'This isn't to do with any complaint, Jack, is it?' the chief superintendent said warily. 'One we haven't been informed about? The arrests were all straightforward.'

'I don't know of any complaint. How did you come to be there? Did you get a tip-off?'

'One of our lads in the CID has a well-placed grass.' He hesitated and saw Jack Bentham's look. 'A homosexual who works for one of the animal rights organizations. He was caught importuning young lads. He bought his liberty with a few animal activists. He's given several useful tip-offs. A pity he wasn't a bank robber. All we had to do was wait for them. They were pretty pissed off at being caught, of course, but apart from one or two incidents they behaved themselves.'

At the research station security was surprisingly brisk, and Bentham wondered how they had effected it so quickly after the raid, especially with the weekend intervening; then he realised that this was their regular line in security. Their need of such high-level protection made him curious. Was the animal rights movement that effective, or were the researchers so sensitive about what they were doing that they were afraid of it being seen by the public, or *were* they illegally importing heroin?

Bentham wasn't long in making up his mind when he and Jim Sloman were shown around by the institute's director, Dr Peter Strange. He was a young, urbane, besuited PR man, who expressed great concern for the welfare of his primates – mostly *cynomolgus macaque* monkeys about two feet in height – and likened them to family. None of which convinced Jack Bentham that these animals weren't suffering, nor from the ashen look on his fleshy face did it impress Jim Sloman. He was the type of copper who reacted in a second to a situation and justified it at leisure. The housing alone was enough for Bentham to appreciate the rightness of Helen's case, if not justify her breaking the law. The monkeys were in small, metal cages, without community areas or play areas – assuming any were in a fit state to play. Few seemed to be, most looked rather withdrawn and reminded Bentham of a cruelty-to-children case he had come across as a constable: five children all under seven were cowering in a bedroom littered with faeces when he had broken into the flat; they had recoiled when he approached to reach them out of their mess. There were four dozen or so monkeys here, some in cages with barred floors through which faecal matter dropped, others on wire-mesh floors where droppings had built up – they obviously hadn't been cleaned in a while. A number of monkeys cowered in the corners of their cages as the three men approached, eyeing them suspiciously. Some were unable to see them at all as their eyelids were sewn together. A marmoset monkey lay unmoving and didn't stir when Bentham tapped the cage door.

'Don't put your fingers through there!' Dr Strange said in alarm, then smiled when the danger was over. 'They're vicious little bastards. They'd bite your finger off.'

'Is he dead?' Bentham said.

'Probably asleep, they're lazy beggars some of them,' the director said, ushering them towards the door. 'It pongs a bit, I'm afraid. All this activity with these lunatics breaking in rather put us out of our routine. Normally this would be spotlessly clean.'

'Did the raiders get in here?' Bentham asked.

'Yes, they did,' Dr Strange said. 'They upset the animals terribly.'

'They were collared before they did much damage,' Chief Superintendent Sloman said.

'The psychological damage to the animals is immeasurable,' the director tried.

'Can we see where else they got to, doctor?'

'Well, I'm not sure ... we have experiments going on. It's better if they're not disturbed. We do like to keep a sterile field and not have people traipsing in and out.'

'If it is possible, Dr Strange. Mr Bentham has come down from Scotland Yard especially to help out on this case. He's looking to bag the entire ring of animal activists,' Jim Sloman said, surprising Bentham, who said nothing. He wondered if Sloman was affected in the same way by what he saw. Nothing lessened that feeling, when, after putting on white overalls and rubber boots, they got into the labs.

The distress caused to the primates by their housing didn't compare with that produced in the laboratory. Monkeys with slightly odd, unco-ordinated movements were trying to operate a set of reward and punishment levers and buttons in a large, smooth-walled cage. When they got the wrong button or lever they received an electric shock which sent them careening and squealing around the cage. Occasionally a monkey would creep back to the control panel and try to find the right action for a reward. Researchers were noting the effect – how many times the monkey got the wrong lever or button, how few rewards it received. One monkey had 'Crap' tattooed across its forehead.

'Is that what he's called?' Jim Sloman asked a technician.

The researcher, who was in white, laughed, 'It does.'

It was the defensive laugh of a man who knew he was wrong-footed, Jack Bentham realised. The degradation here was similar to that gaolers sometimes inflicted on their prisoners, and he found it strange that these researchers, who, if only by educational advantage, were less primitive, should degrade their captives. He assumed the process was similar to that which his father had experienced when he came to kill his first cow as an apprentice butcher. Initially he hadn't been able to do it, but had overcome his revulsion for the act by starting to hate that cow. Then what he did became easier.

'It's the Latin description of the monkey,' Dr Strange explained, and moved them on.

Bentham said nothing when they saw one monkey with 'Moron' on its forehead, and another called 'Lucre', but remembered the words of George Bernard Shaw, whom he had read at university: 'Anybody who is prepared to experiment on animals would not hesitate to lie about it.'

'What's happening here?' Bentham tried to make his question sound like idle curiosity.

'These primates were trained over a period of time to carry out various intelligence tests. Then they were operated on and brain-damaged. We're now testing to ascertain whether they can remember what they have previously learned. We vary the brain damage and measure the degree of unlearning.'

'Wouldn't it be more beneficial to make clinical observations on victims of brain damage?'

Dr Strange laughed throatily. 'It might, if we knew what they had previously learned, and were allowed to experiment on them.'

'What are those you arrested being charged with?' Bentham asked as they drove away from the research station. He knew, having made it his business to find out, but wanted to see if Jim Sloman would offer anything.

'A bit grim, Jack. Makes you think twice about some of those kids protesting.'

'D'you want to take on the possible heroin connection with the import of these monkeys? Now would seem like a good time. Maybe your inside contact could get something.'

'We'll give it a go. He's smooth enough, our Dr Strange. You wouldn't question him twice if he was fronting that. I'll alert the CID. You'll be sending something down?'

'I'll have someone from our drugs intelligence unit contact you. That would be a very worthwhile result,' Bentham said, finding satisfaction at the prospect of that creepy doctor being involved in smuggling heroin sewn into the chest cavities of monkeys.

Chief Superintendent Sloman glanced over at him. 'We could slip those kids through on illegal entry, drop out criminal damage and conspiracy – they only forced open a couple of cages. Seeing the state of some of those cages, who could tell?'

The co-operation from Sloman made the trip out to Surrey

worthwhile and Bentham was pleased for Helen, but decided not to tell her; nor would he give her the name of the plant the police had made in the activist organisation that carried out the raid. It was better that she didn't know that he could influence what charges went in; and as for the plant, there was a tradition of protecting informants, for without them the police were less than effective. The tradition was frequently broken when policemen traded their grasses, either for money or for more worthwhile relationships with grassed villains.

There was a particularly bright DS on the drugs intelligence unit of C11 called Gwyn Gee – or Gee-Gee as he was known. Gee-Gee had a degree in psychology, which was always referred to by his less educated colleagues as a degree in knitting. Bentham wondered if his own degree was referred to similarly.

'You want me to go to work at this lab, sir?' Gwyn Gee asked when Bentham suggested the job to him.

'If you can find an opening. It won't be easy – they're very jumpy down there.'

'Who would I liaise with, the local CID?'

'You'd better send anything up here first,' Bentham glanced at the DI who ran the drugs unit and was in on the briefing. 'We'll pass it on to Surrey.'

Bentham had some expectation that DS Gee would run to earth anything worthwhile on the drugs import rumour, if there was anything in it.

Among his messages on his return to the Yard was one from Commander Mitchell and one from Terry Sneed, who had requested to see him out in Swanley. Bentham guessed he would be looking for help, and thought it ironical that Sneed should think he was the man to help him. Sneed had been at it a long time, but so had a lot of others in the job, Bentham reasoned, policemen who, unlike Sneed, weren't particularly good thief-takers. He would certainly get around to seeing him, but not today. Nor did he respond to Commander Mitchell, but went instead to see his governor, before going out to Hackney to resume interviewing policemen from the DSU.

'What help had you planned to give David Lane, Jack?' Commander Wiseman said, opening a packet of diabetic chocolate, believing that because it was less fattening than regular chocolate he could eat any amount. He didn't offer Bentham any.

'Whatever we can. He's given more than enough names.' Bentham didn't add that a lot were policemen, or that his name had been included, feeling it would have been impolite. 'I'd like to let everything go, so he's really on our side when he gets up in the box.'

'Ordinarily I'd've said yes, Jack. But these are no longer ordinary times. I'd have to get the DAC to talk to the DPP. Why don't we wait and see what comes from the raids you're planning? We'll know what sort of bargain we're getting then.'

'I promised him I'd try and secure his deal for him.'

'Can't you just leave him on a promise? I mean, either way, Jack, he's not going to be let go,' Wiseman said.

Bentham shook his head. 'I might want him to confront some of the villains he's putting in it. Where I make that sort of promise, Ernie, I try and keep it. That's how he stays working for me.'

'Fuck me, Jack,' Wiseman said, rising angrily out of his chair and grabbing a fat file from the open drawer of a filing cabinet. 'Someone't got to end up in the frame. Most of these villains the Wiltshire lot picked up are looking for a deal. The commissioner's saying it's got to stop – I expect the DPP is saying it to him, and the Attorney in turn is saying it to the DPP. Even Terry Sneed's sending messages up here that he wants to see me. It's not to ask how my diet's going.'

'I got a message as well,' Bentham told him.

'Then you go and fucking well see him. I'm not. Every villain who's ever nicked nowadays looks for a result through informing. Where's all that old-fashioned honour among thieves?'

'You tell me,' Bentham said, feeling very pissed off. He would work something out for David Lane, even if he had to raise the matter at tomorrow's planning meeting with the ACC, Peter Vyvyan.

'Chief superintendent, have you got a minute?'

DCS Bulmer was by the vending machine on the wide bridge that connected the Tower Block to the Victoria Block at the fifth floor. Bentham was heading for the Victoria Block lifts to return to the fourth floor, but gave Bulmer his minute.

He was about to insert a ring-pull from a coke can, which Assistant Chief Constable Alan Leeper had discovered fitted these machines perfectly. It was a small enough way to get back at the Met for all the indignities they had to suffer.

Bentham came along the adjacent corridor. 'I'm not getting much help nicking villains. I might as well help you nick policemen.'

'How's your investigation out at Hackney?'

A smile crept across Bentham's face. He wasn't going to be drawn on that. 'Everyone's being very co-operative.'

'I heard you found a cache of weapons they'd been using.'

That surprised Bentham. 'I'm not sure that they used any of them.'

'Can I get you a coffee?' Bulmer offered, pushing in the ring-pull. He glanced at Bentham, unconcerned about him seeing this peculiar coinage. 'We arrested DCI Sneed. A very busy policeman that.'

'He's turned in some good results,' Bentham said.

'He's asked to see you. He's been making all sorts of threats about what he'll do if he's held much longer. He said if he goes he'll take as many with him as he can. I think he's looking for his superiors to bail him out.'

'Has he put his hand up to something?' Bentham ventured. It didn't sound like Terry Sneed, but he knew what pressure a long time in a cell could bring.

'My guess is he knows quite a few corrupt policemen,' Bulmer said, avoiding the question.

'What does he want from me, absolution?' Bentham quipped.

'He'd take it from anyone he thinks could give it. He's asked to see a number of senior policemen, including Assistant Commissioner Vyvyan. They all turned him down.'

Unease crept over Jack Bentham as he wondered what he might be left holding if Peter Vyvyan was involved in the firm that Sneed now expected to respond and help him. He considered Bulmer frankly, realising that this man obviously believed he had something to fear from what Sneed might say. 'Swanley's not exactly handy.'

'Don't we know it.' Bulmer's response suggested a good deal of inconvenience. 'He's not going anywhere, if you decide to see him . . .' He threw his unfinished coffee into the litter bin and went off along the corridor, leaving Jack Bentham to wonder if that remark was an oblique warning about Peter Vyvyan.

'How's your hand, Frank?' Bentham asked with a smile when he stepped across the corridor into the DCI's office.

'Does he want to add something to his statement?' David

Lane's statement already ran to over six hundred pages, all of which Frank Burroughs had taken down in longhand over the past four days.

'I can't say I got him much help,' Bentham said, 'Ernie Wiseman's getting very jumpy.' They exchanged a look, both remembering where his name cropped up.

'Well,' Frank Burroughs said philosophically, 'we might not need him any more.'

Bentham shrugged, remembering his promise. 'We'll see. Organize the raids on all the villains he gave us, Frank. And anyone on the computer who is connected with the targets. It's going to be fairly big.'

'Who do you want to do it? Local CID?'

'It'll have to be with this size of operation. We'd better invite the Robbery Squad, if there are enough of them. Fill in with uniform branch if you have to. No one is to have any of the targets yet. I'll do the briefing with you downstairs at one a.m. I'll be at Hackney for most of the afternoon.'

Bentham didn't get to leave before Commander Mitchell rang him. 'Didn't you get my message, Jack?' he asked.

'I've been out all morning.'

'I promised my lads immunity over Paul Bailey's death,' he said. 'They had a legal order to use their truncheons. They were in a riot situation.'

'I can't say it's helping much, Doug. No one's put his hand up.'

'Of course not. I promised them, Jack. Do what you can.'

When he had put the phone down, Bentham thought about his own promise to David Lane. Policemen didn't readily do the bidding of other policemen any more, they took sides instead. This was the result of the new kind of policing required for public-order situations; it eroded those traditional loyalties that policemen had previously felt towards their collective family. They had become responsible for maintaining a political idea. He began to understand that this was why Paul Bailey had come to be killed. Policemen no longer simply responded to the rule of law, or acted within the control of the civil servant, but, as they became more polarized individual units like the DSU or SPG – or even the Robbery Squad – became a law unto themselves.

*   *   *

'Which of you struck the first blow after you and the men directly under your command piled out of Uniform Carrier G/60 at the junction of Well Street and Tudor Grove?' Jack Bentham asked, reading from one of the many statements that were spread over the table before him in the interview room at Hackney police station.

'I don't understand, sir,' Sergeant Robert Wolf replied, giving himself time to think. He found it unnerving to be brought back to an interview, given a seat, left in silence for all of five minutes, which to him felt like five hours, then have that sort of question put to him. He was worrying about what had been found in his locker, and what he had said when it had been found. He couldn't remember anything of his early statement.

'It's fairly straightforward. You got out of the van, to be faced by an angry mob. What did you do?'

'We set about dispersing them, sir,' Sergeant Wolf said.

'Isn't that what they were already doing – dispersing?' Bentham reached for another file.

Anticipating him, DI Joe Russell pulled out one of the witness statements and passed it to his chief.

'Like any number of other witnesses interviewed, this one said, "We were dispersing, making our way out of the area. The mounted police had charged us in Ricketts Way and were stopping us turning back to the laboratory. Most of us had had enough, what with the police tactics outside the laboratories, with all the arrests and people who were hurt. We were going home. We were scared and wanted to get right away when we saw the two police vans form a road block in Well Street. We were trapped. We just wanted to get away. We turned into Tudor Grove to get away." How did you set about dispersing these people, Sergeant Wolf?' Bentham pushed the statement back onto the file.

'But they were animal rights protesters,' Sergeant Wolf declared.

'Most of them. That doesn't make them any less truthful than policemen, does it?'

'But they're not one of us, sir.' He thought for a moment, then said, 'We followed them into Tudor Grove. There was a detail of policemen waiting at the other end. The side streets had been cordoned off.'

189

'Your vans had formed a road block in Well Street so in fact stopping them dispersing?'

'Well, yes, but not completely. It was on the order of Inspector Hern who was in Uniform Carrier G/59. There was room to let the demonstrators through in ones and twos.'

'In an orderly fashion?' Bentham prompted.

'That was the idea, but they were anything but orderly. A real rioting mob.'

'That's what you saw them as,' Bentham said.

'That's what they were. There was no way they were going to respond to a reasonable order to disperse. No way.'

'So the order was given to draw truncheons and disperse them? Who gave that order?'

'I don't know, sir. I'm not sure anyone did. It was one of those situations where you had to think for yourself, and decide instantly.'

'At what point did you decide to draw your truncheon, Sergeant Wolf?'

'I don't know, sir. I think it was when I saw a colleague being attacked.'

Bentham picked up the three different statements from this officer, all of which carried discrepancies. 'He was being attacked by Paul Bailey?' he said, as if reading that from the page.

That confused the sergeant further. 'I'm not sure, sir. It could have been.'

'Which colleague was he attacking?'

'It's difficult to say, sir. I think it was Constable Westbrook.'

'You went to his aid, with truncheon drawn?' The question elicited a nod in response. 'So was it you who first struck Paul Bailey?'

'No, sir, I didn't. I'm not absolutely certain it was Bailey.'

'You seemed fairly certain in the first statement you made after the incident.' He reached up the statement in question. '"Paul Bailey launched a furious and unprovoked attack on PC Westbrook with the placard he was carrying. I, along with two of my colleagues, went to his assistance." It's what you said. Even though it seems that Bailey might have had his fingers broken when he and others were being cleared from around the laboratory area. According to civilian witnesses, he had been hanging onto a drain grid and his fingers were

190

stamped on. The post-mortem showed his fingers were broken.'

'The situation was very confused, sir, with the rioters coming down at us like that, hurling sticks and stones and bottles.'

'I appreciate that, sergeant,' Bentham allowed. 'But your conflicting statements don't seem to be leading us out of this confusion. The majority of witnesses seem to imagine they were fleeing from you rather than coming towards you. That would be consistent with Paul Bailey's wounds. However, what you are sure of is that it wasn't you who struck Bailey, with either your truncheon or any other implement?'

'No, sir, it wasn't.'

'What implements did you have on you besides the truncheon?'

Sergeant Wolf waited, uncertain about that question or how to answer it, as anxiety shot acid into his stomach. He felt slightly sick, although he had realised that the matter of the unauthorized weapons found in their lockers would be raised. 'None, sir,' he said, his mind momentarily black, unable to remember if his previous statement contradicted that. Unfortunately, they had been separated after the locker search and there hadn't been time to compare stories before statements were taken.

'There was nothing left behind in the van?'

'No, sir. They were just mementoes, sir, that's all.'

'What are an American police night stick, a Bowie knife, a flick knife and knuckle dusters mementoes of?'

Sergeant Wolf said nothing, but wondered if this was going to cost him his job, despite what Commander Mitchell had said.

'Fortunately for you, sergeant, none of those weapons were used on Paul Bailey, and none of the other protesters who were injured and made specific complaints bore identifiable wounds. We'll see what we find as we progress. We are going to progress on this, sergeant. We're going to come back to it again and again, and eventually we'll get it right. Tell Constable West-brook we want to see him.'

'You were a bit hard on him, guv,' DI Russell commented after the uniformed sergeant went out. 'He is a policeman, after all.' Bentham looked at his aide, but said nothing.

The prospect of this inquiry going on and on daunted Sergeant Wolf, and the coroner's inquest would extend it further. He knew procedure well enough to know that the more time and money that were spent on any investigation, the greater would be the pressure to produce a result. He didn't fancy being that result, and would have preferred to clear things up quickly and be done with it. He understood not at all why so much fuss was being made over the death of a protester. The way he and his kind behaved on the streets, they were no better than animals. All they wanted was a total breakdown in law and order, anarchy. He felt like a veteran for having spent so much time on picket duty with the miners. He expected some sort of gratitude for his contribution there, and saw no reason why he should have to put up with this nonsense; nor any reason why he or any of his colleagues should be made scapegoats when they had done what everyone wanted them to do: remove the rabble from the streets and restore some sort of order so that decent people could go about their business unimpeded.

He went with his angry thoughts up to the recreation room, where his colleagues from the DSU were waiting, not knowing which of them would be called for an interview next.

'That bastard's going to nick us all,' Sergeant Wolf announced as he came in. There was a game of snooker in progress, but no one was concentrating on it. Everyone was awaiting his return. 'He wants you again, Phil.'

'What, me?' PC Westbrook said, throwing his cue onto the table. 'He tries to nick anyone he'll get my resignation along with half the unit's.' He stormed out.

'What's the story, Bob?' Inspector Hern asked, as if everyone didn't already know.

'Who used what weapon to whack that protester?'

There was silence in the room, fear permeated the atmosphere: regret that each of them hadn't emptied their lockers after Bailey's death, and anxiety that any one of them might not hold out under interrogation – it gnawed at them inexorably.

'If I was to have a bet on the outcome of this inquiry,' Bentham said, staring across the table at this hostile policeman, 'I'd say you were going to carry the can, as it seems you struck Paul Bailey the fatal blow.'

'I don't think so, sir,' PC Westbrook said, avoiding his look. 'If I'd been quicker off the mark I'd have got him with my truncheon, which I had a legal order to draw. I'd've prevented him attacking me.'

'I expect he was inflicting real damage with his broken fingers.'

'I don't know anything about that, sir.'

'Who gave you the order to draw truncheons?' Bentham asked.

'I can't say, sir. I mean, the situation was very confusing. We were in a riot situation.'

'But you are sure it was a legal order?'

The large man opposite, whose uniform was showing pressure at the seams, hesitated, then said, 'Commander Mitchell said it was, sir.'

'Commander Mitchell wasn't there, was he?'

'With the greatest respect, sir, nor were you,' Phil Westbrook said, knowing it could go down on his record as showing a bad attitude. He would loathe that as it went against all he felt his being a policeman stood for. 'We were in a riot situation there, sir. We had to deal with it as best we could.'

'By coshing the rioters at random?'

'No, sir, that's absolutely not true.'

'But you did take your coshes out on duty with you.'

'No, sir. They remained where they're always kept. In my locker.'

'That's not the information we've been given. We've been told that on numerous occasions you had taken your sap on patrol and kept it in your truncheon pocket.'

'No, sir,' Westbrook said, with a slight tremor in his voice that didn't pass unnoticed.

'You have the weapons, it's logical to take them out and use them.'

'I don't think do, sir. They were presents from a fellow policeman in America.'

'Does it not strike you as odd, constable, that all your colleagues on the DSU, without exception, had in their lockers a range of weapons that would get the average kid on the street two years?'

The PC thought about that, then said, 'No, sir. We deal with violent situations.'

'You deal with them violently,' Bentham ventured, feeling he wouldn't get far with this man, despite instinct telling him that Westbrook was the most likely candidate. No single piece of usable evidence supported that contention, not even the statement from one of the other members of the DSU who had said that he sometimes took his coshes out with him. Neither the sap nor the sewn fire hose full of sand could be forensically connected with Paul Bailey. Bentham guessed that the one that had been used to kill Bailey had been disposed of.

'There's no denying that Paul Bailey was struck on the back of the head while trying to flee from the trap that Uniform Carriers G/59 and G/60 completed in Well Street.'

'But not by a policeman, sir. Anyway, we all had truncheons drawn.'

'Then who do you think struck him?'

'I'd say at a guess it was one of the other protesters.'

'Even though they were running from the police?' Bentham asked.

That was the best he got from this officer, one more slight contradiction over what his colleagues were saying. Shifting from riot to protesters retreating might not have seemed like much, and possibly even wasn't much in the circumstances of that demonstration. But it further confirmed to Bentham that these officers were lying in order to hide the truth and spare themselves disciplinary action at best, a possible murder charge at worst. He pushed on until late into the night, then had to leave for the briefing at the Yard. He had made only minimal progress, but he was convinced it was in the right direction.

16

There was an air of excitement in the fifth-floor lecture theatre which doubled as briefing room when large numbers were involved. There were about a hundred and sixty tip-up chairs, but insufficient to seat everyone. Detectives from various squads drifted in noisily, found seats and colleagues they hadn't seen for a while; caught up on news, or speculated about this raid. Some thought it related to the Wiltshire police investigations, and resented being there. The time was a little before one o'clock and none of these men had been to bed – most had been in after-hours pubs. Some had had the foresight to eat; others hadn't risked it, knowing what tension did to their bowels. There was no drink or food around now.

Some two hundred detectives had gathered in the room by the time Bentham arrived with DCI Frank Burroughs and a superintendent from the Robbery Squad, who was going to act as his deputy co-ordinator. Bentham was tired and wasn't sure that he could stay the course, but hoped that he might perk up when the results of arrests began to come through. Most of the detectives loathed those long hours waiting in cars, but the moment something went off and adrenalin started pumping, then almost to a man they loved it. The capture and bringing in of the suspect for interrogation was always an anti-climax, and often left policemen stranded emotionally, strung out, not knowing how to wind down. That was the cause of a lot of the violence in police cells.

'For those of you who don't know me,' Bentham said, stopping the burble of voices, 'I'm Chief Superintendent Bentham. I'm going to co-ordinate these raids tonight. That's Superintendent Mike Embley of the Robbery Squad, Chief Superintendent Ray from Sussex and Chief Inspector Frank Burroughs. There are a lot of you here. But then we have sixty-eight targets, so we're going to pick up local CID officers, and some uniform branch if they're needed. They will be briefed by individual squad officers when you've been given your targets. I know there's been a lot of speculation about these raids being part of Operation Bad Apple that is being conducted by the Wiltshire CID, but they are nothing at all to do with that investigation.

195

The targets you will be hitting are villains who have been involved in major robberies, and are planning further robberies, which is why we're moving against everyone tonight. An officer from C11 will be going out with each of the target squads; they have been briefed by Mr Burroughs, and they in turn will brief their teams individually. But in the best tradition of C11 they will hang back and be the last in, if in at all.' That brought a ripple of laughter around the room.

Bentham waited for it to fade. 'One or two general remarks. Some of the targets are going to be pretty desperate. They're not going to like it when you feel their collars, so I want every one of them, and I mean every one of them, cuffed to the arresting officer from the moment you nick them. A lot of these targets are dangerous, and will have shooters. Don't worry about it, so will you. Just worry about getting the first shot in.'

The laughter that erupted Bentham recognized as a nervous response to the uncertainty of their position; it reminded him of that lab technician's laughter out in Surrey this morning.

'I want one officer from each squad to ring in immediately after the collar. When they're nicked, let us know here. Radio silence is to be maintained at all times. No chatter on the air unless it's a real emergency and you're in serious trouble. And you could be. One more thing: I don't want any phone calls going out of here from now on. Not to anyone, for any reason. I don't care if you've left the gas on or your old Mum is in hospital. I will treat communication made with anyone outside before the bodies are in as a grave disciplinary offence.' That warning had become increasingly necessary. But there was still no guarantee that any one of the targets wouldn't get a bell. Corruption was often as resourceful as it was stupid, and the resourceful policeman found ways around an obstacle.

All that remained was for him to wish them good luck, and he did so with all sincerity.

'Let's be sensible how we go about this,' Frank Burroughs said when he did his part of the general briefing. 'The way some of you go about searching premises you couldn't find the kitchen, much less the swag that might be hidden in the frozen-food compartment of the fridge. As soon as you lay hands on chummy, get that search under way and take him into every room you search or they'll scream fit-up. Be methodical, don't take stuff out of drawers and cupboards and throw it every-where, then find yourself having to move it to continue the search. All of you will have tape measures, and what you're going to do is measure the outside of the houses, then the inside rooms to make sure a foot or two hasn't been turned into a cavity to hold swag. We're looking for a lot of money. Some of it will have been spent, but a lot will have been carefully hidden about their homes. Floorboards – rip the fuckers up if they look remotely like they've been disturbed, especially if any are screwed down. Don't just roll back the corners of the carpets and lino, get it all back. They'll have hidden the wedge, or their floor safe, in the middle of the floor. Don't forget those freezers. Get everything out, break open packets – that's where the silver bullion was that the Squad missed out at Essex last year – all of it laid along the bottom of the freezer floor, a new floor put in and food packed on top of it. Freezer cabinets have thick insulated walls also. Take out the fibreglass – a villain could get a lot of banknotes in there instead. Remember, you've virtually got to rip these places apart. Don't do unnecessary damage, but don't leave anything untouched where there's the remotest chance of swag being hidden. One other thing: if you make phone calls from the house, which you will to phone in, either pay for the calls or reverse the charge – these poor fuckers won't have a brad by the time we've done.' There was more laughter. 'Right, are there any queries?'

'Are all the suspects coming back here?' a voice from the body of the room asked.

'No. The provincial police liaison officers attached to C11 will give you your destinations. There'll be three locations where the bodies will be taken to, but we don't want a troop of bent lawyers turning up to worry the life out of us. It would be a good idea if we all set our watches to the same time, so you get in more or less at once.' He glanced at the large electric clock on the wall.

The detectives began to organize among themselves: how they would approach the target house, how they would gain entrance, and in what order they would go in so there was no one between the armed detective and the targets.

Nervous tension started to build from the moment Jack Bentham wished them good luck, and was only fleetingly relieved by the activity of finding their squads, then later getting to their cars. Seventy-three vehicles finally left the underground car park at the Yard to drive out to targets as far apart as Bristol and Sidcup in Kent. Time had to be allowed for those with upwards of a two-hour drive to get in place, which meant those with closer targets had more waiting around to do. By 4.00 a.m. everyone was in position. The sky was dense and heavy with rain that had been falling for the past two days. This sort of darkness suited the detectives – it covered their activities, while the rain helped mask any noise they made approaching targets' houses.

No amount of rain would have masked the sound of DI Les Norman's axe swinging against the door of a house on an estate in Abbey Wood in South East London. As the finely-honed blade bit deep, Norman wondered fleetingly if he had the right door. Every house on this council estate looked identical, especially in the small hours of a dark, wet morning. He could have delegated this job, but actually enjoyed smashing doors down. As the axe was wrenched out a fourteen-pound sledge-hammer, swung by a local uniform man now in plain clothes, landed in the same place, sending shock waves through the house as the wood burst away from the lock and the door crashed open.

The door was caught on the rebound and detectives raced up the stairs, having drawn their .38 Smith and Wessons. The special .38 cartridges they were loaded with would enable them to shoot a suspect through a door. The local man went with them, while Les Norman went through to the rear to admit the two detectives, who as it turned out were watching the wrong house.

Denis Rattigan knew it was on top the moment the door burst open. No one other than the police came calling in this way. He stood frozen on the landing in underpants and vest, his three-year-old son in his arms – the child had woken in fright and Rattigan had gone to comfort him.

'Put the fucking child away!' the leading detective shouted, his gun levelled at Rattigan.

The child rubbed its eyes, then started to cry.

'Who are they, Denis? Den, who are they?' A woman in the doorway screamed. She knew as well as her husband who they were.

The detective swung round, cocking his gun nervously, and

glanced back at Rattigan, deciding that neither was armed or dangerous.

Rattigan, a tallish, stooped man in his mid-thirties with thinning light brown hair, set the child down and patted him towards his mother.

'Go to your mum, Josh. There's a good boy. Go to your mum. Go on, there's a good boy.'

Before the child had reached his mother, the detective grabbed Rattigan, snapped a bracelet on his wrist, and firmly attached the other end to himself.

'Denis, what's going on?' Mrs Rattigan said, scooping up her son.

'It's all right, Reet,' he replied. 'Go in the bedroom, put some clothes on. Go on. Go on, take Josh. Make some tea. Gonna be a long morning.'

The other police officers came up the stairs, followed by Les Norman. His presence reminded the DS on the Robbery Squad that he hadn't cautioned the suspect; such niceties often went by unobserved in the excitement.

'Denis Rattigan, we're Robbery Squad officers. Listen carefully to what I have to say. Listen,' the DS remembering the Rule Two Caution as Rattigan's glance went over to Norman. 'I'm arresting you for the robbery of Securicor Ltd at Faversham in Kent, and for conspiring to rob Brinks-Mat at Gatwick airport. You're not obliged to say anything, unless you wish to do so, but what you say may be taken down in writing and given in evidence.' He waited a moment. 'Do you wish to say anything, Den?' The familiarity added to the mockery.

Rattigan shook his head. 'I wouldn't mind putting some clothes on, it's a bit nippy.'

The Robbery Squad DS glanced over at Les Norman, then nodded when he didn't respond.

'What do they want, Den?' his wife asked, appearing at the bedroom door in a jumper and skirt.

'Something about a robbery being plotted up,' he said, suddenly feeling depressed, and wanting to shift the emphasis from Faversham. He had had a decent run of work and earned a fair bit of money. He still had the most of it and was hopeful of it not being found. Rattigan guessed he had been grassed, but no one knew where he had put the money, not even his wife. If the police found it, he would put his hands up and try and get himself some help; if they didn't, there was something worth holding out for.

'We're going to search these premises now, Den,' the DS said from the bedroom doorway where he watched white legs disappear into grey flared jeans, wondering briefly what this villain did with his money. He was a careful dresser himself – spent quite a lot on staying fashionable and paid seven pounds for a haircut. The detective who Rattigan was attached to uncuffed him to allow him to pull on a cheap, nylon rollneck jumber. 'Perhaps you'd like to accompany officers while they search up here, Mrs Rattigan.'

'I'd like to see you all get cancer, that's what,' she said, suddenly angry.

'Leave it out, Reet, they're only doing their job.' The last thing Rattigan wanted to do was upset these policemen. After all, he might need to deal with them.

'We'd like to make a phone call, if we may,' Les Norman said. 'We'll pay for the call.'

It was time to let them know back in the office what had happened.

Awaiting word on the other sixty-seven raids was stressful, and Jack Bentham wasn't able to put his mind to anything else. He wondered how he was going to contain all that might result from these raids, especially if it led deeper into the corrupt heart of the Met. There were only so many things he could keep closed up for so long, and only when other policemen had limited access to that information. If police corruption emerged from this lot there might be pressure on him to turn it over to the Wiltshire CID, despite the resentment felt towards that investigation by the Met heirarchy. That could mean either an indefinite, morale-destroying investigation, or a blanket cover-up. Jack Bentham wasn't sure which would be worse. At one time he might simply have avoided such questions as it wasn't his decision, but, increasingly, the decision was becoming one he couldn't avoid.

As if reading his thoughts, Detective Superintendent Mike Embley said, 'D'you hear anything about Terry Sneed, Jack?'

Bentham glanced round at him, leaning back from the big table, which had eight telephones on it. The co-ordination room was rank with stale tobacco smoke and anti-perspirant. Mike

Embley was making a big contribution to both. 'Only that he's been nicked.'

'You didn't hear how it looks for him?'

'I wouldn't have thought he'd have too many problems,' Bentham said. 'He's asked me for a bit of help. Fuck knows what he thinks I can do.'

'Be handy if someone did something, Jack. He's well liked.'

'Doesn't mean much in the final analysis. No one's rushing forward. He's been asking.'

'I heard he was fitted?'

With a lift of his dark eyebrows, Jack Bentham posed the question: 'Why?'

'A good thief-taker, that's his problem. Bit unorthodox, Jack, a bit swift, but you do the job as best you can. Give me Terry Sneed any day rather than some of the fucking wallys. Fucking uniform carriers. Half the CID can't tie their shoelaces now it's controlled by uniform. That lot would be happy if it disappeared altogether. Then I s'pose it might as well, what with your lot making themselves so busy and computers popping up everywhere. You just send a uniform out with a warrant. You ever see Terry Sneed conduct an interview? I don't look forward to the day when there's a computer with his edge, cunning bastard. Villains end up thanking him.'

'I thought the problem was supposed to be that he let too many buy their liberty, Mike,' Bentham said casually, as if uninformed.

Mike Embley screwed up his mouth and shook his head. 'You've only got to look at his record.'

One of the telephones rang and both turned as Burroughs picked it up. 'Laurence Simons,' he announced, 'he's nicked.'

Bentham marked his co-ordination sheets, as did Embley and Burroughs. Simons was a fairly minor number tonight, one of many who could be done for running flops for villains, supplying cars or handling stolen property. Two more phones rang, and Bentham found no opportunity to come back to his conversation with the superintendent, or none that would have shown something other than a casual interest. The conversation so far did, however, make him decide to visit Terry Sneed, if only to see what sort he was looking for. He could live with being the only senior officer to do so. He had a reason to go.

By five o'clock all sixty-eight calls had been made, and all but two of the suspects arrested. None of them had been brought in as detectives were still searching premises. Having thoroughly searched Denis Rattigan's council house, Les Norman took his men into the garden; there they found a three foot length of rigid plastic wastepipe with one end sealed. It had been hammered into the ground with a rubber stopper bunged in the top end just at ground level and covered by a flower pot. Almost twenty thousand pounds in old notes had been rolled and stuffed along it. This find almost caused Rattigan to crack. That didn't happen until the open bag of plaster found in the garden shed brought them back into the house, where they re-examined all the plaster walls. Eventually, behind new plaster under the sink, they discovered another plastic pipe, this one buried vertically in the wall, with fifteen grand in it.

That was just one result of many. They came in all morning. At seven o'clock Commander Wiseman called in to catch up on the night's events and prepare himself for the press conference that had been called for nine o'clock.

As operational head of Cl1, Jack Bentham had not the same need of a low profile as his officers, who gathered the information to put on the computers, and could have given the press conference himself, but was happy for the commander to cope with it. Wiseman presented the police case well. He was more articulate than a lot of that old school of policemen, even though he hadn't been on one of the special media courses. That was an area where the police, if rather late in the day, were becoming smart: media manipulation. Despite the very clear in-built bias of the media in favour of the police, with selected journalists given special passes which gave them preferential treatment in most police matters, time and again policemen would emerge looking stupid, indifferent or corrupt, simply because they handled their relations with the press clumsily and took their support for granted. Finally the problem had been recognized by the commissioner's office; officers were selected for grooming on media-training courses at Bramshill Police Staff College. Jack Bentham had been on such a course when he was running the RCS. He had found especially useful the techniques for winning television debates by taking the argument to your critics or shifting the argument itself, as politicians did when they found themselves in a difficult spot. He found such ploys invaluable in policy meetings with senior officers. To make absolutely certain of an improved press, a policy was introduced to restrict the issue of Metropolitan and City police press passes to selected journalists in order that more responsibly-written articles would appear. Editors nominated their journalists, who were then either approved or rejected, and the commissioner issued a circular to all Districts stating that preferential treatment was to be given to holders of these passes. Some journalists objected when finding that their ordinary NUJ cards didn't give them any right of access, but the police rejected their overtures simply because they had no control over who issued NUJ cards. The system worked fine, but Jack Bentham had no doubt who got the best bargain. Despite his own bias, he recognized that the commissioner blatantly manipulated the public through the media – fear being his best weapon – when he needed to expand or push through an unacceptable piece of policy. What surprised Bentham was that no one else seemed to notice – or if they did, they didn't care enough to protest.

'Looks like a good night's work, Jack,' Ernie Wiseman said, taking four biscuits off the tray on the table and eating them as he ran his eyes down the ticked columns on the co-ordinator's sheets.

'We've missed a couple,' Bentham said. 'Trevor Whitfield was one. He was on that blag in Faversham.'

'There's always some you miss. You'd have nothing to do tomorrow otherwise.' He ate another biscuit.

'C8 might go a bit light. We'd find enough to do.'

'Not the same though, Jack, is it? Feeding dirt into the computer. Half of it's tittle-tattle.' There was a note of disgust in his voice.

'More than half, Ernie. What looks like rubbish on first appearances looks like something else entirely when you flag it alongside three hundred other bits of inconsequential rubbish that the computer allows you to collect.'

'If it eventually results in something like this . . .' Wiseman said, and regretted it immediately.

'David Lane is what helped bring this about. What about that bit of help now?'

Wiseman nodded his head reluctantly. 'I daresay the DPP will accommodate you part of the way. He can't go out entirely.'

Thinking about that, Bentham said, 'D'you want to talk to the DAC, or do you want me to?'

'You may as well. You'll make more of a case than I will. None of the lot arrested this morning can go out, Jack,' Wiseman said firmly, and the DCS's agreement made him feel he had saved face.

That wasn't of any concern to Bentham now. He had done his job – seen a lot of villains nicked, some for very major crimes, either commissioned or being plotted up.

It was now up to the Robbery Squad to see it into court, and he didn't even much mind that they would probably get the credit. This result was better than all the politicking and public-order policing, though he was realistic enough to know it wouldn't set that aside for long.

'Nice result, Frank, makes it all worthwhile,' Bentham said, as he pressed his feet back into his shoes, fastened his collar, straightened his tie and rose out of his chair.

'Pity about those other two.'

'You going down with the commander?'

'I'll see it through here.'

'I'm going to have a run down to Swanley. See what's happening.'

'Mind how you go, guv.' Frank Burroughs sounded concerned.

Bentham looked at him, then nodded, wondering if this DCI ever had any doubts about him such as he harboured about Commander Wiseman. He wondered about that some more as he stepped out of the smoky room, where a weary strain of jubilation was in the air, and down to the car park, to find his driver asleep behind the wheel of his car.

17

Standing at the greasy truck-stop van in the lay-by on the A2, Jack Bentham thought about the raids that his department had set up for the Robbery Squad and Terry Sneed, and about connections between the Robbery Squad and the RCS when he had been running it. He wasn't going to come to grief over anything Terry Sneed might say. Any dealings he had had with villains for personal gain had been fairly closed up affairs, no one other than the villain concerned and himself knowing about them. Perhaps he would be implicated by association. The robbery at Faversham was a case in point, for according to David Lane Sneed had taken money from both him and Denis Rattigan, and had put Peter Forster away by prior arrangement. Wiltshire had been particularly interested in Bentham's involvement, and now that Sneed was in police cells they might become more interested. He wondered if Terry Sneed had had any contact with David Lane prior to his departure for Spain, contact that Lane had neglected to tell him about. Had Lane told Sneed about Bentham taking money off him for helping Lane's younger brother to avoid a prison sentence? If Sneed was in possession of that information, he would doubtless try and use it. Bentham briefly considered heading back to London and getting some sleep, as all this anxiety was probably the product of a tired mind.

'Two fried-egg sandwiches and two coffees,' the truck-stop owner said above the throb of traffic heading nose-to-tail towards London.

Bentham looked at the man in the greasy apron and thought about challenging the order – his driver had wanted a bacon sandwich. Instead he paid and went back to the car with the bagged food.

'They didn't have any bacon,' he lied when his driver opened the bag and looked disapprovingly at the egg sandwich. 'That's more healthy. Bacon gives you cancer of the colon.' It was said as a joke, but since hearing Helen's cancer argument against eating meat, and especially pork, he hadn't eaten bacon. Unlike her, he took the view that what anyone else did was up to them.

'Is that right, guv?' the driver asked, turning in his seat, his mouth full of egg sandwich.

'About as harmful as cigarettes, it seems.'

'Why don't they tell us about it then? They ought to put government health warnings up in butchers' shops, or some adverts on telly.' The driver sounded outraged; he tended to believe whatever Jack Bentham told him, he being one of the ubiquitous 'they'.

'Too much vested interest, I expect.'

Breakfast over, the driver took Bentham's bag and disposable cup, rolled down the window and threw them out onto the lay-by, before they continued on their journey.

Apart from still being without a bath or change of clothes, and wilfully refusing to let it grind him down, Terry Sneed got different, even preferential, treatment compared to other prisoners in cells at Swanley police station. One of the differences lay in the time he got his meals – mostly when he felt like eating. All other prisoners had breakfast before being collected in the prison van for court. Sneed might have suffered an earlier breakfast for the sake of such a trip.

When the uniform gaoler brought a tray of food to the cell, Sneed looked for the personal touches that this man was trying to achieve which signalled their developing relationship. He would put a paper napkin on the tray and use real cutlery and a china cup rather than plastic and styrofoam, and would get hurt and try harder the next day if Sneed ever complained. The food didn't improve noticeably, but Terry Sneed complained less so as not to upset the man; he didn't even complain when this gaoler started putting the marmalade in the microwave oven along with the rest of the food. One morning, as they went through the familiar 'What no bath?' routine and Sneed splashed himself with water on being let out to wash, he had said, 'Why is it I can't get a bath do you think, Selwyn?'

'To be honest, sir, I don't think this lot from Wiltshire bath themselves very often.' He had glanced over his shoulder as he said this in case any of those detectives were in the cell corridor.

There was a slightly pained expression on the gaoler's face this morning when he brought the tray, and for a moment Sneed thought it signalled the end of their relationship. 'Would you follow me, sir,' he said, handing Sneed the tray.

'Going home, Selwyn, am I?' Sneed responded cheerfully, despite himself. 'Or do I get to eat in the karsey today?'

'There's not much I can do about the conditions, Mr Sneed. You're only going next door, sir. The plumber's coming to fix the WC in here.' Someone had broken the flush. He couldn't think that it was this prisoner, since he would be the one to suffer. Cooped up as he had been for days on end it was possible that he had lapsed into mindless vandalism, out of boredom; but more likely, the gaoler suspected, this was the handiwork of one of the Wiltshire detectives who wanted to hasten Sneed's crack-up. The gaoler admired the way this man was holding up, refusing to break or become short-tempered with either the Wiltshire detectives or the policemen in charge of their cells. Mr Sneed understood their job, and seemed to recognize that they were human, too. Without judging anyone, Selwyn Roberts hoped that this detective would walk clear of his current trouble.

Delight chased surprise through Terry Sneed and he almost dropped the tray when he saw Jack Bentham come through the door at the far end of the corridor. Whatever his motives were, seeing him was like seeing a friendly face after a long journey through hostile country, and Sneed wanted to run forward and greet him, show these country coppers that he wasn't entirely deserted. Instead he tightened his grip on the plastic tray and paused at the doorway of the new cell, permitting only a faint, amused smile to creep across his face.

'Nicked you as well, Jack?' he said, trying to make the words sound casual. He wasn't sure that he succeeded.

'Glad you've still got an appetite, Terry.'

'It's a long time since I've eaten shit like this. Not since Hendon, I don't think,' Sneed responded cheerfully, and preceeded Bentham into the cell, his special relationship with his gaoler forgotten. There might be no need of it after Bentham's visit.

The gaoler stepped back while the sergeant who had shown Bentham to the cells pulled the door to. 'I won't lock the door, sir. But if you could ring the bell when you've finished.'

The two detectives listened to the footfalls as the gaolers went away.

'Looks like you're in a bit of trouble, Terry,' Bentham said, helping himself to a piece of Sneed's toast and putting marmalade on it. 'It's hot,' he said. 'The marmalade's hot.'

'An old Kentish tradition, Jack. The cunt puts it in the microwave oven.' He shrugged dismissively. 'They're making a big thing of it, but I can't see that it's fuck all. They wouldn't have held me like this 'they had fuck all. Fucking liberty, pulling those strokes with a fucking stroke-puller like me.'

'What they're probably doing, Terry, is claiming one or two more to make you look better. You know how people are once they see you nicked,' Bentham said, getting to like hot marmalade and spreading a second piece of toast. 'They start to see you as a lost cause. You've not been getting any offers? Someone as active as you ought to have got an offer. Ernie Wiseman was entitled to have had a go, I'd've said. Even the DAC or Peter Vyvyan.'

Sneed was very conscious of the fact that no senior officer had come by with an offer of help; it made him angry, but he was determined not to show it. 'I know how it looks, but I can't believe I'm being offered the prick, Jack, not even after all this time here and no shower or bath. If I thought otherwise, I'd pull every cunt who's ever had sixpence into the frame.'

'It looks to me, Terry, as if you're the victim of excess, the need to re-establish some sense of balance. When you think about all that's been going on,' Bentham said speculatively, guessing he didn't know one tenth of it and not sure that he wanted to, 'it had to stop somewhere. That sort of policing is becoming an anachronism. It doesn't really fit the needs of policing the sort of society we have now. It's political crimes that are making everyone jumpy nowadays. Even kids without work who are going for opportunistic crime are making a political statement. You can't let politically-motivated villains buy their way out. It's not like the old villain who only hurt the insurance companies, or those paid to guard property.'

'I understand the problem, Jack,' Sneed said. 'But I'm being made the scapegoat for the total failure of those cunts running Operation Bad Apple, that's all. I can see there's a need for a public fuss to help mask the transition, I can see that the Wiltshire could be no more than a subterfuge. All I'm saying is, I'm not going to be part of it. They've got to elect someone else. I won't stand alone in the frame.'

Bentham wondered about his being used in a similar way by

Harry Streeter with his investigation out at Hackney, whether that hadn't been to divert him from the levels of corruption he suspected and had laid out to the deputy commissioner.

'This isn't the usual CIB2 investigation, Terry, where I could pick up the phone and talk to Commander Parker and ask him to do a bit of evidence shuffling. If it was, you wouldn't be here. You might be right about being a scapegoat. The Wiltshire investigation's got out of control – everyone's pissed off at them, from the commissioner down. They couldn't get rid of them by sabotage. You might seem like a cheap price to pay to get them back on the train to Wiltshire.'

Sneed nodded slowly, accepting the reality of the situation. 'There are too many senior officers at it for me to stand the prick like that. They'd have to be put in.'

With a piece of toast half-way to his mouth, Bentham paused and looked at Sneed. He was amazed that this cunning detective didn't recognize the tactic of appearing disinterested. He must have used it himself hundreds of times when interrogating suspects.

'There are more than enough,' Sneed said. 'Assistant Commissioner Vyvyan, Deputy Assistant Commissioner Doc Holliday, Commanders Burland, Shaw and Parker. It's about right that he's running CIB2 – set a thief to catch one. We'd better not forget Ernie Wiseman, he's been well at it. There's DCS Markham and Tim Whittal. They all had money out of that Securicor blag at Faversham, the one that got Operation Bad Apple started.' He laughed. 'There were so many senior policemen earning there that I don't think the villains had anything, Jack. Look what Commander Franklyn's taking out of video porn. More than those pricks running shops. I thought I'd been very cautious. In fact I know I have. You know me, Jack, when I do something it stays done. The mistake I made was in underestimating how desperate them other cunts are. Did you hear how it was done?'

'They put someone into you with a wire,' Bentham said.

'That fat bastard Lenny Feast. They put a gun to his head. There's fuck all I can do about that now. If it goes to court I'll slaughter them, but I'd sooner take a bit of help.'

'Like I said, Terry, who's rushing forward?'

Despite the fact that no one was, Terry Sneed didn't feel everything was lost. All he needed to extricate himself was a contact with the outside, a link to the police hierarchy. He could have wished for someone more amenable than Jack Bentham, but Bentham would do.

'Do you remember that architect I nicked? Laurence James?' Sneed asked in a threatening voice.

It wasn't likely that any of the police hierarchy would ever forget, for the result had truly reminded them all how impotent they were when dealing with other than street crime. He hadn't in fact arrested the architect, whose income was far bigger than his firm out in Richmond could have generated. Those crimes wouldn't have been handled by the Robbery Squad, for they were far more sophisticated than one across a pavement with a shotgun; yet it was one of the cruder variety, a robbery on a bonded warehouse which James's firm had designed out at Heathrow Airport, that had brought him to light. Sneed's instinct for crime had set alarm bells going inside his head when he had sat in on an interview with James's employee, who had supplied the raiders with drawings of the air-ducting system. Under pressure, the man had traded a bigger fish: he knew about large-scale computer fraud. Sneed had involved both Bentham, for access to C11's computer, and Detective Superintendent Stern of the Fraud Squad for his assessment. What they pieced together was massive fraud on both local and national government contracts. A cartel of construction companies had been set up to tender for projects at highly-inflated prices, while their nominated company for the current project obtained the contract at merely inflated prices; money appeared to be lost on the work, which actually made large profits. The computer records would show a loss for the tax inspector, while another set were kept for the profit-takers within the cartel, which included not only the architects and their accountants who kept the computer database, but also local-government officials, and both civil servants and ministers in the Departments of Trade, Environment and Housing, not to mention the Ministry of Defence. There was no doubt in the minds of the policemen involved that they had a scandal of epic proportions, one that never surfaced publicly, wasn't even hinted at in the back pages of *Private Eye*.

'It was all very much the ethos of the market place, Terry,' Bentham said paraphrasing the commissioner. 'And something likely to seriously embarrass the government.'

'No one wanted to do that, uncle,' Sneed said, being perfectly amenable. 'And what happened? All that evidence managed to get lost!'

'As I recall it went into the paper shredder on the seventeenth floor.'

A smile flashed across Sneed's face. 'Not before it went into the xeroxing machine out at Barnes.'

'You made a copy of that file?' Bentham asked. The surprise he expressed was intended to deflect Terry Sneed from the possibility that he had done exactly the same thing – only had it committed to the C11 computer under a secret code – he had a number of items filed there. Terry Sneed seemed to believe he was the only policeman blessed with cunning.

'It's all on microfiche. I thought I might want to go into them at some time for my whack. I've got that, Jack, along with details of everything I've ever known policemen to bend or earn. There's a lot involved.'

'There've been a lot at it, Terry,' Bentham said equitably. He hadn't decided to help Terry Sneed simply because he feared his knowledge being used against others, but because he saw his information as being too useful to risk in an orgy of publicity. Sneed had such a sharp brain, always six moves ahead. Bentham didn't know if he played chess, but imagined he'd be formidable. Such a mind could be finely retuned to the needs of present times, and shouldn't be lost to the police. Set on a new path, he might bring a degree of political acumen to the job that was rarely, if ever, seen in policemen. Bentham saw no point in trying to cling to the old maps of police work when the streets were changing so fast. One had simply to accept the new ground rules, or retire. Terry Sneed had made it abundantly clear that he didn't wish to retire.

'What are you offering if I find you the sort of help you expect, Terry?'

'What d'you want?' Sneed asked a little surprised. 'Money?'

Bentham shook his head. 'All the information you hold will do.'

'I hadn't thought about taking on a partner.' Sneed smiled at the prospect.

'I hadn't thought of our becoming a partnership,' Bentham said, and smiled also.

*　　　*　　　*

211

'The question we must consider, Tony, before we can even think about proceding further is: does Sneed have hard evidence against the senior officers he's named here,' indicating the tape recording on his desk, 'or is he clutching at straws? Personally, I'm afraid this might turn out to be an enormous hoax, with us ending up with egg on our faces if we're not careful.'

They were in Assistant Chief Constable Leeper's temporary office. Also present were DCI Brian Humpfress, a superintendent from Wiltshire, and one from Surrey who had been seconded to the investigation, along with the deputy DPP Colin Wells. The assistant chief constable's increasing anxiety after listening to the tape three times dampened the enthusiasm of the rest of the policemen in the room. They had believed they were at last on their way home as a result of this tape. Each occasionally glanced at Colin Wells, who had so far made no comment; they couldn't work out whether that was a good or bad sign.

'In some ways I'd like to believe it was a hoax,' Tony Bulmer said, humouring him, not wanting him to suffer a stroke. 'But it's not a banker's bet. Not in these circumstances.'

'What about Chief Superintendent Bentham?' the assistant chief constable speculated. 'Do you think he's conducting his own investigation?'

'Draw your own conclusions, Alan. I'm betting he wants Sneed's information for the same reason Sneed holds onto it – power. It'll be interesting to see what he does for Sneed. He's definitely implicated in this cover-up involving Laurence James, whatever it was.'

'Laurence James is a big firm of architects out at Richmond,' the superintendent from Surrey put in.

'Is it credible that senior officers like those mentioned would be so venal?' Alan Leeper argued. 'Sneed actually said they've been taking money out of robberies, from pornography. He's even named Peter Vyvyan. No one's been more supportive.'

'There have been rumours about Commander Wiseman's involvement, sir,' Humpfress said, barely able to stay calm at this man's painful avoidance of the truth. 'Mostly from informers we have in police cells, and not one hundred per cent reliable. But Sneed's evidence is entirely different.'

'But we're talking about some of the most senior officers in the Met. We can't simply challenge them without hard evidence.'

'Why not, Alan?' Bulmer wanted to know. 'That's what we'd expect to get from interviewing them. They hate our fucking guts anyway. What's to lose?'

'It's ridiculous,' Alan Leeper said, feeling the upwards rush of pressure towards his head as blood from over-arousal struggled through constricted arteries. 'Senior policemen don't behave like this.'

'They certainly don't behave like characters in an Agatha Christie novel, Alan.'

Colin Wells laughed. It was a thin, reedy sound that didn't infect anyone else.

'I've no doubt about corruption being widespread in the Met, Tony, but in my opinion it's confined to the lower ranks. That's where we should concentrate our efforts. Get someone else in the cell with Sneed, get him talking about that.'

In deference to Brian Humpfress's commitment to this case, and to what the DCI would think of him if this opportunity were let go, Tony Bulmer said firmly, 'There's an argument that corruption starts at the top, Alan, not the bottom.'

'I'm not competent to pontificate on that,' Alan Leeper said pompously. 'What do you think, Mr Wells? You've been silent a long while.'

Considering the question a moment longer, Colin Wells said, 'I don't believe corruption is endemic. For corruption to have reached into this stratum it would need to be. There was no catalogue of evidence found against senior policemen when you searched Sneed's flat.'

'That doesn't mean much,' Bulmer said. 'There wasn't a single item at Sneed's flat that shouldn't have been there, not even a hotel spoon. Sneed's a cautious man; I didn't expect we'd find the evidence, or the catalogue.'

'But you surely expected to find something, Mr Bulmer, or why search?'

The two men stared across the room at each other, then Colin Wells leaned forward and switched on the tape recorder, held the re-wind button, stopped it at random, then pressed the play button. The echoing but recognizable voice of Terry Sneed came out in mid-sentence.

'... Vyvyan. Deputy Assistant Commissioner Doc Holliday. Commanders Burland, Shaw and Parker. It's about right that he's running CIB2 – set a thief to catch one. We'd better not forget Ernie Wiseman, he's been well at it. There's DCS Markham and Tim Whittal . . .'

The deputy DPP shut off the machine and dismissed it with a flick of his hand. 'It's a list of names.'

That did it for Tony Bulmer. Unlike Brian Humpfress, he was unable to hold in his anger. 'For Christsake! Whose side are you on?'

'I'm on no one's side,' Colin Wells said, turning white, which was the way his anger manifested itself. 'I resent the continual inference by the Wiltshire CID to the contrary. I have been dealing with these policemen a long time and expect to go on dealing with them when you leave. That doesn't make me corrupt or in their pocket. So just shut up and present me with evidence, then I'll present you with an opinion as to whether or not you are likely to secure a conviction. On what you have to date, I can tell you, as any other lawyer will, you won't come near it. If you're in the business of narrow-misses, Mr Bulmer, fine, but I'm not. What we need is this unseen evidence Sneed claims to have committed to paper. Once you get that, I'm sure the situation will change dramatically.'

'Oh, we'll get it,' Bulmer said quietly. 'We'll get it even if it takes another eighteen months.' He closed the thick folder in front of him, rose and went out.

'Mr Bentham. Jack Bentham,' Helen Daniels said to the two uniformed policemen at the desk on the Broadway entrance of Scotland Yard.

'No, madam, I'm not,' one of the constables said without smiling. He understood what she was asking and was merely relieving the monotony of his duty.

'No, I know,' Helen replied. 'I've a meeting with Jack Bentham. I just want him informed I'm here.'

'He's expecting you then, is he?' the constable asked.

The questions went on like this until Helen finally lost her patience. 'What do I have to do, rape you or something before you'll call through to the fourth floor?'

'How do you know Mr Bentham is on the fourth floor?' the uniform asked.

'I don't believe this,' Helen said. 'You're out of *Alice in Wonderland* – no, I'm not Alice, I'm Helen Daniels, and I've called to see Detective Chief Superintendent Bentham.'

'If you talk nicely to that gentleman there, miss,' the constable said, indicating the security officer at the end of the desk, 'he'll telephone and find out if we have a Mr Bentham.'

Jack Bentham came down to meet her in the wide reception area, and Helen kissed him by way of greeting, as if to establish her identity and her relationship to him. She didn't say anything about her encounter with the uniformed policeman when Bentham booked her in at the desk, but glanced back at him as they stepped across to one of the four lifts off the lobby. He was blanching, causing his spots to glow like neons.

'I'm not sure about this, Jack, coming here. It might compromise my position on the loony left. I mean, foaming-at-the-mouth animal activist seen entering Scotland Yard – God, what if my friends saw me?' Her manner was slightly manic. She was aware of how it surfaced whenever she was in a potentially compromising situation with him, which seemed to be any that reminded her that he was a policeman, and not simply a man she was having an affair with.

'I shouldn't worry about it, we have all your friends locked up. It's only because of my influence that you keep your liberty.' He smiled, wondering if he would ever break through the barrier she had erected. He felt it had become stronger. He wanted it to be different. She went through the motions with him, was friendly, loving, considerate – she was an actress after all – but somehow remained out of reach. The invitation here was a PR exercise to try and break down the barrier, to show her that his job wasn't so different to running a bank or a theatre company, notwithstanding the fact that he mostly dealt with the negative aspects of life. Such PR seemed to work on schoolteachers and pupils, journalists and everyone else who was ever shown around. When he thought about it, he realised that most of his relationships had been like this one – held back, uncommitted. Jack Bentham chose to blame the fact that he was a policeman rather than any shortcoming or deficiency in his own emotional make-up. Perhaps the problem wouldn't have arisen with a less intelligent, less sensitive woman.

'I can't contact half my friends,' Helen said. 'I've lost my address book. Could you set the resources of Scotland Yard to finding it?'

'No problem. It'll be in my office by the time we've finished lunch.' They stepped out of the lift and started across the landing to the canteen used by senior officers. 'We've transferred all the names onto our computer and drawn up detailed profiles on them. We can lift them anytime.' His flip humour was by way of mitigation.

Helen felt a sudden chill, despite his wicked grin. There were lots of animal rights activists in her book, any number of whom the police would like a point of contact with. An address might be the only piece missing in the computer's jigsaw of details. There was always a danger in writing down the addresses of such people – especially as some members of the movement had their address books lifted by the police – but there was no alternative if one needed to stay in contact. She certainly needed to, with the movement becoming so disparate. She laughed, trying to dismiss her unease, but the mistrust and uncertainty remained.

'You left it in the flat the other day.'

'You've really got it? Great. It was like losing an arm. I felt bereft.' The relief at the prospect of being reunited with her address book made her forget the threat that his joke had posed.

Bentham glanced around the canteen. Among those gathered were one or two whom he might have joined had he been on his own, but none he wanted Helen to meet. It appealed to Jack Bentham's sense of mischievousness to bring Helen in here, knowing where she stood in the political spectrum in relation to most senior policemen; but the joke might easily get out of hand in a direct clash. He steered her to a vacant table. A little more effort was made here than in most police canteens. There were water carafes, napkins and cutlery. Any number of the officers who used this canteen had, after all, been to Bramshill, where among other things candidates were taught what cutlery went with what dish, and not to tuck the napkins into their collars.

They ordered salad with baked potatoes and wine. The waitress brought the bottle opened to the table and filled both their glasses straight away. Clearly she hadn't been to Bramshill.

'How's the play going?' Bentham asked, making awkward small talk.

'What play?' she asked.

'Aren't you doing a new play?'

'I went for an audition; I didn't get the part.'

'You audition for a part every time?' he said, a little surprised. 'Doesn't that make you a little insecure?'

'Desperately insecure. Most actors are. Some hide it better than others. You just try and act a tough exterior, pretend it doesn't matter, pretend you weren't right for the part. Sometimes the feeling of insecurity is even worse when you get a part, especially if it's small. You try not to admit that this is your level. The director or writer will tell you it's only a small part, but vitally important. You try to convince yourself that to make a character in such a short scene is an enormous challenge.'

'How often do you succeed?'

Helen shrugged. 'That depends on how much of a basket case the people who know me think I am. I suppose I hide those sort of feelings.'

Suddenly Jack Bentham understood why Helen was always half a reach beyond his grasp emotionally, or thought he did, and felt slightly guilty about her address book. He had looked through it, and somehow he imagined his joking about it would exculpate him. A confession was still a confession if presented so as not to be believed. On taking those addresses from her book, he had faced a dilemma familiar to most policemen; the conditioned response versus personal commitment. 'How would you deal with a member of your family who had committed a crime?' was the clumsy way it was put to them in training college. Almost to a student, the response was that they should be treated no differently from any other member of the public. It was the response student policemen believed made their existence acceptable, and from then on the conditioning process took an inevitable course. Bentham had argued with himself about putting the names and addresses of Helen's friends onto the Criminal Intelligence computer. He told himself he would probably never use what he had taken, that it was merely a list of names and addresses. As a computer exercise they would possibly identify the known activists and flag the other names and details in the 'associates' index.

'D'you mind if I join you?' Peter Vyvyan said, approaching their table and pulling out a chair, not expecting to be refused. He appraised Helen openly, as if waiting for her to leave so he could have a private word.

'If you don't mind having your ear bent about not eating dead animals for lunch.' Bentham's grin suggested that he was humouring either or both as he introduced them. 'Helen's big on animal rights.'

'It's you who's been tying up half our men on District with your protests,' Vyvyan said, as if believing it was her responsibility alone.

'It's your men who are restricting our freedom, Mr Vyvyan,' she said.

Peter Vyvyan was more used to women who didn't respond, much less challenge him on his own preserve. He looked away and reached for the menu.

Out of deference to Helen and partly as an unspoken apology for what he had done, Bentham said nothing to ameliorate the antagonism between these two.

'You saw Terry Sneed out at Swanley this morning, Jack,' Vyvyan said, deciding to ignore Helen. 'The cell was wired.'

Jack Bentham looked at Helen to try and read in her face what she thought of that. He showed none of his own surprise, but felt it nonetheless. He hadn't even considered the possibility. 'With Terry's knowledge?' he asked casually.

'He didn't do himself any favours,' Vyvyan said. 'I had a visit from Alan Leeper. What a prick – excuse my language, dear. He came to ask me what to do, and to warn me to advise you against helping Sneed. He doesn't want to see brother officers in trouble, Jack. Not senior officers. Sneed was looking for some help?'

'Don't they all when their collar's felt?' Bentham said. 'He was threatening all sorts of mayhem unless he gets some help.'

'Terry Sneed's too smart for that. He knows where his best interest lies.'

'He doesn't believe it lies in prison without any help.'

'Well, what do you think, Jack? You must have got a clearer impression than that tape gives.'

'If you're wrong about him there'll be an epidemic of retiring senior policemen. Politicians as well, maybe.'

'He has got a copy of the Laurence James file?'

'He's cunning enough.'

Peter Vyvyan thought about that, then consulted the menu again as the waitress arrived. 'I'll have the trout and a pint of bitter, dear,' he glanced at Helen, than back to the waitress. 'The trout's quite dead is it, dear? This young lady is concerned about cruelty to animals.'

The waitress took the order with a bemused smile and went away.

'You feel I should give Sneed a bit of help?'

'The best thing, Peter, would probably be to pull him out of there, send him to Bramshill, then promote him and put him in CIB2. Who would be better suited to catching bent coppers?' Bentham smiled, determined not to give the ACC any more. He could take the advice any way he chose. With a glance at Helen, and a flash of clear insight, Bentham knew they would never come any closer; whatever expectation she had of him wouldn't be fulfilled. At that moment he didn't know if he was disappointed or not.

18

The twice-daily excursions around the pound at the rear of Swanley police station were the high spots in Terry Sneed's day – something he looked forward to, even though it meant shuffling round without laces in his shoes or a belt to support his trousers. He was embarrassed by the smell that followed him, and surprised that no one else noticed it. What also surprised Terry Sneed was how close he was to cracking without the Wiltshire CID realising it – unless they were more cunning than he imagined. Selwyn Roberts, the old police constable who looked after the cells corridor, had more notion than anyone what was going on inside him, but for reasons Sneed couldn't work out he wasn't letting on. It couldn't have been out of loyalty to the Met.

Eleven days he had been in custody, or at least believed he had; without reference to the real world it was difficult to keep track of time. He hadn't seen a newspaper or heard the radio so knew nothing of what was happening outside. The only contact he had had was with Jack Bentham, and nothing had resulted from that, as far as he knew, not even the shower and change of clothes he had asked him to arrange. Sneed knew that putting the facts in a straightforward way to a suspect and expecting a positive response was a pointless exercise. Effective interrogation required isolation, an intimidating atmosphere – full of uncertainty – created by rejection and extended hope; the object was to break the suspect's will as quickly as possible, while ensuring that any statement was made voluntarily. Terry Sneed was less disadvantaged than most suspects because he felt at home in police stations, knew the moves there, what the functions were, why the decisions were made, how they were made. But he didn't know how the Wiltshire CID had guessed he would be so ground down by not being allowed to shower and change his clothes. While he believed it inhuman to deny him this basic right, he also understood that the more fuss he made the worse it would be for him.

Sometimes Brian Humpfress would join him during his exercise period. He would often talk about the church, or God, or the need man had to unburden himself and so free himself of sin. It was an interesting interrogation tactic, Sneed thought, but only likely to break a suspect eaten up with guilt. He hadn't met many who were, and they usually poured everything out as soon as a finger was on their collar. This evening when Humpfress fell into step, causing the gaoler to drop back a few paces as they circled the car-littered yard, Humpfress had something else in mind – a new tactic he hoped might appeal to an obscured sense of fair play in this man.

'This gets to be a right little treat, these excursions,' Sneed said. 'Mind you, Brian, I'd swap a walk around the yard for a shower. Everything's an object of barter in this game. It's all part of the treatment.'

Humpfress didn't respond. He felt Sneed was being mocking, and that wasn't the right atmosphere for his proposal. But soon the opportunity would be lost altogether: the assistant chief constable and the deputy DPP had decided that if there was no imminent breakthrough with Sneed they were going to release him, as there was a limit to the length of time they could hold even a policeman.

'I used to jog, not regularly, enough to keep me fit.' He glanced over his shoulder. 'Selwyn'd think I was legging it.'

With a quick glance at the gaoler, Humpfress said, his pulse rate quickening, 'Would you say I've treated you fairly? I have, haven't I?'

'Oh very fair, uncle.'

The irony was lost on Humpfress. 'Why not play fair by me, then?' he asked, whining slightly. 'Make a statement, Terry. Give it to me. Let me take it from you.'

'That would help you out, Brian, would it?' Sneed said, feeling the man's desperation.

'I've done most of the work. It was me who found you, me who made the arrest.'

'Always the way. You do the work, run the risks doing the fitting, your governor takes the credit.'

As if not hearing this, Humpfress asked, 'How about it then, Terry? We could get it wrapped up quite quickly. Put an end to all this uncertainty.'

Sneed stopped walking and turned to look at Humpfress, then smiled. It took a lot of effort. 'I don't have any uncertainty about the outcome, uncle. You know as well as I do how it's going to come out for me. Sick'ning isn't it. All that fucking work.'

With that Terry Sneed turned away and continued to walk, leaving Humpfress angry and frustrated. His feelings were precipitated by the knowledge that Tony Bulmer would soon be down to continue the interrogation. And he had got nowhere. Humpfress didn't turn as he heard one of the rear doors to the station squeak open and slap shut, knowing it was Sneed's summons back to the interview room.

Detective Chief Superintendent Bulmer was sitting at the table with papers spread before him when a smiling Terry Sneed came in, followed by a morose-looking Humpfress.

'All right, Terry, are you?' Bulmer said cheerfully. He had had a good dinner and had drunk almost a whole bottle of wine – in anticipation of its either being a long night or their last with Sneed. 'Getting everything you want are you? Apart from a bit of the other.' He laughed.

This period in cells was the longest Sneed had been without sex for some while, but it only bothered him when he found himself with a random erection; he refused to masturbate. 'I'm not getting my liberty.'

'To be frank, that's becoming about as remote as the yeti.'

'So's that fucking shower and change of clothes. I couldn't even pull a policewoman smelling like this.'

'Oh, didn't Chief Superintendent Bentham fix that up?' Bulmer said, watching the uncertainty cloud this detective's face. 'I thought that was the purpose of his visit, to see if there was anything you needed. "Any little thing to make life more bearable, Terry?"' Bulmer read from a typescript on his desk. '"A shower or a change of clothes would be handy." Should be "and" not "or". The standard of typing is atrocious. I'd say Mr Bentham forgot you existed the moment he left your cell. I daresay he has more important things on his mind, Terry, along with Commanders Wiseman and Burland et al.'

Sneed nodded slowly and purposefully as a way of outwardly controlling the rage that was building inside him, understanding now why, of all people who had good reason to help him, it was Bentham who had visited him. 'You snaky cunts,' he said, as the truth dawned. He would hurt as many policemen as he could, that was his immediate thought, especially Jack Bentham for pulling such a stroke. 'I stood the prick over that change of cell. Especially after the way you wired Feast. I should have been more slippery.'

'I wasn't hopeful about getting anything as good as this,' Bulmer said, fanning the edges of the transcript.

With a sense of impending disaster, Sneed's thoughts raked the remnants of his conversation with Jack Bentham to discover how much damage it may have done him. He could only remember fragments, but he recognized an ominous picture. He didn't hear Bulmer's words, most of which were self-congratulatory, but knew now why Humpfress had been trying so hard out in the yard. His thoughts were scrabbling frantically over the hummocks of his career, not believing he could have come so far only to have it all go like this. Then, through the panic, the scrabbled fragments of thought that wouldn't string together, he suddenly saw his way out: it would prove irresistible to the brass. A cloud lifted off him and he felt like doing a little dance. Terry Sneed wasn't a man who had ever known the sweetness of miscellany in his emotions, and certainly never responded unthinkingly or in a way that might bear any resemblance to spontaneity.

'Even the most cunning detectives have off days,' Bulmer was saying, mellowed with booze and feeling nothing but goodwill towards this man, who he believed would vindicate all their mistakes, disavow all the criticisms they had received. 'Sit down, Terry, come on. It's time we started some serious trading. I'm the only one who can help you now, do some bargaining for you with the DPP. You have to give me something to bargain with. The right sort of statement. It's save-yourself-time, Terry. No one else cares a fart about you, apart from me and Brian.'

Sneed looked between the two men, who appeared to be holding their breath together in anticipation. He resisted the urge to laugh. What Tony Bulmer said sounded about as genuine as any of his own promises to villains.

'Sit down, Terry. Let's have that natter, shall we?'

In spite of the decision he had made, and knowing it was the only way to save himself, still Terry Sneed hesitated. Once he had crossed the Rubicon, there just might be no way back. 'Fuck it!' he said finally. He pulled the chair out from the table and sat. 'Those cunts can't say I didn't warn them.'

The two Wiltshire detectives started to breathe again.

'Do you want to write your own statement, or do you want us to write it down for you to sign at the end.'

'We'd better get something straight, uncle. What I'm prepared to stick up is a lot of names of bent Old Bill, so many in fact there'll hardly be a CID left in London. That's the sort of level of corruption we're talking about. I'll also put up the sort of evidence that you'd never have got if you were here another eighteen months. What I'm not prepared to do is sign a statement. I won't do that.' Once he had made a verbal admission to these two policemen, there was no logical reason not to sign a statement, but Sneed had an illogical objection to it. In theory, anything in a statement could be altered and changed at any point, and should carry no more or less weight with a judge and jury for having been changed. But Sneed knew that things didn't work like that. A signature on the bottom of a statement, regardless of how the confession was obtained, set the seal on its veracity once and for all. Rarely did courts understand that in illegal and unlimited circumstances, such as those in which Sneed had been held, admissions of guilt could be turned out in much the same way that Ford turned out motor cars.

Tony Bulmer wasn't bothered about Sneed's declaration. They had, he suspected, a long way to go before he was required to sign anything.

'What made you change your mind, Terry?' he asked, while Humpfress went off to get some statement forms – that was how unprepared they were for this turn in events.

Sneed thought for a moment, then said, 'When I started as a young detective – a TDC in fact – the first DS I worked with gave me a piece of advice about taking earners or fitting anyone up. He said, if ever it came on top and you got nicked, always deny everything, and go on denying everything, even if you're bang to rights.' He glanced at Humpfress as he returned. 'I soon realised when I came to pass that advice on to other detectives that it wasn't given for my sake, but for his. All the while I went on denying whatever was put to me, I couldn't involve him.' He smiled. 'It's exactly the same with this lot. All the while the brass is kept out of the frame, they're not going to help me. They're obviously relying on me being a real brick, or a prick. The only way I'm going to get some help is by naming them and putting up what I've got on them.'

224

Silence fell over the room as the significance of Sneed's statement enshrouded these two Wiltshire detectives, and they too saw this possible way out for him.

'Just for the record, Terry,' Bulmer said, clearing his throat and squaring the thick wad of statement sheets with the edge of his thumb, 'you're not making this statement or giving any information as a result of duress, or any threats or promises we've made you?'

Sneed laughed at that unintentionally funny statement. 'How could you threaten me, Tony?'

'Right, in your own words then – you going to take it down as well, Brian? Be as well if we both do it,' Bulmer said.

'You've got some names of the firm from the wire you put in that cell,' Sneed said thoughtfully. 'They are some of the ones at the top. There's always been a firm within a firm in the CID. The CID have always earned well. How can they avoid it? No one wants to lose his liberty. Villains get desperate when they're nicked, they'll do anything. That's why so many turn out to be grasses. We nick them and put them away, but we have no real conception of what it really means to go down the road for ten, fifteen, maybe even twenty years. I mean, you have to wait two minutes to be served a pint or ten minutes for a fucking bus, and it gets intolerable. Imagine all those minutes stretched into years before you taste another pint or even see a bus. Even the thought of it slaughters most villains – they never think about it until they are nicked, otherwise there'd be no villainy. Then, once they're captured, there's so much money on offer that a detective would have to come from another world not to go for it. What harm is there, really? It makes not one bit of difference to the level of crime, certainly none that anyone's going to notice.

'You must have heard me mention the ACC. Well, Peter Vyvyan's been at it ever since he was a chief superintendent on division. I'd say he was at it long before that. You don't suddenly go bent at that rank. It takes a bit of practice to be as greedy as he is.'

'What do you know about Assistant Commissioner Vyvyan's activities on division, Terry?' Bulmer asked, not lifting his pen from the page. 'We'll fill in the gaps as we go.'

'The first thing I was directly involved in with him was a shipment of silver hijacked from a train at Barking. Two bodies were put up. One was called Foot, I can't remember the other name. They were truly fitted – makes the way you fitted me look very amateurish. It was done partly as a favour to some villains who were running the manor at the time – Foot and his partner had been taking liberties. That was Peter Vyvyan's earner – no one else saw anything. But we had two bodies, a nice result.'

'How much did Mr Vyvyan receive for this accommodation over the silver bullion?'

'About a grand. That was the going rate for a DCS in those days. I mean, then a DS would cop a fifty and think he'd had a good earner. Anyone tried bunging a DS fifty pounds nowadays he'd nick them for their cheek. When Peter Vyvyan became a commander and moved over to the Yard, with responsibility for vice and pornography among other things, that was the worst bit of news the dealers had had since I don't know when. It was during that period that the current payment system was worked out. I don't think there was anyone there who wasn't weighing in. Mind you, that level of operation upset a few. That was how Ron Drake came to be nicked.' He paused, realising that they might not know who Drake was. 'He was the commander running the Flying Squad in those days, Wiseman's predecessor. The Squad had fuck all to do with Soho as such, but Commander Drake thought he was entitled to earn something, as he wasn't exactly unknown there. He thought he could just steam in and nick a few quid whenever he liked. Peter Vyvyan decided otherwise. The upshot was Ron Drake being put in over a holiday he had at a villa in Spain owned by a villain called Stevie Collins. Vyvyan made the information available to the *Sunday Mirror*, and the Rubber Heels – the firm before we had CIB2 – they nicked Drake. Ernie Wiseman, who was my governor at West End Central at the time, got Drake's job, and things were back sweet as a nut again. Everyone getting their whack – what they were entitled to.'

'Who did the collecting and sharing out, Terry?' Bulmer, asked, having stopped writing. He was spellbound at this account of recent Met corruption, and would remain so over the next sixteen hours. Only the need of sleep would drag him away from the statement sheets.

'There was a DI called Michael Bryant and a DC Frank Bedsted. Peter Vyvyan saw the writing on the wall over the levels of corruption involving porn – not long after he went up to deputy assistant commissioner there was an awful fucking row over corruption in the Porn Squad. A few detectives were nicked – you might want to talk to them, I expect they're still pretty pissed off. The Porn Squad was disbanded and responsibility for that area given to the uniformed branch. Who found himself sitting at the head of it again? Deputy Assistant Commissioner Vyvyan. So it was business as usual.'

'Are you speculating there,' Bulmer asked, 'or do you know this for a fact?'

Sneed chuckled. 'How many complaints have you had from porn dealers in and around Soho – they've complained enough to collectors. I was well active on the Robbery Squad by this time, so I was less involved with the firm. But if you pull Superintendent Ron Monday of C1, he'll have most of the details. He's only got about a year to go before he retires on four-sixths pension and he shitting himself in case anything prevents that. I'd say you'll find him very co-operative.' Sneed broke off, then said thoughtfully, 'Peter Vyvyan's actually a very practical copper. A lot who go that high get out of touch – I suppose he is a bit. Your values are bound to change when you have to take an overview all the time. But he knows how to put policy to work on the streets, knows how to formulate the sort of policy the lad in the job enjoys. He understands that you have to be seen to have a purge every so often when things seem to be getting out of hand. That's why we got ourselves saddled with Operation Bad Apple. There's no denying things were getting out of hand.'

'Well, it's nice to know we've been of some benefit,' Bulmer said peevishly. 'Made some little contribution to ending corruption.'

'What you've done, uncle, is made us all be a lot more careful.'

'You weren't careful enough,' Humpfress put in.

Sneed nodded, deciding to give them a free ride on that.

'Can we have some details of the wrong-doing he's been up to?' Bulmer asked.

'We'll have a go,' Sneed responded. 'It's not something I carry around in my head – not all of it. But everything where anyone was involved, I noted down and filed for future reference.'

'You should have joined CIB2, Terry. With a talent like yours, I'm sure they would have welcomed you,' Bulmer said drily. 'Tell us about the Securicor robbery at Faversham, since that was what got us started.'

'It was a straightforward business,' Sneed told them, and watched Humpfress's hand move jaggedly across the page. 'The villain who plotted it up wanted to know if I could go into anyone in the Kent police. I know enough CID at it down here, but not enough to keep them all out of any investigation, so I brought in Commander Wiseman. He did the business, with Detective Chief Superintendent Taber.'

'Let us get this straight, Terry,' Bulmer interrupted, sitting forward in his chair and glancing at Humpfress to make certain he was taking down every word. 'They all knew that robbery was going to happen?'

'Well what do you think? The funny thing was, C11 had been plotting that one up. They passed information to us to be there waiting for them. But there was business to be done. It wasn't easy freezing them out. Wiseman and Ted Taber had seven grand each. I had four. A couple of DIs copped four. There were about a dozen on the squad and more than a dozen down here who copped a grand apiece.'

'Did the robbers get anything?' Humpress asked.

'The blag came to about a hundred and seventy grand.'

'How do you know these sums were involved?'

'I acted as the go-be – go-between. I delivered the money to everyone who was due.'

'You said Mr Vyvyan was involved,' Bulmer reminded him.

'So was Doc Holliday. They took a drink out of it. They both had five grand – which I delivered to the ACC's house in Esher. They've been fairly regular, those trips.'

'Those policemen actually knew the robbery was taking place and did nothing to stop it?'

'They'd have earned fuck all for that – not even reward money. Insurance companies don't pay rewards for prevention.'

'I can't believe this,' Humpfress said in a censuring tone.

But for the loyalty he owed him, Bulmer would have told Humpfress to stop moralising before he antagonised the prisoner. Instead, to diffuse the tension, he said, 'As a matter of interest, Terry, how many working policemen would you estimate to be involved in corruption?'

'That I know personally?' Sneed asked while he thought about the question.

'Indulge us with some speculation, why don't you?'

'I'd say you'd be looking at something like ninety-five per cent of the CID. But then I suppose that depends how you define corruption.'

'I suppose we're talking about arrestable offences.'

'It's not that straightforward, Tony. Unless it's a very different breed of animal in your part of the world and there are different laws to deal with them. You know yourself, you can't let dangerous men who you know have committed crimes walk free for the want of a bit of evidence. You have to do it, you have to put those sort of people away, anyhow you can.' He waited and elicited a nod from both detectives opposite. 'Now, we know strictly speaking that's corrupt, but it would be a right bastard who nicked you for it. Corrupt policemen who I know personally? I'd say it's got to be a figure in the region of three hundred.'

'Presumably all these corrupt policemen will know others?' Humpfress said, looking up from the sheet, his anger deepening at this man's relaxed, almost cavalier attitude.

'I'd be surprised if they didn't,' Sneed said confidently. 'I warned you you'd regret nicking me.'

'Has Commander Wiseman been involved in as many incidents of corruption?'

'Could be he's had a lot more. After all, he's a lot older.'

'But has he had a piece of everything you've had?' Bulmer persisted.

'You'd only involve Ernie Wiseman when he'd be needed – if evidence had gone too far up the line, or you wanted the DAC to go into the DPP for someone who's buying a result. The sort of whack commanders want, you'd find yourself working for them half the time.'

'Did any of you ever do anything for nothing?' Humpress asked.

'I've never known detectives do fuck all for nothing.'

'Some put in hundreds of hours unpaid overtime on cases,' Humpfress argued.

'I'm talking about business, uncle,' Sneed said, with a dismissive look.

'What corruption is Commander Burland involved with?' Bulmer asked.

'He runs the stolen vehicles branch, C10. One of his ramps

involves a firm of car thieves specialising in Jaguars who ship them to the continent. The firm was nicked, but he saw to it that the evidence disappeared. A lad called Eddie Roseman ran things, still does. He rings cars for blaggers, too.'

'How was Burland involved on the Faversham robbery?'

'The stolen vehicles used on it came under his jurisdiction. He actually kept the cars in one of his pounds until it was time for them to be found. I mean, who the fuck's going to look for a stolen vehicle among stolen vehicles? If they'd been discovered, it would have meant a ballocking for someone, but it would only be a recovery oversight. The idea was that the cars shouldn't be tied into the blaggers in any way, except to the body who was being fitted for it.'

'How was that arranged?'

'The detectives who arrested Frank Tebbutt – he was elected for that one – picked him up in one of the stolen cars. That way Tebbutt couldn't avoid having his fingerprints all over it. Forensic evidence looks very good.'

'Does Tebbutt have any idea what happened?' Humpfress asked.

'He's got to be a cunt if he doesn't,' Sneed replied sharply. 'He's the only one who went up the steps. But then, of course, you've talked to him, what he had to say about his arrest is history. He got you lot started on this, saying how the CID had put them into the blag. No evidence against his partners, though, they got a throw in court. The cunt.'

'He's one standing for *that* in the first place. Although I suppose villains do have a big disadvantage. They don't expect such treacherous behaviour from policemen.'

'You've got to be a cunt, 'you believe that.'

'Maybe it's to my credit,' Humpfress snapped back, 'that after months of hearing filth like this about policemen I *can* still believe it.'

'Believe what you like, uncle, it doesn't cost me anything.'

Tempers frayed more as the night wore on, and information poured out revealing to the two Wiltshire detectives what a waste of time their investigations had been – how far off the beam they were. Weary, and with mixed feelings of despondency and elation, they called a halt at around three o'clock and went to sleep. They resumed at nine o'clock.

They had been taking evidence that morning for over three

hours and were considering stopping for lunch when Bulmer said, 'You keep on hinting at all this evidence you have, Terry. It might make life a lot easier later on if we were to include that in this statement document. Where is this evidence, if it exists?'

'Oh, it exists, uncle,' Sneed said. 'It's in a safe deposit box.'

'Where's the key kept? We explored that possibility when we searched your flat.' He looked at Brian Humpfress, who shook his head to indicate that no key had been found.

'It's kept in a left luggage locker at Victoria Station. The ticket's at the flat. They missed it.'

'We bloody well didn't,' Humpfress said. He was about at the end of his patience, and lack of sleep wasn't helping him. He had supervised the search.

'The way they went through that flat, s'joke. They couldn't have found the tea or teapot to make it in,' Sneed said. 'They wouldn't get away with searching like that on the Squad.'

'We can't all be as sophisticated as Met policemen,' Bulmer said in defence of his men. 'The best thing would be for us to find this ticket and pull up this evidence.'

He waited for Sneed to make some objection. All he made was a condition – that he could take a shower and a shave and change his clothes at his flat.

The feeling of water rushing over him, releasing the itch from his scalp and body, wasn't something Terry Sneed would ever have considered a luxury until now. He opened the red valve for more hot water, until it was almost unbearable. He could feel his pores opening, letting go the sweat and bacteria that had caused him to stink. He intended staying under the shower until the hot water ran out, or until the Wiltshire detectives, who were in the other part of the flat searching for the left luggage ticket and tidying up after their previous search, came knocking on the door. Terry Sneed didn't really believe this would be his very last shower, but the previous twelve days had made him insecure.

The five detectives present hadn't exactly restored the former pristine order of his flat, Terry Sneed noticed as he walked through to the bedroom in his towelling robe to pick through the debris of clothes that had been stuffed back into the wall cupboards. Some were still in the Sketchley dry cleaning bags, others had dropped off the hangers and been left lying on the floor. They hadn't found the ticket they were looking for, and he guessed they wouldn't. He had seen the way they had searched before, when they'd had no idea what they were looking for. They had gone through the place with a vengeance, putting nothing back, and usually having to move it a second and sometimes a third time as they came to search where they had dropped things. With everything dumped on the floor, they had then got round to searching under the fitted carpets. Even that they hadn't done properly, only turning back the corners.

'No luck?' Sneed said, slightly mockingly. Humpfress seemed embarrassed and averted his eyes when Sneed removed the robe, stepped into some clean underpants and adjusted his cock. He ran his hand over the outside of his genitals, enjoying the feeling of clean cotton against his skin. 'It's here somewhere. The way your lads searched before, we'll be all day.' He remembered the photograph of himself with the last commissioner of police. It was the only thing he had made a point of asking them to be careful with. It had been a moment of weakness, and immediately the photograph was dropped and broken. That sort of move, born out of frustration, was very shortsighted, for a pissed-off subject was less likely to be helpful than one kept sweet.

Sneed hesitated over his choice of shirt. He wanted to wear a white shirt, but thought a darker one would prove more practical – they weren't likely to let him slip back here tomorrow for another change of clothes. He picked a navy shirt with a large white weave running through it, a dark tie and grey suit. The left luggage slip was on the back of the cleaning ticket, neatly folded so as to be completely disguised. He removed both, put them in his pocket, found a clean handkerchief and then felt ready to face anything.

In the kitchen, Sneed picked through the debris and made himself coffee. It was black, without sugar, and better than any he had tasted in a long while.

Humpfress followed him to the doorway and watched him, declining his offer of a cup for himself. 'Do you ever go to church, Terry?' he said quietly.

'You asked me that before,' Sneed pointed out. 'I got married there – wasn't any recommendation. They didn't do divorces. I didn't have any need to go again.'

Humpfress guessed that this man wouldn't be redeemed easily. But he wasn't prepared to write him off. Even the most vile sinner could be born again. 'That's a pity. Churches are wonderfully consoling places, very peaceful, full of the prayers that have been said in them over the years. You can derive great benefit from a visit without even realising it.'

'How does sex figure in your belief?' Sneed asked suddenly.

'Sex as part of procreation is very wonderful.'

'What about letting me slip into a woman I know before we go back,' Sneed suggested. 'S'been a long time.'

Anger made Brian Humpfress tremble and he tightened his grip on the edge of the door. He might have known that Terry Sneed would mock him. 'You felt a great weight lifted off you when you started to unburden yourself yesterday evening. Wasn't that a huge relief? We could stop in a church on the way to Victoria.'

'I'd sooner stop in and see this woman. That would give me enormous relief.'

'Temporary relief of the flesh, Terry,' Brian Humpfress said, holding himself tighter than a drumskin. 'It doesn't bring you lasting benefit.'

Sneed considered this man, wondering if there was any advantage to be gained from what he proposed – not spiritually, but materially. Perhaps if he was seen to repent and renounce the past he could be brought back into the fold. But he doubted if Humpfress had enough clout to influence such a decision one way or the other.

'There's just no sign of that ticket in there, boss,' DS Preece said, coming to the kitchen door.

Both detectives looked over at Sneed as he drank his coffee. 'You still can't remember where it is?'

'It's here somewhere.' He casually fished in his jacket pocket, and came up with the ticket as if by chance.

Disbelief gave way to relief; then haste as they raced to Victoria Station to get the key.

The attaché case contained only a few yachting magazines. The safe-deposit-box key was inside one of these, pressed into the spine. A quick trip to the safe-deposit office in Cheval Place in Knightsbridge yielded Sneed's two boxes, both of which contained evidence about corruption within the Metropolitan Police. There were files of evidence that had been lost; lists of policemen who had taken money, or bought help for suspects, or diverted police resources and property for their own use; a plot of all the shares that went to every senior policeman involved in the firm within the CID. But there was nothing about the one across the pavement in King's Road. Sneed didn't want to come within a mile of any corrupt association with that one, on account of the traffic warden being murdered. The evidence on that one would stay in Lloyds Bank on the corner of Baker Street and Marylebone Road.

In their excitement at discovering this Aladdin's cave of evidence, Bulmer and Humpfress didn't stop to consider that there might be gaps. There were more recorded incidences of corruption in their possession than they had dreamt of in their wildest imaginings. All that most of the senior members of the Wiltshire team saw as they waded through it all, feeding everything into the xeroxing machine and getting Xeroxes made of the microfiche records, was a return home in a blaze of glory, rather than the ignominy they had come to expect.

'This is absolute dynamite, Brian,' Bulmer said. He was in the office he shared at Swanley with the two superintendents on the case, reading throught the piles of evidence spread across all available surfaces, and now piling up on the floor. 'It's beginning to make me a little nervous. I should hate at the end of this to find that Sneed was right, that there are too many and too high-ranking officers involved for us to take them.' He looked at Brian Humpfress, then quickly avoided his gaze, not wanting to face that prospect but now fearing that it was a possibility.

A shiver ran through Brian Humpfress and he felt unsteady. Terry Sneed and all corrupt policemen like him had to be arrested. He would entertain no other idea.

Detective Superintendent Stan Prince came into the office with an armful of xeroxed sheets, which he made space for on the edge of the desk. 'That's the last, Tony. That fucking machine is near to melting this little lot is so hot.'

'Let's hope it's not too hot, Stan,' Bulmer said, as doubts etched deeper into his unconscious. 'Start collating it. Get Sneed up here to go through it, help things along. Cross reference it with anything we've got. If we move fast enough, we'll get these buggers in the bag before the Met knows what's hit it.'

Collecting Xerox copies of everything they had got from DCI Sneed, Bulmer took it across the corridor and dropped the whole pile on Colin Wells's desk. The deputy DPP was packing his briefcase, about to leave for the day.

'Not planning on an early night, Mr Wells?' Bulmer said bullishly. 'Not just a list of names, but copies of everything Sneed committed to paper. It had better not find its way onto any Met officer's desk. At least not before we make our move.'

'I find that remark entirely offensive, Mr Bulmer.'

'I don't give a fuck. Just unpack your bag and phone your wife. I'd like your opinion on that lot before you go home. I don't care if I have to put a policeman outside your door.'

'This is ridiculous. I'm not a suspect that you can treat in this way.'

'No, you're on our side, Mr Wells. I'm sure you'll sort out the most suitable charges for when we arrest everyone named in there.' With that he turned and slammed out of the office.

He was being optimistic. They failed to move anything like fast enough with his arrests. There were thirty-seven senior policemen of the rank of chief superintendent and above named in Terry Sneed's evidence, the charges against them ranging from perverting the course of justice through to conspiracy to commit robbery. Most would have more than one charge. It seemed entirely reasonable to everyone on Bulmer's side, apart from the assistant chief constable, to assume that if these men had so many charges against them arising solely out of Terry Sneed's evidence, they would have many more incidences of wrong-doing in their own right. Apart from Alan Leeper, the only other non-believer was Colin Wells, who rang the DPP at home after reading through the evidence. Sir Trevor Rump was not enamoured of the idea of those senior policemen being indicted – to say nothing of the one hundred and seventy-nine other policemen they wanted to proffer charges against.

'The situation seems beyond belief, Colin,' the DPP said, resisting an inclination to laugh. 'Am I hearing these figures correctly?' He was trying to anticipate how the Attorney General would react.

'They are rather staggering,' Colin Wells agreed.

'Good God. Are they planning any arrests?'

'They seem to imagine they can arrest everyone who's named.'

'This gets worse. You'd better stonewall, Colin. Let me have a copy of everything you have. I'll have a word with the commissioner in the meanwhile.'

Collating the evidence took most of the night and the next day, and ran into a third day, with few of the Wiltshire team getting much sleep.

Meanwhile, the assistant chief constable ill-advisedly showed a copy of the collator's provisional report to Assistant Commissioner Peter Vyvyan. Vyvyan felt stunned when he read through it, and his mood didn't improve when Alan Leeper came to see him at the Yard to discuss it. He looked grey and tired, more tired than he had looked in a long while, and his stoop was more pronounced; his stomach was upset and he was suffering from diarrhoea. He should have been at home in bed, but he wasn't because of his not unreasonable fear that if he left his office now, he might not be let back in again. His world suddenly appeared to be collapsing beneath him. His worst nightmare was coming true.

'There's no denying that your detectives have been more busy these past few days than in the whole of the preceeding eighteen months. Sneed seems to have implicated two thirds of the CID,' Vyvyan observed. He avoided looking at Leeper, but instead gazed from the fifth-floor window onto Caxton Hall, which was closed now and forlornly gathering grime. He could hear the rattle of his secretary's typewriter through the door, and remembered for some reason that she had got married in Caxton Hall. He went on to wonder if she would believe in him, come what may. He put great faith in her opinion, as he did that of the man in the job.

'It doesn't give me any pleasure, sir,' Leeper said stiffly, wanting the ACC to deny it.

'I can't say it gives me much fucking pleasure,' Vyvyan retorted, turning with a brief spark of resistance. 'Is this rubbish still pouring out of Sneed?'

'He's still helping with inquiries.'

'A dangerous man, that. Obviously very bitter, if not very disturbed. He's like a wounded animal, trying to hurt anyone he can in order to reduce his own pain.'

'He's put his evidence together very carefully.'

'It's all nonsense, vindictive fucking nonsense,' Vyvyan declared, colour returning to his face. 'I suppose this is his only line of defence, trying to mitigate his own wrongdoing by naming more senior officers. He's obviously stark, staring, fucking mad.'

'He's also named a lot of less senior detectives,' Leeper pointed out. 'You're saying it's not true, sir?'

'I don't say there's no single grain of truth in it,' Vyvyan said cautiously, his small eyes darting a glance at Leeper to see how this went down. The tight red face across the room was expressionless. 'I can believe lower-ranking detectives would be involved. That's why you lot are there, after all. What are your plans?'

'I'm having a job restraining my men. They're impatient to start making arrests.'

'A meeting's been called tomorrow morning by the commissioner to consider the report,' Vyvyan said, pinning some hope on that stay of execution. 'I think the DPP requested it.'

Alan Leeper felt considerable inner conflict over this, all of which added to his tension. He didn't want to believe senior policemen were involved, but was having increasing difficulty in denying it. 'There seems only one way to proceed. That's what we were brought in for.'

'You might make a complete fool of yourself and do no one any good, least of all hard-working policemen.'

'I know what we've been thought of here,' Alan Leeper said, feeling his blood pound as he held his frustration in check, 'but we've been prepared to put up with most things to get the job done. That's what my men want, so they can retrieve a little of their pride to take home.' He paused and considered the tall, sallow-looking man. 'Do you know Vera Smalley?' he said, as if delivering a bombshell. It was Vyvyan's wife's maiden name. He waited, but got only an anxious look from the ACC. 'She has a deposit account at the Midland Bank in Streatham with £68,000 pounds in it.'

'My wife's a very careful budgeter,' he joked.

Alan Leeper said nothing. He was slightly staggered at how DCI Sneed had managed to acquire that information, which had been confirmed by a policewoman pretending to be Vera Smalley telephoning the bank about her account.

A sense of desperation flooded Peter Vyvyan. He felt worse in the knowledge that he could have retired four years ago on four-sixths pension, and taken a good job with BP. He realised what a fool he had been not to have got out then, as his wife had wanted. But he had never imagined it would end like this, and he certainly never applied the thief's dictum, 'doing the crime, then doing the time', to himself. He was a senior policeman, after all, not a thief. He wondered about putting his resignation in immediately, before the report was acted on, but decided to rely instead on a slim hope.

The deputy commissioner was not best pleased with Assistant Chief Constable Leeper, not only because the contents of his report were so shocking, but also because, without decent warning, he and his men now expected to arrest all the Met officers named.

'Not once have you come to me for help, Mr Leeper,' he said angrily. Harry Streeter didn't often get angry. 'You've made blanket accusations that we've hampered or distracted your investigations with no shred of evidence to support that claim. As deputy commissioner, I'm entitled to be kept informed at all times about matters affecting the discipline and reputation of my men. Have you shown me, a brother officer, that courtesy? Have you fuck!'

'I did approach Peter Vyvyan on numerous occasions, sir,' Assistant Chief Constable Leeper said, feeling small and foolish.

'And he's been more than supportive. I know he has. Now you repay that support in this way. You want to act on this corrupt policeman's statement without deliberation from the DPP, the commissioner or anyone else.'

Like most senior members of the Met who had seen the Wiltshire CID's provisional report, Harry Streeter was in a state of shock. Having these Turnips proceed with such obvious lack of expertise was one thing, having them get lucky with Sneed was something else. He couldn't take the responsibility to squash it personally.

'No action must be taken on this statement until after the meeting in the commissioner's office. You owe us that courtesy.'

That increased Leeper's blood pressure – he could feel it in his temples and at the back of his head. Although he could live with such an instruction, and the possible injustice that might result from it, his most pressing problem was that he didn't believe he could restrain his men now they had the bit between their teeth. He didn't want to tell Streeter, for fear of appearing more foolish. 'I'll have to talk to the chief constable, sir.'

'You do that, Mr Leeper. I'd better speak to Mr Phillips also.'

What should have been a sweet triumph was now turning to ashes in his mouth. He relished the meeting he now urgently needed with Tony Bulmer less than this one. There was a real possibility that Tony Bulmer would ignore any order to hold off and completely undermine his authority.

'How the fuck do they justify that?' Bulmer demanded, when he met with the assistant chief constable later that day. 'There are eighty detectives out there waiting, Alan. Am I to tell them we're too scared to move against these corrupt bastards? That we've been told to hold off? It's a joke.'

'I know how you feel, Tony, I do.'

'The fuck you do or you'd be saying fuck the Met, fuck the commissioner and fuck the DPP and everyone else – let's arrest the buggers. You know that's what we've got to do, and the sooner we get it done the less likely they are to wriggle out of it. We're almost there now, Alan.'

'They're saying we mustn't proceed – we are here at their invitation.'

'But it's our investigation. We were promised no interference.'

'No one expected this, Tony.'

'Then I want to speak to Mr Phillips,' Tony Bulmer demanded. 'You've let those bastards up here fuck you every which way. I want the chief constable to decide where we go from here.'

When, reluctantly, Alan Leeper rang the chief constable of Wiltshire and explained the situation, there was a lot of anger down the phone. Sydney Phillips exploded often, but acted less often. He had been in constant touch with his investigating team in London, and had made frequent noises of frustration about the sort of treatment they had had to put up with. But none of it had helped the men on the ground.

'This is intolerable,' Phillips said, 'they're pulling a real flanker. We won't have this. I'll make sure I'm at that meeting tomorrow. I'll make sure we do things our way.'

That didn't reassure Tony Bulmer, and he told the chief constable so when he picked up the phone extension. 'The thing is, sir, either we see this through, and we can now we have the means, or you can have my resignation – effective immediately. Then I'll go public.'

'There's no need for that, Tony,' Phillips said. 'I'm on your fucking side, after all.'

'I'm sure I speak for a lot of the lads down here. They'll put in their papers, too. We've really had the brown ass of this lot down here. Really shitty treatment we've received. We expect it from them, but not from our people.'

'Why not just hang on for the meeting tomorrow, Tony?'

'They'll outmanoeuvre us again if we do. There's only one way to stop that: we take the initiative and start arrresting these men, go to the meeting with a lot of them in the bag. See how they cope with that.'

'But we haven't got the charges from the DPP,' Alan Leeper cut in, the telephone providing distance and making arguing easier.

'We know what most of the charges will be.'

'We could get one of our solicitors up from here to look at the charges,' the chief constable suggested helpfully. He didn't wish to risk losing experienced officers.

'That will cause a lot of bad feeling, Sydney,' Alan Leeper advised.

'We'll have to risk it, Alan. We don't exactly have their goodwill as it is.'

'You can argue at that meeting from a position of real strength with these arrests under our belt,' Bulmer said cheerfully. 'We'll show the fuckers we're not just a bunch of Turnips.'

'I'll get someone up there to assist you this afternoon.'

Feeling more uncertain than he had felt about anything in his life, Assistant Chief Constable Leeper agreed to proceed, hoping that once it was started it would be unstoppable – that was the only way they would win. But he still wasn't happy about what they would be doing to brother officers, not even these unconscionable policemen. 'Can I suggest a compromise, Sydney? Let them have their senior policemen. Just bring in those up to chief inspector for now. You can discuss the others with the commissioner tomorrow.'

'What numbers are we talking about?' Sydney Phillips asked.

'About forty,' Bulmer informed him.

'No, I mean how many officers above the rank of chief inspector?'

'Yes, it's about forty,' Bulmer said.

There was silence down the telephone. Finally the chief constable agreed that they shouldn't proceed to arrest those officers until the outcome of tomorrow's meeting.

Bulmer was about to argue, but knew this wasn't the time, if for no other reason than that with only the eighty detectives he had, plus a few more on loan from the Kent Constabulary, he couldn't possibly arrest two hundred and sixteen policemen in one swoop. The break point might as well be the rank of chief inspector as anywhere else. But they would have to try to get as many of the others as possible, and as quickly as possible, before additional evidence went missing or was destroyed.

'We're on our way home,' Tony Bulmer said jubilantly to the assembly of detectives who were spread across the briefing room on the first floor in Swanley police station. He had wondered if this day would ever arrive. At last it had. It was eleven o'clock. Their arithmetic showed that each squad had to arrest three Met officers. They would be hard put to do it, and in a number of cases would have to take an arrested officer with them to the next arrest – except those who lived outside the Met's borders, who'd be taken to the local police station. By the time the solicitor had arrived from Wiltshire, he, Bulmer and the two collators had spent all afternoon and most of the evening working out the charges and the logistics of these arrests, deciding which policemen would cause the least damage if left out at this stage. If they were lucky, they would arrest seventy policemen before the start of the next working day, and perhaps another seventy or so during the day. The numbers were optimistic, Bulmer realised, but he felt positive about their planned move. 'At last we are going to get done what we came here to do, and what some of you must have begun to believe we might never get done – and what the Met believed us incapable of doing. We'll fucking well show those sods that they're wrong.'

That brought a loud cheer from the detectives, some of whom clenched their fists and raised them. Bulmer waited for it to die away, sharing their enthusiasm. He glanced at Brian Humpfress, who was standing on his left, and wondered if he shouldn't be asked to lead them all in a prayer for success. A smile started across his face at that thought, for he believed they'd need something more than prayer to bring this off. But maybe Brian Humpfress knew something more than he did, Bulmer thought generously. Of all the detectives on this case, he was about the only one who hadn't lost faith, who had always believed they would get there in the end.

'You all know what the targets are, and how long we've been waiting, so don't let's balls it up in any way, because they won't invite us back for another crack. As you leave, your team officers will brief you about your targets. The secrecy isn't that we don't trust ourselves or our hosts out there, rather that we don't trust *anyone* from this point. There are seventy targets tonight, let's get them all. It'll be a long night on top of a stream of late nights, but remember, this is the finale. The targets are all policemen, so at least you won't have too much trouble with them.' He paused as laughter welled up. It faded as he spoke again. 'Let's do everything correctly, show them we don't need to stoop to their level to make a pinch. Caution them; search their homes in their presence; then bring them in.' He paused again and glanced at the assistant chief constable who was standing near him. 'Mr Leeper wants to say a few words.'

'Just a couple of general points. Some of these policemen will be senior to you, some have rank as high as chief inspector. We haven't got enough more senior detectives to make those arrests, so just remember to treat them with respect. They're all Met officers, but they are still only suspects.'

Laughter was slow following that joke, but built up when finally they all got it. 'Don't tell them where they're being taken and when they get there don't let them make phone calls or contact anyone.'

'Any questions?' Bulmer asked and scanned the room in the brief silence that followed.

'Is it right that the Met are trying to stop us at this stage, boss?' a DI asked.

Bulmer stared straight out over the room, avoiding the chief constable's look.

'It's come as a bit of a shock to them, that's all.'

That wasn't intentionally funny, but policemen laughed none the less.

'We heard that policemen with a lot more rank than chief inspector were coming, boss,' another voice put in.

Bulmer identified the questioner and glanced at Alan Leeper, who didn't seem as if he was about to answer. 'That's not just a rumour, Tim. There are a number who are going to come, but they are many and we are few. They'll be brought in by prior arrangement.' He glanced round the room, enjoying the look on the faces of these men, and cut short any more questions before spirits were dampened. 'Well, good luck.'

19

The Met's most senior officers, with some noticeable absences, filed silently into the commissioner's conference room on the seventeenth floor, some helping themselves to coffee from the small urn that had been set on a side table along with cups and a plate of biscuits. Those who spoke did so in subdued tones and avoided eye contact, less out of respect for absentees than in apprehension about what was to come. Most of them felt a sense of shock, even outrage, rather as they did when a terrorist offence shattered the relative tranquillity of their lives. No one wanted to be seen to be unable to cope, yet most needed to turn somewhere for comfort, without knowing where. Most of them busied themselves by stirring sugar or milk into coffee, or re-reading the large report each had in front of them. Most glanced up as Sydney Phillips, the chief constable of Wiltshire, came into the room with the assistant chief constable who had been running this operation. Both were wearing their best uniforms and looking quite impressive. A couple of senior officers who had had contact with him over the last eighteen months nodded grudgingly, but no one spoke to them as they got themselves coffee and sat down at the long table on their own. They dipped into the report, and had a whispered, self-consciously animated conversation about different points.

Jack Bentham considered using the excuse of getting more coffee to go and speak to Leeper as they all waited for the commissioner. But he decided that he and his boss were being isolated not because this report named so many corrupt police-men, rather because withdrawal was a response of men who didn't know how to cope with the feelings it had dredged up.

Finally the door to the commissioner's adjoining office opened and Denis Whites stepped into the room with Deputy Commissioner Harry Streeter. The atmosphere became alert. Some of those officers sitting down, including Sydney Phillips and Alan Leeper, rose out of respect; before others could follow, the commissioner told them to be seated. His manner was brisk, but he looked far from in control, and gave the impression of someone in need of sleep. No one doubted that the commis-sioner had been up most of the night. He showed no surprise at the chief constable's presence and made no gesture to welcome him.

'You will have observed that a number of people are missing from this meeting,' Denis Whites said, darting an accusing glance at the two Wiltshire men. 'Officers whom you would ordinarily expect to be present. Deputy Commissioner Streeter purposely didn't invite the senior officers named in Sneed's statement – not because we presume them guilty. Not at all.' He glanced across at the two Wiltshire policemen again, then let his gaze settle on the wall behind them where a painting of Sir Robert Peel hung. He had no more time for Phillips than he had for the assistant chief constable, both of whom he considered low grade. 'In fact, I presume them innocent. I wanted to spare them any embarrassment today. I also wanted to avoid the spectre of collusion or cover-up, just as the Met has assiduously avoided the spectre of interference with the progress of Operation Bad Apple.' He looked directly at Alan Leeper and waited, finally drawing a grudging nod from him. 'You've now stopped arresting Met policemen, I understand?'

'Yes, sir,' Leeper said, glancing at his chief, expecting him to answer. 'On the instruction of the DPP.'

'The Home Secretary,' the commissioner said, to set the record straight and convey to this man, who obviously understood little of Met politics, the gravity of the situation. 'You should never have started arresting them. Not on this scale, not without top-level consultation.' Hostility and fear were endeavouring to erupt through the superficial civility of the meeting.

'We've been hampered at every turn on this investigation,' Sydney Phillips said suddenly, ending the pretence at civility. 'I want them to finish what they came here to do so they can get back to Wiltshire where they belong.'

'We'd all be very happy for them to go back to Wiltshire,' the commissioner said. 'What is doubted is their ability to achieve what they set out to do.'

'They'd have done it long ago but for the resentment of Met officers.'

'We've offered you every assistance.' Realising an open row wouldn't help them to progress or enhance his stature, the commissioner pulled back: 'The Home Secretary's feeling is that we must seek a way through this before irreparable damage

245

is done to the service. There's no doubt that we are being damaged by the uncertainty.'

'With respect, sir,' Leeper said, bravely trying to stay calm but feeling his pulse quickening, 'more permanent damage is likely to be done the longer corrupt policemen are left in place.'

'Are you suggesting there are even more corrupt policemen other than those named in your report?'

'We haven't had time to interview all the policemen in custody, but those we have indicated that there are others. But I was referring to the corrupt detectives we've named but haven't picked up yet. They could destroy evidence, tamper with witnesses ...'

'That presumes them guilty,' Deputy Commissioner Streeter said. 'At the moment most of the evidence hinges on Sneed's statement.'

'Certainly without Sneed we wouldn't have achieved a quarter of what we have. Cracking Sneed was a big break for us.'

'I believe you proceeded against Chief Inspector Sneed in an illegal manner,' an assistant commissioner said, 'keeping him incommunicado for twelve days. Not charging him, or taking him before a magistrate to sanction his detention. The Federation is taking a pretty dim view of that.'

'We were invited to take on an investigation into police corruption,' the chief constable interjected angrily. 'It seems to me you don't like the finding. Then that's no more than we've come to expect from you.'

'But there are rules to observe, chief constable. Just because they're policemen, doesn't mean we can ignore the rule of law.'

As he listened to these arguments, which increasingly gave the impression that Leeper and his boss were in the Star Chamber, Jack Bentham reviewed his own plans regarding the police corruption involved in cases he was investigating. Something had to be done with that sort of evidence. He could hardly ignore it, and obviously turning it over to the Wiltshire police was of no use. In an instant he anticipated the outcome of all this, and knew what he would do. The Wiltshire officers were being outmanoeuvred and didn't have the political clout to avoid what was happening. Their only alternative would be to go public, but it would be astonishing if they did, knowing the damage it would do overall to the job.

'For all we know,' Deputy Commissioner Streeter was saying,

'Terry Sneed may be completely mad, the entire plank of his evidence the product of a very sick mind.'

That idea came alight around the table like touchwood, everyone understanding its implications. Bentham wondered if the deputy commissioner was merely playing Devil's advocate, or if he believed, for whatever reasons, that simply prosecuting all those policemen wouldn't do the job that was wanted. Perhaps he had something entirely different in mind.

A little breathlessly, Alan Leeper said, 'I'm a policeman, I collected the evidence and I presented it to the DPP. It's not for me to pontificate on Sneed's state of mind. I'll leave that to the psychiatrists.'

'Has he been examined?' the commissioner wanted to know.

'Not while he's been in custody with us.'

'Perhaps he should see the chief medical officer. The sooner the better, I'd say. After all, his mental state might have a very serious effect on this.' The commissioner indicated the report, feeling a little relieved. Seeking a psychiatric report would provide a stay of execution, even though finally it might reprieve neither Sneed nor the Met. 'In the meanwhile, the deputy commissioner is going to interview the senior policemen named in your report.'

Wearing a double-breasted suit with a tiny lovat check, and brightly-polished tan shoes, Sneed looked impeccable. He might have been mistaken for the psychiatrist, but for the fact that he was sitting in the stark reception area of the psychiatric department of St Thomas's Hospital. Its attempts to brighten the area with cheap wall prints were a dismal failure. There were crushed cigarette ends and burnt-out matches on the floor, redolent of the burnt-out lives of some of the people who came here. The psychiatrist's secretary glanced up from the report she was checking through on the desk and caught Sneed staring at her through the open doorway. She quickly looked away, then looked back, feeling that she shouldn't be the one to give ground.

'I suppose you'd think it too risky to go out with clients,' Sneed said, still staring at her.

The receptionist said nothing, but looked around her as if deciding whether or not to feel embarrassed. There was no one around to embarrass her. She was in her late twenties, blonde, with large breasts and good legs. Her teeth protruded slightly from her wide mouth, but she had a good smile, which she offered in response to Sneed's comment.

'I thought perhaps you'd like to go for a drink lunchtime.'

'Oh, I have a lunch, I'm meeting someone,' she said, becoming flustered and apologetic. 'A friend.'

Sneed nodded, accepting this, deciding that he had a good chance here since he hadn't had a straight knockback. 'What about this evening? What time do you finish up here?' He didn't imagine that anything would happen today with the psychiatrist that would affect his future as immediately as this evening. He had been suspended on full pay and given his liberty, but had to make himself available to the Wiltshire for questioning. He would rather have been working, but suspension wasn't the end of the world, especially as the prospects for his future were, according to his interpretation, improving all the while. If he was wanted as a public sacrifice, he argued, he wouldn't have been steered to this psychiatrist by the Met's CMO. He wasn't prepared to consider that he might be found mad, or that, if he were, this might end his career and exonerate all the senior officers he had named. 'I'll call back and pick you up.'

'Well, I'm not sure.' She glanced at the door to the consulting room.

'I won't tell your boss if you don't,' Sneed smiled. 'About six o'clock? Let's hope he doesn't commit me to a nuthouse.' Sneed smiled again.

'Oh, that's hardly likely,' the receptionist said, and smiled.

Pursuing women was something Terry Sneed had applied himself to over the past two days. He found it easy and never understood the problem many men had in that area. He supposed the majority feared rejection, which wasn't something that bothered him. He simply took the view that there were more lonely women than not, and all they wanted was for someone to reach out to them.

The door of the consulting room opened and a man in a blazer and well-cut grey flannels put his head out. He jerked it around the reception area agitatedly, as if fearing he'd find it full. The man was about fifty and wore a Wykhemist's tie. 'Mr Sneed. Do come in,' he said expansively.

'I'm Dr Bosé.' He shut the door after Sneed and waved him towards the low chair opposite the desk. 'Do have a seat.' He gingerly felt the well-designed coffee percolator which stood, along with some thick, gold-rimmed Apilco cups, on a small side table like an affectation in the drab, uncomfortable room. He turned sharply as Sneed took his chair behind the desk. 'Some patients prefer to walk; while we talk, they prefer to walk about.'

'I'm fine,' Sneed said, pretending not to notice the doctor's agitation at losing his chair.

'I see. Would you like some coffee – I don't have any milk.'

'Black's fine.' Sneed leaned back in the chair and waited for the doctor to bring his coffee.

'There seems to be a move afoot to have you declared insane,' Dr Bosé said, as if breaking a confidence. 'That seems to be the hope according to your chief medical officer. How do you feel about that?'

'Sounds about right,' Sneed responded, without missing a beat. 'Those cunts are looking to survive, like everyone else. It's the sort of stroke I'd pull.'

'Survival matters a great deal?' Dr Bosé asked as he walked about this small office.

Sneed watched him, wondering if this was a trick question. 'If it didn't I wouldn't be fucking around like this.'

'Then faced with two options, Mr Sneed – on the one hand your being declared insane and allowed to resign, on the other prosecuted and sent to prison – which would you choose?'

'What about the third option?' Sneed wondered if it had escaped this man. 'Staying on in the job?'

The possibility had been dismissed by the psychiatrist, on account of the way the chief medical officer had approached him. What was implicit in his brief was that Sneed was to be found unstable and quietly let retire. He had undertaken similar examinations for the Metropolitan police, and had found no difficulty convincing himself that his opinion only coincidentally accorded with their wishes. 'You believe that to be realistic?' From the circumstances surrounding Sneed's arrest, Dr Bosé doubted it was, even if his sanity wasn't in question.

'It could be arranged easily enough. Who the fuck would question it?'

'Isn't that the purpose of Operation Bad Apple?' Dr Bosé asked. 'To question such wrongdoing?'

'There's been an extensive investigation, that's enough to satisfy most people. It won't matter now whether six or six dozen detectives end up in the frame. No one is going to make trouble, not with the stakes so high: not the media, not Wiltshire – certainly no one in the Met. They all stand to lose too much. The public thinks law and order is breaking down. If that wasn't so, we wouldn't have politicians falling over themselves to increase police powers. Having increased those powers, the Home Office is hardly going to proceed to render the Met ineffective.'

Dr Bosé went across to his desk, retrieved his pad and some pencils, and reluctantly took the lower chair which Sneed should have been sitting in. 'You expect to be allowed to go back to work?' he said casually, without looking up from his note-taking.

'Unless someone decides I'm mad,' Sneed said with a smile.

'Can someone do that, do you feel, regardless?'

'I can decide if someone's a villain, regardless.' Sneed looked directly at the psychiatrist. 'All you'd need is another doctor to sign the Section.'

Dr Bosé smiled, enjoying the client's openness. 'How important is your work to you?'

Sneed hesitated, believing that if he told the truth he would be in this man's power. 'I'm a good detective.'

'What does that mean?'

'I claim more than my share of bodies.'

'As long as no one questions the methods?'

'When someone's afraid of something and they employ some-one to remove that object of fear, it would be a bit perverse to then shout foul. People are perverse, of course, but their need to have their world made safe usually overrides all other feelings.'

'You believe that the police are in a position to conduct themselves in any way they choose as long as it makes, or appears to make, the world safe?'

'That's what we do – our price is high, but not so high it's unacceptable. I doubt if it ever will be. You must know what the solution is,' Sneed said, but ventured it all the same. 'You have to get people to stop being afraid.'

'Do you get a sense of achievement, satisfaction, a sense of power from what you do?'

'How do you feel when you commit someone to the bin?'

'You frequently answer with a question, Mr Sneed,' the doctor observed. 'Why is that, do you think?'

'I'm used to asking questions,' Sneed said directly. He smiled, believing he saw the doctor's tack. 'I don't get a hard-on when I send a villain down. I see it as a tragic waste of human resource being written off in prison. I sometimes even wonder what sort of society we have that requires the likes of me to pursue the likes of him.' Sneed smiled again, feeling really quite pleased with this 'right' answer. He waited as the man opposite scribbled a note on the pad that was resting on his knee, and wondered if he had taken him in.

The interview continued for over an hour, with Dr Bosé filling fourteen pages with notes, often angry comments on Sneed's arrogant assumptions. Roald Bosé had long since learned to confine his anger to his notes. Only when asking the detective if he considered himself sufficiently well paid did the interview take a turn which seemed to lead towards Sneed's true character.

'The job's what you make of it. I work hard. I take something nearer to what I feel I'm entitled to,' he said candidly. 'If you want your dustbins emptied, the rubbish tucked tidily out of sight, you have to pay for it. I've got some property in Spain that can only go up in value; a nice flat here; some of the creature comforts. I work too hard to end up with nothing. I'm a survivor – that makes me a good copper. I've a pretty shrewd idea of my own worth. It's not inflated, and it's certainly not undervalued. I've yet to nick a villain who's been anything but a loser. Successful villains I can count on the fingers of this hand. We don't nick them. They're survivors.'

Dr Bosé smiled. 'You've been nicked, as you say.'

Sneed nodded. 'I expect to get a result. At worst it'll mean quietly retiring. That leaves me poncing around in my boat in Spain. How bad?'

'What sort of boat do you have?' the good doctor asked, his interest coming alive. His passion was boats, and he was twice divorced on account of it – sailing out on his own on warm misty mornings at weekends, not to be seen until it was time to return to the office.

'I have a forty-foot sloop with a fifty-five horse Perkins,' Sneed said.

'That sounds first rate. Do you race her?'

'Never really had the inclination,' Sneed said, noticing the change in this man. 'I suppose it would be quite nice to try. I might have the time soon.'

'What age is she?'

'The keel was laid in seventy-nine,' Sneed said. 'Solid mahogany. There's so much rubbish on the market.'

'Paint and plywood, paint and ply. Have you never seriously thought about racing?'

'Needs a regular crew and hard work. There's a judge who goes out with me mostly. We're happy enough doing what we do. Would you be interested in racing?'

'That sounds very attractive. I have a small catamaran at Cowes. I race a bit. Always been meaning to try and organize something for the Around Britain.'

'Maybe we should have a deal,' Sneed ventured with an uncertain laugh – not because he believed doctors incorruptible, rather because he felt he had no need to take that route. The proposition seemed to pass the doctor unnoticed. 'How long have you been into boats?'

'Ever since I was at Medical School. I organized a crew to sail across to America. Unfortunately we sank off the coat of Ireland. When did your interest in boats begin?'

'A few years ago. An old governor of mine put me onto them as an investment. Boats were better bargains than houses. You could pick up a six- or eight-berth ocean-going yacht for forty-five grand. There's only any value buying when the bottom's out of the market. You have to stay optimistic. Same as I was about the house market in Northern Ireland. I picked up three houses there at just over five hundred pounds each a few years ago. If they never settle their troubles, I'm still earning rent.'

'Are you optimistic about the troubles being solved out there?'

'People have got to live there whether they are or not.'

Dr Bosé nodded thoughtfully. He had made up his mind about Terry Sneed's mental state. 'I have a colleague next door, a psychologist. I'd like you to take some tests with her, then we should talk again.' He rose, and waited for Sneed. 'Would you like to think about entering your boat for the Around Britain next year?'

'It might be a go,' Sneed said as he went out. 'Judge Wertham might be very keen.'

The psychologist was in her early sixties and gave Sneed intelligence tests, but no indication of how well he did. He felt he came out all right, and only at the end of them, when she smiled warmly, did he know he had. They were only slightly harder than some of the tests that were given to would-be policemen when they applied for the job.

'I don't know what you said to Dr Bosé,' Linda, the psychiatrist's secretary, commented when Sneed took her for a drink in the evening, 'but he was very impressed with you.' They were in a wine bar in Clapham – Sneed wasn't known on this manor.

'Does that mean I might get to make love to you tonight?' Sneed said, looking directly at her and smiling.

The young woman giggled and looked around to see if anyone in the bar had heard him. 'I said you impressed Dr Bosé.'

Sneed smiled again; those lying blue eyes suggesting he hadn't a worry in the world. 'At least you've decided I'm not mad. I suppose that's a start.' He poured her some more wine from the bottle of Chablis on the table. Not only was that a start, he decided, but a head start.

After interviewing each of the senior policemen who had been named in the Wiltshire CID's report, Deputy Commissioner Harry Streeter wasn't surprised that, to a man, they had denied involvement. In fact, he didn't know how he would have handled the situation if any had admitted it. He was looking for some face-saving move that would get the Met out of its current predicament. He would have preferred to eradicate the corruption instead; but because of the way the external inquiry had been allowed to spread and get out of control, to do that now would almost certainly mean throwing the baby out with the bath water.

Assistant Commissioner Peter Vyvyan was the last on his list. As he was the most senior officer named in corruption allegations, it was a courtesy to see him either first or last, but had he seen him first and the man he had confessed – and the evidence was perhaps strongest against ACC Vyvyan – then the others might have fallen like a house of cards. The similarity of their responses indicated either that they had all got together to corroborate what they would say, or that they were innocent. Harry Streeter didn't believe the latter.

He waited for Peter Vyvyan to play his stroke and watched the ball lift and bounce twice on the green near the fourth hole. He would make that a hole in three, Vyvyan guessed, which was one over par. It might have been more prudent to let his interrogator win.

On the fairway they had been discussing the psychiatric report on Terry Sneed. Harry Streeter had seen a copy and had précised it. They had made only the most oblique references to Vyvyan's involvement in corruption.

'To be honest, Peter,' Harry Streeter said, resuming the thread of their conversation as they walked towards the green, 'it would have solved an awful lot of problems had the psychiatrist found Sneed mad. We could have slipped him into a private psychiatric unit and waited for the dust to settle.'

'Unless any senior officer you've interviewed supports Sneed's outrageous claims?'

'None has so far,' Harry Streeter said candidly.

Peter Vyvyan stopped on the green and set his caddy back on its stand, all but the remnants of his anxiety having gone. 'I'm not about to spoil the record, Henry. Most of what he said is ballocks. Oh, I don't doubt friend Sneed knows a lot of detectives who are at it. I'd be surprised if they weren't, and we have to take some responsibility for that, of course. But they'll be lower ranks.'

'Even that presents us with a considerable problem, especially in the numbers that have been named.' He played his stroke, which still left him another two from the hole. He waited a few moments until Vyvyan had squared up to his ball, then said, 'There was a lot of money unaccounted for in your wife's bank, Peter. Sixty-eight thousand pounds in her maiden name.'

His knuckles turning white as his fingers tensed on the putter, Vyvyan tried to stop an involuntary trembling running down his arms. He slowly raised his head and forced out a laugh. 'So she does. S'all circumstantial, Henry. I suppose if it got out it wouldn't look too clever, especially in the circumstances. But it's only a minor tax fiddle: Vera's old man gave it her for safekeeping, to avoid death duties. He's got quite a bit put by from his shops. The account's in her maiden name because she doesn't want to get clobbered for capital gains tax. The greedy fuckers take it every way they can.' He waited a moment then, satisfied that the lie had bedded down, played his stroke. The ball rolled around the rim of the hole and stopped a foot or so beyond. 'The way to solve the Met's little dilemma, Henry, is to send those fucking clods back home to Wiltshire where they belong, then second Terry Sneed to CIB2 and let him catch corrupt policemen.'

There was a pause while Harry Streeter thought about that. He expected the ACC to laugh, or at least smile and indicate that he was joking. But he didn't. 'Are you quite serious, Peter?'

'Never more so. As my old gran used to say, set a thief to catch one. Who better than Sneed to look at police wrongdoing? If he can't catch them, who can?'

Harry Streeter laughed. 'It's fucking outrageous,' he said. 'I've never heard anything so outrageous.'

'It's bold and imaginative. Look at the man's record. Eleven commendations – one from the Queen, even. You tell me a better way out of this.'

Outrageous as he continued to find the ACC's proposal Deputy Commissioner Streeter had to admit, albeit only to himself, that he couldn't see a more viable solution. In the absence of one, it was more than possible that a suggestion such as Peter Vyvyan's might even be adopted.

20

Jack Bentham could only speculate as to why the deputy commissioner had invited him to this afternoon's conference at the Home Office. They were to discuss the proposals for concluding Operation Bad Apple following the arrest of Terry Sneed, but Bentham couldn't say he enjoyed hearing the sort of proposals that were being mooted. Although he had no real objection to Terry Sneed walking clear, Bentham somehow felt it offensive that it might come about by intervention of the Home Secretary. If that happened, it would mean the hierarchy hadn't the courage to grasp the nettle of police lawlessness and deal with it regardless of consequences. It would mean they were more concerned to parade an acceptable image for the police than provide a service to the public. That would amount to a tacit admission that any level of corruption was tolerable provided the Met wasn't seen to be corrupt, and that, of course, was political expediency. Bentham wondered if Harry Streeter had invited him along to the meeting to somehow upset their plans, to force the issue of mass prosecutions out of some perverse streak in his nature. If that was the deputy commissioner's plan, Bentham wasn't sure that he had the goods, much less the will, to do it. What he *was* going to do was try a couple of moves that might enable him to pull the plug in his own way and in his own time, if it became necessary. Perhaps that time was now, he thought, with all the pressure that was being put on his inquiry out at Hackney. If he got the information he wanted, he would still only have the option; having the courage was another matter.

Denis Rattigan was part of that option. Since his arrest in the C11-organized raids eighteen days previously, he had been held in police cells at Tooley Street. He was one of only six out of the sixty-eight suspects to be held in this way; the majority had been remanded at Brixton Prison; a couple had been released without charges. Although Rattigan hadn't been charged in connection with the robbery across the pavement in King's Road, his involvement was strongly suspected, as part of the money found at his house was believed to have come from that bank. It was all in old notes, money that could go straight back into circulation whenever the villain had felt safe to start spending it. In the circumstances Rattigan probably regretted not having done so immediately. Some of the notes had been identified by a couple of the cashiers in the King's Road bank as bearing their personal marks. But any good barrister would make much to a jury of the fact that hundreds, if not thousands, of similarly-marked notes would be in circulation, and that it might not be unreasonable for his client to have the three that he had among his 'savings'. How he would explain his unemployed client's thirty-five thousand pounds' worth of savings was another matter. But when he went across to Tooley Street, Jack Bentham had in mind something other than securing evidence to convict this villain on the King's Road robbery. There was enough to convict him for his part in the Faversham Securicor truck robbery, and he wouldn't gain any more time for King's Road. But by firmly implicating Rattigan in that blag, he believed he could implicate Terry Sneed also. Rattigan and Howie's evidence together might do what Howie's statement alone could not, as Howie hadn't actually had any direct dealings with Terry Sneed.

Eighteen days in a police cell had brought Denis Rattigan no philosophy that might help him resign himself to prison; every minute would probably drag as if it were a life sentence. Jack Bentham recognized this the moment he walked into the ground-floor interview room where Rattigan had been brought by two gaolers. He paused long enough from his agitated pacing to grind out his cigarette stub.

'You couldn't spare another one?' he appealed. He had given up smoking on the outside but, confined where access would be difficult for a long time to come, he had perversely resumed the habit. Even among policemen, it was difficult nowadays to find enough who smoked to ensure some sort of steady supply. 'This is only my second smoke all day,' he apologised to Bentham.

'Life could be a lot easier for you, Denis. You won't get your liberty, but you could have cigarettes, visits from your wife, see your kids.'

'What do I have to do, become a grass?' Rattigan glanced at the two uniforms who stepped outside at DCI David Evans's bidding. 'Thanks for the smoke, pal.'

'Everybody else does it, Denis. They can't all be wrong,' Bentham said, gently mocking him. 'You're bang to rights over

Faversham. Frank Howie has put you in for the one across the pavement in King's Road.'

'Who the fuck's Frank Howie? I keep asking him,' indicating Evans. 'I don't know the man. In fact, I don't know anyone else on that one apart from Ronnie Letts. He gave me the work.'

It wasn't a classic slip but a casual yielding to the inevitable. He was weary of the continual uncertainty and depressed by his prospects. He knew the detective wasn't lying when he said everyone grassed. People who Rattigan never thought would do it in a hundred years turned to it. No one in their right mind wanted to do a long prison sentence. 'I'll take any help I can get over King's Road. It got a bit nasty. Wasn't meant to happen like that.'

'It never is,' Bentham said, without showing his anger. 'But that's often the way, someone getting hurt when you take shooters.'

'Bit difficult trying it without, I'd say.'

Bentham conceded this with a nod. 'We'd like the Old Bill who put you into it. Word is it was a detective.'

'Why's that? So you can pull him clear?'

'Probably,' Bentham said casually.

There was a pause. Rattigan was unsure, now, realising that he had committed himself to something he couldn't complete. 'You'll have to go out to Spain and talk to Ronnie Letts. There was an Old Bill involved. I think the bank manager was involved, too. But Ronnie stayed very closed up about that. I just made up the number. Funny thing is, Ronnie would say, "If you don't know, sunshine, you can't grass no one." S'cunning fucker. I mean, he's out in Spain with his bit of poke, here's us nicked.'

'Only you and the body – Frank Howie,' Bentham told him. 'If it's any consolation, we will nick the others.'

'S'only any value if it gets me some sort of result.'

'Who was the fourth man on the blag, aside from the driver?'

'Fuck it, a cunt, I am!' Denis Rattigan said, almost in tears. 'I don't fucking know. That's the truth, I don't. I never got to meet them other than for the blag. All I know was that he was called Brian – Ronnie called him "Bri", it's got to be Brian. I didn't know any of them apart from Ronnie. They didn't know me.'

'Frank Howie knew you,' Bentham lied.

'How? Ronnie said there was no need for us to have that sort of information.'

'Who was it did the shooting? Killed the traffic warden?' Evans asked.

Denis Rattigan hesitated, looked at Evans, then away. 'I'm not sure. It may have been Ronnie. It might have been Bri, but I think it was Ronnie.'

'How often does he come back to England?'

'The cunning bastard he is. You won't nick him. Not now he's out there with his bit of poke. He's got no reason to come back, apart from to see his old Mum. He thinks the world of her. He could get by without seeing her – I know I could.'

There was a long pause while Bentham thought about the extradition possibilities now existing with Spain. But more of a problem at the moment was the evidence they would have to place before the court in order to secure a warrant. The case had to be made, and that was the case that then had to be put at any subsequent trial. What they needed was Ronnie Letts tucked up in a cell somewhere here.

Out of the uncertainty created by this silence, Denis Rattigan said, 'I can give you the geez' who put us into that one at Faversham, if that helps. He was Old Bill.'

Bentham smiled encouragingly. 'Every little bit helps.'

The rain that had been falling since early morning was torrential when Jack Bentham's car passed through the security barrier and into the inner courtyard of the Home Office. He waited a moment, as if hoping someone might emerge from the glass doors with an umbrella. No one did, so he ran across the pavement. Because he lived in well-heated offices and cars, Bentham rarely wore a coat or mac and got wet in those few paces to the door. That, as well as his being late for the Home Secretary's meeting, made him very conspicuous on the seventh floor when he was shown into the large, modern office. He slid into one of three vacant places at the round table, mumbling an apology. No one was interested. The fair, diffident-looking Home Secretary glanced at him, as if uncertain who he was or why he was there, or why he was wet, and went on talking about the psychiatric report on Detective Chief Inspector Sneed. Each of the nine other people present had a copy. Bentham glanced at

Deputy Commissioner Harry Streeter, but wasn't acknowledged with so much as a raised eyebrow; Bentham began to wonder if he had in fact been invited.

'This is all quite unequivocal,' Charles Freeman, the Home Secretary, said, his small, watery eyes passing over the sombre-looking faces.

There was only courteous agreement. The whole polite tone of the meeting was a veneer covering fear and ambiton and seething hostility. The participants had had a lot of practice at presenting a civilized facade.

Julian Brind slid a copy of the report across to Bentham.

'Unfortunately, Charles, the doctor found the fellow as sane as any of us,' Sir Walter Pursar, the fifty-five-year-old Attorney General, said. 'Or as mad – I fear we're all a bit touched in our handling of this. It's ridiculous.' Such impetuous statements prevented Pursar stepping into the Lord Chancellor's shoes, so rumour had it.

The Home Secretary gave him a deprecating look, deciding he was wetter than the detective who had arrived late. 'The possible consequences of prosecuting all those policemen are causing a good deal of unease in Cabinet. To say nothing, I'm sure, of the feeling among policemen on the street.' He glanced at Jack Bentham, but didn't find any sort of response. 'Leeper has actually stopped arresting policemen?'

'He has for the time being,' Harry Streeter said. 'He's holding a lot in police cells and continuing to question them.'

'There have been a great number of complaints from solicitors about their clients being held without charges – also from the Police Federation,' Sir Trevor Rump informed them. 'You could start losing their goodwill, Charles.' The DPP was less than happy about the situation; he thought things were all but out of control.

'Oh, I still have their goodwill, Trevor?' Charles Freeman said with a boyish laugh. He wondered where the voracious demands of the police would end, or at what point he might dare to refuse them.

'We have to presume there is sufficient evidence for more arrests, Trevor?' Sir Walter Pursar said.

The deputy commissioner replied, 'They only got around to arresting about half those named by Sneed. More names of policemen are being put forward. I can say no more than that.'

There was an uneasy silence.

Finally the Home Secretary said with a note of irritation, 'This situation can't be allowed to continue. If all these police-men were prosecuted, and possibly many more besides, it would devastate the Met. Policemen the world over look to them for help, see them as a model for enforcing the democratic rule of law.' He was proud of that, and felt ashamed that two weeks ago a hundred uniformed policemen with truncheons drawn, some with dogs, had turned and run from a crowd of football hooligans at Chelsea. Fortunately that element of the story hadn't emerged. But the damage the football fans had done on their rampage through the grounds had made good copy, which had helped him launch his new, tougher measures for dealing with such violence. However, another humiliation for the police might not meet with the same silence from the media.

'We can't presume these officers guilty, Home Secretary,' Sir Trevor Rump said, 'simply because they're in police cells or being interviewed.'

'Perhaps it's time to shift the emphasis of all this mess away from the Met,' the police commissioner said. 'That would happen if we started thinking in terms of a national police force.'

'The danger there, as I see it at present, Denis, is that in the public's mind the Met may be seen to contaminate the rest.' These were the considered words of Sir Roger Weaver, the permanent secretary at the Home Office. He was in favour of a national police force, and through Neville Masham, the deputy undersecretary with responsibility for the police department, he was fostering that notion. But such a move would be a disaster in other than the right circumstances. The fears engendered by the setting up of a National Reporting Centre by the Association of Chief Police Officers during the miners' strike was a clear indication of that. The centre, based at Scotland Yard, had collated by computer every scrap of information and intel-ligence from up and down the country at different pits, and responded with manpower and resources to 'on paper' situat-ions, regardless of the local feelings.

'I'm inclined to agree, Denis,' the Home Secretary said. 'I can't think why the public would have any more confidence in a national police force at this stage.' He glanced over at Julian Brind. 'I thought you were telling us that that was what we already have, more or less, through our police computer network?'

'The network isn't complete, Home Secretary,' Brind said. 'Nor will it be until we have the master computer. At the moment it relies on goodwill and co-operation from individual police forces. As most policemen know, because of rivalry and jealousy, that isn't always forthcoming. We can't start such a computing operation unless we have some national force to run it – unless the Home Office were to run it directly. That's hardly practical for the obvious reason that we're not policemen.'

'The Met seems to run the CRO computer well enough,' the commissioner pointed out. 'We hold thirty million records indexes there.'

'That's purely an information service,' Brind pointed out. 'The master computer would work through all existing police computers, as well as being able to link up with DHSS, schools, banks and so on. It would work on information held, not just indexes.'

'Is that possible?' Sir Walter Pursar asked, a little shocked.

Julian Brind smiled. 'All that's lacking is the political commitment.'

'If we don't win back the hearts and minds of the general public,' Jack Bentham said quietly and unasked, 'not only are we not going to be able to introduce a national police force that will have the support and trust of the nation, but policing will be an increasingly uphill affair.'

'Are you going to tell us what the secret is, chief superintendent,' the Attorney General asked, 'for winning hearts and minds?'

'With respect, sir, unless we get our act cleaned up, or at least give that appearance, we won't even get to Go.'

'Isn't that what has been happening?' Sir Trevor Rump asked. 'It's that which has brought the Met almost to its knees.'

'It's been painful and fairly destructive,' Bentham said. 'But to go through that sort of pain and wreak that sort of destruction without deriving any benefit seems a stupid exercise.'

'In other words, Mr Bentham,' Sir Roger Weaver said, 'you believe we should tear the centre out of the Met?'

'We might need to suffer a little more before we get well.'

'The danger is that the patient could die on us.'

'That's what we're trying to prevent.'

'We certainly are,' the Home Secretary put in.

Bentham looked at him and decided not to further his argument. It was fairly obvious that the minds around this table were made up about the best course of action. No one had come to this meeting undecided.

'Whatever the virtues of a national police force or the master computer, neither will help the Met out of its current predicament,' Charles Freeman said, shifting the argument as he poked around in his ear with his finger and examined what he brought out. 'Unless someone has a more constructive proposal, I believe we might implement your suggestion, Denis. Promote Mr Sneed and put him where he will do most good rather than least harm, CIB2. Let him catch corrupt police.'

'This amounts to a tacit amnesty for all those policemen under arrest,' Sir Walter Pursar pointed out, neither approvingly nor disapprovingly. He glanced at the permanent secretary. 'We can assume that some are corrupt, Roger.'

'The emphasis should very much be on the "tacit",' the Home Secretary said. 'It would rather defeat the purpose of these endeavours if the public lose the image of the police as guardians of their security, and my new proposals dealing with riot and public order might be undermined.' He shot a glance at Jack Bentham, but didn't allow his eyes to linger. Everyone present knew how fine a balancing act was required to keep the public behind the police regardless of their tactics.

The decision had been taken, Bentham realised, not to prosecute hundreds of Met policemen. If any at all were to go to court, there would certainly be no senior policemen among them. All that remained was to arrange the details of the whitewash. He caught Deputy Commissioner Streeter's look and held it for a second or two, trying to read what was going on behind those grey eyes. Whatever it was, Bentham knew he couldn't help him out, not here.

'I couldn't get the evidence I was after in place,' Bentham said to Harry Streeter when the meeting had broken up. He regretted not having been able to amass the evidence he had been looking for that would corroborate Sneed's claims about corruption. It would have been satisfying to have presented it as a *fait accompli*, if only to have observed how they fielded that one. But the system wasn't designed to respond to individual, heroic gestures. Realistically, all he could do was go along with the censensus opinion about how things should be, or resign.

'Perhaps it was as well.'

Bentham looked, but said nothing.

'We're none of us so naive as to believe that you can have a police force without a certain amount of corruption, Jack. A man comes to me and says help this man up the ladder, overlook this because he's in my lodge – it's no less corrupt than what Sneed and the others have been doing.'

Harry Streeter paused as he slipped his papers into his briefcase. 'What we can't abide is having to admit it, even to ourselves. No one in my time has ever come to terms with it and dealt with it, and I doubt they ever will in your time. It's a fact of life.'

'Maybe,' Bentham said, seeing no point in arguing about the self-justification when the decision was already made. However, that made him feel he was part of some uncontrollable institutional corruption, and redundant as a result. He didn't enjoy the feeling, and wondered about Harry Streeter's apparent change of direction.

Julian Brind was waiting for him in the outer office. 'Couldn't give me a lift back to Horseferry House, Jack?' he asked.

'I think it very unfair that your lot have cars at your constant disposal and assistant secretaries have to take taxis,' Brind said humorously in the back of Bentham's car.

'You could always draft a proposal to change that situation,' Bentham said.

Brind smiled. 'In the current economic climate a discussion paper on why all policemen should go back to bicycles might be more appropriate. It would be a real contribution to new computer hardware.'

'At those sort of prices we'd have to go into the bank-robbing business,' Bentham said, and wished he hadn't.

'It seems a number of your colleagues are already. But, as ever, it's the wrong approach. The real robbers are the banks, of course. Borrowing money as the Met has been doing to pay for its computers is a ridiculous way of approaching the technological revolution. Far better that the government provided resources on a national basis. The Met has just borrowed twenty-eight millions on the money market – far more than it can afford to repay in any one financial year, or can carry forward as a deficit to the next financial year. The interest, of course, is crippling.'

'So losing our cars is a serious prospect, Julian?' Bentham ventured, wondering why he was being put in this privileged position, if indeed that was what it was.

'Do you think the Wiltshire police will accept what was proposed by the Home Secretary?' Brind asked.

'Of course. With the DPP deciding there is insufficient evidence, they'll have little choice. They won't like it, but that's another matter. I'm sure you'll be able to rely on the traditional silence of the police. One or two might want to go public.'

'Which do you feel will be the most put out by it?'

'I don't know them well enough, Julian. There's a DCI named Humpfress. He might feel disgruntled. Rumour has it that he sees this as a moral crusade.'

Brind looked over at him and smiled. 'Has anything by way of rumour about him found a place on your computer?'

Bentham hesitated. 'CIB2 have a few entries in their computer going idle. He's into violence. Mostly towards his wife, but it has been rumoured to spill outside the family, mainly in the direction of women working at some form of prostitution.'

'Cleaning up the city, making it a decent place for women and children to walk abroad.' Brind was amused. 'Anything indictable?'

'With a little pressure on the witnesses. Rex Parker at CIB2 would probably welcome the excuse.'

'We'll have to see how vociferous Chief Inspector Humpfress wants to be. There is a fairly major police scandal brewing in the Wiltshire according to the chief inspector of constabulary. Their chief constable's been spending money on all sorts of things he shouldn't. He may have to be suspended pending an inquiry. If we choose our time well, it will deflect attention away from the Met and its troubles. How is your inquiry out at Hackney progressing, Jack?'

'It's almost done.' He hesitated. 'It looks messy. The selection and command structure of the DSUs is a shambles. The units have attracted the worst sort of copper – the unthinking, gung-ho cowboy, the sort who bash heads and ask questions after-wards. They could function fairly effectively had they comman-ders who thought on their feet. All they seem to be interested in is the unit identity, the more macho the better. They appear not to be able to cope with anything outside of what was planned for – which, as I understood it, was their purpose. They seem to see themselves solely as mopping-up units.'

'Is this all going into your report?' Brind wanted to know.

'It wasn't my brief to write a critique of the DSUs. All I was asked to do was conduct an inquiry surrounding the death of Paul Bailey. That's what I've done. If the policemen involved are to be believed, then they didn't kill him. But I'm inclined to believe the witnesses who were on the demonstration. Of course, both have a vested interest in their own particular version of the truth coming out. The murder weapon wasn't found, but going by the collection of weapons those DSU officers had in their lockers it seems reasonable to assume that a similar cosh or sap was used to hit Bailey.'

'That could prove very damaging to the police, Jack,' Brind pointed out.

'How long are we to go on pretending that nothing is amiss, that men in the job are acting like reasonable, rational, impartial enforcers of the law when they're anything but. Maybe, Julian, just maybe, it's time to put our house in order. Because things aren't going to get better, they're going to get worse.'

'For who?' Brind wanted to know.

'For the public. Laws will inevitably become more restrictive, dare I say draconian? Parliament won't need much persuading to vote in the Home Secretary's new proposal. What other way can they go? Never in our recent history have so few had so much to protect from so many.'

'Oh, I like that, Jack – paraphrasing Churchill is always well received,' Brind said with a smile. 'I'll use that, if I may.'

'Laws inevitably get to be more repressive in these circumstances.'

'Are you suggesting that the alternative is a fairer distribution of wealth and power?'

Bentham laughed. 'That's about as realistic as expecting to have a police force without corruption. What I'm saying is, if we expect to maintain order in confrontation policing, which is what we're getting further and further into, then we have to be seen to be as straight and fair-minded as we can be.'

'It occurs to me, Jack, that the Metropolitan Police face two potentially very embarrassing and damaging situations: one, the death of Paul Bailey; the other, this revelation of widespread corruption. It seems rather unfortunate that the Met should be burdened with both at more or less the same time.'

'Neither is going to get up and walk away to a more convenient time.'

'Is there ever such a time? My assessment is that the latter is possibly the most damaging in the long term. Would you agree?'

'I'd say so. Charging a policeman with murder or unlawful killing will cause a lot of anger, but then people will quickly forget once the offenders have been seen to have been dealt with – assuming they're found guilty.'

'Precisely my mind. Possibly it would be sensible to go in hard in that area in order to deflect attention away from corruption. That vociferous section of the public which is against the police on all fronts simply needs a focus for its invective. If the policemen involved over Paul Bailey's death were to stand trial and were found guilty, no one could accuse the police of acting with favour towards their own.'

'If they were found not guilty, Julian?' Jack Bentham asked.

'That would surely depend on how good your evidence is.'

There was a pause. Bentham considered this approach in relation to his earlier conversation with Julian Brind – about precipitating discontent among animal rightists over Paul Bailey's death, by exonerating the police with the intention of leading them to engage in unlawful acts that would cost them public sympathy.

'That's a shift in emphasis in favour of the animal rights protesters,' he pointed out.

'The stakes are higher now. We'll find something else with those people. They're not going to abandon their ideals and stop what they do. However, if we're left with a thoroughly discredited police force there's no telling what chaos might ensue.'

This was game-playing, as far as Bentham could see, manipulation of events for advantage in a way that had nothing at all to do with truth, or rightness, or justice. He wondered fleetingly what Helen would say if he told her of this sort of trading. He wouldn't tell her, of course.

'Where does all this leave us at the end of the day?'

Brind smiled winsomely. The car was now stationary outside the west entrance of Horseferry House, and he stopped with his fingers on the door handle. 'I'm very ambitious, Jack. I'm going to get Neville Masham's job eventually, deputy undersecretary – possibly even Sir Roger Weaver's job, though I probably went to the wrong university for that. I'm certainly not going to advance over the remnants of a broken, ineffective police force.'

'Where do you imagine all this leaves me, then?' Bentham wanted to know.

'If I have anything to do with it, Jack,' Brind said evenly, looking him directly in the eyes, 'you can go as high as you like, assuming that's of interest to you.' He smiled again at Bentham's silence. 'Perhaps you'd let me take a dekko at your report on the Bailey killing before it's finalized.'

'That can be arranged, Julian,' Bentham said. He had agreed to do the same for Harry Streeter – only the deputy commissioner hadn't offered him anything.

'Thanks for the lift.' Brind slipped out of the car and across the pavement into the inelegant building.

Bentham sat unmoving, knowing he should have been feeling pretty pleased, but paradoxically feeling depressed. He had no doubt that Julian Brind was going to get where he wanted to get, but wasn't sure he wanted to go with him – not if it meant clinging to his shirt tails, doing his bidding. He guessed that was how all bureaucratic institutions ran.

His driver looked round at him, waiting for his instruction. He thought about going back to his office to work on the Paul Bailey death report, but decided to visit Helen instead.

The press conference signalling the rundown of Operation Bad Apple was a well organized and well attended affair held in the fifth-floor lecture hall at the Yard. This delicate situation had to be handled sensitively, as it was essential to the police that they received the right sort of media coverage – the sort which explained the success of the operation and at the same time sealed off the loose ends, cleared the air of the putrefying smell of a cover-up. The kind of coverage wanted by the deputy assistant commissioner with responsibility for public relations was assured by virtue of the fact that the eighty-odd journalists present were all holders of the special-privileges press card issued by the Met. DAC Andrew Rapsey made a couple of jokes, then read a short statement to remind journalists how the investigations into police corruption had come about. He stated how the Met had invited this – after wild allegations from a known criminal – in order to be seen to be clean, despite knowing themselves to be clean; and how, once they had started, the Wiltshire CID was encouraged to pursue every rumour that any criminal put up about possibly corrupt policemen; and how, in order for there to be no suggestion that the Met was in any way interfering with the investigation, the Wiltshire lads – many of whom had incidentally formed solid friendships with brother officers in the Met – were encouraged to move in with the Kent Constabulary. Having taken a long, hard, close look at the Metropolitan Police, they had concluded that there wasn't, in fact, any widespread corruption. However, there were odd incidents of individual corruption, which would result in criminal proceedings. Having said that, he handed the briefing over to Assistant Commissioner Peter Vyvyan.

'By and large, ladies and gentlemen,' the ACC said, 'there is less corruption within the Metropolitan Police force than there are impurities within the metropolitan water system, and I see no evidence of people refusing to trust the water.' The press laughed. From this point, he coasted right through to opening the session to questions. There were many, all of which were fielded easily. Because of the obviously unacceptable consequences, no one truly wanted to believe that police corruption was endemic, or even widespread, so relatively few of the questions were awkward; those that were met a firm rebuttal and weren't pursued.

'The police corruption investigation is completely run down now, assistant commissioner?' asked a lady journalist, one of the few.

'Not run down, scaled down. Its perimeter is being re-established to deal with matters such as the original complaint that brought the Wiltshire police here in the first place.'

'Does that mean that the investigation has been a complete waste of police resources?'

Peter Vyvyan smiled, humouring her. 'On the contrary, my dear. It's been a huge success. We have charged two policemen, one of them a detective sergeant. But more than this, we've thoroughly examined our navel and found almost no fluff at all.' That brought a wave of laughter. 'What other institution examines itself as publicly and as thoroughly as the police? To be able to say, at the end of such a painstaking examination, that we aren't a barrel of rotten apples after all is quite an achievement, I'd say. I feel very proud about it.'

No one pointed out that it was policemen, yet again, who were looking at policemen. It might have seemed impolite to do so in those circumstances.

'But the investigation is continuing, sir?' a young reporter from the *Mirror* asked.

'Of course. We won't be satisfied until everything has been held up to the light. Detective Superintendent Sneed of CIB2 has been made operational head of the investigation. Chief Inspector Humpfress is remaining behind to help tie up any loose ends. Only then will we be satisfied that the job is complete.'

Both Terry Sneed and Brian Humpfress were sitting at the table on the stage, one relaxed and cheerful, the other so tense he seemed about to burst. It had taken a lot for Brian Humpfress to swallow this; he had been offered a course at Bramshill with promotion to superintendent to follow, but had turned it down. He was determined to see this through.

'Could you tell us what the whole operation has cost, Mr Vyvyan?' asked a reporter who was on first name terms with Peter Vyvyan.

'A lot more than my share of all this ill-gotten gain we were supposed to be having,' Vyvyan said with a smile. 'The final accounting isn't in, Stephen, but I think we're looking at a figure adjacent to two million pounds.'

'This will have to be borne by the Met?'

'Unless we take the hat round. This is how effective the criminals are with their malicious, unfounded allegations. That's two million pounds that will never go into fighting real crime. Two million pounds' worth of police hours that won't go onto the streets preventing criminal behaviour. But that's how highly we prize our reputation.'

That was the stuff of a number of editorials the following day. A parting shot from another well-placed journalist about the scandal the Wiltshire police were now facing on their return made the tabloids' main police story.

That proved a satisfactory subterfuge. The effective close-down of Operation Bad Apple was scarcely noticed.

21

The number of times Brian Humpfress had been drunk could be counted on the fingers of one hand, as could the number of times he had been ill as a result. Drink didn't agree with him, but there were times when the pill one was asked to swallow was so bitter that only alcohol could wash it down. So many people found an answer in drink and he was disappointed that he couldn't; however, on these occasions and in the cold reflection of sobriety the following day, he felt more disappointed that he had turned to drink rather than God. Then he would feel wretched and ashamed. But he wasn't approaching that stage yet.

Frustration had blotted out the reasoning process and brought with it a creeping tension that wouldn't go away. Sitting through that mockery of a press conference had been difficult for him, but he had suppressed an impulse to decry the deceit and hypocrisy, because he hadn't found the courage to do otherwise. God had deserted him, just as he in his turn deserted Him by turning to drink. Alcohol had now nicely numbed the edges of his frustration. The palpable centre of pain remained, but it was inaccessible, existing rather as if it was no longer a part of him, as if it wasn't his responsibility. Nothing changed, but it was easier just to go on putting one foot in front of the other. The alcohol had caused the tics in the left-hand side of his face to lose their anger.

How he came to be out at Hammersmith, ringing Detective Chief Superintendent Bentham's doorbell, he didn't know. He had started out with the intention of going to visit Detective Superintendent Sneed, to tell him what he thought of him and what he had planned for him; that idea was chased out by the notion of going to Soho and visiting some of its disease ridden habitués, but he had decided that the dangers were too great. His position in having remained behind while his colleagues had returned home was too tenuous.

The mansion block in which Jack Bentham lived had an expensive atmosphere, the sort created by high ceilings and thick carpet and flowers on the hall table. The doorbell on the third floor had a satisfying resonance and Humpfress left his finger against the bell-push for so long that he forgot it was there until Jack Bentham opened the door.

Looking out into the corridor, Bentham half-expected to see more policemen there, until he noticed the condition Humpfress was in. 'Why didn't you crash it in?' Bentham asked, but the sarcasm was lost on his visitor. He removed his finger from the bell-push and ushered him in.

'I'm going to get that bastard,' Humpfress said, collapsing into a large armchair in the sitting room. 'S'why I stayed on. I was asked to go on a Command Course at Bramshill. But I asked to stay on. Just until I can send him down. I didn't tell them that. I didn't tell anyone but you.'

Bentham switched off the television. Despite Humpfress being fairly drunk he guessed this wasn't a social visit. 'Do you want another drink or some coffee?'

'Coffee might make me sober,' Humpfress said looking glassily across at his host. 'Sneed's going away if it's the last thing I do.'

'You had your chance. All you are now is window dressing. You're better off taking a course at the Police Staff College and getting your promotion. You can help others to stay on the path of righteousness then.'

If Humpfress noticed Bentham's joke he didn't show it. He shook his head. 'I want you to help me.'

'Be realistic. Why not accept Terry Sneed as part of that inevitable pattern of police corruption? It's not going to go away even if you manage to put him down.' He took him a glass of whisky. That was all he had in the flat, apart from some wine that Helen had left. He assumed Humpfress hadn't been drinking wine.

'He's making a fool of honest coppers. He's saying all policemen are corruptible.'

'He's probably right,' Bentham said casually. 'Ours is a peculiarly opportunistic world. Terry's more enterprising than most, makes a few more opportunities. He'll go. He won't always be as well covered as he was this time.'

'I want you to help me make sure,' Humpfress said, with all the earnestness he could muster. He sat forward to emphasise his point, spilling his drink.

Bentham considered him. 'Did you get anything to eat tonight?' He could see Humpfress was going to either pass out or throw up or both, and decided food might help to sober him. The Chinese restaurant on the Broadway were used to catering for drunks.

They ate curried vegetables with fried rice and drank some beer. Humpfress managed to eat and keep it down. He rambled on about his ambitions as a policeman and what his motives were, how he wanted to set the world aright; the frustration he felt that things didn't meet his expectations; he touched on religion, and feeling uneasy Bentham joked that vegetarianism was his religion.

Humpfress stopped eating and looked at Bentham, then down at his food, as if believing himself tricked into eating it. 'There's no morality here, Jack. That's what's needed you know. Scrape off the surface dross. They can all be set back on the path, once they acknowledge their guilt and are prepared to repent.'

'You ought to be on the Parole Board,' Bentham advised him, and signalled the waiter for more beer. He decided to let Humpfress collapse, then pour him into a taxi.

'There's no one else who can help me scrape back to clean bone. There's no one else I can trust. Sneed'll see everything I do now I'm working under him. Can you know what that feels like? What I had to do to stomach that? It made me feel physically sick. It's such a mockery. But I'm prepared to put up with it.'

Jack Benthan didn't want to get involved in whatever this detective was planning for Terry Sneed, as he had ideas in that direction himself. But what he saw before him, or thought he saw, was a man close to a breakdown. If any offer of help would prevent that, then it was little enough.

'Show me whatever you get. I'll try and help you to use it effectively.

That was all Brian Humpfress wanted. He didn't finish his new drink before stumbling quickly out to the toilet. One of the waiters came to the table a short while later and informed Bentham that his friend had collapsed. Bentham paid the bill and got a cab.

The taxi driver wasn't prepared to take the fare when he saw the condition of Brian Humpfress, and didn't want to go all the way to his hotel in Bloomsbury anyway – until Bentham flashed his warrent card. 'If he doesn't get there, friend, you're in trouble.' He paid the estimated fare in advance, and so disposed of his comatose visitor; but he doubted if that was the end of the liability that Humpfress presented.

Jack Bentham wasn't planning to put Terry Sneed under any sort of surveillance, but intended instead to look for evidence resulting from past deeds. However, the high-level surveillance that was being kept on Brian Cayman, whom the computer had thrown up as a probable suspect for the King's Road robbery and a current plotter, discovered Terry Sneed when he made contact with the villain.

Terry Sneed had let Brian Cayman completely alone for what he considered a respectable interval while he got on with his new job and established new routines. The workload was quite heavy – there were still a lot of policemen at it. CIB2 was the largest investigatory department in the Met and still growing. It took up more floor space than any other department in Tintagel House, the tower block on Albert Embankment. No one expected Superintendent Sneed to open any old wounds in his new office; there was a tacit amnesty granted to those who had remained in the job; a few policemen had taken early retirement. The complaints investigated by Sneed were of a serious nature, a lot involving traffic offences where policemen supposedly solicited money from members of the public to ignore speeding offences or excess alcohol; most of the people concerned stood to lose their licences as a result of previous convictions. Sneel generally found these complaints to be unsubstantiated. One particularly nasty case he investigated was an assault by a DC on a man who had been having an affair with the policeman's wife. There was no doubt in Sneed's mind that the detective had used two of his colleagues to waylay the lover, and then worked him over with a cricket bat. He could understand the detective's feelings, but that didn't influence his findings. There were odds and ends from Operation Bad Apple, but Humpfress was mostly dealing with those; and policemen weren't going to be arrested as a result, despite what Humpfress believed. Sneed would make sure of that.

All that Terry Sneed had earned from previous contacts was gone, vanished into the coffers of the Metropolitan Police Receiver. He had settled for his result, and had no intention of pushing his luck by asking for the money back. The evidence he had salted away in two of his three deposit boxes went too, but not the memory of who had been involved, nor of what was still outstanding from some parties. There was a lot outstanding on the one across the pavement in King's Road, and he wasn't about to give those blaggers a free ride, especially as none of that evidence had been traded for his freedom.

Having no intention of going to Cayman's home, or even telephoning him, Terry Sneed picked him up in the street near his flat. Cayman had an old, well-maintained Mercedes, and walked nowhere when he could drive. Sneed spotted him on a five-hundred-yard trip to a bookmaker's in a nearby shopping precinct. The car drew up outside the bookmaker's, and Cayman dived out and went inside.

Sneed parked further along the pavement and climbed out, leaving his driver behind. He got into Cayman's car and was casually checking through the large glove compartment when Brian Cayman came back across the pavement. He looked up from his betting slips and shortened his step.

'What the fuck ... ' He started angrily foward until he realised who it was rifling through his personal effects.

'Getting in, Brian? Or do we talk like this?' Sneed asked.

Reluctantly Cayman climbed behind the wheel of the Mercedes, which was parked on the wrong side of the road facing oncoming traffic. He started it and swung across the road. Neither he nor his passenger noticed the baker's delivery van that started off with them, nor the unmarked mini van.

'You're about the last person I expected to see.'

'You owe me money, Brian. Did you forget?'

'All the aggravation you had. I didn't think you'd want to put yourself on offer.'

'I had a right result.' Sneed smiled uninvitingly. 'Now it's business as usual.'

'I'm not holding. That's straight. Too many horses still running's the problem.'

'That might be your problem.'

A pained expression etched its way deeper into Cayman's lined face. He knew Sneed wouldn't leave him alone until he was paid. But no way could he pull up the sort of money that was due. 'Didn't Ronnie Letts take care of what was outstanding? I thought Ronnie was gonna weigh on.'

'I've not exactly been in a position to get down to Spain. But I still want what you owe me. Either that or you'll find yourself in the frame.'

'Fuck me, Terry, I ain't got it. I ain't holding.'

Sneed looked over at him, unmoved by his obvious distress. 'Then do some more villainy. I want to hear from you by the weekend. You know what it comes to. Drop me back at my car.'

'It was definitely Terry Sneed, Frank, was it?' Bentham asked.

'Alan Cheesman, the DC on obo, recognized him when the villain dropped him back to his car. He ran a check on the car. It's a Met car, allocated to CIB2 for Sneed's use. The driver was a Met driver, Ted Hazell.'

'Sounds like it's business as usual,' Bentham observed. 'It didn't take him long.' They were in the DCS's office at the Yard.

'Do you want obo kept on him?' Burroughs asked.

Bentham thought about that then shook his head. 'We'd have to get up too early, Frank. Concentrate on Brian Cayman. At least Terry's confirmed we've picked the right suspect there. See if we can't get Ronnie Letts back over here. His old Mum might be the lever.' He picked up the criminal intelligence file on Ronnie Letts. In it was not only information on what he had been convicted for and was suspected of committing, but also multifarious details about family and associates. Some of them, like his mother, had no criminal record in their own right, but a fairly thick dossier nonetheless on everything from school reports through medical reports to their current financial status. Databanks were a huge boon to criminal intelligence: information that was freely given and innocently gathered for one purpose often proved revealing when laid beside information dug out for the purpose of putting a person to a crime.

Mrs Ethel Letts was the sole blood relative of her son Ronnie, and at seventy-four she wasn't in the best of health, according to the copy of her medical record in the C11 file. Continuing problems with her stomach and colon had resulted in a couple of exploratory operations, which hadn't pinpointed the trouble. She was a widow, living on a pension and supplementary benefit, and lived alone in a rented council flat; she saw her son about three times a year when he visited her from Spain. She didn't hold a passport and had never been out of the country. She had two thousand pounds in a post-office savings account, and spent the interest she got from it.

'She's the obvious way to get Letts back here, Frank,' Bentham said. 'I can't see anything else that might do it.'

'There's probably enough to apply for an extradition warrant.'

'Not to have it stand in court. He'd get a throw, for sure.'

He looked at the file again. 'Go and see Dr Hanif, her GP. Ask him to call the son or something, tell him his old Mum's ill.' He passed the file over. 'Keep the connection with Terry Sneed closed up for now.'

'What if Brian Humpfress gets it?'

'He won't unless we give it him. I might do that at some point, but not yet. What else are we looking at?'

The DCI passed over a folder, one of several he was holding. Bentham read the suspect's name and scanned the intelligence for details, his thoughts still occupied with Terry Sneed. He had had his chance. Sneed had remained a dinosaur of a policeman, unable to get his head around the new ground-rules. It was a pity, Bentham thought, because he liked Terry Sneed and his bold front; but he felt no regrets he couldn't live with.

Dr Hanif was most accommodating when Frank Burroughs went to see him, so much so that the DCI wondered if his status in this country was dodgy. He had been treating Mrs Letts for her stomach trouble, he explained, and knew all about her son. Mrs Letts often talked about Ronnie, and said what a good boy he was.

'Would he come back if she were ill?' Frank Burroughs had asked. The doctor had replied that he was sure he would if the complaint was sufficiently serious; but although the old woman had a recurring stomach problem, it wasn't acute or life-threatening.

'However, it could reasonably be mistaken for stomach cancer,' the doctor had told him. 'If she were got into hospital they would keep her under observation for a few days. She would benefit from that. Perhaps then we can discover what is wrong with Mrs Letts. Would that help?'

After a late evening visit by Dr Hanif, Mrs Letts became an emergency admission to the Mayday Hospital in Croydon, with a bowel obstruction – question carcinoma. Frank Burroughs was present in the ward sister's office when, in the early hours of the morning, Dr Hanif put in a call to Ronnie Letts in Spain.

The sun was still well below the rim of the horizon on the sea outside Ronnie Letts' bedroom window when the telephone startled him from a sleep which it seemed had only lasted minutes. He heaved his muscular body onto the side of the bed and stared into the darkness at the instrument, feeling anxious. His Mum came into his thoughts for some reason. Perhaps he had been dreaming of her. He put on the light and took up the receiver, but said nothing. That was his way of answering the telephone, not just at three o'clock in the morning.

'Hello. Hello,' the lilting Asian voice of Dr Hanif said. 'Hello. May I speak to Mr Letts. Hello. I'm trying to contact Ronald Letts. Is there someone?'

'What is this, a joke?' Letts said, rubbing his tanned arm to take the chill off. 'D'you know what the time is, ringing at this hour?'

'It's even earlier here in England.'

'You sound like you're in Pakistan, pal. Who is this? S'that you, Sam?' He was the only friend Letts could think of who could imitate an Asian accent, but there was no reason why he would ring.

'I'm Dr Hanif, Mr Letts,' the voice said down the phone, ignoring the racist remark. 'I'm your mother's GP.'

'Why the fuck didn't you say so?' A note of alarm came into Letts's voice as fragments of his disturbing dream crossed his mind, just out of reach. 'What's wrong with Mum?'

'I've just admitted her to Croydon Hospital. There seems to be a bowel obstruction, Mr Letts. There is a possiblity it may be cancer.'

'Cancer?' The word struck a keep chord of fear. 'I'd better come over. I'm all she's got.'

'I don't want to alarm you, Mr Letts,' the doctor said, not minding at all, happy to pay him back for his racism. He wasn't, after all, telling one single lie. 'It's only possible they will operate and find cancer.'

'Operating . . . I'll come over, doctor; I'll come right away. Tell her I'll get the earliest plane I can. Tell her not to worry, doctor. Is she all right? She in much pain?'

'I don't believe she's in very great pain, Mr Letts.'

'She never lets on, that's her trouble,' he said in an admonishing tone. 'You tell her not to worry, doctor. I'm coming back. Give her the very best treatment.'

Frank Burroughs avoided smiling when he replaced the telephone extension – it would have seemed inappropriate in the face of this doctor's earnestness.

'They'll know soon enough if the obstruction is adhesion from old scar tissue,' he said. 'I suspect it's not cancer at all.'

'So long as no one finds out before her son gets there, doctor,' Frank Burroughs said, feeling truly grateful to this man and forgetting momentarily his own racial prejudice.

'I will ask hospital please to refer any inquiry Mr Letts makes about his Mum to me,' the doctor added, to make certain of his help.

'I appreciate that,' Burroughs said, and meant it.

22

'CID office,' Sneed said into the phone on getting the switchboard at Ealing police station. He waited to be put through, glancing around the unadorned green partition walls of his sixth-floor office: it was lifeless, and he wondered if he would be there long enough to make it feel any different. He had plans to move on from CIB2 as soon as an opportunity presented itself. Although he was adept at gathering information on fellow policemen, actually nicking them went against the grain; he enjoyed collecting knowledge and holding it to himself because he enjoyed the power it gave him over a powerful section of the population. There were many opportunities for such information-gathering in his present office, but he took none of them, suspecting that any of them might be a trap for him. He dealt with each case as required, or as his discretion as a detective superintendent in CIB2 allowed. Everything he did in his present office benefited only the service. He wasn't without offers from policemen he had nicked, and nor was he slow to notice where other CIB2 detectives were taking advantage of their position to earn by dropping out evidence.

'DC Squires,' Sneed said abruptly into the phone when a voice answered. Colin Squires identified himself, as did Sneed. There followed a brief silence. 'How's life back on District, Colin?' Sneed had been instrumental in his departure from the Squad.

'Oh, not too bad, guv,' Squires said, his thoughts working hard, trying to anticipate the purpose of the call. What leaped to mind was the possibility that Detective Superintendent Sneed might be ringing to nick him for his past misdemeanours, and anxiety overtook him at the prospect. 'It's a very busy nick out here, guv,' he said garrulously, 'a lot going on. Plenty of overtime.' He suddenly regretted those words and wished he could pull them back.

'I hope it's all straight these days, uncle – without me around to sort out your duty sheets.'

Squires laughed nervously. He waited, apprehension filling his lungs instead of air. He realised that Detective Superintendent Sneed wouldn't ring him without a reason.

'I want you to do me a favour, Colin. You owe me one. I've a bit of work for you.'

That sort of involvement was the last thing Squires wanted, but he didn't know how to respond. He feared that if he said no he would then face a corruption charge for past deeds; if he said yes, he might find himself on a similar charge anyway. He wondered if perhaps this was a test. 'I'm a bit busy, guv. There's a lot on,' he said.

'Won't take long. I know you won't let me down. Not after the favours you've been done.' He explained what he wanted.

Afterwards Squires felt confused and sick. He feared his career was going to come to a crashing halt, with him being arrested as he collected money from the villain Sneed had named. After agonizing for the entire afternoon, and deciding against speaking to his own governor in case he knew Terry Sneed and telephoned him, he finally made a desperate move; one which, ironically, found him going to the meeting that Sneed had arranged anyway.

He recognized Brian Cayman when he entered the pub and approached the bar to order a large vodka and tonic. He swallowed half of the drink and then went out to the toilets. DC Squires hesitated. He looked around the bar, checking out the other customers, none of whom he took to be detectives. Two men playing pool looked as if they had just come from a football match at Chelsea.

Trying to maintain control of his panic over what counter-measures Detective Superintendent Sneed might take, Squires went out to the gents.

'He's a right greedy bastard and no mistake,' Brian Cayman said bitterly as Squires joined him at the urinal. He hated him and all his kind, and if there was some way he could get even without putting himself in jeopardy, he would take it. 'Someone's going to put him away, and fucking soon, I hope. He wants the lion's share. He's gonna get hurt, I promise you that.' He passed over the package of money. He had had to put himself dangerously on offer to raise it.

'You want me to tell him?' That wasn't what Squires had intended to say; he wanted to encourage this man to pay back Terry Sneed.

'Tell him what the fuck you like. The greedy cunt, I hope he gets cancer.'

Brian Cayman turned and went quickly out, leaving Squires trembling with anger and wondering if he should flush the money down the WC. Then he heard the arrest, what sounded like 'Oh, fuck me!' from Cayman, and felt relieved it was over.

The two Chelsea supporters at the pool table laid hands on Squires when he stepped into the bar-room as Brian Cayman was being led out. Squires wanted to protest, but said nothing.

In the street, Brian Humpfress broke off from a conversation with the detectives who had collared Cayman and came across to Squires smiling thinly. 'Well done, Colin.'

Relief swept through Colin Squires, but it was short-lived and he questioned now if he had done the right thing after all. 'I'm glad that's over, guv. When I rang you I wasn't sure if Mr Sneed would get to know.'

'He'll know soon enough. Just as soon as you get this money to him,' he said, squeezing the package that a detective had removed from Squires's pocket. 'First we'll dye-mark it, just to make absolutely certain of Mr Sneed.'

The breathless unease he had felt on and off ever since Sneed's phone call recurred. His prospects for the future seemed dim, and could get dimmer depending on who proved to be the most manipulative out of these two senior detectives. But there was no doubt in his mind that Detective Superintendent Sneed had the edge.

Jack Bentham was at Croydon police station interviewing Ronnie Letts, who was being fairly forthcoming about his part in the King's Road robbery, when Humpfress arrived wanting a word. Bentham was reluctant to stop the interview he was conducting along with Frank Burroughs, and so made Humpfress wait. About an hour later, they took a break and he found Humpfress sitting at a Formica-topped table in the large, neon-lit canteen drinking tea. Bentham got some barely-drinkable powdered tea for himself and joined him.

'I want you to look at this,' Humpfress said, pushing a slim file across the table. With a glance across the man's face, which was at once full of excitement and anxiety, Bentham opened the file, which contained details of Squires's involvement as go-between for Terry Sneed. Bentham skimmed through the sheets of the DC's statement, gleaning sufficient information to know that he didn't want this coming up right now in case it prejudiced the investigation he was pursuing. He glanced at Humpfress again.

282

'This time he's going. He is.'

'Why should Terry Sneed leave himself on offer?' Bentham asked. 'Keeping the money in his desk doesn't sound like him.'

'He's a greedy, immoral policeman who thinks he's safe. He's got away with a lot more than this. Who is there to stop him? That's what he thinks.' He gave a series of two fingered taps against his chest.

There was a questioning moment between these two detectives, one that created a chasm of doubt in Bentham's mind. This rang out 'fit-up' in his ears. Brian Humpfress's desperation was obvious. Bentham wanted nothing to do with it, but guessed that Humpfress would go on pursuing Sneed anyway.

'Take it to Doug Markham,' Bentham advised. 'He's Operational Head of CIB2. Not me.'

'Markham was part of the old firm,' Humpfress said scornfully. 'Him and Terry Sneed are in the same Freemasons' lodge. The evidence would just disappear. I want Sneed put away, so I can move on to my course at Bramshill, so I can take promotion.'

He felt on the rack with uncertainty while awaiting Bentham's reply and couldn't understand why he didn't leap at this chance. 'The villain Sneed was demanding the money off wants to put him away.'

'What's the situation with this lad Cayman?' Bentham asked, glancing at the folder as if looking for an unfamiliar name. He was puzzled by what Cayman was up to. Brian Cayman had featured clearly in his previous conversation with Ronnie Letts; but more than that from their surveillance of Cayman – which included tapping his phone and videoing all visitors to his home as well as all the people he met elsewhere, where possible – they knew Cayman was plotting up another robbery. Then suddenly it became clear.

'Part of the deal is that he stays out if he gives evidence against Sneed,' Humpfress explained. 'Provided the DPP agrees, and provided we get a conviction.'

'Why was he paying Sneed money?' Bentham asked, realising that they weren't talking about the same offence.

'He's been dealing in stolen property – bearer bonds. Sneed decided he still owed him money on their previous deal. It's a banker's bet that Sneed has any number like Cayman who he's now trying to collect old dues on.'

Jack Bentham nodded, reluctantly accepting that he would have to let Humpfress go after what he wanted in order for Bentham to get what he was after, despite the possibility that it would precipitate his own plans. It was a shaky deal, and as he didn't pretend to be gifted with second sight, he could only rely on experience. This told him that something was likely to get fucked up in the process; it usually did.

The arrest of Detective Superintendent Terry Sneed was set up the following morning. The money was in place, and all that was needed was for Sneed to have it in his possession. A phone call from DC Squires saw to that.

Sneed was in his office, dictating a report on an incident of alleged rape which he had been called out the previous evening to investigate. Having taken a statement from a woman who claimed to have been raped, the detective inspector in charge of the case had offered to run her home, and had then raped her himself in his car. The DI had been very frank about the whole incident and had made a long statement to Sneed. Although in no way condoning what had happened, Terry Sneed understood the extenuating circumstances that had led up to the incident, and was prepared to put those in his report. He flicked off the microphone switch on the dictaphone as the telephone rang.

'CIB2. Detective Superintendent Sneed ...' Colin Squires identified himself. 'Uncle, I wondered what had happened to you. I rang your nick, they said you were off sick. How did it go last night?'

'Fine, guv, fine.' Squires tried to keep the nervousness out of his voice. 'Did you get the money? I dropped it off at your office last night.'

Alarm bells started ringing inside Sneed's head.

'I put it in the back of your desk, bottom left-hand drawer ...' the young detective continued as Sneed slammed the phone down.

The drawer wouldn't yield immediately and Sneed realised he was pulling upwards rather than out. He told himself to calm down, this wasn't a problem. Squires had been silly enough to simply leave the money in his drawer when he hadn't been able to reach him. But how had he got into CIB2's offices un-challenged, much less his? He would simply walk the money out of the building, put it in the left-luggage office at Victoria Station, then the panic would be over. The parcel was where

Squires had said it would be. Sneed resisted opening it. He would have had no time to anyway before Bentham came in with DCS Markham and Brian Humpfress.

'What a get-up!' Sneed protested. He managed to hold onto his anger; he was more insulted than outraged at their blatant move.

'Looks like it's on top, Terry,' Jack Bentham said.

Sneed shook his head. 'It's a fit-up, Jack. I'm being fitted. Doug? It's a ramp.'

Doug Markham, who had a fleshy face and drooping jowls rather like a spaniel, shrugged, trying to disguise his awkwardness. He hadn't wanted any part of this, but had been invited to the arrest as a courtesy to his office.

'Some chance of that, Terry,' Bentham said despite himself.

Sneed laughed. 'I get a phone call from a bent ex-Squad detective, one who should have been nicked a long while ago. He tells me there's a parcel of money in my desk. He knows there is because he fucking well planted it. Then the next moment you burst in to feel my collar. If that's not a fucking fit-up, I'd like to know what is.'

There was silence in the office, the atmosphere was charged to crackling. Faces of other detectives in CIB2 appeared in the doorway. In other offices of the department, telephones were ringing, printers clacking away, the everyday business of CIB2 continuing. The arrest of Terry Sneed was nothing more than that, it just happened that he was a CIB2 officer.

'This time you'll stay down, superintendent,' Brian Humpfress said, with a display of vindictiveness that brought a sparkle to his eyes.

Doubts that had been submerged in Jack Bentham slid quietly to the surface as Doug Markham cautioned Terry Sneed. He wasn't convinced that this arrest was as sound as Humpfress believed it to be. But he remained silent all the same, and knew that made him as culpable as Humpfress, regardless of the self-justification he found.

23

The atmosphere in the flat was tense and oppressive and Jack Bentham found that moving around was like trying to wade through mud. He was hoping not to be noticed by Helen, as if believing the cause of the tension could be avoided if it were ignored. But realistically he knew they had to discuss it at some point. They could perhaps delude themselves, pretend the problem didn't exist, but it would surface in other ways, probably when they least expected it to. Their relationship had been founded on a lie, or at least a false expectation.

As he entered the kitchen, tying his tie, Jack Bentham glanced edgily at Helen, who was sitting at the table reading his report on the circumstances of Paul Bailey's death. The thick folder was open and her eyes crossed the pages, but he doubted whether she was focussing on the words or concentrating on their meaning. She was aware of him as he busied himself in the kitchen making coffee and toast. She shrugged vaguely when he asked if she wanted anything, and didn't speak until he set a pot of tea in front of her and sat at the table with his coffee and toast.

'You left this out for me to read?' she said, folding back the front cover of the report. 'Your report on Paul's murder.'

He nodded, then said quietly, as if to try and make his statement more acceptable, 'It wasn't murder, Helen, whatever you or your movement wants to believe. Those policemen used the force they determined necessary to deal with the situation.'

Tears of anger and frustration stung Helen's eyes and her head hurt from trying to hold them back. A headache had started soon after opening the report and reading the summary. She felt devastated. How could he have written this? How could she have been so wrong about him? Helen fought an inclination to flee the room, the flat, Jack Bentham's life; she needed to prove herself right about him, to confirm that their relationship had meant something, that he had understood what was going on in her life and had been truly sympathetic, even empathetic.

'Jack, this is your conclusion. You're a policeman, too.'

'I conducted the investigation as fairly as I could. We do the job the public wants us to do, that's all.'

She laughed, 'Killing an animal rights protester or a perfectly lawful demonstrator?'

'No one wanted him to die. We police crime and disorder the best way we can.'

'Paul wasn't a criminal. He wasn't even disorderly. He was a quiet, questioning medical student who didn't think animals should be tortured in laboratories.'

'Crime ... lawlessness.' Bentham made no real distinction, because as a policeman he was no longer being given a choice.

'You know the police aren't interested in that any longer. You know that's no longer their main concern.' She was feeling betrayed, as if he had changed the ground-rules.

'The police are, Helen. I am interested in policing crime. Of course I am.'

'The government isn't. You're the strong arm of government. That's what you've allowed yourself to become. You said yourself that fewer and fewer policemen are looking at crime, but are going armed to political demonstrations instead, and offering more and more a strong-arm response.' Her anger and hurt increased as her sense of betrayal deepened. 'That's what Paul is a victim of.'

'What's your first reaction when your house is burgled or your mother attacked by some sooty?' he said, being purposely provocative.

Helen closed her eyes, not wanting to concede a point.

'I know what you do, you call the police, along with all the other liberals, radicals, blacks, racists, conservatives. They're each as scared as the next and they're all demanding "Protect me, protect my children, protect my property." You call the police because there is no one else to cope with all the shitty problems.'

'But each time something like Paul's murder occurs and the police are allowed to get away with it, the perimeters of what is permissible, what they feel they can get away with, are extended. It's legitimized violence, the same as violence to all those laboratory animals, all the animals in factory farms – why should we be surprised at the increase of violence on the streets? It's an outrageous state of affairs, the police assaulting and killing an innocent person in the street. By calling it a "death resulting from reasonable force", you're helping cover it up, Jack.'

'He was a violent demonstrator who assaulted the police,' Bentham said calmly, as a counter to her hostility. He didn't feel angry or upset. He didn't feel anything.

'Jack, I was there. I made a statement, remember. I was in the street when those two police vans made a roadblock. I saw Paul being struck and killed by policemen. If you don't do something about it, who will? If you don't end it, where will it end?'

'Wherever you want it to end, Helen. You say where. Everything we do as policemen, we do in your name.'

'Not my name,' she protested loudly, rising from the kitchen table, wanting nothing to do with that proposition.

He laughed. 'You'd better believe it, Helen. Until you decide otherwise at the ballot box.'

'Oh yes, that's so easy. We're a democracy, I'd forgotten. All we have to do is elect a new Parliament to change the police state, to change the exploitation of animals. But meanwhile you're going to sanitize Paul's death for the police.'

'I have no choice,' he told her. 'What should I do, make those policemen scapegoats for a system you don't approve of but find necessary for your protection?'

'Everyone has a choice, even policemen. You can choose *not* to police pickets, *not* to arrest animal rightists or anti-nuclear protesters. Just as you choose *not* to arrest corrupt policemen.'

That hurt Bentham. It was something he had told Helen in confidence, trying to resolve his own dilemma, and now she was using it as a stick to beat him with.

'You're not being realistic, Helen.' He knew the choices. 'I'm not a copper with simple options. I have to strike a balance between public needs and how the police can continue to be effective.'

Helen was shaking her head vigorously. 'That's the choice you have decided to make, Jack.'

'The alternative is to stop being a policeman.'

'You enjoy being a policeman too much, Jack.' It was an accusation.

For a moment Jack Bentham thought she would mock him with Julian Brind's prospect for his future – going as high as he wanted to – which he had revealed to her in a moment of weakness. She didn't and he was glad.

'I've never had to make the choice before now.'

But now he had made it. He didn't need to say the words, they hung in the silence between them like a portcullis. Helen turned away to the kitchen window. On the River Thames below an empty pleasure boat was going past. She wished she were on it, going anywhere away from this relationship. She wished it had never started. Tears tipped out of her eyes and ran down her cheeks. She heard Jack Bentham pick up the report, push it into his briefcase and snap it shut. He went without saying goodbye. At least he hadn't seen her tears and couldn't accuse her of using them to pressure him, as men so often did. The conclusion of the report was, it seemed, the conclusion of their relationship. They might have come together for no other purpose.

Stepping into one of the line of phones adjacent to the post office in Broadway opposite the New Scotland Yard building, Terry Sneed dialled Ernest Wiseman's direct line.

'Fuck me, Terry!' Commander Wiseman was unable to disguise his alarm when Sneed identified himself. The caller wasn't welcome; his phone, like most, was regularly tapped, to deter private calls that were helping run up the Met's huge phone bill, and anything criminal or unusual would be reported. A phone call from a suspended detective super-intendent remanded on bail following corruption charges would certainly fall into the latter category. 'You're about the last person I expected to hear from,' – or wanted to. He was suddenly afraid that the crust covering all Terry Sneed's pre-vious corrupt deeds would erupt and everything would ooze out, despite the hard work and best intentions of so many people. The result might be that he, and many like him, would after all find himself facing criminal charges.

'I'm across the road, guv. I'd like a meet,' Sneed said. 'I'd come up, but you know what they are like about letting you back into the building when you're suspended.' That prohibi-tion had been firmly enforced as a result of suspended policemen using Met facilities to pervert the course of justice. Access was only permitted on production of a warrant card, which sus-pended policemen had to surrender.

'I am rather tied up, Terry. Straight, I am.'

Sneed wasn't interested in Commander Wiseman's excuses. 'It's important to us all, Ernie. How about the St Ermine Hotel in about fifteen minutes?'

The St Ermine was a red-brick Victorian hotel around a

courtyard off Caxton Street, which was two minutes' walk from New Scotland Yard. Reluctant as he was to make this meeting with Sneed, Commander Wiseman was too scared not to. He found Sneed in the ornately-furnished lounge, where Americans of both gender drifted about in polyester flared trousers. Sneed had ordered a pot of tea for two and a plate of toasted teacakes, one of which Ernie Wiseman reached for as he settled his weight into the button-backed wing chair. He had eaten three halves spread with strawberry jam before broaching the purpose of the meeting.

'I was sorry to hear about your trouble, Terry,' Wiseman said, wiping a napkin across his mouth. 'I really was. It was outrageous the way they treated you.' He reached for another teacake. 'No one else expected, is there?'

Sneed shook his head. 'I'll need some help when I get to court. S'why I rang you.'

'How? How the fuck can I help now, Terry?' Wiseman said, suddenly feeling a sense of release: he had no dealings with CIB2, and there was no reasonable influence he could bring to bear. He almost smiled. Sneed couldn't reasonably hold a grudge against him. 'I'd help if I could, Terry, like a shot. Anything. But I don't see how.'

'Everything hangs on Brian Cayman's evidence. He's got the needle with me. If you organize his arrest for robbery and murder, it won't look too clever if he goes into court in cuffs with an army of armed policemen guarding him. What jury will want to believe his evidence rather than that of a senior policeman? Better if he didn't get to court at all. I mean, a dangerous villain like that. You'd all need shooters, and marksmen.'

Wiseman sat looking at him, his mouth had fallen open – in surprise rather than to receive the next piece of bun. 'Robbery and murder, Terry? The man's out on bail.'

'That's how desperate someone is to nick me,' Sneed told him. 'They don't know what's involved, that's for sure. Cayman was on that one across the pavement in King's Road. I held those details back when we had that other bit of bad luck with Operation Bad Apple. I like to keep something back.' An edge of menace came into his voice. 'Gives you another start. He's the only one who can put me in.' He smiled an uninviting smile.

'What have you held back on me, Terry?'

Sneed shook his head. 'You'll have no worries, 'you organize something for Brian Cayman. CIB2 have pugged him up in a little cottage in Berkshire, trying to keep him out of the way. The cunt's out there plotting one up, he's shootered up. If that's taken care of we'll all have a result.'

The feeling of nausea Ernie Wiseman had when he left the hotel was not the result of the four teacakes he had eaten. His continuing involvement in corruption, that persistent threat to his career which he couldn't ever quite pull clear of, was like a recurring nightmare. There was, he knew, only one way to be completely free of it, but he wasn't brave enough to face that; instead he found himself doing Terry Sneed's bidding, hoping that this would be all that was required of him.

The cottage in Berkshire lay along a wooded lane off the A4 near Knowl Hill. It had a modernised Gingerbread house look to it, as if it could comfortably have been eaten by the combined forces of the Robbery Squad and the Thames Valley police who turned out for this dawn raid. The morning was cold and still, breath streamed white as officers moved around getting themselves into position. Most of the policemen were armed, and all had been briefed about how dangerous the target was. It was a shoot-first situation. Also present were eight marksmen with their high-velocity rifles, who took up high positions at the front and back of the cottage, dividing the windows and doors between them. Little was said apart from the instructions whispered by the uniformed chief superintendent in charge of the operation. These were passed quietly down the chain of command. Not even the birds were disturbed before the start of their dawn chorus. Brian Cayman had no notion of what was awaiting him, until at first light Chief Superintendent Grower raised a megaphone to his mouth.

'Brian Cayman. Brian Cayman,' he repeated. 'Mr Cayman, can you hear me? This is Chief Superintendent Grower of Thames Valley police. The house is surrounded.' He glanced around at some of the men ranged about with drawn weapons, as if to reassure himself. 'Do you hear me? I want you to throw out any weapons you may have in there with you and come out with your hands raised. Is that understood?' He repeated it all, then issued a two-minute warning.

Although Cayman didn't quite catch them, the first words

woke him and caused him to spring out of bed, wrenching him from the tail-end of a dream where he was being pursued by the police and they shot him dead; only he had woken before being shot. He was anxious and sweating as he crouched on the floor. Quickly he identified what was being said, then anger and hatred for them chased away all fear. He moved to the window. His sleep-filled eyes widened at the sight of this regiment of armed policemen below. He ought to have known better than ever to trust the police, was his last angry thought.

The police marksmen had been briefed to be on the lookout for any movement, however minor, from inside the cottage, and to respond if the movement didn't signal a clear intention on the part of the suspect to give himself up. The marksman covering the upstairs window at front right saw the net curtain being drawn aside, saw the window rise slightly, saw the target in the room behind the glass and saw what he thought was a gun – that's what he would tell the subsequent inquiry which would exonerate him of blame. Then carefully, to avoid tension tremor, he squeezed the trigger. The shot rang out in the still morning, shattering the glass in the bedroom window, the bullet entering Cayman's left eye and exiting from the back of his head with half of his brain. As the crack of the rifle report died away, some nearby rooks answered with their noise, before also falling silent.

Sir Alan Seabrook, the senior partner in Germain, Seabrook and Co., the Inner Temple firm of solicitors that Detective Superintendent Sneed had representing him, was happy to respond to the DPP's invitation to discuss the case at Queen Anne's Gate. Sir Alan knew it could mean only one thing – that the DPP wanted to negotiate a lesser charge in view of the police debacle in accidentally killing their star witness.

Although it was his intention to negotiate, Sir Trevor Rump wasn't very good at it and put forward several stratagems, all of which Sir Alan said would be quite unacceptable to his client. Exploiting what he saw as the strength of his position, Sir Alan said that his client was ready to proceed to the crown court and rely on a jury to decide his innocence.

'He had a very narrow squeak before, Alan,' Sir Trevor said with a glance at Colin Wells, his deputy, who was also present. 'Does he really want to push his luck?'

Sir Alan stared implacably across the desk. 'He believes it was the Met that got off lightly over Operation Bad Apple. He feels he's the victim of a vindictive detective who isn't satisfied with that result. He bears the Met no grudge. He wants to see justice done.'

The situation wasn't developing as Sir Trevor Rump had anticipated. He was unclear whether the position Sneed seemed to be taking came out of arrogance or innocence. He could scarcely believe it was the latter, but couldn't take that chance.

'I don't mind telling you, off the record, Alan,' Sir Trevor said, changing tack, 'I'm less than happy with the prospect of prosecuting Sneed. With the death of the prosecution's main witness the case is collapsing. To make matters worse, it seems Chief Inspector Humpfress had pressured Detective Constable Squires to secrete the money in Sneed's office.'

'I see,' Sir Alan said speculatively. 'Presumably you'll be dropping the charges against my client, Trevor?'

'Not quite. Detective Constable Squires did, after all, receive the money from the deceased Brian Cayman on your client's behalf.'

'That's what Sneed's prepared to go to court to disprove.'

'We might do a little horse trading, Alan. Perhaps substituting the conspiracy charge for a minor corruption charge, one that would carry a maximum sentence of three years? If he'd be prepared to plead guilty.'

'I'd have to first discuss that with my client, Trevor,' Sir Alan Seabrook said pompously. 'But my advice, based on the information available, would be to turn down this offer.' He knew he was taking an enormous chance with this line. It was perhaps the best offer Sneed would get, and it might even be withdrawn. But it was his audacity that had got him where he was.

'I doubt I'd be able to improve on the offer.'

'I'll put it to him, Trevor. But I shan't withhold my advice,' Sir Alan said. 'Has the case been set down in the lists yet?'

'Before Anthony Wertham.'

Sir Alan Seabrook gave no sign that this was significant, but knew that Anthony Wertham would have to withdraw because of his relationship with Sneed.

That was what happened. But two days later, Judge Wertham found himself having lunch with the judge who had drawn Sneed's case, and it inevitably became a matter for discussion. Wertham remarked that he held Terry Sneed in high esteem. He needed to tell his colleague nothing else; and indeed it would have been unfair for him to have done so.

The point proved academic anyway. The DPP declined to proceed with the case in the face of the crumbling evidence and Sneed's firm refusal to trade.

24

Bramshill Police Staff College, housed in an early seventeenth-century manor near Basingstoke, was an inter-force training establishment for police officers from England and Wales, most of whom were considered to be a cut above the rest – policemen who were expected to go on to be leaders in their chosen career. At Bramshill everything was taught: from the correct use of cutlery at dinner, through presenting a reasoned and articulate image to the media and strategy in dealing with public order policing, to political awareness. Apart from the regular academic and police staff at the college, many of whom were chief superintendents with specialized knowledge seconded to Bramshill for two years, there were visiting lecturers from various police forces around the country, usually at chief-constable level. The comissioner of the Met made a point of delivering a lecture there at least once a year. It was something he ordinarily looked forward to, but today he had arrived at the college and eaten lunch at the top table in the mess with the commandant and senior members of staff with something less than enthusiasm. The reason for this was the cloud that was gathering back at the Met, where deeds he had hoped were all deeply buried were being resurrected. He had entertained such hopes despite himself, despite knowing deep inside that a cover-up was no solution to acute corruption, that at best it could give only temporary respite before re-emerging in some chronic form. He might have hoped for a longer respite, possibly until he retired and it became someone else's problem. He had been given a knighthood in the new year's Honours list. Although it was traditional for the commissioner of the Met to be so honoured, it had come about at this time, he was sure, as a reward for the tidy manner in which he had brought Operation Bad Apple to a conclusion: a vast section of the Met hadn't had to resign as had been unofficially predicted. He wondered if the knighthood could be withdrawn in view of the present scandal that was now becoming imminent. But he knew that wasn't the way the Establishment worked, it had to be seen to be right, or at least not to be wrong. The problem that he knew Chief Superintendent Bentham and the deputy commissioner were now bringing him, when he saw them enter and find seats at the back of the main lecture hall, was something the Establishment would expect him to deal with in return for his reward.

'. . . Although the problems of policing the Met are increasingly difficult,' Sir Denis said in conclusion, moving away from his scripted text, 'they are not hopeless. If they were, believe me, we would have given up long ago. What improves the situation the whole time, of course, are policemen like you. You are not ordinary policemen, but extraordinary policemen. You know that. If you weren't, you wouldn't have been selected for these courses. You were chosen because of your exceptional qualities, your intelligence, your ability to cope under pressure, your qualities of leadership – all of which will be finely honed here so that you go back to your own forces and instil into the men and women under your command the sort of mettle needed to spearhead the fight against crime, and tackle the erosion of public order that we are increasingly experiencing with riots, on picket lines, at football matches, at political demonstrations. These are areas where policemen are tested to the full, where not only community but also family loyalties are sometimes put under tremendous strain. It is in such circumstances that we have to be particularly careful to be impartial, to enforce the law without threat or favour. The highest tribute that can be paid to any policeman is that he is impartial. If you can set only that example to the young men and women serving with you, then you are doing both the job and the public the greatest possible service. No one can reproach us, no one can dissmiss us as rubbish or call us corrupt while we remain impartial. And, by and large, I think we do.' He paused, as if about to say something else, but glanced at the deputy commissioner and Jack Bentham and decided to end there. He closed the folder which contained his lecture.

Applause started before the chief superintendent running the lecture could rise to call for their thanks. These policemen, the majority of whom were in uniform and ranked from sergeant to superintendent, knew how to respond to Britain's premier policeman. When the clapping faded, the chief superintendent called for questions. There were several, mostly asking him to expand on points he had made peculiar to policing the Metropolis, such as the increasing use of firearms, and his willingness to deploy plastic bullets. There were also questions concerning his ideas for a national police force. One or two provincial policemen were worried about loss of autonomy and a cumbersome bureaucratic chain of command from London, possibly Westminster. The commissioner assured them that the plan he had in mind would leave regional command structure intact for dealing with local issues.

A final question came from DCI Brian Humpfress, who was in the body of the hall. 'Do you feel, sir,' he asked, 'that with the increasing evidence of political crime from the likes of trade unionists and people like animal activists, the expansion of the Special Branch is both necessary and desirable, and their role inevitably has to become more covert?'

'Well, to answer the first part of the question briefly,' the commissioner said, remembering Humpfress and not enjoying his memories of him, 'certainly the expansion of the Branch is likely, but how desirable it is would depend on whose viewpoint you take. Certainly it won't be desirable, I'm sure, to the subversive or lawless activist; those people in the animal rights movement who are prepared to enter into terrorism in an attempt to achieve their ends wouldn't find it desirable. The Branch has had considerable success in these areas, it's becoming very adept at infiltrating subversive movements and reporting back. Inevitably certain civil liberties might be infringed in the process, but we have to remember that it's the liberty of the majority we are trying to safeguard, the silent, law-abiding majority who pay their rates and television licences,' he added with a smile. 'The answer to the second part – whether the expansion of covert operations is inevitable – must be yes, if we are to give adequate protection to that majority. I see covert operations in the same way as I see the expansion of police intelligence. This is the age of the computer, after all, and good intelligence means effective policing. These are simply labels we give to common-sense policing, which is, after all, nothing more than prevention. We're never given credit for the countless crimes we prevent. Covert operations and intelligence are very necessary to the legions of prevented crimes that never become statistics, which we never get thanked for because they are stopped before anything happens. Last year, because of good intelligence, we nipped nine potential riots in the bud. They didn't become Handsworths or Tottenhams. That's successful policing. If some marginal loss of liberty is the price to be paid for it, then we must pay up and not complain.'

There was a final round of thanks with more applause. Sir Denis stepped down, and went to join Harry Streeter and Jack Bentham.

'One of the few real pleasures of my work made less than enjoyable for knowing what's brewing,' the commissioner said when they stepped out into the corridor. 'I wasn't unaware that I could have been talking about Detective Superintendent Sneed just then, when I spoke to these men of their exceptional qualities. I'm sure my predecessor said similar things about him.' He waited for two chief inspectors to pass. 'The bent bastard seems to be mocking us. What he seems to be getting away with is an insult to men like these.'

'This looks like his last manoeuvre, Denis,' Harry Streeter said, and glanced at Bentham. 'With what Jack has there are some more to lift.'

'I'm sick of hearing about police corruption. It's eating the soul out of the Met,' Sir Denis said, as if he hadn't heard, but in fact just feeling a need to complain to someone about the situation. 'I'm sick at heart to think that men I've worked with and trusted could betray me like this. I'm to blame, of course. I blame myself, even though you don't seem to have included me.'

'There are officers I can directly connect with the robbery in King's Road,' Bentham said, emphasising this as a point of information. That wasn't how the commissioner took it.

'In other circumstances I might consider that impertinent,' he said, but didn't pursue the point. 'Is the evidence all in place?'

'Most of it is,' Bentham said. 'I just want the word from you to move. The Surrey Constabulary will make the arrests for us if we want them to.'

'You've not involved CIB2?'

'Not at this stage,' Harry Streeter replied.

'What about the bank manager Sneed got his information from?'

'He can be picked up any time.' Bentham proffered the man in the immaculate uniform a folder with the details, but the commissioner refused it, as if it might contaminate him.

'Will this be the end of it, Jack?' he asked with a note of hope.

'For now.' Bentham wasn't about to pretend that things would be all right.

'I see. We might have another massive police corruption scandal on our hands?'

Bentham raised his shoulders. 'It's what tends to happen. It might remain confined to these officers.' He indicated the folder.

'I want twenty-four hours to consider what action to take. Whatever it is, I dare say it won't be pleasant.' The commissioner paused. 'Yes, you'll know in twenty-four hours.'

As he arrived back at his flat, Jack Bentham got a phone call from Helen. She wanted to see him and sounded ominous. He guessed what she wanted to say to him, and the prospect did nothing to lift the feeling of depression he felt over the delay the commissioner wanted. He knew what that meant and had said as much to the deputy commissioner in the car on the return journey from Hampshire. The commissioner was almost certainly looking for an alternative way out, one he would consult politicians about rather than either Bentham or Harry Streeter. A means of saving face would be found that would leave the Met exactly as it was before: riddled with corruption, and also moving deeper into uncharted territory, with the creeping erosion of civil liberties and the increasing use of computers. That possibility wasn't pleasing to Jack Bentham, but he knew there was little he could do about it; and what he *could* do, wasn't acceptable to him.

'Don't frown, Jack,' Helen said across the table of their favourite Chinese restaurant. They weren't exactly spoilt for choice in Hammersmith. She had so far avoided saying what she had wanted to say to him, but had allowed him to make love to her first, which made saying it more difficult. What she would miss most was that physical contact she had so craved when they had started their relationship. They had barely made contact on any other level, she realised. She had imagined, at one point, that he would make the world safe for her, more secure than she ever could, but found, ironically, that he had made her feel more threatened. That wasn't something she had been prepared to admit to herself until now.

'What will you do if the commissioner doesn't take action?' she asked. She had listened to the reason for his disquiet as a means of avoiding what was on her mind. Hearing what she believed only amounted to the tip of the iceberg, she had no doubt why policemen on demonstrations conducted themselves with such scant regard for either the law or civil liberties.

Bentham looked at her for a while. The truth was that he didn't know what he'd do. 'What's to do? I'll go on doing what I did yesterday.'

'You could resign.'

He laughed. 'God, you really are an extremist. No half-measures, no compromise, no grey bits between the black and white.'

'That's why the police are in such a mess, isn't it,' Helen said openly. 'Why society's such a mess, I suppose. Because we refuse to take radical action to deal with deteriorating situations.'

'But what do you leave in place of the police while you have this revolution? I know you can't fundamentally change the system by picking at it here, and picking at it there. But that's about all we can do in practice.'

'So in the meantime it's business as usual?'

'Have you got a practical solution, Helen?' he said angrily. 'If so, I'll pass it on to the commissioner.'

Helen didn't respond. She decided he didn't want the answer, but just wanted to accept the situation – perhaps out of laziness, because it made him feel comfortable, perhaps because he thought better the devil you know. The situation was much the same, she felt, as it was when she argued for animal rights. When she pointed out that the exploitation of one species paved the way for the exploitation of all other species, or that there could never be a peaceful world all the while people ingested violence and terror because the food they ate came from animals that were held in terror and killed violently, she was perpetually perplexed that sentient people wouldn't accept the argument immediately. She was genuinely baffled that the intelligent and thinking Jack Bentham couldn't accept her argument about the police. But he obviously wasn't going to.

'There is no alternative, Helen. 'Least, I don't know one.'

'I've been offered a job in Stratford,' she said suddenly. It had been something of a surprise to her to be invited to join the Royal Shakespeare Company. The offer would mean her physically removing herself from their relationship. 'It's a three-year contract.'

'That's an alternative of sorts,' he said evenly. 'You'd be daft not to take it.'

She nodded.

Jack Bentham considered her, then nodded himself, taking this information on board and dealing with it. He turned and signalled to a waiter for the bill, thinking as he did so about their earlier love-making. He was comfortable now, without any longing in his speechless genitals, but how long before the longing returned, before that feeling of pressure moved from his genitals to his heart, his mind, until his entire body was filled with it? Then he would want her back more than anything, and would hope for a phone call to say she had an evening free. But he wouldn't ask to see her again after tonight. He wondered briefly about trying to make love once more before they parted, but knew he couldn't store up the feeling against future need.

The meeting in the commissioner's office on the morning following their discussion at Bramshill held no surprises for Harry Streeter. He was only a little taken aback at the ease with which he acquiesced in the commissioner's plans following his promises to Jack Bentham to hold the line, and Jack Bentham's resigned acceptance of this reversal. There was no denying that Bentham had done a job and, given the evidence against Terry Sneed, Assistant Commissioner Peter Vyvyan, DAC Doc Holliday, Commander Ernie Wiseman and the others, it wasn't unreasonable that he had had some expectation of seeing it satisfactorily concluded. But a commissioner was entitled to do things his way, however unjust or wrong-headed that way seemed – only his autobiography would show how right he had been, if he dared reveal any of this. Harry Streeter had warned the eighteen senior officers named in Bentham's report to be on hand at the Yard to await a call from him. The commissioner had made the decisions, but it was left to Harry Streeter to implement them. Peter Vyvyan was the first to be summoned.

He looked ashen as Harry Streeter passed him singly the close-typed sheets of evidence against him. He read the words with difficulty, avoiding any sort of eye-contact with the deputy commissioner.

'You can deny all of it or any part of it if you wish, Peter,' Harry Streeter said in a not unfriendly manner. 'But I'm bound to tell you, as a friend, you'd be daft to try. If you do, the case will certainly go to court, and you stand to lose everything, including your liberty.'

Vyvyan sighed heavily. 'Where did all this evidence spring from?'

'It's been put together with care and intelligence. Not in the clumsy way the Wiltshire lot went about things.'

'Looks like Jack Bentham's work – the snaky cunt.'

The deputy commissioner said nothing.

'I suppose I should have had everything TIC'd with that last turn-out. You get careless, that's the trouble. Things go on for so long, you get used to having it. You start to look for it when it stops. I thought everything was squared away after the Wiltshire lot were sent home. I didn't think anyone would start digging again. But I suppose I knew in my bones that it had to end like this. I mean, it has to, Harry, no other way.' He fell silent.

Retrieving the typed sheets of evidence, Harry Streeter slipped them back into the pink folder on his desk and at the same time removed a typed letter, which he placed in front of Vyvyan.

'This is the alternative. Your resignation. If you sign it, you can walk away, Peter, taking your pension with you.' This was the commissioner's way. 'There's a decent job in security that's been lined up for you if you want it. It's not obligatory.'

For the first time since entering this office, Peter Vyvyan looked at the deputy commissioner, realising that everything wasn't as bleak as he had assumed. 'Is there a directorship?' he asked cheekily.

A smile crossed Harry Streeter's thin face. He liked to think he would have taken the same, even way with this man had he been laying a hand on his collar. 'You won't be the only one brought in here today and given the same choice.'

'I hope they're not all being offered the same fucking job,' he joked, signing the letter with a flourish.

'Clear your desk immediately, Peter,' Harry Streeter said, sliding the resignation back into the folder. He rose.

Peter Vyvyan did the same, suddenly weary and full of remorse, knowing that the longest chapter of his life had ended in ignomy, even though a thin shroud of public acceptability had carefully been drawn over him.

'I'm sorry, Harry,' he said, the fight having gone. 'The

302

ᴵ pressure got too much. Once you're in, you're in. It's like a drug.'

Cutting him short, Harry Streeter said, 'No one at Brinks-Mat knows what's behind your resignation.' He didn't want to listen to this man's whimpered apology, in case he got angry with him. He just wanted him out of the building.

On the seventeenth-floor corridor, Peter Vyvyan broke his step and put his hand out to the pale green wall to steady himself. The fluorescent light made him look even paler than he was. He felt sick and giddy as he choked back a sob. He tried to force back the inner turmoil that threatened to overwhelm him, and succeeded briefly, hoping he could hold himself together long enough to get to his own office.

A stream of senior officers followed the same path to the deputy commissioner's office, and took the same route out. Some whimpered, some were silent, but not one of them denied what was put to him or wanted to take his chances in court – until Terry Sneed arrived at his appointed hour.

'With the greatest respect, sir,' a less than usually confident Terry Sneed said, using from habit that standard phrase that prefaced any challenge to a senior officer, 'this is all ballocks. I don't plan to resign, not for a while yet.'

'If you sign it, I'll accept it,' Harry Streeter said. 'Then you can be out of the building within minutes, all the charges against you dropped.'

'What about my pension?' Sneed said boldly.

'Don't push your fucking luck, sunshine,' the deputy commissioner retorted; the day had taken its toll of him.

'I thought I was being called in to hear about resuming my duties. That's all I'm interested in, to be perfectly honest.'

'Have sense enough to quit while you're marginally ahead. It's the best offer you'll get. There's even a job waiting for you in security, if you want it.'

Sneed shook his head. 'I like being a policeman. I expect to remain a policeman.'

'You're the only one to have refused my offer.'

Terry Sneed expected negotiations to go on longer and was surprised when the deputy commissioner rose to show him out.

'What's the plan?' he asked. 'Dragging all those other senior policemen into court with me?'

'What policemen?' Harry Streeter smiled a clever smile.

'They've all resigned. You'll be in the dock on your own. You had the choice, your decision. You'll be arrested and charged in due course, Mr Sneed.' He inclined his head, indicating him to get out, and closed the door after him.

Harry Streeter felt he needed a drink, but first he had to make a phone call. The speed with which Jack Bentham answered suggested he had been waiting with his hand on the receiver.

'Jack. Sneed refused the commissioner's offer.'

'There's always one. I suppose Terry was a good bet.'

'Do your worst, Jack. Bring in everyone directly involved with the King's Road robbery.' He meant Sneed and all those below him in rank. Bentham understood that. 'We'll have to learn to live with the scandal.'

Besides Terry Sneed, there were four other policemen directly connected with the robbery: Detective Inspector Fred Pyle, who was at Chelsea; a detective sergeant from the same station; a DS on the Robbery Squad out at Barnes; and a detective inspector from C10. With Doug Markham, the operational head of CIB2, having resigned, there was no one from the Bureau to complain when Jack Bentham employed detectives he had worked with on the Regional Crime Squad to make these arrests. As if to reassure the world that the problems which beset the Met were now sorted out, and for the sake of future relations, he requested that CIB2 detectives accompanied them. After the briefing he gave them in his office, they were despatched to arrest the five named policemen. The DI from C10 obviously received a telephone call to warn him, for he disappeared completely. Other detectives went to the bank in King's Road and arrested the manager. After breaking down and crying, he excused himself and went to the toilet. Only when the arresting officers realised how long he had been in there did they interrupt him. He had tried to hang himself, and had to be taken to St Stephen's Hospital rather than the police station.

In order to close off all avenues to Sneed, Jack Bentham contacted Customs and Excise officers and gave them what information he had about Judge Anthony Wertham's smuggling enterprise. Customs claimed they were aware of it and had had the judge's trips with Sneed under observation. Whether that was so, or whether they were attempting to save face on account of the long-standing rivalry that existed between police and customs officers, mattered little to Bentham. They moved against the judge immediately. It wasn't certain that he would have given Terry Sneed any cover anyway, but Bentham wanted to leave nothing to chance.

Having Terry Sneed taken to Croydon police station following his arrest was another means of removing the chance factor. Bentham doubted that Sneed would find many offers of help from the Met, but it wasn't beyond the realms of possibility; so he didn't want him having easy access to Met officers. Because of his relationship with the governor out at Croydon, Bentham knew that Sneed would find no opportunity of advancing his position, other than through the correct procedure with a solicitor, to whom he would be allowed access when it suited them.

Despite achieving what he had set out to achieve when he began looking closely at Terry Sneed and corruption in the Met, when he had realised that information which was gathered by C11 and passed to the Robbery Squad wasn't producing the results it should have produced, Jack Bentham felt no sense of triumph as he drove out to Croydon. Nor did he feel disappointment that eighteen senior officers had been allowed to retire instead of being arrested. He felt nothing at all. He remembered again the story his father had told about how he had overcome his distress at having to slaughter his first cow, by learning to hate it. Possibly he should have started to hate Terry Sneed and all that he imagined the man stood for; but he didn't. Instead he understood how easy it was to fall on that slippery slope; how difficult it was to get off. There but for the grace of God, he thought. Ironically Jack Bentham started to consider how he might help Sneed. That was, he supposed, why he was going to see him. He had no need to get closely involved on the case – Frank Burroughs and DCS Ken Howard from CIB2 were coping fine. But he didn't know how he might help Sneed. and it seemed perverse on his part anyway. Terry Sneed was a good thief-taker and had done more than his share to put a lot of villains away. But on the other hand, he knew that through his slippery-slope activity Sneed had helped a lot of villains stay loose – to say nothing of those he had put into blags, or of the traffic warden who had been killed.

The long cell corridor at Croydon nick was neon lit and had a cold feel, even though it was centrally heated. The uniformed gaoler swung his keys idly on a small chain that was fastened to one of his trouser belt loops. He walked ahead of Bentham at a slow, even pace as if part of a cortège. He drew the bolts on Sneed's cell and swung the door open.

Terry Sneed, looking in better shape than when the Wiltshire police had held him, looked up expectantly. In his jacket lapel he wore a rose that had started to wilt. He had no shoelaces or belt, but he did have access to washing facilities.

'Come to give me back my belt and shoelaces, Jack?' Sneed asked as Bentham stepped into the cell and waited for the gaoler to shut the door. 'Last time you visited me in these circumstances, Jack, there was a wire in the cell.'

'None of my doing, Terry.'

'I'd offer you a drink, but the cunts out here aren't that biddable.'

Bentham smiled. 'That's why you're out here, Terry.'

'They're almost as bad as those cunts from Wiltshire.'

'They have no vested interest in you, Terry.'

'I suppose not,' Sneed allowed. Then, looking at the DCS, 'That DCI Humpfress, he's mad, you know that.'

'He's out at Bramshill.'

'What's his course, advanced Karate?' Sneed said. 'He's a violence specialist. He beats up prostitutes. Did you know that? I've a whole pile of evidence on him, you want it. I don't s'pose it'll do me much good now.'

Bentham shook his head.

'I should think they could use his peculiar talent out at Hendon. Teach some of those new recruits. Really violent fuckers some of the lads in the job nowadays. Give them a weird haircut and some Doc Martens, s'all they need.'

'New breed of policemen, Terry. They don't even bother to promise anyone any help. All they want to do is give some stick.' He thought about the policing of that animal rights demo in Hackney and how Paul Bailey had died and wondered if the way it was handled – policing by confrontation – was anything like fair. Perhaps the new breed was needed to deal with increasing lawlessness, or incite it. 'We should maybe take a few lessons from them. That's the sort of policing that's wanted nowadays. Your sort of coppering has become an anachronism. You don't talk to villains any more, Terry, you talk to computers; you don't feel collars, you thump demonstrators.

Maybe you should have gone on a course at Bramshill.'

'Any chance?' Sneed asked.

'You had your chance, Terry. You can't say you didn't. You couldn't change.'

'There are still worthwhile villains who need putting away.'

'The trouble was, Terry, you were letting too many of them buy their liberty. They're becoming an anachronism, too. As we get more and more into plastic and credit. There'll be nothing going across the pavement.'

'Don't get too depressed about the lads in the job in big boots who have a preference for sandbags and coshes instead of standard truncheons. There's always been that nutter element.'

'Oh, I can live with them. I can live with the rapid expansion of computers, electronic surveillance, and ever-expanding re-cords on people who don't have any criminal convictions,' Bentham said. 'All of that I can get my head around. What depresses me is that someone as talented as you lets the wheel come off like this when all it needed was a little adjustment.'

Sneed shrugged, as doubts about this man's visit sank in. He thought for the first time that perhaps he wasn't going to offer any help. 'The situation's difficult, but not hopeless.' He waited, but didn't get a response. 'Well it's not, is it?'

'There are no arms left to twist, Terry. The writing's been on the wall a long time.'

'There's got to be some sort of help. 'I go and draw the right judge – I'll get a result.'

With a shake of his head, Bentham said, 'Your shipmate's been nicked. Customs and Excise did it this morning.'

'Sounds like you've been busy. I wouldn't have thought they'd get very far – unless Tony Wertham was into smuggling when he wasn't with me.'

'He put his hand up right away. He's already given his resig-nation to the Lord Chancellor.' He watched Sneed's face tighten, and felt like apologising. 'It's a pretty hollow victory, Terry.'

Sneed nodded, not trusting himself to speak immediately in case he betrayed his emotion. Finally he said, 'Goes against the grain nicking one of your own. I had the same problem in CIB2. The trouble is, we're still playing by the old ground-rules. You read the new ones, but they don't make sense. They might to the new breed – I doubt it. Trouble is, you become a bought-and-paid-for police force, bought and paid for by the politicians, by vested interest. That's probably worse than copping off villains – at least there you can walk away whenever you want to. The way things are going now, the demands will get bigger and bigger.' He paused and waited, expecting Jack Bentham to comment. 'No one'll thank you for what you're doing. Whatever sort of result you turn in, at the end of the day they'll give you a pension and say fuck off. So you might as well do it your way. The way you want to do it.'

'Sounds about right.' Bentham said non-committally, neither impressed by Sneed's argument nor wanting to hear it.

There was a long silence between these two men. Noise from along the corridor penetrated the cell as a prisoner was released. Sneed thought about his freedom. It was no longer even an intellectual assumption. Bentham told himself that his way, his decision, was right.

'So what about it, Jack. A bit of help? Can anything be done?'

Bentham didn't reply, and an air of desperation fell over Sneed.

'Well can it? There could be plenty of dough on offer. Jack?'

Laughter started up in Bentham, low at first, a throaty chuckle.

Sneed smiled in anticipation, a smile which quickly faded as Bentham turned away and pulled open the cell door. His sense of desperation increased.

'Jack? What about it? Jack?'

There was real panic in Sneed now, something he could never remember experiencing since his early days as a young constable. It swept through him, making him feel sick. He took a step after Jack Bentham, wanting to stop him leaving, preparing to beg for help. But the cell door slammed shut in his face with a resounding clang. He heard Bentham's laughter as he went away along the corridor.

Following the one-way traffic system leaving Croydon, the route took them past a ballet school on the outskirts of town. Jack Bentham told his driver to stop and back up on passing the sign board. The driver of the car immediately behind blasted on the horn angrily as Bentham's driver did his bidding. Bentham remained in the passenger seat and stared at the large, slightly crumbling Victorian building. He could see the movement of a ballet class through the bow-fronted windows beyond the crescent-shaped drive. Young girls were leaping around the room, imitating the wind, no doubt. He sat and watched them for a couple of minutes, his driver saying nothing. He thought about going inside to explore the possibility of classes for his non-existent daughter, taking time to watch the girls. He noticed he was getting an erection. Finally he told his driver to take him back to the Yard.

Epilogue

Based on information received from Criminal Intelligence, A8 – the branch of Scotland Yard that controlled all demonstrations – had organized a squad of 170 uniformed policemen to be on hand for the first day of the resumed inquest into the death of Paul Bailey at Hackney coroner's court. Mike Regan, the local superintendent, felt uncertain about the need for this many policemen, as they could be made to look foolish for over-reacting. But the commander of A8 had no such misgivings. He had carte blanche to spend whatever he felt necessary on public order events: ultimate control of the streets by the police justified any means. As a result all such demos were over-policed.

The preliminaries to the hearing had hiccuped for a long while before arriving at Hackney. Because of widespread public interest, a decision was taken to hold the inquest in Hackney Town Hall; but with the prospect of possible disruptions, the Town Hall was abandoned in favour of Walthamstow coroner's court. It was there that the jury was sworn in. Walthamstow, being a more conservative area than Hackney, provided a jury that in few respects reflected the people in the neighbourhood where Paul Bailey had been killed, and one more likely than not to support the police. With this jury, selected as was the custom by the coroner's officer – he happened to be a police officer himself – the coroner switched venue back to the district of Hackney. There were protests from the lawyer representing Paul Bailey's estate – hired by animal rights groups since Bailey had no family – and protests from various animal rightists. They wanted to attend the inquest, but were told that there was no space in the courtroom as it had all been filled by press members with Metropolican Police press passes. It all augered for a stormy inquest.

Superintendent Regan had anticipated trouble and had planned to have extra policemen on duty. But he hadn't anticipated needing anything like the numbers A8 drafted in. Along with information from C11 came names, addresses, biographical details and, in some cases, photographs of expected troublemakers. There were enough names for the police to prepare three dozen charge sheets prior to the resumption of the inquest, and clear cells at Hackney police station ready for their arrest. Superintendent Regan willingly organized this particular policing operation, for arresting these people early on in the hearing might make life a lot easier for the duration. Part of the overall policing strategy was to remove the bulk of the demonstrators straight away, get them to court, and see to it that one of the conditions of bail was that they didn't return to the inquest while the hearing was on. That had been included in the briefing to senior officers given by the District commander, and it was proving an effective means of policing whenever there was a threat of persistent or continuing demonstrations. The only surprise was the source of the information – it meant C11 were involving themselves closely in public-order issues, and it was especially strange after the way Commander Bentham had carried out the original inquiry out at Hackney.

The lads on demo duty that morning felt bullish. The fact that this would provide a conclusion to the long-drawn-out policing operation which had gone so badly for the police meant nothing to the men and women waiting to go into action, for none of them had been directly involved in the death. But the mistakes that had happened then weren't going to be repeated.

There was no difference in feeling between those officers held in reserve in the buses parked next to the court and those actually on the pavement and steps outside. They were comforted by the thought that they were in control, and would remain so. The demonstrators would be warned to remove themselves, and if they didn't they would be arrested for obstructing a police officer – or at least thirty-six of them would. If the remainder regrouped themselves and continued the demo, then the police would have to rethink their strategy.

The demonstrators gathered around nine o'clock at Hackney railway station, arriving there by twos and threes. There were two dozen policemen on hand waiting to escort them to the coroner's court. By a quarter to ten the demonstrators numbered around thirty, under the leadership of animal rights activist Sheila Weymouth. Although without a criminal record, the police had considerable information on her, along with a photograph. They suspected her of being involved in various criminal activities – from poisoning Mars Bars to breaking into laboratories, destroying equipment and stealing animals. They moved off without warning or signal to the police, who quickly drew alongside to escort them. At the court building, the police drew back and allowed the protesters to form a double row along the pavement, but no sooner had they done so than Superintendent Regan approached.

'Miss Weymouth,' he said, recognizing her, 'I want you and all these other demonstrators to disperse and not obstruct the highway.'

'But you've just escorted us here. Why are you asking us to disperse?'

'You can't hold a demonstration outside this building. It's likely to prove intimidating.'

'Well why didn't you tell us that before we started? Why didn't you tell me that when I phoned the station and told you about the demo?'

'I'm telling you now,' Superintendent Regan said. 'Move or you'll be arrested.'

'You'd better start arresting us, then. We're not going anywhere.'

'Then I'll have to get the chief superintendent.'

'Will he negotiate with us about our staying?'

'He'll tell you the same thing. Either you move or you'll be arrested.'

The demonstrators didn't move, not even at the request of the chief superintendent, a small man who was holding down a lot of inner anger, as his stabbing finger betrayed. He wasn't about to let the demonstrators stay a moment longer than he needed to tell them to leave. When they refused to disperse, he gave the order to arrest them. A column of sixty policemen appeared from the buses in the adjoining street and, assisted by policemen from outside the court, started to arrest the demonstrators – twenty-nine in all, most of them women. They were led away to the police buses, which meant the inquest conducted by Dr Robert 'Jock' Taylor could proceed without intimidation.

The proceedings inside the building were hardly less demonstrative. Civilian witnesses from the original demonstration, which had taken place almost a year before, were subjected to abuse from both the coroner and counsel for the police.

'You're lying about that,' Dr Taylor told an elderly lady who described from the witness box how she had seen police pile from the two DSU vans and slash into Paul Bailey.

'I most certainly am not,' Marjorie Lodge said firmly. 'I don't see how you can say I'm lying. You weren't there.'

'I most certainly was not, madam,' Dr Taylor said, his face reddening in anger. 'You ought to know better at your age than to get involved in such anti-police demonstrations.'

'It wasn't anti-police. It was an animal rights demonstration, and it was quite in order until those police thugs started their disgraceful behaviour. It was their behaviour which left that poor man dead.'

'Don't contradict me. I would say the police behaved with admirable restraint in the face of such abuse, and the barrage of stones and other missiles.'

'There were no stones thrown or anything else,' the witness said, angered and perplexed. 'None at all.'

'That doesn't correspond to my information,' the coroner argued. 'I have statements from the police to that effect.'

'I was part of the group that was attacked by police thugs when Paul Bailey was killed,' Marjorie Lodge insisted, not giving in to intimidation. 'There were no stones being thrown.'

'And I repeat, madam, that doesn't accord with my information.'

'Perhaps I could at this time make a further request that the report following the investigation conducted by Commander Bentham be submitted to the court for consideration,' counsel for Paul Bailey's estate said. 'I understand there were extensive statements taken from eye-witnesses on both sides.'

'I don't require the production of that report, Mr Seedling,' the coroner said. 'It isn't relevant to the proceedings.'

'With respect, sir,' Simon Seedling argued, 'it is relevant. This was the result of an extensive investigation by a very senior policeman.'

'But we will be calling all of these witnesses, Mr Seedling. This court doesn't require a senior policeman to establish for it how Paul Bailey died.'

Only the civilian witnesses were required to prove anything, and as almost all of these had been on the demonstration, it was fairly obvious that Dr Taylor had scant regard for anything they said; indeed, he frequently mocked them. After a young, Asian-looking man who lived in Tudor Grove had given evidence about the police charge that caused the demonstrators to run in various directions to avoid being hit, Dr Taylor said, 'Presumably you'd need to run pretty fast after throwing stones at the police in India.'

'I wouldn't know,' the witness said, 'I've never been there.'

The police witnesses, on the other hand, were given an easy ride. The coroner was painstakingly fair and reasonable to them whenever Simon Seedling got heavy in cross-examination. They remembered enough to exculpate themselves from any blame over the death of Paul Bailey, but little else. Counsel for both the Metropolitan Police and the Police Federation hardly questioned the police witnesses. Both had read Bentham's report.

Cross-examination by counsel for Paul Bailey's estate, when the coroner allowed it without interruption, showed the police evidence to be confused. Officers were unable to remember who had been in the DSU carriers, where the order had come from to proceed to the point at which they intercepted the fleeing demonstrators, or who had given the order to draw truncheons. They knew quite definitely that they hadn't taken any unauthorized weapons in the vans, and that they hadn't attacked dispersing demonstrators.

'What was the object when you piled from the DSU van and drew truncheons?' Mr Seedling asked.

PC Phil Westbrook hesitated and looked at the coroner, hoping to be helped out with an intervention. 'I don't understand the question, sir.'

'It's quite straightforward, constable. What were the demonstrators doing that caused you to pile out of the van with drawn truncheons?'

'They were running towards us, sir, to attack us.'

'But how was that so? They were coming along Well Street away from another contingent of policemen, were they not?'

'They were running at us,' the constable insisted.

'You had just arrived in your vans from the opposite end of Well Street and formed a roadblock at the junction of Tudor Grove. Is that right?'

'Yes. We were stopped just below the junction.'

'A roadblock?'

'The police form roadblocks the whole time to control traffic and demonstrations,' the coroner interjected. 'There's nothing sinister about that.'

Mr Seedling gave him a deprecating look. 'We've established

from earlier evidence that this "raging, uncontrolled mob of demonstrators" turned into Tudor Grove away from the un-sinister roadblock. You had preceded them into Tudor Grove, had you?'

'No sir, we remained in the vans at that point.'

'So you drew truncheons and pursued the demonstrators after they had turned into Tudor Grove, when Paul Bailey was struck on the back of the head?'

'No sir.'

'Are you saying Paul Bailey wasn't struck on the back of the head, or that you didn't pursue the demonstrators?'

'We caused them to turn into Tudor Grove.'

'Then how do you imagine that they were coming to attack you? Consider how the police had blocked their exit along Well Street; the demonstrators had turned away along Tudor Grove; Paul Bailey was struck on the back of the head. How was this mob attacking you?'

'It's fairly obvious to all but an idiot, Mr Seedling,' the coroner interrupted. 'This angry mob presumably turned on the police, causing them to draw truncheons to defend themselves.'

When one of the policemen giving evidence put forward the suggestion that Paul Bailey's death had been an 'own goal', caused by a rock thrown by a demonstrator, that seemed to provide all the answers for Dr Taylor. A lot of his remarks to the jury confirmed that position, only adding to their confusion, despite Simon Seedling pointing out both that forensic medical reports ruled out the possibility of a rock causing the death blow, and also that no rocks or bricks had been found strewn in the street after the demonstration.

'This was one of the worst anti-police riots I've ever seen,' one of the police officers said in the witness-box.

'That was what you took it to be?' counsel for the police asked. 'Not an animal rights demonstration?'

'I can't say how it began, sir,' the constable said. 'The District Support Units weren't around at the start – we were held in reserve till we were needed. We was certainly needed that day. We had to steam right in.'

'Where were the demonstrators when you "steamed right in"?' Simon Seedling asked.

'I'm not sure. Proceeding along Tudor Grove, I think.'

'From where to where?' Seedling asked. 'Towards or away from the junction of Well Street?'

'It's been firmly established that the demonstrators were going along Tudor Grove and probably turned to attack the police,' the coroner said.

'With respect, sir,' the barrister said, 'I think that is for the witness to establish.'

'All you're doing is taking up unnecessary time, Mr Seedling.'

'They were going along Tudor Grove away from the junction,' the police constable said.

'Then what was it that prompted you to "steam right in", truncheons drawn?'

The police constable didn't answer.

'Well did you find it necessary to pursue the demonstrators into Tudor Grove or did you not?'

'We certainly did.'

'With truncheons drawn?'

'Yes,' the constable in the witness-box replied.

'Then how do you interpret that as an anti-police riot, if the police were pursuing fleeing demonstrators?'

'They ran from us when the two vans drew up just below the junction.'

'But earlier, when answering questions from my learned friend Mr Coulter,' he indicated counsel for the police, 'you said this was one of the worst anti-police riots you had seen. Where was the riot taking place?'

'All around us. They were everywhere.'

'Is not something nearer the truth that you were brought in to mop up after the police had earlier been routed by the demonstrators? That you pursued this group of fleeing demonstrators along Tudor Grove with that one intention?'

'I don't know anything about that.'

Confusion was the only consistent thing about the police evidence concerning what had actually happened. Among the civilian witnesses, most of whom were automatically liars for having taken part in the demonstration – as far as Dr Taylor was concerned – there were numerous eye-witnesses to the killing; however, not one of the police reportedly saw the blow that was struck or the person who delivered it. A number of witnesses had themselves been struck on the back of the head by the police; none of the police had reportedly been hit by the stones

316

and other missiles supposedly thrown by the demonstrators.

It took Simon Seedling most of the afternoon of the eighteenth day of the inquest and part of the following morning to sum up. He tried to lead the jury out of their obvious confusion and into some clear line of understanding. At the end of it, he wasn't sure that he had succeeded.

The coroner sought, it seemed, with a few well-chosen phrases, to have the confusion continue in the jurors' minds. 'It is very obvious,' he said, 'that the police have a duty to the greater public at large to damp down potential violence as quickly and as effectively as possible. We've all seen evidence of this on many occasions, when they have nipped mini-riots in the bud, put down violence on picket lines and at football matches. They have our heartfelt thanks as well as our support for doing that. There is no telling how dangerous our streets would be today without firm and effective action by the police. It isn't difficult for experienced officers to identify the real trouble-makers, and to go in hard and sort them out. One must presume this is what the police were doing when they pursued those rioters along Tudor Grove when Paul Bailey met his untimely death.

'The question you have to consider, ladies and gentlemen, is not whether Paul Bailey was killed by a police officer, for it's reasonable to presume that he was, but whether the policeman who struck him acted lawfully or not – in other words, whether the truncheon was drawn on a lawful order to endeavour to control the riot situation that was clearly happening at the time. You must remember that if there is a riot, and the police have to take action to stop it, and if innocent bystanders are injured in the process, that is, I'm afraid, as far as the law is concerned, unfortunate. There can be no such thing as an innocent by-stander in a riot. In such situations, people are struck by the police, sometimes on the head. You have heard the police say it was the worst anti-police riot they had experienced. But it is for you to decide.' He paused and considered the silent court a moment, then glanced back at the jury. 'You have a clear choice. You may return a verdict of killed unlawfully, and this expression covers both murder and manslaughter by unknown assailants. For the evidence hasn't shown which policeman struck the fatal blow. This is an accident resulting from an intentional act, in other words, one that was attended by unintentional misfortune. The alternative verdict for you to consider is misadventure. However, you can only bring in this verdict if you believe there was a riot in the street, that the police used reasonable force, and that Paul Bailey was one of the rioters.'

The jury were a long time deciding, but finally, after about four hours, they returned a finding of death by misadventure.

The police who were directly involved were hugely relieved, but had the presence of mind not to gloat publicly. The animal rights people who were among the spectators rose in angry protest and had to be removed from the court. Their sense of injustice wouldn't go away. One more outrage had been added to those heaped upon animals, and upon those who tried to do something to protect them.

Helen Daniels, who had given evidence to the hearing, had remained behind that day, hoping she might see Jack Bentham to tell him how hurt and betrayed she had felt. She wept when she heard the result on the six o'clock news. She was getting ready to go to the theatre. She felt sick at heart that she hadn't been able to do more for Paul than give evidence, which hadn't been believed anyway. She felt she had somehow let the animals down again, as she had when she stopped being active on their behalf.

Jack Bentham felt neither surprise nor disappointment at the result. He was busy expanding C11's computer system to take on more intelligence about quasi-illegal organizations such as those who campaigned for animal rights. They were expecting some wholly illegal move by certain elements of that movement as a result of this verdict. Frustrated beyond endurance, these people would feel compelled to strike back at the establishment. Informants within their ranks would convey their intentions. C11, as a result of all the data stored on its computer, was targeting the most likely candidates.

A top secret SBS mission during the Falklands
War soars into explosive action . . .

SPECIAL
DELIVERANCE

ALEXANDER FULLERTON

In the war-torn, storm-swept South Atlantic, a small band of
highly-trained SBS experts embark on a vital secret mission: to
sabotage Argentina's stock of deadly Exocet missiles.

The dangers are unthinkable: the coastline is exposed and treacherous,
the missile base is surrounded by vast tracts of open land, they must
infiltrate and destroy without ever being detected. Some say it's
impossible . . . but no one underestimates the SBS's lethal capacity.

And one man, Andy MacEwan, an Anglo-Argentine civilian recruited to
the team as guide and interpreter, has more than the success of the
mission on his mind. His brother is a commander in the Argentine Navy
Air Force and there is no love lost between them . . .

*'Good rollicking stuff – full of tension and highly authentic on SBS
technique'*
TODAY

'The action passages are superb. He is in a class of his own'
OBSERVER

0 7221 3719 2   ADVENTURE THRILLER   £2.99

A selection of bestsellers from Sphere

FICTION

WHITE SUN, RED STAR	Robert Elegant	£3.50 ☐
A TASTE FOR DEATH	P. D. James	£3.50 ☐
THE PRINCESS OF POOR STREET	Emma Blair	£2.99 ☐
WANDERLUST	Danielle Steel	£3.50 ☐
LADY OF HAY	Barbara Erskine	£3.95 ☐

FILM AND TV TIE-IN

BLACK FOREST CLINIC	Peter Heim	£2.99 ☐
INTIMATE CONTACT	Jacqueline Osborne	£2.50 ☐
BEST OF BRITISH	Maurice Sellar	£8.95 ☐
SEX WITH PAULA YATES	Paula Yates	£2.95 ☐
RAW DEAL	Walter Wager	£2.50 ☐

NON-FICTION

INVISIBLE ARMIES	Stephen Segaller	£4.99 ☐
ALEX THROUGH THE LOOKING GLASS	Alex Higgins with Tony Francis	£2.99 ☐
NEXT TO A LETTER FROM HOME: THE GLENN MILLER STORY	Geoffrey Butcher	£4.99 ☐
AS TIME GOES BY: THE LIFE OF INGRID BERGMAN	Laurence Leamer	£3.95 ☐
BOTHAM	Don Mosey	£3.50 ☐

All Sphere books are available at your local bookshop or newsagent, or can be ordered direct from the publisher. Just tick the titles you want and fill in the form below.

Name_____

Address_____

_____

Write to Sphere Books, Cash Sales Department, P.O. Box 11, Falmouth, Cornwall TR10 9EN

Please enclose a cheque or postal order to the value of the cover price plus:

UK: 60p for the first book, 25p for the second book and 15p for each additional book ordered to a maximum charge of £1.90.

OVERSEAS & EIRE: £1.25 for the first book, 75p for the second book and 28p for each subsequent title ordered.

BFPO: 60p for the first book, 25p for the second book plus 15p per copy for the next 7 books, thereafter 9p per book.

Sphere Books reserve the right to show new retail prices on covers which may differ from those previously advertised in the text elsewhere, and to increase postal rates in accordance with the P.O.